CW00410827

ALL BETS ARE OFF
MARGUERITE LABBE

Dreamspinner Press

Published by
Dreamspinner Press
382 NE 191st Street #88329
Miami, FL 33179-3899, USA
http://www.dreamspinnerpress.com/

This is a work of fiction. Names, characters, places, and incidents either are the product of the author's imagination or are used fictitiously, and any resemblance to actual persons, living or dead, business establishments, events, or locales is entirely coincidental.

All Bets Are Off
Copyright © 2011 by Marguerite Labbe

Cover Art by Anne Cain annecain.art@gmail.com
Cover Design by Mara McKennen

All rights reserved. No part of this book may be reproduced or transmitted in any form or by any means, electronic or mechanical, including photocopying, recording, or by any information storage and retrieval system without the written permission of the Publisher, except where permitted by law. To request permission and all other inquiries, contact Dreamspinner Press, 382 NE 191st Street #88329, Miami, FL 33179-3899, USA
http://www.dreamspinnerpress.com/

ISBN: 978-1-61372-251-0

Printed in the United States of America
First Edition
December 2011

eBook edition available
eBook ISBN: 978-1-61372-252-7

For Melissa K., my fellow displaced New Englander and lover of baseball, I hope we get to commiserate and anguish over future games for many more years.

Acknowledgments

Alaina Pincus was invaluable in helping me figure out the inner workings of college departments. She answered my many notes as I was writing the story and then graciously read through and corrected my many mistakes afterward and offered her own insights into the story.

KJ Reed helped me with military terminology and answered my many questions regarding the Marines and the Reserves in particular, even when those questions came late at night or when she was working on her own deadline.

CM Torrens and Jen McJ provided wonderful critiques and suggestions that helped keep me on track.

I thank them so much for their time and patience.

CHAPTER 1

"OH, FUCK me," Eli Hollister muttered under his breath as he pulled his motorcycle to a stop in front of Dingers Sports Bar and Grill. His heart sank at the sight of the "Closed" sign over the doorway and men crawling all over the roof. Not that he normally minded seeing a bunch of sweaty and shirtless men working hard in the sun, just not when his stomach was trying to gnaw a hole through his spine. Eye candy was one thing, food was another.

He took another glance at the men on the roof, who were tearing up shingles and tossing them into the dumpster below. Eli knew all but one of the men up there. Jonas Quantrill ran the local construction company with Craig and Lee, two of his sons. However, it was the man Eli didn't know who caught his attention.

He had the hard, muscular build of a man who used his body to make a living. It was difficult to make out any more details with the sun glaring in his eyes, but Eli watched his silhouette. Eli liked the sure, agile way he moved across the sloping roof. The man set down the boards he was carrying and straightened, wiping the back of his hand across his forehead. The action sent a quick punch of lust to Eli's gut. He bet the guy had rough hands and Eli did enjoy the feel of rough hands on his bare skin.

"Move your bike away from there before you pick up a nail." Neil Ryder, the owner of Dingers, emerged out onto the sidewalk with his arms crossed over his chest. "I'm not coming to pick you up if you get a flat halfway up the mountain."

Eli could see the sense in that. Some of those shingles were barely ending up in the trash bin. Eli moved his bike further down the street and walked back toward Dingers. Neil stared up at the men working on the roof, his bald pate gleaming in the sun.

"Neil, what are you doing to me?"

"You?" Neil turned a hard look at Eli, who grinned back at him. Neil looked like he belonged more on a lumberjack crew than tending a bar. He was a big, rangy man with a thick, silvering brown beard. Sweat glistened on his bald head, and he mopped it with a handkerchief before glaring back up at the men on the roof. "The damn thing sprang a bad leak over my office. Dumped a shit-ton of water all over the place. Now I've got to replace the whole thing. You know how much money I lost over the Fourth of July? This is going to set my budget back months."

"You're exaggerating. You'll be fine." Especially once the college town of Amwich filled with the autumn glut of students. "Why didn't you use the opportunity to take off for a few days and relax?"

"And leave them to mess with Dingers unsupervised? I don't think so. Not all of us can go prancing about the country like you do." Neil growled, scowling again up at the roof where the men were hauling up supplies through the scaffolding and tromping all over his beloved bar. It looked like a hot mess with a chimney jutting out like the last forlorn soldier standing amidst the carnage of a battlefield.

Once again, Eli's gaze strayed to the newcomer as he dropped a load of shingles over the edge. He thought their eyes might've met, at least he hoped that's what the hot tingle he felt meant.

"It was just a suggestion." Eli pulled his eyes away from the other man. Neil's sour expression made Eli decide not to poke any more fun at him. It was one of those rare scorching summer days, and Neil's face had taken on a florid cast.

"A bad one." Neil turned toward the bar and held open the door for Eli. "It's too hot to stand outside and jibber jabber. Want a beer?"

"Is it safe to go in there?" Eli followed Neil into the slightly cooler, dim space of the bar. Inside, the sounds of the men moving about overhead and tearing up shingles were amplified tenfold.

It was strange to see the bar empty of customers, the flat-screen TVs quiet and dark, covered up by the heavy blankets that movers used. The baseball memorabilia that wasn't nailed tight to the walls had been taken down and stored in more wrappings on the tables, leaving pale patches on the walls. The rock-hewn chimney stood solid amid the polished wooden tables with worn and faded red leather padded benches and chairs. At least that hadn't changed one bit.

"Sure, the break happened over my office, but Jonas says I should get the area over the kitchen replaced too." Neil poured some water over his head and mopped it up with a dishtowel.

"Are you going to listen to him this time?"

"Yeah, smart ass. I told him to go ahead since they're already ripping the rest of the shit up." Neil shot him a sour glance. "I bet you'd like to know where your cousin is, since I'm not feeding you. Lu should be here soon. She promised Jonas and the boys some lunch."

"Oh thank God, I do not want to suffer the horror of my own cooking." Eli would be doing enough of that on his backpacking trip and didn't want to start early. It wasn't that he couldn't cook; he just hated it with a passion he reserved for the New York Yankees and closed-minded bigots in equal measure. And as much as he wanted to eat, he was also looking forward to getting a real look at that new guy. It was impossible to ogle properly with the sun in his eyes.

"I don't know how the hell you'd survive if everyone stopped feeding you."

"Don't even joke like that. Come on, I'll help you push some tables together. Lu is liable to bring enough to feed half the town."

They cleared off two tables and pushed them together, setting up a mini buffet off to the side of the bar. Eli dragged the chairs to the back so they wouldn't get in the way of the hungry workers and cleared some more tables so they could sit and eat.

Eli straightened when the familiar honk of Lu's horn came from outside. "I'll go help her unload." He left Neil setting up sodas and bottled water. His cousin had parked haphazardly in front of the bar, the tail end of her car two feet out onto the street. "Lu, you're the only person I've ever met who cannot park alongside a curb when there's nothing hindering you," he said to his cousin as she emerged from her hatchback.

Lu Pelland paused, hands on her narrow hips, and with pursed lips she surveyed her parking job, then shrugged. "Close enough for me."

Eli enfolded his cousin in a hug. She was all bones and angles, her graying chestnut hair pulled back into a braid. Out of everyone in his family, Eli felt the closest to her. She'd been older sister, confidante, and counselor for as long as he could remember. And when he'd been banished here to Amwich for six months when he was fifteen, it had been Lu who calmed his fears and taught him that being different didn't mean there was a damn thing wrong with him.

"When did you sneak in?" Lu asked. "I woke up this morning to find that crazy mutt of yours gone and a scribbled note that I couldn't make any sense of."

"It was almost two in the morning. I didn't want to bother you." Eli lifted a heavy pot out of the back. "So, what have you gifted me with today?" Whatever it was, the aromas made his stomach rumble even more.

"I didn't make it for you, glutton, but there is enough for you to mooch. It's chilled tomato basil soup, turkey and havarti on ciabatta rolls, and a pasta salad." Lu frowned as she looked over the array of food. "Do you think I made enough?"

"Name me one time when you ended up short," Eli said with a chuckle.

"One time is all it will take to make me neurotic," Lu said, following Eli into the bar with the pasta bowl.

"I don't understand why you insist on waitressing when you could run my kitchen," Neil grumbled as he took the bowl from her.

"If I take over your kitchen it becomes work and no longer fun. I cook when I want to. I get to decide what I'm making, how much, and who I want to give it to. Besides, I'd miss talking to everyone." Lu tied on an apron and flipped her hands at Neil. "Go get the boys while Eli brings in the sandwiches."

Eli shook his head as Neil opened his mouth to retort. "I wouldn't. It's just easier to do as she says. You know, you should marry her," Eli teased, then burst out laughing as Neil shot him a horrified glance.

"Don't I have enough gray hair?" Lu asked.

"Are you crazy?" Neil burst out. "I'd never know any peace. The woman would take over and run the whole thing, leaving me with just the bartending."

Eli refrained from pointing out that Lu had already taken on far more than waitressing and that Neil would be in hog heaven if all he had to do was run the bar, talk baseball, and buy more memorabilia.

"I was just throwing it out as an option." Eli lifted his hands in surrender as he backed out.

By the time he finished carting in the last tray of sandwiches, the crew had climbed down from the roof and congregated in the restrooms to clean up. Lu was nowhere to be seen and Eli took full advantage, loading up a plate with sandwiches and pasta salad before grabbing a bowl of soup.

"What do you think you're doing?" Lu asked as she returned from the kitchen carrying small dishes filled with condiments.

"Getting lunch before the hungry mob appears."

"I can see that."

"Then why'd you ask such a silly question?" Eli gave her a cheeky grin and then took a step back as she brandished a wooden spoon in his direction. "Besides, I had to taste it all to make sure it's okay for the audience you wish to dazzle."

"Don't try to charm me, Eli. I know you too well." Then Jonas appeared and she stopped her lecture to smile at the foreman. "How's Rebecca doing, Jonas? I haven't seen her in a few weeks."

Eli greeted Jonas, then took his purloined food over to his favorite table in the far corner of the bar and cleaned off his space. He bit into his sandwich, watching the rest of the guys trickle in. His gaze immediately honed in on the newcomer, and his senses sizzled. That man was worth any amount of anticipation.

His height and broad shoulders kept his muscles from bulking him up too much. The wifebeater he wore showed off his chest, flat stomach, and tight nipples. God, Lu would flay him if she discovered Eli ogling nipples during lunch, only he couldn't help himself. The man was tasty from head to toe. As he turned to get his food, Eli bit back a groan. The cargo shorts he wore clung to his muscular ass just right, and what an ass it was. Eli would love to get his hands on it, just a quick squeeze to see if it was as firm as it looked.

He'd have to ask Lu who he was and when he had drifted into Amwich. The town held an interesting mix of people. On the northern side were the locals who had lived here for generations and who knew everything about everybody, or so they believed. The southern part of town was where everyone else lived, in a series of refurbished apartments: the students from Amwich State College who didn't want to stay in the dormitories, along with the short-term professors and specialists who wanted to stay close by campus.

At that moment, his cousin caught Eli's gaze and gave him a small shake of her head. Eli could almost hear her tsking under her breath. That he was openly gay did not bother Lu one bit. In fact she had been the first person he'd talked to when he started suspecting that he was different from the other boys around him. Only after Eli had gotten decked for casting glances at a guy had she become overprotective about his discretion.

Eli grinned and shrugged, deciding to humor her. It wasn't as if he really wanted to engage in a flirtation before he left town again anyway, unless that flirtation translated into a night or two of hot sex. Provided that the guy even swung his way. Still, he couldn't help one more glance as the other man turned back around with his loaded plate. His red-gold hair had been cut short in a Marine-type buzz. And damned if he didn't have freckles, too, a nice smattering of them across an open and friendly face.

As the man pulled out a chair at the same table as his coworkers, he glanced over and caught Eli looking. Eli's stomach fluttered, and he couldn't help the mischievous grin that crossed his lips. Hey, no harm no foul, right? Maybe the guy wouldn't take offense. Another, stronger flutter went through him when the other man smiled back with a wink before Craig said something and drew his attention away.

The new guy had a nice smile too. One of those genuine smiles that lit up his face. Eli gave a mental sigh at that and wondered what color his eyes were. Maybe hazel or a warm brown that would offset his hair.

Eli was definitely going to have to grill Lu for details. Neil set an old TV on the bar and fiddled with the cable on the back until the screen cleared and he was able to change the channel to ESPN for a recap of last night's game between the Red Sox and the Orioles.

"The man has only two things on his mind," Lu huffed as she joined Eli. "Beer and baseball. And you, Elijah Hollister, need to keep your eyes where they belong."

"Neither of us are going to change at this point, Lu." Eli chuckled and moved his chair over as Neil approached, so he could sit with them. "So how long is Dingers going to be closed?"

Neil grimaced as he reached for the pepper. "Jonas said it would take about four days to do the job right. Then I figure I'll need at least another day to clean up and put everything back. We should be open by Sunday's game if the damn noise doesn't drive me crazy before then."

"I'm not leaving until Monday so I can help you put everything back together," Eli offered.

Neil's face brightened and he gave Eli a rare smile. "Thanks. You're still not getting that photograph, but I'll agree to feed you in exchange."

Eli glanced at the bare spot on the wall where the picture of Joe DiMaggio and Ted Williams in their respective uniforms usually hung. Eli coveted that photograph and nothing would induce Neil to part with it, no matter how hard Eli tried. He really needed to get a replica of his own. "I think I can agree to those terms. It'll be good to see Dingers back to normal before I go. So catch me up on the gossip. I'm not going to be able to get any messages soon."

"That's because you'll be out in the middle of nowhere, gallivanting about the States with that crazy mutt of yours," Lu retorted.

"That's the second time you've mentioned he's crazy. Did Jabbers misbehave that much while I was in Tennessee?"

"You're the only one in town that doesn't know he's certifiable, Eli." Lu didn't like the idea of him going off on his long, solo camping trips with only a beagle for company. At least she didn't badger him about it too much. "So how was your trip? How are your southern cousins doing?"

"The Smoky Mountains are nice, though not as pretty as the ones in New Hampshire." Lu hadn't asked about his parents, whom Eli had gone to visit. That was one rift he didn't think would ever be healed, and it made him uncomfortable that he was at the heart of the conflict between Lu and his dad. "And the cousins are doing well. Most of them have married and moved off. Only one left is Gareth, and he'll never settle down. He's enjoying life too much."

Eli rose to get seconds. As he did, he was able to get a better glance at his new dream guy. The lighting in the bar was terrible and Eli still wasn't able to catch the color of his eyes, but the man had the undertone to his skin of a true redhead that would never tan, no matter how much time he spent in the sun it would only burn or freckle more.

He did catch Jonas saying his name: Ash. Finally, a name to go along with the face. He wanted to introduce himself, but Jonas was talking business and he wouldn't be pleased with an interruption, so Eli returned to his table with another loaded plate and contented himself with quick glimpses. The crew finished lunch quickly, and as they trooped out again, Ash caught his eye and gave him another wink, a good-natured smile on his face.

"Oh, man, I think I'm in love," Eli said under his breath as the door shut behind Ash.

Neil shot him a skeptical glance. "You say that all the time. Call me when it actually happens so I can point and laugh."

Eli ignored him and turned to appeal to his cousin. "You have to know something about Ash. Is he gay? Is he single? Is he one of those itinerant construction workers who will disappear before I come back home and break my heart?"

"I'm sure your heart is quite safe," Lu said with a dry tone. "He's renting one of Abraham's places. I think the construction gig is part-time. I know I've seen him leaving his apartment in cammies once or twice." Lu rose and started to pack up the leftover food, dividing it into two containers before Eli and Neil could start arguing over who got to keep them.

A military man. National Guard, maybe, or one of the Reserves. Eli thought there might be a Marine Corps headquarters somewhere south of here. That clinched Eli's interest. He'd always had a soft spot for military men, and it seemed that the worst trouble he'd ever gotten into followed them, but that had never stopped him before. Eli cast Lu a look of appeal. "So you'll ask around for me while I'm gone, right? Inquiring minds need to know these little details, Lu, and it's your duty as my loving cousin to investigate them when I can't."

ASH GALLAGHER returned to tearing up rotten shingles as the hot July sun beat down on him. He'd laughed when the rest of the crew had complained about the heat. This was nothing compared to the summers in Savannah, where he grew up, where the air was liquid and heavy and sweat would just pour off a body. And Savannah hadn't prepared him at all for Iraq's dry heat that blasted right off of him and sucked every drop of moisture from his body before he even had a chance to bitch about how hot it was. At least in Iraq, shade had provided welcome relief.

Dingers sat in the middle of a long row of connected buildings lining one side of the street. The town common sat across from it with the red, white, and blue bunting still decorating the gazebo from the Fourth of July celebration earlier in the week. Ash had enjoyed the small town festivities more than he'd thought he would. He wiped the beads of sweat from his forehead with the back of his hand. He needed a bandana. His short hair did nothing to soak up the sweat that ran into his eyes and stung.

"So who was that with Neil and Lu?" Ash asked Jonas, who worked beside him. He thought he'd met all the locals since he'd moved into town. Clearly he hadn't or he would've remembered that guy, for sure. The sudden brilliance of the man's smile had caught his wholehearted attention. There had been no embarrassment or coyness when he'd been caught staring, just that boyish "oh well you can't blame a guy" smile.

Jonas gave him an odd, measuring look that made Ash wonder what was going through his head before he shrugged. "That's Eli. He's Lu's second cousin on his dad's side. He's good people."

The culture of a small town would certainly take some getting used to. Everyone had deep-seated opinions about each other that they often didn't hesitate to share. Ash had found that he didn't get introduced to a person without finding out who else they were connected to and how long their particular family had lived here.

Sure enough, Jonas continued, and a smile tugged at Ash's lips. "He took over the Hermitage from his grandfather about five years ago. Cared for his grandmother till she passed a year later. Unlike most of the rest of his family, it doesn't look like he's leaving the area anytime soon."

Ash supposed that was pretty good praise in Jonas's mind. So Eli was a man who had put down roots, unlike Ash, who was still wandering about, searching for a place he could claim. An old restlessness tugged at him. It was the same restlessness that had caused him to join the Marine Corps right out of high school. Then he'd been looking for an exciting challenge; now he was looking for a place where he belonged.

After the way his second tour in Iraq had ended, he'd started questioning what he wanted out of his life. As much as he'd loved being a Marine, he'd opted out and gone into the Reserves so he could go to school. Now that was almost over with. One more year and he'd have his degree and the freedom to go where he wished. Even if he wasn't sure where that was yet.

Eli. He tasted the name. A strong name for a man with such a quirky, sexy smile.

Jonas exchanged a quick, concerned glance with his sons, but didn't offer any further details when Ash didn't ask. Ash set aside the roofer's spade and gathered an armload of shingles that hadn't already skittered down the roof. He spotted Eli walking out of the bar and watched him help Lu load up her car with empty trays, a bowl, and a Crock-Pot. He hugged her and kissed the top of her head in a gesture that reminded Ash of the way he was with his youngest sister Katie.

Eli wasn't at all like the men Ash normally found himself attracted to. There was a bohemian look about him with his long, auburn hair caught back in a neat braid, clad in scarred boots, worn jeans, and a fitted black T-shirt. Eli glanced up at him, another broad smile crossing his face as he waved, and the flash of desire that struck Ash took his breath away.

Yeah, there was definite interest there, and it was mutual. Not like there were many other options off campus, and Ash definitely hadn't found anyone on campus who came close to catching his eye. They all seemed so incredibly young.

Not that Ash was that old, even if he'd been on his own for the past ten years. He'd seen war and blood. He'd witnessed the worst acts of depravity someone could imagine, yet some of the most compassionate too. He just didn't have anything in common with the rest of the students in his classes. This was his final year at Amwich State College. Once he had his degree he could move on.

He was glad that he'd moved closer to his school instead trying to stay halfway between there and his Reserve unit in Londonderry. Concord had been okay, and he'd liked his roommate and the dating opportunities in a larger town, but when his roommate had gotten serious about his girlfriend, Ash had decided it was time to move on. This year's classes were going to be intense enough without having a long daily commute on top of them.

Once Lu had driven off and gotten her car out of harm's way, Ash dropped his armload of shingles into the trash bin below. Eli was walking back toward the motorcycle Ash had noticed earlier, a gorgeous dark-blue Valkyrie. A motorcycle was one of those things he'd always wanted, but had never gotten around to buying. He planned to rectify that once he graduated.

Jonas glanced up from where he was testing the wood for rot as Ash returned. "Some might say Eli's odd. He can be a bit of a loner, and it's no secret about town that he doesn't prefer women," he said, his eyes sharp on Ash. "Not sure what he did to catch your attention, but whatever it was, he didn't mean anything by it and isn't looking for trouble."

Ash chuckled and shook his head as he grabbed his spade again. "I'm not looking to cause any. I don't judge what a man does on his own time or who he does it with." It would be rather hypocritical of him, all things considered. Ash had known he was gay since he was fourteen. All of his friends had been hot for this one girl at school, and he'd only had eyes for her older brother.

"Just making sure." That being said, Jonas went back to what he was doing without another word.

A bit surprised, Ash returned to tearing up shingles. He hadn't expected the people in Amwich to be so broad-minded when he'd moved here a month ago. Maybe it was the influence of the college, or maybe it was just easier to accept people as they were when you'd known them their entire lives. The reasons didn't matter. It was just nice to be in a place where he could be at ease in his own skin.

ELI spied Wayne Grayson's truck, bristling with compartments for tools, parked by the town common and paused, struck by a pang of empathy. Remembering the grim news he'd received while he had been in Tennessee, Eli stored his leftovers in the saddlebag of his bike and turned back. He waved at the other man as he jogged across the street. "Hey, Wayne."

Wayne dragged along a large trash can as he systematically cleaned up the common of debris from the Fourth of July festivities. Confetti covered the grass in a colorful carpet, with the added adornment of empty beer bottles and spent sparkler sticks scattered about. "Back already? Thought you'd be gone the whole summer." He straightened as Eli approached, and tied off another bag of trash. Though they were close in age, Wayne's long, narrow face had new lines etched around the mouth and eyes. The thick, black framed glasses on his upturned nose gave him a studious look, but the other man was far more comfortable with tools in his hand than a book. Wayne had always been like that, ever since they were kids.

"I'm home for a week and then I'm off to Colorado and northern California for a while. I heard about your dad being rushed to the hospital last week."

Mr. Grayson and Eli's dad were best friends until after high school, when they both went their separate ways. Eli had never understood what had happened, and the few times he'd tried to ask his dad about the antagonism between them, he'd been rebuffed. But when he'd heard that Mr. Grayson had been hospitalized, his dad had unbent enough to send him a letter with Eli.

"What happened? What have the doctors said?"

"He had a pretty bad stroke in the middle of the night." Wayne took off his stained work gloves and stuffed them in his back pocket, the lines of tension on his face deepening. "He's still in the hospital. They're trying to make sure there aren't more complications. He's got a long rehab ahead of him. Can't barely talk, and now he's stuck riding in a wheelchair for a while until the physical therapists get a go at him."

"I'm sorry. Tell me if there's anything I can do to help. You know Lu wouldn't mind fussing over your dad too."

A smile lifted some of the anxiety on Wayne's face. "She's visited every day. Keeps bringing food too. Enough to feed a whole family, not just me. My freezer's likely to burst."

"That sounds about right, knowing her. Don't complain; just savor the bounty while it lasts." Eli clapped Wayne on the shoulder in sympathy as the man's face fell once again. He couldn't begin to image having to watch his dad recover from a sudden illness like that, estranged or not. "I'll stop by the hospital before I go. And like I said, let me know if there's anything I can do."

"Actually there is." Wayne took a swig of water from the bottle hanging from his belt. "I need to hire a live-in nurse for him when he comes back home and I've got to pay for Tilly to run the store full time now. I don't know where the money's gonna come from since Dad didn't have any medical insurance. So if you could put in a good word for me at the college for anybody looking to have some jobs done around the house or yard, I'd appreciate it. I'd even be willing to go out of town to Concord or Dartmouth to drum up some business, just as long as it's not too far away."

"Not a problem. I'll post something up on the community board, and if anybody asks I'll drop your name. Speaking of which, I have some stuff around my house that could be taken care of since I'm going to be gone pretty much for the rest of the summer. The gutters won't last another winter, and the door on my shed is starting to sag."

A relieved grin broke out over Wayne's face. "I'll tell you what, Eli. Write out a list of what you need, and I'll work up an estimate for you. Then when you come back, all you have to worry about is a bunch of smart-mouthed kids and Britton."

"Please don't invoke that name," Eli said with a grimace. "I refuse to let him in my thoughts over the summer."

"Forget I mentioned him, then."

"The kids are fun and I can handle Britton. I think what irks him the most is that I don't get upset with him," Eli said with a chuckle. "Sometimes it's even fun."

They talked for a few minutes more, catching up on news, until Eli could see that Wayne wanted to get back to work. Eli promised to drop off the work list at the hardware store, and then headed off across the square toward his motorcycle.

"Hey, Eli," Wayne called after him. "You think you might have some time before you leave to show me the baseball card collection our dads had?"

"Ha! My dad saving something sentimental? Remember who you're talking about." A flash of acute disappointment crossed Wayne's face, and Eli wished he could've told him otherwise. "Sorry, Wayne, he's not that kind of a guy."

Wayne grunted and pulled the trashcan to another section of grass that needed to be cleared. "Well, if you get a chance, ask your dad if he kept them."

Eli wasn't looking to talk to his dad anytime soon, especially over something he'd consider frivolous. "I'll keep it in mind. See you, Wayne."

He glanced at Dingers' roof as he turned away and immediately picked out Ash's silhouette from the others. Smiling to himself, he returned to his bike. He could count on Lu, being the gossip that she was, to find out more about him while he was on his vacation.

In the meantime, it was a perfect day for riding, with the brilliant July sun shining and puffy, low flying clouds dappling shadows on the hillside as he left town. Eli wanted to make the most of such a day.

The motorcycle roared along the curved road, and Eli opened the throttle, grinning and whooping in delight when the bike sped up in response. The wheels kicked up dust as he turned off the main road and headed up Mount Abenaqui toward the Hermitage. It was good to be back home among the weathered, exposed granite and tree-covered peaks, and all the more poignant because he would be leaving again in a few days.

CHAPTER 2

ASH felt the ache of every battered, tired muscle in his body. It never failed after a drill weekend. No matter how much he worked out beforehand, no matter how many construction jobs he took on, he still left drill feeling like he'd spent the intervening weeks lazing around on his ass, doing nothing.

At least it was the tail end of summer and not the dead of winter, when they did their two-week cold-weather survival training exercises. For the last five years, that alone made Ash question why he'd settled on a college in New Hampshire when he'd entered the Reserves instead of one back home in Georgia.

He pulled his battered truck into the grocery store parking lot, mentally going through his shopping list. This chore was last thing he wanted to do, but after he'd gone home and changed out of his cammies and showered, he'd felt marginally better. Once he wasn't in danger of starving he could sprawl on the couch in his boxers and watch TV for the rest of the day.

Ash forgot about his aches as he emerged from his truck and spotted a familiar Jeep covered in hiking and national park stickers. Eli Hollister drove that Jeep when he wasn't on his motorcycle. Ash had seen it a few times around town before Eli had disappeared for the rest of the summer, depriving Ash of a chance to talk to him.

Ash had hoped to get a chance to introduce himself to the man to see if the vibe he'd sensed between them was real or imagined, only to be disappointed when Eli disappeared. Energized, Ash grabbed a cart, and as soon as he entered the small grocery store he spotted his quarry. Eli stood in the baking aisle beside a half-full cart, studying two different bags of sugar with the air of a man making a momentous decision. His brows were furrowed and his lips pursed as he examined them, oblivious to the other customers moving up and down the aisle around him.

Today Eli had his long, auburn hair caught back at the nape of his neck with a tie and a dark-gray fedora perched on his head at a rakish tilt. Ash would love to see that hat off his head and his hair spread in a burnished tangle around his shoulders. His black, gray, and cream vest over a plain T-shirt and a pair of jeans gave him a sense of casual style.

With a little nod, Eli set one of the sugar bags into his cart and strolled off, whistling to himself. Ash was smitten. There was no other word for it, and he wasn't going to miss another opportunity to talk with Eli. He wanted to see whether or not those teasing glances they'd exchanged had meant anything or if they were just the product of his lustful imagination and too many months without sex.

Ash took his time following after him. Eli's jeans were cut just right, faded, and clinging to an ass that seemed too round for a man who was as long and lean as he looked. It was a truly inspiring, erotic sight. Eli had to be a good couple inches taller than Ash, though not as broad in the shoulders. Ash noticed other details that he had missed before, such as the warm, gleaming highlights in Eli's hair and the way he didn't seem entirely aware of the world as he went about filling his cart. The way he moved spoke of lean muscle concealed beneath his clothes.

Ash closed the distance between them as Eli paused halfway down the aisle, cocking his head. Abruptly the man turned his cart around, almost crashing it into Ash's. "Oops, I'm sorry, I...."

Eli's eyes widened in recognition as he focused on Ash, startled out of whatever he had been thinking about so hard. He had beautiful eyes. They were a blue-gray, the irises outlined with a much darker gray, and framed by long, red-brown lashes. They reminded Ash of a seer's eyes, of someone who had his attention riveted on some other time or world. His eyes were the color of the sky on a winter's day, that pale steel in the morning when the day hovered between the promise of snow and possible sunshine.

Dear God, at this rate, the man was going to have him composing bad poetry. With Ash's skills, very bad, make people laugh poetry.

Damn, he must be punch-drunk tired. He was going to make a fool out of himself.

"It's okay, no harm done," Ash said, his anticipation rising.

Eli's gaze flicked over Ash in his jeans and T-shirt. "My cousin told me that she saw you in cammies a couple times. Marine Corps Reserves?"

"Very good," Ash said, another slow grin crossing his lips. "Out of Londonderry. How'd you guess?"

"The haircut is a dead giveaway. And I don't know of any other Marine Corps units within driving distance, except for the Reserve one. It does help that half my family is in one branch of the military or another. My dad was Air Force." Eli moved his cart over, nodding to another woman Ash vaguely recognized from around town.

"Ma'am." Ash nodded and pulled his cart over as well, so they'd stop blocking the aisle, and then turned his attention back to Eli. "A flyboy?" Ash didn't really have anything against the Air Force, not like some of the guys in his unit, who thought they all were a bunch of pansies. It had always been Ash's opinion that they were all serving, each in their own way.

"Yeah, he loved flying, loved taking off in a Strike Eagle, and would've given his left arm to have jumped a Tomcat off an aircraft carrier just once. Mom used to tease him about joining the wrong branch. He finally retired last year after saying he was finished God knows how long ago, but kept reenlisting. Thought my mom was going to tear out her hair." Eli paused, then his mouth quirked in a self-deprecating grin. "I'm sorry; I'll ramble forever if you let me."

"You don't have to apologize. I don't mind." Eli had the kind of rich voice Ash could listen to for hours. Add to it his expressive features and slightly upturned nose, and Ash was entranced. Ash realized he was staring and stuck out his hand, not wanting to appear rude. "I didn't get a chance to introduce myself at Dingers. I'm Ash."

"Pleasure to meet you, Ash. My cousin told me you'd gotten a place nearby." When Eli shook his hand with a firm grip, a little ripple of awareness went through him. Eli's eyes widened just a fraction as if he felt it, too, and the reaction filled Ash with a warm sense of pleasure. "Small towns being what they are, and all, when anything new happens it's discussed to death until the next new thing appears."

"And you're Eli," Ash said with a grin, realizing that Eli wasn't kidding when he said he had a tendency to ramble. There went his bit of hopeful conceit that he had Eli flustered. "Jonas told me your name." He'd tried to get more details out of Neil during one of their poker games only to be told that he was there to play, not to jibber jabber.

"I'm sorry, I'm not normally so rude," Eli said. "I think you caught me on a scatterbrained day. I just got back into town a few days ago and I'm still trying to get settled before the week starts."

"Maybe just a little," Ash said and the affable grin on Eli's face told him Eli was probably used to the teasing. "It's not necessarily a bad thing." In his opinion, it was damn cute.

"Lu is going to be upset if I don't get these to her. I'm already running behind as usual." Eli gestured to the cart with a look of regret. "Are you on duty tonight? Dingers is going to be hopping with the Red Sox playing the Yankees. Why don't you come on by? We could talk some more."

Got him. Ash grinned. His intuition had been dead-on, and he hadn't been this glad to be right in a long while. "Should be a good game. Aren't they battling for the wild card?"

"They're focusing on the pennant race. I'm sure it'll heat up and get exciting before it's settled." Eli's eyes gleamed with the zeal of a true baseball fanatic, and Ash laughed in recognition of a fellow lover of the sport. He was sure the night was going to heat up and get exciting too. If it was up to him, baseball would have little to do with it.

The initial interest that had struck Ash when he'd first seen Eli was quickly replaced with longing. He wanted Eli. He wanted to see him stretched out naked underneath him, all long limbs and tumbled hair, his eyes darkened with desire and that playful smile on his lips.

"I'll take you up on it." Ash moved his cart again as someone tried to reach between them for an item on the shelf. "Sorry, sir." They were monopolizing the aisle, but he couldn't bring himself to really feel bad about doing so. "What time does the game start?"

"Seven thirty, but you might want to get there a little earlier. Tables tend to fill up, especially on game nights."

"And I suppose it's strictly American League territory."

"That's a safe bet. As long as you don't wear a Yankees cap you'll be okay. Neil lets that slide with the college kids who come, but anyone else is asking for a night of mocking." Eli paused and gave Ash a considering glance. "You're not a Yankee fan, are you?" The tone of his voice said there were some things that just couldn't be overlooked.

"Please, the accent isn't a dead giveaway? Atlanta Braves all the way, my friend. Though my baby sister is living in New York City now and has been converted."

"Oh well, there's one in every family." Eli gave a mocking little sigh, his eyes flashing with humor. "Atlanta Braves, hmmm? The man of my dreams couldn't be in the military, have devastating looks, and be a Red Sox fan, as well. There just isn't that much luck in the world. Maybe you're not a grand slam, but I'd definitely say you're at least a three-run homer."

Oh wow, a teaser. Ash had missed that. The last guy he'd dated had been entirely too uptight. Ash laughed and murmured an apology to another customer trying to reach around him.

"Well, I'll see what I can do to change your opinion by the end of the night. See you at seven, Eli." With that, he strolled off, anticipation making him forget all about his earlier intention to sprawl and not move for the rest of the night. All he needed was a quick nap and he'd be good to go if his night ran as late as he hoped it would.

WAYNE'S stomach jumped with nerves as he watched Eli ride into town. True to Eli's habits, he parked his motorcycle in front of Dingers and disappeared inside. It would take an emergency to get him to move from there until the game was over, which gave Wayne at least a couple hours to poke around his place.

There was a part of him that shrank back in shame for what he was about to do, violating the trust of someone who considered him a friend, but dammit, he'd been wronged first. If it wasn't for Mr. Hollister cheating his dad out of his most prized possession all those years ago, he'd have the money he needed to take care of his dad properly. Wayne climbed inside his truck and slammed the door. The frustration and worry was damn near eating him alive. Now he had guilt to deal with too.

Eli's house stood halfway up the mountain, overlooking a series of sloped, wooded hills and broad meadows. His nearest neighbor lived half a mile away, so there was no one to see Wayne pull into the driveway. He stared at the Hermitage, gnawing on his lip and trying to work himself up into taking this step. His stomach had gone from jumping to mad flutters that made him feel faintly sick, and his knuckles turned white as he gripped the steering wheel harder. If he got caught....

He shouldn't even be thinking of doing this, but that argument had grown weaker over the past month as the bills started to pile up. Wayne drew in a deep breath and squared his jaw. This wasn't about his friendship with Eli. Wayne hadn't been able to believe it when he found the series of letters between Mr. Hollister and his dad. His dad had begged the asshole to make it right, and he'd refused over and over again to admit how he cheated on their bet.

That reminder was enough to make Wayne forget his little crisis of conscience, and without any further internal argument, he climbed out of his truck. A beagle appeared in the window, his baying shockingly loud to Wayne's ears. "Damn fool dog," Wayne muttered, wiping a nervous hand across his brow.

A hundred excuses for his presence crossed his mind as he checked the unlocked door to the mudroom and let himself in. He wanted to have one ready just in case Eli came home early. Those excuses flew out of his head as a brown, white, and black blur bounded toward him. The beagle skidded on the smooth wood floors, barking loud enough to make Wayne cringe and almost knock over the stand full of walking sticks.

"Jabbers, sit!" he pleaded as the dog jumped on him.

The beagle plopped his haunches on the floor and cocked his head in an inquisitive expression. He barked once in question and then jumped up again, putting his paws on Wayne's knee, his tail wagging in welcome, before running off to check the window. "Sorry, Jabbers, your owner isn't here."

It wasn't really breaking and entering. Eli was a friend. It was more like a recovery operation. It was a kindness, really; Eli didn't need to know how much of a jackass his dad really was, and Wayne was damn well determined to get what was his back. A little look-see wouldn't hurt. Generations of Hollisters had lived at the Hermitage. There was a chance, a slim one, that Eli's dad might've left the baseball cards behind when he'd left home.

Finding it would mean the difference between being able to take care of his dad at home, making sure he had everything he needed to recover, or seeing him stuck in some damn nursing home while the state liquidated his dad's business to pay for his care. Wayne would never let that happen.

He took a deep breath and forced himself to continue on into the kitchen. He'd give himself an hour to look, start one room at a time. Those damn baseball cards had to be here somewhere. He refused to think that they could be in Tennessee with Mr. Hollister. That just couldn't be allowed to happen.

Jabbers followed him from the untouched kitchen to the living room. Crammed bookshelves lined the available spots against the wall, and a stack of books sat on the end table by the armchair. Wayne's heart sank. All those books. It would take forever to go through them. He took a framed photo of Eli and his grandparents down off the mantle. Of all the pictures there, only one had his parents, and Eli was noticeably absent. Well, perhaps Eli had no loyalty to the old bastard.

Jabbers barked and Wayne jumped, almost dropping the picture in the process. "For chrissake, will you stop that?" He mopped the fresh sweat off his forehead and checked between the photo and the backing to make sure the card wasn't there. "You're going to give me a heart attack, Jabbers."

The beagle showed no signs of remorse as he followed Wayne out of the room. Wayne would just take a quick glance around the entire place first to see if the baseball card collection was out in the open before he started looking in earnest. Jabbers stayed right on his heels, staring at him and making those questioning barks as if asking him what he was doing here.

It was not helping his state of mind, and after an hour of fruitless searching Wayne thought he was about to sweat out of his skin. Those fucking baseball cards were nowhere in sight.

Wayne glanced at his watch and swore. He'd have to poke around the attic another day, when he had more time. Jabbers danced at his heels as Wayne came back downstairs and did another sweep just in case he'd missed something critical the first time. The place was pretty neat, except for Eli's study, which was littered with books and stacks of paper. How he ever found anything in that mess, Wayne would never understand. The man should invest in some built-in bookshelves and a file cabinet. Only Wayne couldn't suggest it without admitting being inside his place. Still, his hands itched to impose some order on the chaos.

He spent another thirty minutes shifting through stacks, resisting the urge to neaten them. Eli probably wouldn't even notice. All he found was old papers, grade ledgers, and multiple copies of the same books. Who needed more than one edition? Jabbers had sprawled out under the desk, peering at him with his head on his paws, looking as if Wayne were the most boring companion he'd ever met.

"Will you stop that, Jabbers?" Wayne complained.

At the sound of his name, Jabbers rushed toward him and knocked over a box teetering on the edge of a chair, sending papers and books scattering across the floor. The beagle promptly forgot about Wayne and pounced on the mess with a happy growl. Wayne gasped, his eyes opening wide in horror and sweat broke out on his brow as Jabbers grabbed one of the books in his jaw like it was a chew toy.

"Jabbers!" Wayne jumped forward, making a swipe for the book. Eli loved his books. "Love" wasn't even the word. The man was obsessed. Eli would die if he knew. "Gimme that."

Jabbers danced out of the way, his tail wagging, his brown eyes lit up with glee, as if Wayne had invented the best game ever. Cursing, Wayne lunged for him again and managed to get his hands on the book. The dog dropped his hindquarters, shook his head, and mock growled as they tugged back and forth.

"Drop it. Drop it! Bad Jabbers!"

With a whine, Jabbers released the book, sending Wayne stumbling back. The beagle opted for a strategic retreat and disappeared into the hallway with a reproachful look over his shoulder as Wayne began cursing.

Wayne cringed as he looked at the cover, the binding pierced through and slobbered on, the spine cracked. At least it looked like an old book. If Wayne put everything back to rights, maybe Eli wouldn't notice or he'd think it happened a long time ago. He was picking up the last of the papers when one of them caught his eye, an appraisal for a range of baseball cards from the fifties and sixties.

No fucking way. Wayne clenched the paper so hard in his hand that it crumpled. No damn way. That lying bastard. He examined the paper again, then stuffed it in his pocket, and with his heart racing began going through every paper he'd just replaced in the box. There were several bills of sale, some even for baseball cards, but nothing for a 1954 Ted Williams.

Wayne sat back on his heels, a sick feeling of betrayal clenching his stomach. Eli had lied to him. Not only had he lied, but now he was seeking to make a profit off his dad's theft. At first he'd been grateful for the work Eli had sent him, only the more he'd thought about it over the summer, the more he realized that the offer had just been a token gesture, or maybe a salve for Eli's own conscience. Damn him.

Well, that settled it; he refused to feel guilty any longer for doing what he had to do. He had to look out for his dad. Screw Eli. If he hadn't sold the card yet then it had to be here somewhere, and Wayne was going to get it back.

CHAPTER 3

ASH found Dingers more crowded than he had seen it all summer, when just the locals had been the patrons at the bar. As students had trickled in to take up residence during the past week, the population of Amwich had tripled. Every table was occupied, and people were crowded two deep around the bar.

Ash's gaze roamed, searching for Eli. He found him sitting at the same small table as when Ash had first seen him. He'd ditched the fedora, and his hair was once again back in its braid.

Ash began to wend his way toward him, greeting those he knew and waving to Neil, who was busy working the taps behind the bar. Living in Concord had kept him from discovering Dingers, which had quickly become a favorite hangout, especially on Wednesday night when they served their fish and chips.

Eli glanced up as he approached, his smile lighting up his face. He had one of those genuine smiles, the kind that Ash found impossible to resist. He grinned back, a tug of desire taking hold of him deep inside.

"I'd be disappointed that you can't wear your cammies out," Eli said, his eyes flashing with teasing, "only you still move like a military man. Bet you were glad for a chance to relax. You looked a bit worn out earlier."

"It was a long weekend," Ash admitted, pulling out a chair and angling it next to Eli's so they both could see the giant flat-screen TV perched on the wall behind Neil. He was still exhausted. He'd never managed to get that nap, but the promise of seeing Eli had revived some of his energy. "Sometimes they bust our ass at drill and sometimes it's dead boring, with little to do. This was one of the bust our ass weekends."

Lu Pelland came up then, shaking her head and leveling an exasperated glance at Eli. "Wretch," she said to Eli and then gave Ash a warm smile. "Ash, it's good to see you again. Do you want your usual?"

"Yes, ma'am." Ash glanced in curiosity at Eli as she walked away. "What did you do?"

Eli's mouth dropped open in mock astonishment. "Me? Nothing, I swear."

Ash leaned back in his chair, not believing his attempt at innocence for one moment. The highlights in Eli's hair glinted with a warm fire, and his eyes held such wicked humor that Ash wasn't fooled. "Uh huh."

Eli laughed, glancing at the older woman as she reached the bar. "Lu's my cousin, friend, incurable gossip, and mother hen all wrapped up in one. She worries about me terribly when I have a date that she hasn't met. I hadn't told her that I had one tonight and still she managed to guess and has been hounding me incessantly about who it was since I arrived."

"And you held out? Or did you deny having a date at all?"

"I didn't want her to start any rumors until I had a chance to warn you," Eli said, his expression turning serious. "I wasn't sure if you were out or not, and she'll behave if we ask."

"Don't worry about it," Ash said, touched by Eli's forethought. "We're a long way from my unit, and rumor would abound in a town like this whether or not your cousin talks."

In truth, it didn't matter to him anymore. He was tired of hiding who he was. When he'd enlisted in the Marines, he'd thought it would be easy. After all, his private life was his own business. His parents had tried to change his mind, being far more worried about him being a gay man in the military than him shipping off to war. They'd tried to talk him into joining another branch, but in his opinion he couldn't sit back and let others fight on the front lines for his freedom. He'd wanted to be in the thick of things.

It had been far harder than he'd thought it would be. He wasn't a man given to deceiving others, and it had felt like he was living in someone else's skin. That was why he had chosen not to re-enlist a third time, instead moving to the Reserves while he attended college. Once he was done with the years he'd promised the Reserves and had his degree, he was done. It didn't matter whether the "Don't Ask, Don't Tell" law had been repealed or not. Besides, the repeal was still uncertain, and people weren't rushing to come out of the closet until it was really settled. Attitudes wouldn't change overnight, and he was ready to move on.

"True," Eli said with a rueful smile. "Amwich does like to discuss who's keeping company with whom. They've known all about my scandalous relationships ever since I was fifteen, after being sent here one summer in disgrace."

"I suspect there's quite a story there," Ash replied. Eli's expression was mostly amused, though a glint in his eyes also spoke of an old anger and regret.

"Quite," Lu said as she appeared at their table with a loaded tray. She set a frosty glass of beer in front of Ash and a glass of red wine for Eli, followed by a bowl of popcorn. "Eli has been driving me batty ever since then. Always seems to me that he picks the perfect guy at the worst time."

"For the love of—" Eli broke off and flipped his hand at Lu. "I don't need a running commentary during my date, thank you."

She leveled a glare at him, and he looked back at her with exasperation. "Been a mighty long time since you've been on a date," Lu said. "You should've told me that it was Ash. I've been going crazy thinking that you'd hooked up with a stranger online. There's some crazy people on the Internet, I've heard."

Ash covered his laughter with a handful of popcorn before Lu decided to include him in her dressing down.

"Lu, the Miltons are crazy, and they live just down the street from you," Eli said with a note of exasperation.

"Yeah, but that's a crazy I know." Lu swiveled her head around as Neil bellowed her name from the bar, then huffed and tucked her tray under her arm. "I'm coming, you old goat," she yelled over the din of the bar, then muttered as Neil shouted for her again, "Can't give a body a rest."

"So what part of Georgia are you from?" Eli's eyes flicked to Ash's Atlanta Braves cap. "Your taste in teams must be homegrown, and then there's your accent. My dad was stationed in Georgia for a few years while I was in high school, so I recognize it."

"Savannah. My family has been there for generations." Over on the flat screen, the players started to line up for the national anthem, but Ash found it hard to put his attention anywhere but on Eli. "What base were you on in Georgia?" Ash could just imagine Eli in high school, too pretty for his own good, not gawky like Ash had been. He was a little sorry he hadn't run into him then.

"Moody. Savannah's nice, we visited it a couple of times. I loved the historic feel of the place. And the architecture is amazing."

"Yeah, I love it. You, on the other hand, don't have much of an accent," Ash said. Eli's voice was smooth and cultured. There were hints of one, but nothing like the broad Boston accent most of the locals possessed. Ash found it hard to decipher the twang at times, even as he was being accused of talking funny. "There's a bit of a twang, but there's also a drawl on some words. How did you do that? All the different bases you've been on?"

"Mom's from Tennessee. I spent almost as much time there as I did up here," Eli replied.

Lu returned and took their orders before disappearing amongst the swirl of customers crowded close to the bar. A few people glanced in their direction with disapproving expressions, but no one started any trouble or said anything. Ash wasn't sure if it was because Amwich was more cosmopolitan than other small towns because of the college or because people had known Eli a long time and adopted an unspoken mutual agreement not to harass one another. Ash had been in town long enough to know which people were the most intolerant. He didn't see any of them tonight, but that wasn't a surprise. Neil wouldn't put up with any kind of flak at Dingers.

There had been a few families eating dinner when Ash had arrived. As game time approached, most of them had cleared out, to be replaced with an almost unbroken wall of red and white. The real disapproving looks were saved for the little knots of navy that had banded together.

Ash shook his head. "It's nice to see there's still room on the bandwagon for everyone around here. How many of these people were baseball fans before 2004? I feel like I'm in the middle of a combat zone."

Eli chuckled and took a sip of his wine. "I would have said you should be safe, but you live on this side of town, not the school side. You keep talking like that and you'll be setting yourself up to get as good as you can give if anyone overhears you."

Eli's clear, blue-gray eyes possessed a mischievous glint as he watched Ash. Oh, the challenge was clearly there, and Ash felt it right down to his toes. And he wanted to take Eli up on it. "So are you trying to say that you're the only man in here that won't accost me if you lose?"

"You've definitely got me thinking about accosting," Eli replied with a smile tugging at the corners of his sensual lips. "But we're not going to lose."

"Spoken like a true fan." Ash laughed. Red Sox fans were certainly in a league of their own. He brushed the back of Eli's hand with his fingers, savoring the little thrill of awareness, before picking up his own beer. "You want to place a bet on the outcome?"

"What are the stakes?" Eli asked as Lu returned and set two platters of fried whole-belly clams in front of them.

"His hair," Lu replied, tugging on the end of Eli's braid. "He'd have far less problems at work if he'd just cut his hair."

"That would be a crime, ma'am," Ash said, and Lu shot him a look that said not to encourage Eli. He leaned over, lowering his voice as Lu walked away again. "I have been thinking about seeing your hair loose ever since I first saw you."

Eli's gaze heated as the sense of anticipation jumped higher in Ash's gut. The crowd cheered over something that happened on the screen, and Ash was pleased to see that Eli didn't even steal a peek. If Ash was caught up in Eli's spell, it was only right that Eli be caught as well in Ash's. "I'm sorry to say that my thoughts of you weren't quite as tame," Eli murmured.

Well, hot damn, Ash wanted to know what every single one of those untamed thoughts were. Heat surged between them. It had been a long time since a guy had gotten Ash this worked up, and he briefly considered abandoning dinner and the game to lure Eli back to his place right now. Not that it seemed like it would take that much luring. Then he dismissed the idea. He was enjoying their date and when they did fall into bed, the experience would be all the more intense if they kept up a keen edge to their anticipation. Just the thought of leaning over to steal a kiss had Ash's heart beating faster. He wanted to know how those lips would taste and feel. Years of ingrained discretion kept him where he was.

"You'll have to give me more details later on." The gleam in Eli's eyes, the wicked little quirk to his mouth, told Ash that he intended on doing just that. "I'm curious to find out what wicked thoughts you've got going on in that head of yours."

"Just to whet your imagination"—Eli leaned closer, his voice dropping to a conspiratorial whisper—"one involved licking every one of the freckles on your body. I hope you have them all over."

A punch of pure heat hit Ash right in his chest, and his dick came awake with a vengeance. Damn, Eli was a wild one. Ash could see it written all over his face. A flirtatious, playful smile hovered on Eli's lips, and his eyes were quicksilver with humor. He was like the dancing end of a candle: impossible to catch, and if you managed it, you got singed. Ash's thoughts scattered as he vainly tried to get his raging hormones back in control.

Ash had been through flames before. He didn't want to repeat the experience, ever, but Eli was a whole different kind of fire altogether.

The bet, ah yes. That's what they had been discussing. Ash cleared his throat and drained the rest of his beer. "How about stakes? Is there anything I've got that you want?"

Eli took a sip of his wine, glancing at the screen before looking at Ash with undisguised interest. He leaned in a little closer, and his lips twisted in a teasing smile. "Your Atlanta Braves cap," he said, flicking the brim of Ash's hat. He grinned as Ash groaned. "If you're going to bet, the stakes should mean something."

Ash had not been expecting that. Not with that gleam in Eli's eyes. Damn, he loved that cap. It was nice and broken in, fitting his head perfectly. Still, this was not an opportunity he was about to pass up.

"You play a hard game, but I accept your terms," he replied, as he wracked his brain for something to demand in return. Something that would also make Eli pause. Only the fantasy of Eli naked kept intruding on his thoughts. Ash was horny and distracted, a dangerous combination.

Why pretend this wasn't headed where both of them knew it was going? Ash had no intention of playing it safe, and he'd bet that Eli had one hell of a wild streak in him. Either Eli would be game or he'd back off. Ash chuckled softly, his gaze intent on Eli. "But if I win, I get your boxers and I get to watch you take them off."

There was a moment of startled silence, then Eli laughed as well, the sound rich and wicked. "What if I don't wear anything underneath my jeans?"

Ash couldn't decide if Eli was teasing him or not, and frankly he didn't care if he was. The image of bare naked ass against soft, worn denim almost made him groan out loud. No, it was fine by him if Eli went commando. Ash gave him a crooked grin. "Then I'm sure I could come up with something else."

"You've got yourself a deal. And for the record, yes, it's boxers."

"Are you sure you don't want to change the stakes up a bit?" Ash offered. "A hat for boxer shorts hardly seems fair. To you, I mean."

"Nice try, Ash. But I'll stick to my wager. Winning your Braves cap would be just fine with me."

"Anyone ever tell you that you're a cruel, devious man?" Ash asked, glancing at the screen and wincing when he saw the Sox up by two runs. It was only the second inning, though. There was no telling what would happen in the next couple hours.

"I have to protest being called devious," Eli said as Lu returned with fresh drinks for them both.

"Don't believe one word of it, Ash," Lu said, picking up their empties. "Eli doesn't have a mean bone in his body, but he is devious. He'll make you think he's all laid-back and easygoing, which he is, but he's got more layers than that. Just when you think you've got him going your way, he digs in his heels and gets stubborn and rebellious, tougher to get out than a deer tick."

Ash burst out laughing as Eli leveled a look of loving exasperation at his cousin. It spoke of a long history of teasing and banter between the two. "Really, Lu, a deer tick? You're not helping me, here. Go harass your man before he starts bellowing for you again."

He watched her go and then turned to Ash. "You mentioned a sister. Can I call her and get the dirt on you to even the odds?"

"Actually, I have two sisters, and they would be more than happy to answer any questions you have. The only problem is they expect to have all their questions answered in turn. You might be stuck on the phone for quite a while."

They continued to banter back and forth, watching the game as it progressed. Ash had always found baseball to be a game of anticipation and now, with the stakes involved, it was even more so. He was intensely aware of the man sitting next to him, of every expression that crossed Eli's open face, the timbre of his voice and the way there always seemed to be laughter in it. Eli's knee brushed his under the table, increasing his awareness of the man even more.

Lu came and took their plates away, leaving behind another beer for Ash and a glass of water for Eli. Ash relaxed back in his chair, nursing his drink. He was already mellow enough as it was. "So which is your favorite position?"

"That's such a loaded question." Eli glanced at the screen, cursing under his breath as the Yankees pulled ahead.

"It's meant to be," Ash murmured.

"Let's see, then. I've always been particularly fond of third base." He cast Ash a significant glance, an unspoken promise of what would happen when they were alone. It made it hard to have a coherent thought other than *yes, please*. "They don't call it the hot corner for nothing. You?"

Ash shifted in his chair, the insistent ache in his cock making it difficult to keep up with Eli's sinful tongue. "I preferred batting to outfield. I loved blowing the ball out of the park." He grinned as the sound of Eli's soft groan sent another thrill through him.

"How long did you play for?" Eli asked.

"From T-ball all the way through high school. I wasn't good enough to get a scholarship, and at the time, I wasn't much interested in going to college, anyway. I wanted to get away from home and do something meaningful, or at least ridiculously dangerous. So I enlisted."

Ash shook his head as the Red Sox surged ahead by one, and Eli laughed with delight. "How about you?"

Eli didn't respond at first, and when Ash glanced at him, there was something in his eyes and in the set of his mouth that made him wonder if perhaps he'd brought up bad memories. Before he could ask or back off, Eli shrugged. "Till my sophomore year, then we were stationed in Alaska and my dad signed me up for hockey instead."

"I see you managed to escape with all your teeth," Ash said lightly, and Eli flashed him a smile.

"My short-lived hockey career ended in an epic battle, I'm afraid," he said, with such relish in his tone Ash was sure that Eli cherished the memory. "I don't like being cornered into something I don't want to do. Never have. I might've acted out a bit."

Ash reached under the table and took Eli's hand, brushing his thumb over the knuckles. "You'll have to tell me that story sometime."

"Maybe someday when we have several hours, a bottle of wine, and nowhere to be in the morning."

No one seemed to be paying them any attention anymore, and Eli didn't seem as if he wanted to hide at all. He certainly didn't pull his hand away and Ash liked the feel of it in his own. He was more aware of every heartbeat, every intake of Eli's breath, than he was of the game. And when the Yankees tied the score in the ninth inning, the heat and tension between them had little to do with the game going on or with the bet.

Ash laid his hand on Eli's leg as the sexual tension slid up another notch. He'd been right about there being muscle underneath his clothes, and not the bulky kind, either. Ash grinned slow and easy as those expressive eyes met his. "Now here's the real question. Do you want them to win or lose?"

Eli laughed softly and leaned closer himself. "I don't think it really matters, does it?"

"Nah, not really. I just wanted to hear a Red Sox fan commit blasphemy."

"If I get struck down by lightning it would really put a damper on the evening." Eli sucked in a breath as Ash's hand drifted higher up his thigh.

"Admit that you'd rather be doing something else."

"Yeah, I would. But I have to say that I'm also enjoying this slow buildup we're having," Eli said, moving his own hand to Ash's leg under the table. His fingertips slid to Ash's inner thigh, sending a spark of heat straight to his groin. "Are you that afraid of losing your hat?"

"Oh, I can play as long as you can, Eli."

Another roar came up from the crowd near the bar, but Ash barely heard it. "I think someone just scored."

Eli glanced toward the screen and grimaced. "No, we just went into extra innings."

Ash drained the last of his beer, tossed some money on the table, and caught Eli's hand, giving it a squeeze as he shot his companion a sideways glance. "Come on, let's get out of here." He wasn't about to deny himself. He'd had his share of one-night stands, though not with anybody he'd known for such a short amount of time. He'd been thinking of being with Eli for weeks now and did not want to wait a moment longer before having the chance to kiss him. "My place is just up the street, within walking distance."

"If we take my motorcycle, it'll be even quicker," Eli said with a heated gleam in his eyes and added money to Ash's to pay for his half of the meal.

Ash bit back another groan and headed for the exit. He wouldn't turn down an opportunity to have his arms wrapped around Eli as he pressed against his back.

Chapter 4

Eli's heart thrummed as he caught Lu's gaze, and he nodded toward the door to let her know they were leaving. Her brows shot up and then she gave him a little grin and a shooing motion before going over to the bar to distract Neil. His friend would never understand the necessity of leaving a game early, and Eli didn't want to draw attention to himself before he slipped out.

In fact, he'd be all for skipping the rest of the game. He couldn't wait to get his hands on Ash's body. He had been hungering for the feel of the man's skin since he'd first seen him. He joined Ash out on the sidewalk, and they walked in silence over to his bike. It was getting late and as a result, Main Street had emptied. Dingers was the only establishment left with lights on. Eli appreciated the solitude as Ash climbed up behind him on the motorcycle.

"You know, I do like a man with a bike," Ash murmured against his ear, his hands lingering in a slow slide down Eli's ribs to rest on his hips. His voice was husky, with that drawl that was melted honey over his senses.

"Fair enough," Eli replied with a smirk back at him. "Because a military man has always pushed my buttons."

Ash laughed, his grip tightening as they took off with a rumble. Eli was almost sorry the ride was only a few blocks. He enjoyed the intimacy of Ash pressed up against him and the cool night air rushing over them. It was a beautiful night for riding, with the moon full and the town quiet. The trip ended far too fast.

They pulled into the little lot behind Ash's apartment, and as Eli slowed to a stop, Ash stuck his hands in Eli's back pockets and kissed the side of his neck. "That was nice," he drawled next to his ear. A shiver of awareness rippled down Eli's spine.

"You've got my complete attention, Georgia," he said as he shut off his engine. He loved that accent that had only thickened with the desire in Ash's voice.

"Does that mean we can forego the bet and skip the rest of the game?"

The heat of Ash's breath against his ear distracted him, and it was all Eli could do to not turn around and capture those lips that teased his senses. He bet that Ash kissed just the way he sounded, all slow, liquid, southern heat, as potent as twenty-year-old whiskey.

"Is that lust or fear talking?" Eli asked with a chuckle, turning his head to look at Ash in the moonlight. He flicked the brim of Ash's cap. "Unless you want to go ahead and forfeit; seems only fair since you're going to be able to watch me strip down."

Ash swung off the bike and pulled his keys out of his jeans. "I suppose my ego can handle not being able to distract you from the rest of the game." He caught Eli's hand in his, twining their fingers together as he led him up the outside staircase to the apartment on the second floor. To Eli's amusement, Ash actually locked his front door, unlike most of the other residents in Amwich.

"I'm sure I can be persuaded, after all you did get me out of the bar. I might, however, find the persuading quite fun." Ash drew him into the apartment, and Eli blinked as the lights came on. He caught the brief impression of a rather bare living room with a poker table in the corner and two giant pictures, one a framed poster of Hank Aaron and the other the famous print of the dogs playing poker.

"I'll keep that in mind," Ash murmured, turning his Atlanta Braves cap around and pinning Eli to the door. He smiled slowly. Eli liked the way his eyes crinkled up at the corners as he did. Ash had gorgeous eyes, a dark green with flecks of gold. They were even better than what he'd imagined. Only right now they were shadowed, and lines of weariness were etched on his face.

Perhaps Eli should call it a night and let Ash get the rest he obviously needed. Before he could voice that thought, Ash leaned closer and their lips met. It was a soft, sweet kiss, a promise of more to come, and Eli savored the sensation of Ash's firm lips as the heat between them smoldered. Eli's lips parted, but before the kiss could deepen, Ash stepped back, leaving Eli wanting more. His breath caught, stomach fluttering as Ash smiled and led Eli over to the longer mismatched couch with a tug of his hand.

His focus remained on the sexy man standing before him while Ash clicked on the game. "Not that I think I'll be able to pay much attention to it, but at least we'll know who won," Ash said and then tugged Eli down onto the couch with him.

Eli glanced at the screen and winced. That was a mistake. The Yankees had managed to score during the short time since they left Dingers. "You've let me jinx them," he sighed mournfully. "Don't you know you're not supposed to walk out before a game is over?"

In truth, he couldn't seem to muster up any kind of upset over the game. Not with Ash drawing him closer with a teasing light in his eyes. He had a clean, tantalizing scent that stirred Eli's senses as Ash started to nuzzle his jaw line. Eli shivered, turning his head and arching his throat for those wandering lips.

"It's not taking much effort to distract you," Ash said, grinning against his skin. Eli lifted his head, and their breath mingled on each other's lips as their eyes met.

"I don't even want to watch until we're at least tied." Eli's stomach fluttered as those smooth lips met his own for a brief touch before pulling away. Ash was such a wicked, sexy tease. "But the truth is, I don't believe that I can resist your brand of temptation for a moment."

"Ah, Eli, flattery will get you everywhere."

They kissed again, deeper this time, their tongues brushing against each other as they tasted and explored. Ash's thumb rubbed along Eli's jaw, and he wondered what it would be like to have those fingers elsewhere on his body. As impatient as he was to feel it, he was really enjoying this slow, drawn-out seduction. Eli cupped his hand around the nape of Ash's neck, seeking more contact as hot, little licks of fire filled him.

As they drew back again, Eli's heart pounded harder. For a moment Eli considered pulling away to take things slower. Ash seemed to be just too perfect, and Eli knew all too well his luck with those few guys that he clicked with. Some strange twist of fate seemed to conspire against him, every time. Right guy, wrong time.

Then Ash grinned, and Eli couldn't decide what was sexier, the hint of a dimple on his cheek or the stray freckle near his mouth that begged to be kissed. He did just that, tongue flicking out to taste that tiny spot. Eli leaned back into the cushion, tugging Ash against him so that he was sprawled over him. His misgivings melted away with the sensation of Ash's hard body against his own.

Ash glanced at the TV. "Your boys managed to keep them from scoring again. Do you think they can catch up?"

"They'd better at least get one run ahead, because I'm not interested in drawing this out for a whole other inning." Ash's cock stirred against Eli's hip as he shifted, followed by an answering tingling in his balls. Screw the game and any lightning that might come down to strike him for thinking it.

"That's good to know." Ash nuzzled at Eli's lips before claiming them, his tongue thrusting deep into his mouth this time. Eli groaned and kissed him back, the heat kicking up another notch. He itched to slowly take off Ash's clothes and feel all that naked skin against his own. They both drew long shuddering breaths as they parted and glanced at the baseball game on the screen.

"One man on base," Eli murmured.

"Then there's still hope for me." Ash's green eyes gleamed as he looked down at him. "Do you prefer pitching or catching?"

"I've gone both ways," Eli replied with a grin, his hands skimming down Ash's sides. "We could always wrestle for top or bottom since we already have one bet between us tonight." His hand slipped underneath Ash's T-shirt and flattened against his hard stomach. "Given the way you're built, I don't think I'll stand a chance."

"Try ten years in the Marine Corps combined with construction on the side. You should've seen me before I enlisted. I was an awkward, lanky reed."

Eli laughed with Ash, remembering his own teenage years, when he seemed to grow taller every day without any weight to back it up. "Well, I have ten years of teaching under my belt. I don't think it's going to hold up against your experience."

"Maybe, but I bet there's plenty that you could teach me." Ash sucked in a breath as Eli slid his hand upward, exploring his chest. The reaction sent another punch of lust straight to Eli's gut. This was far hotter than any of his fantasies had ever been and they were just getting started.

"We'll see, won't we?" Eli replied, groaning as Ash's mouth came down to tease his throat. He slid his fingertips along the muscle over Ash's ribs. There was an unnatural roughness to the skin there, and before Eli could make out the reason, Ash kissed him again. Coherent thought skittered away, and Eli slid his hands up higher along Ash's back and shoulders.

Ash lifted his head at the cracking sound of a bat striking a ball and glanced at the screen. "Your boys have another man on base."

"Do they now? That's promising." Eli gathered his disjointed wits together and tried to think past the insistent throbbing of his cock to look at the stats on the screen. "Damn, but they've already struck out once."

"Don't you have any faith?" Ash sat back on his heels and tossed his Braves cap on the couch arm before tugging his T-shirt off to join it. Eli's gaze roamed over his chest and stomach like he'd been longing to do since he'd first seen Ash working on the roof. He had the build of a man who worked hard for a living, instead of spending hours at a gym. Livid scars marred Ash's skin along his side, from the length of his ribs down to disappear underneath the waist of his jeans. They looked like a combination of healed burns and shrapnel scars.

Ash tensed, a haggard, guarded expression crossing his face. "Do they bother you?" he asked in a clipped voice.

"Not at all," Eli said, meeting Ash's eyes so the other man could see he wasn't bullshitting him. Eli sat up and kissed Ash's dog tags lying against his bare chest as he slid his hand up to caress the roughened flesh again. Sympathy welled up inside of him. He couldn't even begin to imagine how much that had hurt. He had no frame of reference at all to base it on.

Ash relaxed, an apologetic smile coming to his lips. "Sorry, I'm not normally so touchy. I tend to get that way when I'm running on too little sleep."

"No need to apologize," Eli said, wrapping his arms around Ash to draw him closer. If anybody rejected Ash because of those scars, they were idiots. He wanted to ask Ash how he'd gotten them, but there was a lingering tightness about his eyes that warned Eli to leave it alone.

The question must have been in his expression when he looked at Ash, because before he could ask it, Ash shook his head. "That's a story for another time."

"Understood." Eli smiled and nuzzled Ash's lips, his hands not stopping their slow exploration of Ash's body. Questions could wait for another day, because he would damn well make sure there was another day for the both of them, and right now desire made him ache. "Now, where were we?"

Ash kissed him hard before starting to undo the buttons on Eli's vest. "Getting you half-naked too." He stripped Eli's vest and shirt off, his hands settling on Eli's shoulders. His mouth quirked into a pleased smile as he looked Eli over.

Eli might not have been ripped like Ash, but he was active enough to not feel self-conscious under Ash's scrutiny. Ash's hands slid over his lean chest and stomach in a lingering caress. "Very nice, guess you don't just watch baseball."

"Hiking, every day. There's a ton of trails around here," Eli said, his fingers running along the waistband of Ash's jeans. "Some rock climbing too, when I can find a buddy to go with."

"I might have to join you sometime."

Their mouths met again in a hot, consuming kiss. Eli groaned as Ash's fingers deftly undid the button of his jeans. A hand cupped him through his boxers, and his cock surged in response, pressing against Ash's palm. He broke his mouth away, arching the lower half of his body with a groan. How a simple touch could feel so good he didn't know. "Damn, Ash."

"Even though I have a chance to win your boxers, I was still imagining you going commando," Ash said, giving his cock a light squeeze that had Eli's hips bucking for more contact. "You only said that to screw with me."

"Maybe." Eli kicked off his shoes and unzipped Ash's jeans. A little reciprocation was in order, and, as his hand slipped inside Ash's jeans, the crowd roared on the TV. They looked over, and Ash let out a short bark of laughter. "Jeez, you have got to be kidding me. How much longer are they going to drag this out?"

Eli grinned. Normally at a moment like this he'd be sitting on the edge of his seat, tense with anticipation, but now a whole different kind of anticipation thrummed through him. "It's the bottom of the tenth. They're ahead by one. We have the three men on base and two outs. Sounds like a typical Red Sox/Yankees game to me, exciting to the end."

"So the fate of my hat rests on the next hitter? Are you sure you won't strip for me if I lose?" Ash teased, his lips moving along Eli's throat, making his pulse pound.

"You're screwed, my friend. Look who's up next." Eli tugged him back down until Ash sprawled over him. He wrapped his arms around Ash's waist and maneuvered so that they were reclining side by side. "That hat is as good as mine."

"Not if he can't hit the ball. Strike one." Ash snickered as Eli nipped his shoulder.

"All we need is one run to tie and another to win, unless it goes into another inning or two. Or you could just forfeit now and give me the hat." Eli shut up as Ash growled and attacked his mouth. The rest of his teasing thoughts fled as Ash's hands seemed to be everywhere at once. The game had better not go into another damn inning.

Eli's hand slid into Ash's jeans again. His hand curved over warm, naked ass, and he thought he would have a coronary. Good thing he hadn't asked for Ash's boxers or he would've come up short. And his ass was as tight as it looked. Hot damn.

A roar of protest came from the TV, and they both glanced over as they kicked their shoes off onto the floor. "Strike two." Ash's eyes were warm with laughter. "Do you want me to put on some music for you to strip to when you lose? I think I have 'Hot for Teacher' somewhere here."

"Trust me; you don't want to watch me attempt to dance. But, while we're waiting for the outcome...." Eli kissed him as his hand slid to Ash's hip, where the scars extended down another couple inches before tapering off. For once, he didn't feel the disappointment that he usually did when the Red Sox were on the verge of blowing a game. How could he when Ash was sprawled out half-naked next to him?

For a final time, the crack of a bat drew their attention, and they both looked in time to see the ball sail out of the park. "Oh, fuck me," Ash said, shaking his head. "Really?"

Eli laughed and shot Ash a triumphant grin before nipping his lower lip. "Looks like you'll have to get that strip tease another time, Georgia. I'd really much rather you fuck me."

Ash's eyes lit up, and a shiver of awareness went down Eli's spine. "I sure as hell won't turn down an offer like that." Ash stood up with a soft groan and stretched. For a split moment, Eli saw the exhaustion cross Ash's face again before the other man held out his hand to him.

Eli kissed the back of his fingers and then stepped forward, slipping his hand around the nape of Ash's neck, stroking it with his fingertips. "Where's your bedroom?" Ash looked as if he could use a bit of pampering, and Eli didn't mind volunteering, especially if it meant an excuse to get his hands all over him.

Forget one-night stands. He wasn't leaving without Ash's phone number and the promise to see him again.

Ash grinned and led him down the hall to a darkened bedroom, walking backward. His jeans rode low on his hips, red-gold curls peeking out from the gaping zipper. He flipped on the bedside lamp, revealing a surprisingly neat room that was stripped of everything but the basics. "You're still in the barracks mindset, aren't you?" Eli teased.

"I'm working on it." Ash tugged on the end of Eli's braid and slipped off the rubber band securing it, deftly undoing the braid until Eli's hair brushed his shoulders. He buried his hands in its softness, grinning. "I've wanted to do that all night."

"So you've said." Eli's heart thumped in anticipation as Ash drew him closer. He slipped his hands in Ash's jeans and pushed them down, leaving him completely naked. Ash kicked them to the side to lie in a heap as Eli looked him over. "Damn, Georgia," he breathed, his cock throbbing.

He slipped his arms around Ash's waist as the other man pulled him close again. The kiss started out slow and exploring before quickly escalating. Eli tugged off his own jeans and boxer shorts, shivers racing through his body as he pressed against Ash and felt the delicious sensation of naked flesh against naked flesh that he'd been craving.

Ash's cock nudged between Eli's thighs, bobbing against his balls, and Eli groaned against his mouth.

Ash's hands slid from Eli's hair down his back and cupped his ass, giving it a good squeeze. Bed, that's what they needed. That single coherent thought emerged from the chaos of his brain trying to take in every bit of sensation. Eli began to maneuver backward in the general direction of where he thought the bed would be. He wanted nothing more than to get his hands all over Ash in a slow and sensual exploration.

They broke the kiss long enough to tumble back on the bed before they kissed again. Their tongues stroked together, tasting, exploring, and making Eli hungry for more. Eli straddled Ash's thighs, sprawling on top of him, deepening the kiss as Ash's hands moved all over him.

"I wouldn't suppose you have any massage oil handy, would you?" Eli panted against Ash's mouth. His senses reeled, thoughts scattering as Ash shifted and their cocks rubbed against each other. "Oh fuck."

Ash chuckled and gently bit Eli's jaw before his mouth moved down to devastate Eli's throat. "Didn't I tell you I was also a Scout when I was a kid? Always prepared."

Eli shook his head and laughed, somehow not at all surprised. Ash must've spent most of his life in one uniform or another, while Eli had spent most of his life bucking the system in any way he could. He'd never understood that about himself, how he could get so worked up over a man in uniform when he'd always known that he'd never be able to handle that kind of a lifestyle for himself.

"What's so funny?" Ash kissed the pulse at Eli's throat.

"That's another one of those things for later." Eli slid his mouth down Ash's chest until he found one flat nipple. He gave it a gentle bite and a flick of his tongue, then met Ash's gaze. "Right now, my brain isn't wired for conversation."

"Good point." Ash cupped Eli's ass, blunt fingers teasing the cleft until he found Eli's entrance.

"You wicked man," Eli said with a breathless laugh. He slid his hand down, palmed Ash's cock and began to stroke it. Ash groaned, lifting his hips, his eyes hot on him.

"I'm just getting started."

Eli had come up with any number of fantasies since first seeing Ash, and after realizing that the man harbored similar fantasies about him, Eli had been increasingly impatient to get to this exact point. A delicious excitement had taken hold of him, and Eli lifted his head to nip at Ash's earlobe. "Are those just words or is that a promise?"

Ash groaned, sliding his hand down Eli's thighs. "You tell me after. Damn, you have the longest legs. Are you sure you're a teacher? You're the hottest teacher I've ever seen."

Eli laughed and squeezed Ash's cock. "You're losing track, Georgia. Massage oil?"

Ash twisted and leaned over to fumble at the stand of drawers beside the bed. He pulled out a bottle of oil as well as a box of condoms and lube. Eli's brows rose as he caught a glimpse of all kinds of other interesting things in that drawer before Ash shut it.

"Here you go, projecting this all-American, boy next door vibe—who would've known you have a kink drawer in your bedroom," Eli teased.

"Who says kink isn't all-American?"

"Point taken." Eli pushed Ash back against the sheets. "You look like you could use a wee bit of pampering. Indulge me." Ash looked done in after a weekend away at training. Eli had no idea what that entailed, but he was sure it was enough to make the body ache. Not to mention that he wanted to slow things down a bit and draw their evening out. He kissed Ash's shoulder and ran a hand down his side.

Ash shook his head with a chuckle. "Only a fool would say no to that."

Eli leaned over to grab the bottle of almond scented oil as Ash tucked his hands under the back of his head. Eli straddled Ash's thighs, unable to take his eyes off of him. There was a smattering of freckles and hair on his chest and his arms were lightly sun-kissed, the freckles darker and more numerous there.

Eli poured some oil onto his hands and rubbed them together to warm it before bringing them down to Ash's shoulders. He rubbed the oil around and over, slicking his skin, flexing his fingers, and began to knead away the tension he could feel. Ash groaned, his eyes fluttering shut as a smile tugged on his lips. "Oh God, yeah."

Eli chuckled, stroking down his chest with long, smooth sweeps of his hands, watching with pleasure as Ash relaxed.

"Man, you're the one who won the bet," Ash murmured. "Shouldn't I be doing this to you?"

"You're the one who spent the entire weekend busting your ass doing combat training." Eli leaned over him, pausing to kiss the scar on his side. "Maybe you can return the favor some other time." His stomach fluttered for a moment as he hoped for a next time.

Ash's answering smile held a promise. He opened half-lidded eyes, casting Eli a heated glance through rusty-tipped lashes. "You're on."

Eli scooted lower, rubbing the oil more gently along the scars on his side, and Ash gave him no indication that they still caused him any pain. Once again, Ash's eyes had closed, and with a wicked smile Eli grasped Ash's still hard cock, giving it a firm stroke.

Ash groaned, rocking his hips up as his cock throbbed in Eli's hand. "Tease. Just you wait until I get my hands on you."

Eli chuckled, stroking him a few more times before warming some more oil between his palms. "That doesn't sound very threatening." More like amazing. He slid his hands down to Ash's strong thighs, kneading down them. The hair on his legs had been bleached golden by the sun. Eli liked the texture of it under his hands.

"Roll onto your stomach," Eli said, scooting out of the way for him.

"I don't know if that's such a good idea," Ash murmured as he obeyed, pillowing his head on his folded arms. "Between the beers and your magic hands, I'm feeling very mellow."

Eli leaned over him and nipped the nape of his neck, smiling as Ash's breath caught. "If you pass out on me, can I tease you for going AWOL?"

"I'm sure you can come up with something a lot more inventive than teasing."

Eli drizzled oil down Ash's spine. He had a beautiful back, broad, but not so bulky that he made Eli think of those 'roided out guys in some of those home gym commercials. The lingering tension in those muscles eased as Eli worked his way down, kneading from Ash's shoulders to his firm ass, the sounds of Ash's soft groans urging him on.

"Damn, your hands are lethal," Ash sighed.

Eli grinned and scooted down between Ash's legs, trailing a finger along the shadowed cleft of Ash's ass. He loved the image of a nice butt, balls peeking out between strong thighs. He began massaging down Ash's legs, savoring the sensations. He could touch Ash for hours. It had been a long time since he'd been able to indulge in this kind of pampering. His last lover had been a bang-and-go kind of guy.

By the time Eli reached Ash's ankles, the man was lying limp, his eyes closed, his breathing even. "Ash?"

A light snore answered him. Eli sat back on his heels, both disappointed and amused. Well, Ash had warned him. He debated whether or not to wake him before reluctantly deciding against it. As much as his cock protested, it seemed cruel to wake Ash when he had such dark shadows under his eyes.

Eli set the oil aside before drawing the sheets and blankets up around Ash. He murmured, shifting before starting to snore again. Eli dragged on his boxers and jeans, trying without much success to stifle the desire still hot in his blood.

He flipped off the light, plunging the room into darkness before returning to the living room to grab the remainder of his clothes. They'd forgotten to shut off the TV in their eagerness to get back to the bedroom, and the memory sent another hot, aching throb through his cock.

Eli grabbed up Ash's baseball cap with a grin. Hey, he'd still won that. And if the man wanted to have it back, he'd have to come looking for Eli. He quickly scribbled a note and left it on the coffee table, chuckling to himself as he left.

He roared home on his bike, the late night air cool on his skin. He was invigorated and wide awake, and his mind kept drifting back to the picture Ash made tangled up in the sheets in the bed. It was going to take Eli forever to get to sleep with that image in his head and he was going to be exhausted in the morning for the start of the school semester.

Didn't matter. Knowing he would be seeing Ash again would more than make up for being tired.

The light from the Hermitage's front door shone through the trees, and Eli heard Jabbers as he turned into the long driveway. The beagle was framed in the front window, head thrown back as he bayed in welcome. And when Eli opened the front door, Jabbers was there waiting for him, his whole body wiggling before he pounced on Eli. He laughed, rubbing the beagle's silky ears. "You certainly know how to make a man feel welcome."

Jabbers sniffed all over him, resting his paws on Eli's shoulders as he investigated him. "Smell someone new, huh, boyo? I've got a new friend." Eli wished that there was more of Ash's scent on him. His balls still ached.

He let Jabbers out and frowned as he saw a closet door ajar. He was usually pretty good about remembering to shut it. A quick check inside showed that all of his shoes had been unmolested, so Eli closed it with a shrug, making sure it latched. Jabbers rarely missed an opportunity for mischief.

He let Jabbers in when he scratched at the door, and the beagle dropped a worn work glove at Eli's feet, looking up at him with pride as he thumped his tail. "What did you swipe this time, you little heathen?" Eli picked up the glove and tossed it on the kitchen counter. "I swear you're worse than a magpie. Come on, it's time for bed."

CHAPTER 5

ASH awoke to the sound of rain sheeting down on the roof. He groaned and pulled the blankets back up over his head, determined not to move until the sound let up. He was cozy with the sheets curled around his naked body, scented with massage oil. The memories came back in a slow progression of erotic images. Eli naked, with his unbound hair around his shoulders and a teasing light in his blue-gray eyes.

Only the last thing he remembered was not orgasmic bliss, it was Eli's hands on him. And while they had been blissful, the end result had been him passing out. Ash buried his face in his pillow with another groan. He could not fucking believe he'd done that, no matter how hard the weekend had been. It was his own damn fault, letting his sisters and mother pamper him while he'd been on vacation, and for having those beers when he'd already been exhausted.

Great way to make an impression on the man he'd been lusting after for weeks. His mission to get laid had ended in utter failure, and he'd lost his baseball cap in the process. The next time Eli saw him, he'd probably laugh his ass off or ignore him. And Ash wanted to see him again.

At least the alarm clock hadn't gone off yet. After the weekend of hard training he was disinclined to move until he absolutely had to. And he needed to come up with a way to get Eli out on a second date. Only the thought of the silent alarm kept nagging at him, not letting him relax until he stole a reluctant peek.

8:53 a.m.

"Fuck me."

Ash leapt out of bed, cursing nonstop under his breath as he scrambled to get his clothes and books together. Outside, thunder rumbled, bringing with it a new torrent of rain. What a miserable start for the semester.

ASH felt like he'd been running behind all damn day. Between that and dashing through the incessant rain between buildings, his temper had been simmering, mostly directed toward himself. At least this was his final class of the day.

Ash dragged his feet as he made his way through the corridors of the English building. He had put off taking his final English credits as long as possible. Hell, he would've waited until the final semester in the spring, but he was already pretty loaded down with what he wanted to take. He had finally decided to suck it up and fit it in this fall. And he'd managed to find a class that actually piqued his interest. If nothing else, he wouldn't be reading a stack of books that made no sense, written by people who had died centuries ago.

He reached the classroom with only two minutes to spare and frowned when he found it empty. Cursing, Ash pulled out his itinerary. He'd printed out the new one just this morning before he left because the school was terrible about changing rooms around the last week leading up to the start of school.

"The Dying Art of Correspondence: An Intimate Study of Historic Letters" with Dr. E. Hollister, Room 113, English Building.

Ash was in the right room. They wouldn't have canceled it on the last day, would they? Fuck.

He spied a taped piece of paper fallen near the door and scooped it up. *Meeting in the Allie B. Martin Library, ground floor, back of building.*

Ash sighed and stuck it back on the door in case he wasn't the only one running late and took off for the room at a jog. It was like he could see his drill instructor up in his face and telling him to get a move on unless he wanted to find himself doing double duty for being late. The memory of that voice sent him from a jog to a dead run.

At least it wasn't far. Ash dashed across the quad to the renovated library on the other side. The guy behind the counter looked up with a bored air as Ash rushed in. "If you're looking for the class, it's in the back," he said and went back to flipping through his book. Ash headed back toward the historic part of the library. It had high ceilings, dark paneling, and cozy nooks between glass display cases of documents and artifacts.

Ash hurried past rain-lashed gray windows toward the murmur of voices. Low, cushy chairs had been pulled into a circle near an old fireplace that had been fitted with glass and had an electric fire installed. Warm light danced behind the glass, and Ash's steps quickened again as he noticed that all the chairs but one were taken.

"It's only five minutes after." Ash slowed at the sound of the familiar voice. He stared at the back of Eli's head, his long, auburn hair caught back in a tie at the back of his neck. The last time he'd seen Eli, it had tumbled about his shoulders in a sex-tangled mess. Right before he embarrassed himself by passing out like a tipsy prom date.

Holy fuck. He froze and rubbed a hand over his damp hair. He'd definitely intended on looking Eli up and apologizing later on today. He just had an opportunity to do it sooner, now. And this was not the old, boring professor he'd been expecting. A grin broke out across his face as he stepped closer.

"It looks like we're only waiting for Ashley," Eli said, leaning back in his chair. "We'll just give her a few more minutes since it's particularly nasty outside this afternoon."

Ash bit back a groan. "Only my mama dares call me that. I prefer Ash."

Eli's head whipped around, his eyes widening and lips parting in pure astonishment. Ash gave him an apologetic smile, hoping that expression wouldn't change to one of disdain. The stunned look in those blue-gray eyes flashed to desire then to an "oh shit" look as Eli seemed to realize that Ashley was not the girl he'd been expecting, but the man he'd been naked with the night before.

Well, at least Ash hadn't completely blown his chances with Eli, not if that brief flash of heat meant what Ash thought it did. He grinned as his day went from crap to "oh hell yeah." He strolled around the chairs to the empty one directly across from Eli and took a seat, stretching his legs out in front of him. His opinion on having to take an English class went up a hundred notches.

He was aware of the other students looking at him, but he only had eyes for Eli. "I apologize for being late," he drawled, as amusement over their situation struck him. "Unexpected room change."

Two faint spots of color appeared on Eli's cheeks and the corners of his mouth twitched as if he were fighting a smile. "That is my fault. I prefer a more intimate setting for my smaller classes. I figured it would be a more comfortable place to meet and have discussions than a classroom. And since you all are going to be doing the majority of your research in here, I wanted to show everyone how to access the online archives."

I like intimate settings. Ash pressed his lips together before he said the comment that flashed into his mind. He had to behave, but oh, was it going to be hard when he knew very well how good Eli was at bantering right back at him.

Eli had said he was a teacher, but for some reason with his laid-back, easygoing attitude, Ash had pictured him teaching little ones. Like kindergarten or first grade. He'd never met a professor who had long hair, rode a motorcycle, and hung out at sports bars.

Ash let his gaze drift over Eli. Judging from the way he kept shuffling his papers, not quite looking at him, Ash was sure that seeing him in his class was the last thing Eli had expected. Ash hadn't seen him anything but confident and this hint of uncertainty on Eli's face was kinda cute. Unless it meant that Eli regretted last night, and that thought didn't settle well with Ash at all.

"Well, then, now that we're all here...." Eli cleared his throat and slipped on a pair of gold-rimmed glasses as he looked down at the stack of papers in his lap. "Why don't we take a few minutes to look at the syllabus? Then we can discuss what you're looking to get out of this class and get to know one another a bit before calling it an early day."

There were so many things that Ash wanted to say with an opening like that and none of them were appropriate. He wanted to get to know every inch of Eli, and his expectations for this class had entirely changed. Ash set his book bag down at his feet and pulled out a pen, trying to figure out what he should say when class was over. He definitely wasn't about to suggest talking over a couple of beers. Lord, he was disgusted with himself for passing out like that.

"As you can see, I have a strict attendance policy," Eli said as the girl next to Ash passed a stack of bound papers with a shy expression on her face. There were only ten of them in all, Eli included. Oh damn, what should he call him? He'd have to work hard not to slip up and say something that would embarrass Eli. "A good portion of your grade will be based on discussions, and you can't discuss if you're not here."

He stole a glance at Eli. What did he think about this? The firelight glinted off the frames of Eli's glasses and brought out the deep red highlights in his auburn hair. There was a serious expression on his face, a look Ash had not seen before and one he couldn't decipher. He kind of liked this side to him and those glasses were sexy.

Ash glanced down at the syllabus, not really seeing the words, nothing except the location of Eli's office and the hours when he could be found there. Eli's voice washed over him as he asked one of the other students a question. Heat pooled in his stomach. The sound made Ash remember how husky it had been last night when they'd been entangled on his couch, teasing each other over the outcome of the game. And that made Ash remember how Eli had looked naked, with his hair free of that tie and…. He shifted in his chair as a punch of unfulfilled lust hit him in his gut.

He needed to concentrate on unsexy thoughts. Ash pictured his drill instructor at boot camp as the voices of the other students murmured in the background. The man's face had been shaped like a misshapen lump, with a mole on his cheek that had always made him think of a potato eye. Ash would always be grateful for the guidance the man had given him, but sexy he was not.

Ash stole a quick look at his watch. Really? Only fifteen minutes had passed? He was going to go out of his skin by the time class ended. He needed a chance to speak to Eli, personally, even though this situation might be a little awkward, between last night and the fact that Eli was now his teacher. That didn't stop Ash from wanting to get with him again. They were both grown adults, and he didn't see the harm in continuing, as long as they were discreet. As discreet as you could be in a small town where everyone knew Eli and his entire family.

He wanted to groan and bury his face in his hands.

"Ash?"

Ash glanced up to see the rest of the students and Eli staring at him, and he scrambled to recover the thread of the conversation before he completely embarrassed himself again. Something about reasons for taking the class, and he gathered that so far everyone else was an English major, so he was the odd man out.

"Is there a particular reason you chose this course?" Eli prompted him. He'd taken off his glasses again, hooking them in the collar of his shirt, and Ash wondered how often he forgot they were there.

"Well." Ash tugged on one earlobe and cast a quick smile around at the group. "Don't shoot me for this, but until now, I'd always thought English classes were dead boring. And I didn't particularly want to take another one, but my advisor didn't leave me much of a choice. So I put it off until this one caught my eye."

One of the other guys in the group smirked, and the girl sitting next to Eli leaned forward, the hem of her short shirt hiking up another inch. "What was it about this class that did?"

Ash looked back at Eli, who had his head cocked with a silent question in his blue-gray eyes. Ash thought that his reason for taking the class was silly, but if anyone would understand, it would be Eli, so instead of giving some bullshit answer he told the truth. "When I was in Iraq, nothing meant more to me than the letters I got from back home. Even more than the e-mails, because I could carry them out on the field with me and re-read them. And somehow the handwriting made it more personal."

Eli's eyes warmed and a gentle smile crossed his lips as Ash shrugged in embarrassment at the admission. "Sounds like you'll really connect with the class, then, and offer some good insights." Eli turned to the girl next to him as if he knew Ash would rather not elaborate further. "Hannah, how about you?"

Ash relaxed and gave him a grateful smile in return. Words actually couldn't express how much those letters had meant to him, or to the other men in his unit, especially to those men who'd had no one back home to get letters from. He made it a point every week to send one to his best friend, Kurtis, who was in Afghanistan now, and another through one of the organizations that collected letters and care packages for those who had to do without.

He glanced at his watch again and only hard-won discipline kept him from shifting in his seat. He preferred action to waiting, even though he knew that sometimes waiting was a better option. He still didn't know what Eli thought about the whole situation. And his expression wasn't giving Ash one clue. The not knowing drove him crazy.

Not that Ash was looking for anything long-term. Hell no. But boning his hot professor would be far more preferable to sitting near him all semester and knowing he'd totally blown his chance.

By the time class ended, Ash still had no answers. He'd never been in a situation remotely like this before and somehow he was sure Eli hadn't either. He just couldn't picture Eli starting up relationships with students on a regular basis. And Ash had never been one to hit on a superior officer when he'd known the guy had swung his way. It had seemed too much like trading sex to get ahead.

Ash lingered, putting his new materials in his bag with deliberate care as the rest of the students wandered off. All except one, the leggy brunette with the short skirt. She cast Ash a look, as if silently telling him to shoo, and his brows rose. He glanced at Eli as she gave him an inviting smile.

Sorry, honey, that one's mine.

"Is there something I can help you with, Whitney?" Eli asked, tucking his reading glasses in a hard case before stowing it away in a battered leather satchel stuffed haphazardly with papers and books.

The girl cast Ash another glance, and he grinned back at her. She seemed to realize that she was not going to get a few minutes alone with Eli and she bristled in irritation before bestowing a smile at Eli. "It's private," she murmured and leaned in to whisper in Eli's ear.

Ash shook his head and fought a smirk. That one had eyes for Eli, and it amused him that Eli didn't seem to see it at all.

"Just get here when you can and have a good day," Eli said as he straightened.

Ash watched Whitney go with a grin, and then Eli turned to him and squared his shoulders. His grin faltered; that couldn't be a good sign. "Ash, want to talk in my office?"

"I really think we should."

Eli was grateful for Ash's silence as they went up to the third floor, where his office was tucked way in the back. Randall Britton had decided that as the youngest professor of the English department, Eli should have the most out-of-the-way space and finagled for him to be stuck back there. In truth, it suited him, so Eli had let the man think he won that one.

The view was amazing. The windows looked out over the tree-covered mountains behind the school. And its remote location usually kept him from receiving too many students just looking to drop in and complain. Eli liked the stillness up here, it let him think.

Only this time neither the walk nor the stillness helped him come to any easy answers as he had hoped they would. His initial surprise at seeing Ash in his class had been replaced with acute disappointment. He'd been jockeying to get more Cultural Studies classes offered and finally felt like he was making some headway with getting permission for this class. And then one of his students was the same guy he'd been naked with the night before.

Damn, Ash had to be the hottest guy on campus. And now he was hands-off. Normally, Eli wouldn't care, since no one had to know what wicked fantasies went on his mind. With Ash, he had memories to give potency to said fantasies. And Ash would know Eli's thoughts were anything but pure every time Eli looked at him. Plus he genuinely liked Ash on top of the chemistry between them.

Eli hadn't been able to tell what Ash thought, beyond his initial amusement when he'd first shown up. A couple of years ago Eli would have been just as amused, even if he'd unwittingly broken one of his few rules. He didn't get involved with students. Period. It would just open up more trouble than he wanted to deal with, especially for something so fleeting as lust.

Ash was different, though. Dammit, why was it that all the guys he really felt a connection to came with complicated situations as well?

Eli unlocked his office door and motioned for Ash to go first. How the hell did one start a conversation like this? He'd been in many strange circumstances before, but this one had enough fodder for a situation comedy. He had no desire to star in that kind of a show.

To be honest, if it was just between him and Ash and there wasn't all this other bullshit going on at the college, he'd say fuck the rules.

"Look, I'm so sorry about last night," Ash said as he shut the door. "I shouldn't have had those beers, not with how tired I was."

Eli faced Ash, leaning back against the desk, his arms crossed. "You don't need to apologize, Ash. I knew you were exhausted when I offered the massage. I wanted my greedy hands all over you and was thinking of that first. You did warn me."

He still wanted his hands all over Ash. Last night had just been a taste, a tease. Just thinking about it woke up the heat and hunger inside of him. He had very vivid memories of how Ash looked naked on his bed. How he tasted when they kissed. What Eli didn't know was how it felt to be fucked by him, and he hated an unsatisfied curiosity.

"Senior year?" Eli asked, going back over their conversation the night before. He didn't remember Ash saying anything about being a student.

Ash tossed his book bag down on the chair and remained standing as well. He looked good in his jeans and faded U2 T-shirt, and when he met Eli's gaze, heat sparked between them. "Yeah, I'm majoring in Criminology and Criminal Justice. I plan on joining the state police or one of the federal agencies after I graduate. Haven't decided where yet. I guess anywhere that'll have me."

Eli heard the quiet pride in Ash's voice and had to smile. Somehow that revelation did not surprise him at all. "I could easily see you as an agent." And his major explained why he'd never seen him before. The Behavioral Sciences building was on the other side of campus, and Eli didn't venture that way often.

"Thanks." Ash shifted and cocked his head, giving him a speculative look. "I have to say, when you said you were a teacher I was thinking elementary school."

"I'm too much of a nerd to do elementary school. I like books too much and I like sharing them with people who get as excited as I do." Eli sighed. Neither one of them were getting around to what they had really come here to talk about. "I shouldn't see you again outside of class, Ash. At least not until the semester is over with." There, it was said, despite Eli's reluctance to do so.

Ash's green eyes brightened, and he took a step closer, making Eli's pulse race. "You're hedging. You said shouldn't, does that mean you'd be willing? Because I'd sure as hell like to pick up where we left off last night."

Temptation thrummed in Eli's blood. He couldn't see harm in a little consensual nookie. It wasn't like Ash was a kid straight out of high school, and it wasn't like Eli was the kind of guy who let his dick decide grades. "You do entice me to break my own rules."

Ash took another step closer, and his husky chuckle had heat rippling over Eli's skin. "I haven't even started on the temptation, Eli," he drawled.

Eli was about to say fuck caution and lean in to kiss those teasing lips when the sound of very familiar footsteps echoed down the long hallway toward his door. He swore, pressed his lips in irritation, and gently pushed Ash back.

"And the reason why I cannot give into that temptation is about to come in here and chew my ass off because he wouldn't understand creativity if it shoved its way past the stick in his ass."

Surprise crossed Ash's face as Eli slipped behind his desk and the door opened without the courtesy of a knock. He sat down, schooling his expression so he wouldn't scowl at the tall, older man with silvering wings in his dark hair. Britton was the head of his department at Amwich State College and the thorn digging into Eli's proverbial paw. He'd probably get along much better with the man if he conformed to all of his ridiculous, bullshit nagging. The perverse part of his nature would not allow it. As long as there weren't official rules about how long he kept his hair, or whether or not he really had to wear boring suits, or if it was appropriate or not to conduct a lecture outside on a beautiful day, he'd continue to do things his own way.

Britton would love to see him axed. At least for now, Eli was on good terms with the dean, and he figured that as long as he never broke any real rules, his tenure track was safe. At least Britton's days as head were almost over. This was his last year, and Eli was careful not to give him any true cause to have him sacked. Too bad the other man had tenure. He'd lost touch with the times two decades ago and his classes were among the most unpopular.

Britton strode in, his mouth tight and Eli cast him a look of irritation at the interruption. "Excuse me, Professor Britton, but I am meeting with a student." He forced himself to keep his tone civil and to stop before he said what was really burning on his tongue. This had to be a record: day one and already Britton was hounding him. He was probably still pissed over Eli strong-arming him into allowing his Historic Letters class.

"That's okay, Doc. I can wait outside." Ash grabbed his bag and was gone before Eli could stop him. He pressed his lips together as the door shut behind Ash. It bothered him that he didn't know what Ash was thinking.

"Well, now that you've chased him off, what can I do for you?" Eli gave in to the urge to lean back in his chair and prop his feet up on his desk, knowing how much it would irk Britton. And sure enough, the man's mouth tightened even more.

The system sucked. Britton was safe, but if Eli irked the wrong person, he could kiss his chances of ever making tenure goodbye. It wasn't like he didn't have other options at other colleges, but Eli loved Amwich. He loved having the option to hike to work when he wanted to. Besides, he toed the line on all of the actual rules. He had no real interest in outright rebellion. He just couldn't stand to have his every little action scrutinized. Not when he was good at teaching and at making his classes interesting.

"Why did you switch rooms again without authorization?" Britton snapped. "The upper-level classes are supposed to be taken with the utmost seriousness. I knew you weren't ready for the responsibility."

"I did put in a request, which you ignored. Twice," Eli said mildly, crossing his hands over his stomach.

"And you went ahead and switched the rooms anyway." Britton drew himself up, a hard light appearing in his eyes. "This time you went too far and I have grounds to take this to the dean. You need my authorization to change rooms. What you did was a blatant disregard for the rules and chain of command. I won't have it."

The man had to be the most pompous ass that Eli had ever met. One look at his face was all Eli needed to know that he believed Eli couldn't handle teaching the class. It was all Eli could do not to roll his eyes. Especially since what just came out of his mouth was utter bullshit.

"With all due respect, I didn't change the room." Eli paused as Britton blinked and lost some of his bluster. "I had the students meet me in the library today so I could introduce them to archival research methods over the first couple of classes." To be honest, he'd prefer to continue to meet in the small room at the back of the library. He wanted to generate intimate discussion, which was why the class size was kept down. A regular classroom didn't do that. The best he could do would be to draw the chairs in a circle.

When Eli had gotten permission to meet in the library from the woman who handled all those assignments, he hadn't bothered to tell Britton because that wasn't really his job as head. He had enough things to see to. Besides, the department was tense enough between those loyal to Britton and those eager to see him step down at the end of the year. Eli didn't think he needed to aggravate matters more.

The amusement he got out of knowing the man would make an ass out of himself if he complained soothed some of Eli's irritation, if not his disappointment that he wouldn't be able to carry on his affair with Ash. The last thing he needed now was to give Britton more reasons than he already had to scrutinize everything Eli did. Maybe it was catty of him, or even malicious, but Eli had never claimed to be an angel.

"Don't talk about respect, Hollister. You haven't shown me any with your flagrant disregard for the reputation of this college." Britton stabbed the air with forceful gestures. "For example, your appearance. You look more like a student than a professor, for God's sake. How do you expect anyone to take you seriously?"

"Actually, I've never had one problem with the students taking me seriously. The only one who seems to have a problem is you." Eli paused to let that sink in, though he doubted it would make an impression. "Cutting my hair wouldn't change your opinion, nor would staying in the assigned room. Since the papers I've published have brought quite a bit of positive attention to this college, I've had few problems with most of the people here." Only the ignorant jackasses who clung to the old ways like shit to toilet paper.

For a moment, Eli thought that Britton would grind his teeth in acute frustration. No matter what he did, Eli had not lost his temper with him yet and it about gave the man a fit of apoplexy. And Britton absolutely hated to be reminded of Eli's papers, since he considered Eli a hack. "You don't respect me or the fact that I head this department. You never have."

Eli bit the inside of his cheek before he could retort that Britton was right. "Respect tends to deteriorate when you're not shown any in return. Look, I know I pissed you off when I forced the issue about having more Cultural Studies classes—"

Randall Britton's features twisted into a snarl, and he stabbed his finger one last time in Eli's direction. "Those classes do not belong in the English Department. Their focus is more on external circumstances, not textual elements."

That was an old argument and not one that Eli cared to rehash again. "Which is why I suggested to the dean that we make them Liberal Arts classes." Britton had been quick to veto that idea because then he would've lost all power over those courses and he'd taken his defeat with ill grace. "I thought this was all resolved."

"Fine, the class can continue to meet in the back room of the library if you keep them under control." He strode toward the door as Eli stared at him, surprised by that concession. "And get a haircut, Hollister. We should have a little more decorum in the appearance of our professors. I swear you'll be gone by the holidays if I have anything to say about the matter."

Britton could beg on his knees for that haircut and it would never happen. There wasn't a dress code, so Eli didn't consider it a reasonable request. However, he kept his mouth shut and let Britton leave without antagonizing him further. To his surprise, Ash immediately popped his head back in, his expression set. "Don't you dare cut your damned hair, Eli," he said in an undertone so it wouldn't be heard by Britton as he strode back down the hallway.

Eli touched the tie at the nape of his neck. The way Britton spoke to him made his common sense disappear. He should at least consider the idea. If it would get Britton off his back a bit, it might be worth the temporary sacrifice. Then again, it might not. Britton might decide that since he'd won that battle he could move onto something else he wanted to change about Eli. The next thing he knew he could end up wearing tweed suits and hideous ties and be locked up indoors on even the most beautiful days. One more year, and then it would be over.

"Don't worry. It's not likely to happen."

"What a horse's ass." Ash tossed his bag back down on one of the chairs and took the other. "So did you do something to piss him off? Or did he just not like you from the start? It's not because you're gay, is it?"

"No, Britton has no gaydar. It was pretty much hate on first sight. You know how it is when you meet someone and they just rub you the wrong way? Well, I seem to do that for Britton. He hates the fact that I was hired just before he became head, so he had no say. He hates that my emphasis is on Cultural Studies, because in his opinion it is the worst development to ever happen to literary studies. Most of the time he isn't so bad. He just seems to be getting worse the closer he comes to stepping down."

Eli massaged one aching temple and peered out the window. The downpour had eased off into a gray drizzle and the slowly brightening sky gave promise for sunshine later on. Maybe he wouldn't be soaked through two minutes into his hike, and after this day, he really needed the peace of one of his long walks.

"Hey, are you interested in going on a hike with me? We can finish the conversation as we walk. I just want to get the hell out of here."

Ash came to stand beside him at the window. "You're serious? You really want to go hiking out in this mess?"

"Every day, doesn't matter the weather." Eli laughed at Ash's surprise. "Come on, I know you've been out in much worse. I'll even give you your baseball cap back so you don't have to worry about your fuzz getting wet."

Ash ran a hand over his buzz cut and shot him a sour glance. "Yeah, I may be used to worse, but it doesn't mean I like it. Sadist."

"Maybe." Eli started to shove his books and papers into his satchel. He couldn't have this conversation with Ash in his office. "Are you done with classes for the day?"

"All done. You serious about giving me my cap back?"

"Absolutely." It wasn't like Ash would have the opportunity to win it back anytime soon, and it seemed mean-spirited to keep it when it was clear that Ash had a fondness for the cap.

Ash turned away from the window and kissed the side of Eli's neck, sending a shock through him. He wanted to lean back into his arms. Damn, this wasn't going to be easy.

"So where are we hiking and how long do you go for?"

"At least an hour, and since it is so wet, I'll leave it at that today." Eli eased away from Ash and scribbled quick directions. "Meet me at my place. There are plenty of trails back there."

Eli still didn't know what he was going to do about their sexual tension, but one way or another he needed to figure it out. It wouldn't be fair to leave Ash hanging. Ash grabbed his bag from the chair and slung it over his shoulder as Eli gathered his fedora and poncho from the coat rack.

"You know, you could antagonize him a little less."

"Yeah, but it wouldn't change anything, and then I would get no satisfaction at all out of our skirmishes." Eli shrugged and gave Ash an apologetic glance. "As much as I love military men, I wouldn't have lasted ten minutes in boot camp. I've been told that I have authority issues."

"I don't know if I'd say that," Ash said thoughtfully as they made their way down the staircase. "I think it's more a case of that you're a free spirit. If you go into a situation and know the rules ahead of time, you wouldn't buck the situation so much, but if somebody comes after you and tries to make you conform to their own rules then you outright refuse."

Eli stared in surprise at Ash. "Damn, I think I may have finally met someone who gets me. Either you're really good at reading people or I'm very transparent."

"Maybe a little bit of both." Ash grinned at him then sighed as they reached the front entrance and he looked out on the drizzly day. "One thing is for certain, Lu was right when she said you were more stubborn than a deer tick."

CHAPTER 6

BY THE time Ash had dropped off his schoolbooks, changed into hiking boots, and headed toward Eli's place, the drizzle had softened into a light mist. He was just as unsure about whether or not he'd get to have another shot at Eli as he had been when he woke up that morning. At least this time it wasn't because he'd fucked up the night before.

After overhearing Eli's confrontation with that asshole, Ash had waited for Eli to say they couldn't fool around during the semester, and he understood that. Didn't mean he wasn't disappointed, but he understood.

Then Eli asked him on the hike, and now Ash didn't know what to think. The simplest solution would be to call it off for now and let what happened happen. If they were still interested in each other come December, then cool, and if not, no feelings were hurt. It wasn't like they weren't ever going to see each other.

Maybe that was the difficulty. He'd have to see Eli a couple days a week, in close proximity, and try to concentrate on class instead of screwing his professor. If Ash was told that he couldn't take Eli to his bed after all the buildup of sexual tension, it would guarantee wandering thoughts of necking in the library or bending Eli over his desk in his office.

Ash's cock stirred at that all too vivid picture. Eli's office was in the back end of nowhere. No one would ever hear them, and damned if the idea of getting it on in such a taboo place wasn't a major turn-on. And now that he'd thought of it, Ash wanted it. He wanted to hear Eli trying to stay quiet while he fucked him in his office. He wanted to go to class knowing that's what Eli was remembering when they looked at each other.

Ash understood Eli's hesitance. For the past ten years, Ash had avoided scrutiny over his private life. One of the reasons why he had decided to opt out of the military when his term was over was because of that scrutiny. He wanted to be with who he wanted and not have the threat of the wrong person finding out hanging over his head.

Eli had that worry now, and judging from what Ash had come to know of the man, he had a feeling he knew which way Eli would decide. Eli had a streak of rampant rebellion in him unlike anything Ash had ever seen before. It went counter to everything that had been drilled into him all his life, first at home and then when he'd enlisted.

It gave Ash quite a bit to think about. He did not want to be the cause of Eli losing his position at the college when he really seemed to love being there. Damn ethical dilemmas. This was not what he'd been looking for last night. What had happened to a nice, uncomplicated good time?

As Ash pulled up in front of the wood-shingled home, he saw Eli poke his head out of a side door and wave at him to come on in. He parked behind Eli's Jeep and just looked at the house for a minute. His sister Melanie would love it. Hell, *he* loved it. Growing up in an older home in Savannah had given him an appreciation for historic places like this. The Cape Cod-style house was beautiful, with white trim that set off the weathered red-brown shingles, and two brick chimneys set over the long sloping roof.

The sound of a dog's joyful bark came to Ash as he went around the side and let himself into the mudroom that seemed to have its place in so many New England homes. He'd never understood the reason for it until his first winter in New Hampshire.

"Jabbers, don't you dare jump on him. Sit," Eli commanded as a beagle launched himself at Ash. The dog practically vibrated, he was so excited, but he sat himself down and looked at Ash with soulful, pleading eyes and pitiful whines for attention.

"It's okay." Ash knelt down and rubbed Jabbers's silky ears, grinning as the dog took that as permission and swarmed over him, tail wagging as he offered sloppy kisses. "Eli, that's cruel. What kind of a name is Jabbers for any self-respecting dog?"

Eli appeared in the door and leaned against the frame with a soft laugh. He'd changed into heavy hiking boots, worn jeans, and a faded hoodie. He'd taken his hair out of its tie and it hung in loose auburn waves around his shoulders. Ash's hands itched to bury themselves in it, but if he did, he'd end up kissing Eli and one kiss wouldn't be enough.

"Actually, his name is Jabberwocky, because he was supposed to be a fearsome beastie to the rabbits. But he turned out to be the opposite of fearsome. I think he would make friends with a skunk. Trust me, Jabbers fits. He never stops talking. Isn't that right, Jabbers?"

The beagle twisted his head around to look at Eli and proceeded to give a series of half barks and a soft, drawn-out undulating growl that sounded so much like conversation that Ash had to laugh. "I get your point."

There was a peculiar expression on Eli's face, an almost perplexed tightening around his eyes that hadn't been there when they'd parted. "Did something come up?" Ash asked. "You look worried about something." He hoped Eli wasn't regretting his invitation to go on the hike.

"No, just confused." Eli shook his head and glanced back over his shoulder. "It's nothing. I thought I put this glove Jabbers found last night on the counter. I was going to ask Wayne if it was his, but it's not there. Now I'm wondering if I just dreamt the whole thing."

"Wayne?" Ash frowned, trying to place him and ignore the uncomfortable prick of jealousy at the same time. He had no claim on Eli and he wasn't looking for one. They'd only really talked for the first time yesterday, but he couldn't help the little possessive surge at the thought of another guy hanging around Eli's enough that he left things around for Jabbers to find. When a face came to him, Ash felt a little foolish for his momentary reaction. "Wait, he's the standoffish guy who owns the hardware store?"

"Yeah, he's been helping me out with some odd jobs around here. Things are tight for him right now." Eli furrowed his brow, his eyes worried. "His father had a bad stroke, and since it happened in the middle of the night, it gave him some complications. Wayne's always kept to himself but he's a good guy when you get to know him."

Ash rubbed Jabbers's ears one last time then stood up, grateful that he'd kept his mouth shut and not said something stupid. And, if he was honest with himself, glad that he wasn't competing with Wayne for Eli's attention. That was almost irksome in itself. He was letting himself get into knots over a sorta relationship that might not be there after their hike. He needed a distraction.

"Before we go, do you mind showing me around your place? How old is it?"

Eli's eyes lit up, and he stepped back into the house. "Come on in. My great-grandparents bought it, but it's older than that. About two hundred years, I think." Eli showed him around the home with obvious pride, pointing out the original floors and their handmade, square, iron nails, dark wood-pegged beams, and old brick fireplaces bearing the ghosts of soot above their openings. "Gram and Grumpy took me in during the summers. I always loved this place, and when Grumpy passed, he left the place to me, much to my dad's irritation."

Ash touched his fingers to Eli's as the other man's mouth tightened. This wasn't the first hint that Eli and his father had a rocky history together. "You don't get along with your dad?"

"Let's just say we don't really understand each other. We never have. And we've come to a point in our lives where we've accepted that it's not going to change and we just have to take each other as we are."

Ash didn't believe Eli's easy dismissal, not when there was remembered sorrow in those clear, blue-gray eyes. "I think I understand," he said and left it at that. "So are you ready to drag me out into the wet wilds around here?"

Eli shot him a grateful look. "Let me grab your baseball cap."

He came back a few moments later, cap and binoculars in hand. "I know I won it fairly," Eli said as he handed it over, "but it just didn't seem right to have it lying around never used. It would be a crime."

Ash grinned and sat the Braves cap on his head. "Thank you. I didn't want to break in a new one. This is my favorite."

Eli grabbed two walking sticks from the mudroom. Jabbers bolted outside, but once he saw Eli and Ash heading off, he fell in beside Eli at a sedate trot. "How did you get him to heel so well?"

"He's putting on his good manners for you. Wait until he smells something interesting and takes off to make friends."

They headed out toward the trees behind Eli's house, the air cool and damp against their skin. There was a quiet solitude about the afternoon, broken only by the sound of Jabbers snuffling along the path, his tail whipping the undergrowth. There was a look of contentment on Eli's face, as if his argument with the other professor just a bit ago had been completely forgotten.

Much to Ash's surprise, he found himself enjoying the hike despite the wet. The scenery was spectacular, and Eli kept pointing out things that he missed and telling him about some of his favorite trails he'd been on over the summer. Neither one of them brought up the reason why they had come out here: to talk about the next step between them. Ash was content with the company, and if Eli wasn't inclined to murky up the day with relationship talk, then that was fine by him.

The trees opened up on the right side of the path as the ground dropped away to follow along a creek rippling over rock outcroppings. In the distance Ash could hear the muted roar of a waterfall. The rain had stopped completely, though the air was still heavy with moisture. White mist gathered around the rocks, obscuring the trees except for a few ethereal branches. It was like there was no one left in the world but the two of them and Jabbers.

Ash kept stealing glances at his companion. Eli's long legs moved over the uneven ground with the ease of long practice. He set a hard pace, not flagging at all, and Ash had to revise his opinion that most professors were soft. Not that Eli had seemed at all soft last night. "Okay, now I believe you go hiking every day. I thought you were just bullshitting me."

Eli flashed him a grin. "Lu swears I was one of those crazy trailblazers in a past life. Out by myself for months on end, hiking, rock climbing, camping. I love it all."

Ash's gaze slid down to Eli's ass as the trail narrowed and he took the lead. Maybe they could strike a deal. They'd behave on campus and misbehave off of it… misbehave several times. The trail widened again, and Ash moved up beside him and was about to take Eli by the hand so they could talk when Jabbers broke the silence with excited baying, his whole body stiffening. Ash followed the dog's intent stare as a raspy, eerie shriek rent the air.

"What the hell is that?" It sounded like something out of a horror movie.

Eli lunged forward and grabbed Jabbers's collar just as the beagle prepared to bound across the creek to confront the caterwauling creature that looked like a mutant cross between a beaver and a ferret. "It's a fisher cat," Eli said, crouching down to look his dog in the eyes. "Jabbers, stay," he said firmly. "Remember what happened the last time you tried to take one of them on?"

Ash watched with bemusement as the animal gave one last defiant screech before scampering off into the trees. Jabbers whined, casting Eli a look of betrayal. "I guess you run into all kinds of animals around here," he said as Eli let go of Jabbers's collar and straightened after waiting a moment to see if the dog would bolt.

"Mostly deer, and up at my camp you can often spot moose or bear too. Moose are so curious, it's not unheard of to find one peering in a window. I think you'd like it there." Eli cast him an unreadable look, and Ash wasn't sure if it was an invitation or regret. "Some of my cousins and I built a camp up north. They use it for hunting, and I go up for hiking and fishing about once a month for a long weekend."

Ash started an ongoing argument in his head. Half of him wanted to be the one to call it off to save face and keep Eli from risking his career and the other half wanted to say to the hell with everyone else and kiss Eli until there wasn't any other thought but the heat between them.

"Sounds like it would be fun sometime." He would not turn down a weekend of privacy, naked Eli, and a bit of camping. Ash came to a halt as the creek fell away a few yards later to tumble down in a long, silver cascade into a wide natural pool below. "Oh wow, that's gorgeous."

"Yeah, some days I'll hike all the way down and go swimming. It's far too cold for that today." Eli scrambled up onto a rock by the path and gave Ash a look filled with regret. Ash echoed that feeling with a pang in his chest. He'd totally missed his chance.

"We should've fucked like rabbits last night," Ash said in response to all the unspoken things he saw echoed in Eli's expression. "I understand. You want hands off till the end of the semester. I'm disappointed, but I understand."

Eli smiled with relief in his eyes. "I know you do. Britton, the dipshit you saw earlier, would love nothing more than to see me lose my chance at tenure. So much so that I'm surprised he hasn't invented something yet. I guess his lack of imagination is what thwarts him."

"And if he had any idea about us he'd make trouble." Ash had seen and heard that for himself. "I didn't think there were any set rules about relationships with students."

Eli pulled a canteen off a clip on his belt and took a swig before recapping it and tossing it to Ash. "There aren't. Too many people would get caught up in scandals if that were the case. It's frowned upon, though, and Britton would twist it around to make it seem like some kind of power play on my part, a using my charisma to coerce students into being my sex slaves kind of thing. Definitely not my style."

Ash choked on his sip of water. "Didn't think it was. Sounds like he'd be much happier if he got some himself."

The idea that someone would actually believe that Ash would let himself be coerced into a situation he didn't want was ludicrous. Still, those who were in charge didn't know him from any other student. If Eli had been a professor in the Criminal Justice program, that would be different. A man like Britton wouldn't investigate the situation as much as take the fact that a teacher and a student were carrying on a sexual relationship and twist it into the most sordid scenario possible.

And that thought just irked the hell out of him.

"He wouldn't know what to do with sex if it was freely offered. I'm surprised he hasn't moldered in his office yet." Eli's lips twisted in a sour expression. "I hate having someone else dictate my actions, but he's the head of the department so I'm stuck with him until the end of the year."

"I was half afraid he was going to send you into open rebellion and then I'd have to be the voice of reason." And Ash didn't want to contemplate what it would take to turn Eli from a course of action once he'd decided on one. There had been a wicked glint in his eyes earlier when he'd faced Britton that had reminded Ash of his best friend Kurtis Wakefield. Heaven help the person who crossed Kurtis. His notion of retaliation was inventive and pointed. He never went over the line into cruelty, but his target would remember what had happened for a long time.

"Oh, I considered it," Eli said.

"What changed your mind?" Ash found another boulder and pulled himself up to sit. The rock was cool and damp, the skies still a solid gray, but it was good to be outdoors after a day of being cooped up. Even better to be in Eli's company. If they were going to have to behave, he wanted to get what he could, while he could.

"Because if we were to have an illicit affair—" Eli's lips quirked in a wicked, heated smile that stirred Ash's desire. "And believe me, I love the words illicit and affair, and we were to get caught, then it would be a scandal." His expression turned serious, his blue-gray eyes as somber as the sky. "And that could affect you as well as me. I don't want people thinking you're a dirty secret or that there is anything at all sleazy about what we're doing together. I'd rather be with you openly."

This time, the warmth that filled Ash had nothing to do with sex. There had been several times, when he was on active duty, that he had wished for the same thing. To be able to be with the guy he was seeing without living a lie. He wasn't an idiot: things would be tough in the DCIS, or FBI, or the even the police. There were repercussions in all the careers that interested him. He could handle those. But he hated the lying. It ate at him.

"Well, then, now that's been decided. Do I get to flirt with you? I don't know if I can pretend for the next several months that I don't find you sexy."

"I don't see anything wrong with a little harmless flirting," Eli responded with a gleam in his eyes.

"What about fantasizing?" Ash asked, flashing a grin at him. Surprisingly, he realized that he kind of liked this idea. The heat they could build up over the next couple of months would be epic. "You are the hottest professor I've ever had. My thoughts are bound to stray from time to time."

"Just as long as you don't let it affect your class work." Eli turned his mouth into a prim line, eliciting a laugh from Ash, before he let it relax. "I'm sure I'll be having a number of fantasies myself. Our thoughts are our own. And it's not like when I see you about town I'm going to ignore you. Who I'm friends with outside of work is my own business, and that I can defend."

"Sounds like you intend on walking the line."

"Walking the line is what I do best."

WAYNE'S heart clenched and adrenaline shot through him as pulled down Eli's road and saw his Jeep along with a strange truck outside the house. He almost turned right back around until he reminded himself that he had a legitimate reason for being here. It would look odd if he started avoiding Eli now. And the truck didn't belong to Sheriff Cooper, so there was no reason to freak out.

Wayne counted on Eli being unobservant and forgetful after Wayne had fucked up his first and second break-in. It was that yapping mutt's fault. Somehow, Jabbers had stolen Wayne's glove without him noticing. He'd almost had a coronary when he'd seen it on Eli's kitchen counter. At first he thought he'd dropped it, but then he'd seen the teeth marks. He'd grabbed it without thinking it through and now he regretted his rashness. Eli might dismiss one odd occurrence, but he wasn't likely to dismiss several.

Stupid idiot. He was going to blow it all if he didn't get his shit together. He wasn't cut out for a life of crime. He didn't understand how people found it to be thrilling. He was more likely to end up with an ulcer.

He'd explored the attic earlier and ground his teeth at the decades' worth of junk that had been collected and stuffed up there. It would take forever to search, but if the baseball cards were there, no one would know or remember if he took them. And it was better to have them there instead of in some damned hidey-hole safe, or in Tennessee with that thieving, cheating rat bastard.

Wayne didn't hear Jabbers when he got out of the truck, which meant that Eli was probably off on one of his hikes. He glanced at the mudroom door and saw that only the screen door was shut; the other was wide open to allow a breeze to go through the kitchen.

He frowned in thought as he tugged on his gloves and started to unload the cordwood. Now might be a good time to lift Eli's office keys. He'd have to search there too.

Wayne chewed on his lip as he started to stack the wood against the shed. He had no way of knowing how long Eli had been gone or who he was with. Wayne had better wait for another opportunity. He'd watch Eli for a few weeks, get his routine down, and then he'd have plenty of time to grab the keys, make copies, and return them before the man even realized they were missing.

Feeling better with a plan in mind instead of picking the impulsive option, Wayne began to whistle as he went to work with more confidence. He had only stacked a few armloads when the sound of Jabbers's barking alerted him to Eli's return. His stomach churned. Good thing he hadn't tried to make a copy of the key this afternoon.

Wayne steeled himself as Jabbers ran up to him, tail wagging. It was easier to look at the dog than in Eli's direction. The betrayal still burned hot in his mind, and he'd give anything not to have to look the man in the eye. Wayne finished stacking his load and then grabbed a rawhide treat from his truck. Bribery worked wonders, and he needed to stay friends with Jabbers if he was going to keep on snooping around.

He waved the treat in the air and Jabbers jumped, trying to snatch it out of his hand. "Not this time, troublemaker. Sit, Jabbers!" The dog immediately plopped down, baying in his excitement. Wayne tossed him the treat, and Jabbers jumped up and caught it midair. "Now remember what listening to me gets you." Last night was not going to happen again. No siree.

"How's it going, Wayne?"

Wayne glanced over as Eli emerged from the trees with Ash Gallagher. He'd seen him on Jonas's construction crew over the summer and again last night with Eli at Dingers. And here he was, looking all cozy with Eli. Wayne narrowed his eyes. It had been awhile since Eli had dated, and on another day he'd have been happy for him. Today he just wanted to tell Ash to get out while he could.

"It's going." Wayne nodded to Ash and grabbed another armload of wood. Eli's expression was open and friendly, and some of Wayne's anxiety eased. Eli mustn't have noticed anything odd, then. Damn, how could the man have looked him in the eye and said that he knew nothing about those cards? It still made him sick. "Dad's recovering slower than the doctors would like, but he's a stubborn one."

"I'm sorry about that," Eli said as they walked up, and Wayne ground his teeth at the false sympathy. "Wayne, have you met Ash Gallagher?"

"Not officially. Jonas had good things to say about you." Wayne stripped off his glove and reached out to shake Ash's hand. He had the oddest feeling that the man was measuring him. Those eyes studied him the way he'd seen Sheriff Cooper watch someone he didn't trust. "We don't get many outsiders settling into our part of town."

"It's a good town, suits me for the time being." Ash's eyes flicked to Wayne's hands and the chewed-up glove. Wayne stuffed it in his back pocket and cursed his guilty flush. "I see you got your glove back from Eli's kitchen."

"How'd you know?" Wayne blurted out without thinking, as a little spurt of panic grabbed his throat.

Ash met his eyes again. If anything, the man made him more nervous than Jabbers. "Eli mentioned that Jabbers found one, and I can see that he gnawed the hell out of it. Eli couldn't figure out where it had disappeared to."

"Oh, good," Eli said with a smile. "I was wondering if it was yours. That solves that mystery. I'm glad you got it back."

To Wayne's relief, Eli let it go at that, though Ash was still looking at him with speculation in his eyes. Anger blossomed into a hot knot. Who was this fucking outsider to question what he did? "I needed them to haul the wood today." He winced at his defensive tone. That sounded like he was feeling guilty and he wasn't, dammit. Not one bit.

"Just let me grab my gloves and I'll give you a hand." Eli looked at Ash and seemed to hesitate. "You sticking around?"

Ash cast him a look of regret, and Wayne took the opportunity to exit out of the conversation. He turned and began to grab an armload of wood, listening intently in case he came up as a topic.

"I wish I could. I have a standing date with my best friend once every couple of weeks to chat online. He's stationed in Afghanistan right now."

"So I'll see you Wednesday?"

"Definitely, Doc," Ash said in a teasing voice.

Wayne trudged away with his armload, grateful that conversation seemed to be entirely about the two of them. When he returned, Ash was gone. Good. Those sidelong looks of his made him nervous. Eli didn't seem inclined to chatter, so that was another bonus. He wasn't sure that he could stomach being pleasant with him. With Jabbers off somewhere, gnawing on his prize instead of underfoot, the day had taken a turn for the better.

ASH frowned as he drove off. There was something not right about Wayne. The man had been skittish from the start of the conversation and he had not liked being questioned about that glove. Now, maybe things were different up here in this small town, but if Wayne had just needed that glove to haul wood, then why the hell did he act like Ash had caught him in the middle of being where he didn't belong? It didn't make any sense, especially when Eli didn't seem bothered by Wayne going into his house to fetch it. Other unanswered questions bothered him, like where did Jabbers find that glove and how had Wayne known to look for it in Eli's house?

Ash flexed his hand, feeling the scar tissue tug on his arm. He'd learned the hard way about not trusting his instincts. He'd made that mistake during his second stint in Iraq. He'd looked into those eyes and had been fooled, right before the world exploded around him. A fanatic's gaze was soulless, all personality burned away and replaced with one driving goal. And he'd dismissed that gaze and let that woman's outward appearance fool him. Not anymore.

Right now his instincts said Wayne was twitchy. What kind of man just walked into a person's house when they weren't home? He didn't seem that friendly with Eli because Wayne hadn't met his eyes once. And there was that look on his face when Ash had mentioned the glove, that flash of panic. If there wasn't something off about the situation, why the fear? It struck him as dishonest. Only he couldn't figure out why he'd be in Eli's house snooping; even if he did need the money, Eli hadn't noticed anything missing but the glove.

Those thoughts kept Ash's mind occupied until he pulled up to his apartment. Ten minutes later he was sitting in front of his computer with a glass of sweet iced tea beside him along with a folded note he'd found on the coffee table. Ash eyeballed it as he slipped on the headset and turned on the webcam.

Eli had to have left it last night, and he wished he'd seen it this morning when he'd been rushing around. He signed into his account, and as he was waiting for Kurtis's call he picked up the note.

Georgia,

> *I won the first round, thank you for the hat. You think you're up for another bet? Call me and next time I promise I won't knock you out again.*

> *Eli*

Ash could almost picture the teasing smile on Eli's face as he wrote the note. Well, damn, Eli hadn't said one word about whether or not seducing was allowed. Ash was up for another bet. Only this time Eli would be the prize. Now he just needed to figure out a way to get Eli to agree to a bet like that. Maybe it wouldn't take much, not if Eli really did intend on walking that fine line.

The call came through and Kurtis appeared on the screen. There were dark shadows under Kurtis's eyes, and his face was haggard. Ash sat back, careful not to let his shock at his best friend's appearance show. This last tour had taken its toll, and it worried Ash to see it so plainly.

"Man, Kurtis, you're even uglier than usual. Your wife will have a fit if you show up looking like that."

Kurtis grinned, breaking the tension in his expression. "Still prettier than you, ass. How are things stateside?"

Though Ash wanted to know how things were going for Kurtis, he refrained from prying. He remembered how welcome distraction was at times, and Kurtis looked as if he needed to have his mind on other things. If he wanted to talk, he'd bring it up, but those discussions were best on late nights with a couple of beers.

"Nothing much is new since last time. Melanie's trying to get knocked up, and you know once she sets her mind on something she usually accomplishes it. So expect her and Jamie to be out baby shopping when you get back."

Kurtis groaned and shook his head. "That means Jamie is going to want another one."

"I call bullshit on that look, buddy." Ash snickered. "You dote on your twins. I hear they're climbing now."

"Like a pair of monkeys. Jamie's about to tear out her hair. Brandon got over the backyard fence for the second time last week while she was hanging the laundry. She swears she only had her back turned for a minute."

"I heard about that, in vivid detail. With many colorful words aimed toward me and you both." Jamie swore Brandon had inherited every single one of Kurtis's mischievous genes and Ash's simply because the boy was his namesake. At least they had been merciful and given the boy his middle name instead of his first. It was a kindness he'd make sure Brandon understood when he was older. There was nothing like going through boot camp with the name Ashley. "I also heard about Danielle getting up on top of the fridge and dropping down the doggie treats to a very happy bulldog."

"I didn't hear about that one yet," Kurtis said, and Ash smiled at the soft look in his eyes. "I think Jamie likes to string out these tales in little doses so I don't worry about her taking care of it all by herself."

"Jamie's stronger than the both of us. Besides, Melanie and Bruce are twenty minutes away. They make sure she gets breaks and help."

"What about you? Classes started yet? You gonna do impressions of Keanu Reeves when you finally become an agent?"

"Ha ha, no I'm thinking of going more toward the Spooky Mulder route. Gillian Anderson is much better to look at than Gary Busey on a daily basis, even if I don't swing her way." Kurtis was Ash's only friend in the military whom he'd come out to, six months into their first tour, after an attack in the middle of the night. Neither of them had been able to sleep afterward and they had sat up talking for hours.

"Just don't start quoting conspiracy theories at me. I will have to bury you alive."

"I'll keep that in mind." Ash glanced at his watch. He didn't want to keep Kurtis up too long. He looked worn out enough as it was. "So before I let you go, I wanted to tell you something."

Kurtis sat up straighter and lowered his voice. "You met someone."

"Oh, Lord, do I have it tattooed on my forehead?"

"Nah, I've seen that look before. When we were in Hawaii and you met that surfer you thought was so hot and—"

"Don't remind me," Ash groaned. The guy was gorgeous and had ended up being an utter ass before the night was over. "That was a mistake I blame on Jägermeister and you egging me on. No, this guy is different."

"Then what's the problem?" Kurtis asked when Ash hesitated. "He's married, is that it?"

"That wouldn't be a problem because once I found that out there wouldn't be an interest. No, we met in town last night, had a kickass evening together, and then he ends up being one of my professors today."

Kurtis burst out laughing, his head falling back in his glee, the fucker. "Oh damn, I wish I was there to see you squirm."

"Squirm? Me? Please, jackass. I don't squirm, not ever."

"Yes, you do, like a worm on the end of a hook. I can already see it in your eyes," Kurtis snickered. "Wait till I tell Jamie."

"Don't you fucking dare. Jamie will tell Melanie and she'll tell Katie and then baby sis will find an excuse to come up to see me. Let me get through this tangle myself." Ash had no idea what the semester would bring and he didn't want any more complications. He should just walk away from the budding relationship. It wasn't like he was going to stay in Amwich past graduation, but Eli was the most interesting man he'd met in a long time, and he kissed like the devil.

Kurtis yawned, and Ash could see how the exhaustion and stress had added up, giving him new lines on his brow that weren't there before. He wasn't sure what was different during this tour for his friend. Maybe it was one too many, too close together, or maybe it was having his family away from him so long and the twins growing up without him, but it seemed like Kurtis had aged years since he left.

"Another three months and you'll be home, just in time for the start of the holidays," Ash said quietly.

"You're damn right, buddy. You have to come down for Thanksgiving."

"I wouldn't miss it for anything. So before you go, I have another joke for you."

Kurtis groaned shaking his head. "Please tell me it's not another gay Marine joke."

"What's the difference between a straight Marine and a gay Marine?" Ash chuckled as Kurtis dropped his face into his hand. "A six pack."

"You're probably right, ass." Kurt shook his head again, laughing, just as Ash hoped he would. "God help your professor because he's going to need it dealing with you."

CHAPTER 7

ELI lived for days like this. Early October was his absolute favorite time of year. The air was crisp and the sky an amazing intense blue that provided a perfect backdrop for the changing foliage. The tree Eli sat under had turned a brilliant yellow, and some of the leaves had already fallen to mix with the dark-green grass. His students were sprawled under other trees bedecked in varying shades of orange and scarlet.

He loved this spot. It was a cardinal sin to be indoors on a day like this, especially knowing the freezing winter was coming soon. The trees provided a screen from the weathered brick and stone buildings covered in ivy and blocked out some of the noise from the students going to their classes. He had a view of the chapel's bell tower in the distance and the footbridge over one of the many brooks bubbling through campus. It was his little slice of heaven. Add in Ash sitting himself down directly across from him, as usual, and the afternoon couldn't get much better.

Unless of course there was the promise of stolen kisses later on and hot sex in some out-of-the-way place. A quickie in his office had become a favorite fantasy of his after spending an hour and fifteen minutes every Monday and Wednesday staring at Ash. Only that wasn't about to happen. And if it did, Eli was pretty damn certain that a quickie wouldn't do anything to satisfy him.

"Hey, Doc," Ash drawled as he leaned forward toward Eli and rested his arms on his knees. "Did you have a good weekend?"

The man was up to something. Eli had not had Ash in his class for the past four weeks without learning to recognize when his thoughts weren't quite on the subject at hand during class. Not that his attention wandered. No, those green eyes would look right at him, and Ash's lips would tug in a secret smile that made Eli want to pull him aside and demand to know what was going through his mind.

Right now, there was an extra glint of devil in Ash's gaze that sent a hot shiver of pure anticipation through Eli. The way the man's gaze flicked over him, as if he was mentally taking off each article of clothing, made Eli's heart beat harder. At least Ash had given up on the idea of roping him into another bet. Ash's teasing was hard enough to withstand. Ash trying a full out seduction would've been impossible to resist.

"I did, though it was quiet. How about you?"

"About as far from quiet as you could get. Drill was this weekend." Ash tugged out a notebook and pen and sent Eli a sideways glance. "I was pretty sore afterward."

That put the image of Ash dressed in cammies right into Eli's thoughts, followed by the memory of massaging all those aching muscles after Ash's last drill weekend. And judging from the small smile on the man's face, that was his intention.

Eli would dearly love to kiss that smirk right off Ash's face.

"I hope you're not too sore today." Eli's lips twitched with laughter as Ash's gaze heated. "I've heard massage therapy works wonders."

"I suspect I'll survive. Those massage therapists can be dangerous." Ash leaned back against his tree, hands tucked behind his head. Damn, if that wasn't an invitation to explore. Eli flicked a quick glance at the way Ash's T-shirt stretched across his chest and shoulders, and his imagination went wild. Today would be a perfect day for sex on a blanket outdoors with the sun warming their skin and a breeze cooling them off. That little field behind his house would be the perfect spot to guarantee their privacy. He'd start by taking off that T-shirt and—

Eli pulled his thoughts away before he had another night of lying awake, staring up at his ceiling and unable to sleep. Thoughts of Ash and seeing him naked, touching and tasting him, had kept intruding on his mind over the past month.

Especially after the ass had sneaked that picture of him in his full dress uniform into Eli's notes. Ash knew what that picture would do to him, and the smirk on his face during the next class proved it. And Eli had retaliated by wearing his hair loose most Mondays and Wednesdays and smiling when he saw Ash's hands twitch, as if he was thinking of burying his hands in Eli's hair. It took two to play the game right.

Still, the weeks had given Eli an opportunity to get to know Ash better. He liked the insights that Ash brought to their discussions in class. He enjoyed watching the serious expression that would cross Ash's face when he thought something over before speaking. How he would get that tiny line between his brows or he would unconsciously rub his scarred arm. So the past four weeks had been just as much about learning and anticipation as they had been about sexual frustration.

Ash glanced down at the papers in his lap and grinned. "You have a lot to look forward to today, with the presentation, I mean. I think you'll like it."

Eli was sure that whatever wickedness Ash had in mind was tied in somehow to his presentation today. It was his and Nori's turn to bring in copies of historical letters they'd found and discuss their relevance to the culture and time period. From what he'd learned of Ash, he would take this opportunity to get Eli worked up. He would say things he wouldn't normally be able to get away with in class. So Eli expected a message within a message. Very appropriate, considering the class content, even if Ash would use it to be downright wicked.

Maybe he dug up something from Casanova. God have mercy on him. The last thing Eli needed was Ash reading erotic letters in that sexy Georgia drawl.

Eli glanced at his watch and cleared his throat to get the other students' attention. "Since it looks like Whitney will not be joining us today, let's get started."

"Again," Bron muttered under his breath with a sour glance at Isaac, who thought that Whitney could do nothing wrong. Isaac looked as if he were about to retort, but then changed his mind after one glance in Eli's direction.

"Ash, Nori, which one of you would like to go first?" Eli looked at Nori, who paled and bit her lip, and then at Ash, who grinned.

"I don't mind going first, Doc," Ash said, gathering his papers together as Nori shot him a grateful look. That poor girl had to be the shyest person Eli had ever met, and he worked hard to draw her into their conversations.

"You have my complete attention." It was on the tip of Eli's tongue to call him Georgia, but he managed to catch it in time. One of these days he was going to slip up and call him that in class, especially with as much as he did it in his head.

The look Ash cast him said, "I bet I do." Eli stretched out his legs, set his notebook on his lap, and hoped he wouldn't embarrass himself. Though every single one of the girls in the class had their attention on Ash and weren't likely to notice. Not that Eli could blame them. Not with as good as Ash looked, and there was that smile on Ash's lips again as he glanced at his papers.

"Okay, I found several letters from Oscar Wilde to Lord Alfred Douglas. A few of them were used against Wilde in his trial for gross indecency and the last one was sent to Douglas after Wilde was released from prison."

Gross indecency? What the hell was in those letters? Eli bit back a groan as Ash glanced at him through his lashes.

"Gross indecency? What he'd do?" Bron asked, sprawled out on his stomach on the blanket he'd brought, doodling on the notebook in front of him. "Expose himself to small kids and married women?"

"Ew." Hannah wrinkled her nose and tossed her head. "You would say that."

"Here, let me tell you in his own words. This is the letter he sent to Douglas after he was released." Ash pulled one paper to the front and cast Eli a quick, laughing glance before reading the short letter, his accent seeming to thicken. Eli resisted the urge to close his eyes and just listen to the sound of his voice.

My own Darling Boy,

I got your telegram half an hour ago, and just send a line to say that I feel that my only hope of again doing beautiful work in art is being with you. It was not so in the old days, but now it is different, and you can really recreate in me that energy and sense of joyous power on which art depends.

Everyone is furious with me for going back to you, but they don't understand us. I feel that it is only with

*you that I can do anything at all. Do remake my ruined
life for me, and then our friendship and love will have a
different meaning to the world.*

*I wish that when we met at Rouen we had not
parted at all. There are such wide abysses now of space
and land between us. But we love each other.*

Goodnight, dear. Ever yours,

Oscar

Eli bit the inside of his cheek and for the eleventh time since class
had started, wished they were alone together so he could speak openly.
Wicked man. He went for seduction and sentiment over eroticism. He
had not been expecting that from Ash. And damned if it wasn't
effective too.

"I don't get it," Elsa said. "What's so indecent about that? Are
you censoring the good stuff, Ash?"

"They were gay. That was, like, illegal back then or something,"
Isaac said, looking a bit uncomfortable. "Bet there didn't have to be
much in those letters at all to get them in trouble."

"I think it's sweet," Nori said softly. "What happened after that?
Did they meet up again?"

"Actually," Eli replied, drawing everyone's attention to him,
"Oscar Wilde died a few years after he was released from prison.
Complications stemming from the hard physical labor he had been
sentenced to, I believe."

"That bites. I bet he died from a broken heart." Kerry had a
slightly dreamy look in her eyes as her nimble fingers wove colorful
leaves and bits of sticks she'd gathered together into a rough wreath. "It
sounds like he really loved that guy."

"Don't be ridiculous, nobody dies from a broken heart," Bron cut
in. "What else did he write? What were the letters they used as
evidence? I bet the stuff Elsa is looking for is in them."

"Well, the defense brought out this letter first, before the
prosecutors could, so it couldn't be used against Wilde." Ash pulled out
another piece of paper, his lips curving in a small smile as he stole

another look at Eli. "Wilde testified that this was just an example of the way poets talked to one another, and at first the jury bought his excuse."

> *My Own Boy,*
>
> *Your sonnet is quite lovely, and it is a marvel that those red-roseleaf lips of yours should be made no less for the madness of music and song than for the madness of kissing. Your slim gilt soul walks between passion and poetry. I know Hyacinthus, whom Apollo loved so madly, was you in Greek days. Why are you alone in London, and when do you go to Salisbury? Do go there to cool your hands in the grey twilight of Gothic things, and come here whenever you like. It is a lovely place and lacks only you; but go to Salisbury first.*
>
> *Always, with undying love,*
>
> *Yours, Oscar*

Bron was snickering and shaking his head before Ash even finished reading the letter. "Shut up, they really bought it? Come on."

"They did, at least for the first trial." Ash met Eli's gaze. "Though maybe the talk of kissing and meeting up someplace out of town should have clued them in."

An idea took hold of Eli, and he wondered if that had been Ash's intent. It would be nice to get away for a few days, just the two of them. Who the hell would ever know? Especially with the way Ash left town once a month for his weekend drills and Eli often left on weekend trips to go to his camp. No one would comment if they were gone the same weekend.

Or he was just overthinking it and nobody gave a damn what they did with themselves off campus. Britton had been too mired down in his own affairs to bother Eli much lately. And he could be reading too much into Ash's presentation and he wasn't really thinking about a weekend away. It was enough to make him crazy.

"Your minds could just be in the gutter, you know," Hannah said. "It could be just as he was saying. It's pretty fancy talk. I can picture poets talking like that. And he was married, wasn't he? With kids? Are you sure he was gay? Maybe he just pissed off the wrong noble or something."

"Gay men get married nowadays too, because they want to feel normal or it's expected of them by family or their careers," Eli cut in quietly.

"You're not going to do that are you, Dr. Hollister?" Kerry asked. "Get a beard, I mean?" The other students all looked at her, their mouths falling open in the sudden, awkward silence. Isaac snickered behind his hand, and Nori turned a painful red. "What? It was a just a question."

The rest of the class immediately erupted into a heated argument, and Ash mouthed, "Sorry" at him. Eli shrugged with a small smile. He'd never made a big deal about his orientation on campus; on occasion people picked it up and he never denied it. He held up his hands, whistled to get their attention, and smiled as they all looked at him again. "Let's get back to Ash's presentation, but to ease your mind, Kerry, I promise I won't ever marry just to hide who I am."

Eli turned his attention back to Ash, who looked bemused as he pulled out another piece of paper. "You're right, Hannah, he was married and he did piss off a noble—Douglas's dad, in his case. In the next letter I have, he mentions renters. That was slang for prostitutes back then. The prosecution brought a whole bunch of the renter guys to his trial to testify about what he'd paid them to do, and that pretty much clinched it for a conviction."

> *Dearest of All Boys,*
>
> *Your letter was delightful, red and yellow wine to me; but I am sad and out of sorts. Bosie, you must not make scenes with me. They kill me, they wreck the loveliness of life. I cannot see you, so Greek and gracious, distorted with passion. I cannot listen to your curved lips saying hideous things to me. I would sooner be blackmailed by every renter in London than to have you bitter, unjust, hating. You are the divine thing I want, the thing of grace and beauty; but I don't know how to do it. Shall I come to Salisbury? My bill here is 49 pounds for a week. I have also got a new sitting-*

room over the Thames. Why are you not here, my dear, my wonderful boy? I fear I must leave; no money, no credit, and a heart of lead.

Your own, Oscar

The whole story was rather tragic, now that he thought about it. Over one hundred years had passed since Oscar Wilde's death, and attitudes were just really beginning to change. He listened to Ash and the class discuss the letters he'd chosen, making notes as he went.

For someone who claimed to hate English classes, Ash certainly put forth all his effort. And given what he'd learned of Ash, Eli wasn't surprised at all. Even with this project, yes, he had no doubt that Ash picked the topic to flirt with him in class, but the presentation hadn't been quickly thrown together.

Eli shifted as thoughts of getting away with Ash for a long weekend made his blood heat. His camp was only a couple hours away, though he'd have to make sure none of his cousins were using it to hunt over the weekend.

"Good job, Ash," Eli said when he'd finished, and then the sound of high heels came from the direction of the bridge.

Bron groaned as Isaac perked up, looking over his shoulder. "The princess is arriving. Why'd she even bother? She's already missed half of class, and I bet you that she dressed stupidly even though she knew we'd be out here. I don't want to hear her bitching for the rest of the time."

"What's wrong with you? You don't like girls? Whitney is one hot piece," Isaac said, still staring in the direction of the bridge.

"I don't like prissy prima donnas who act like they're entitled to everything. I like real girls," Bron retorted, casting a quick glance at Nori, who was clutching her presentation papers with a pale face.

"Enough, you two. We don't talk about people behind their backs. Understand me?" Eli said.

The boys nodded as Whitney came into view. Eli sighed as he saw that once again she'd chosen to wear a skirt that was really too short for sitting on the ground, and it didn't look as if she'd bothered to bring a blanket. He'd just have to stop having classes outside on good days. Maybe that was why she missed so much.

Whitney stepped off the path and immediately her heels sank into the grass. She lurched with a startled squawk and almost fell over. With a sigh, Eli sprinted over and offered her his arm.

"Thank you, Dr. Hollister." Whitney clutched at his arm as he led her toward the class. "I'm sorry I'm late. I'd forgotten we were supposed to meet out here."

"You were with us when we discussed it last class." Eli wasn't about to let her continued absences and lateness slide this time. "You won't have that excuse next time, since we'll no longer be having class outside."

There. That should settle it. As they neared the others, Isaac moved over on his blanket, making room for her. "You can sit here with me," he offered.

Eli steered her over there before she could argue and returned to his seat, trying not to show his aggravation. Whitney stared after him for a moment before folding her legs under her gingerly and kneeling, exposing far too much of her thighs.

Ash frowned and came over to hand Eli his report. He looked as if he wanted to say something. There was a tiny line between his brows and his lips were slightly pursed. Eli's eyes were drawn to that one little freckle near his lip. "I don't know whether to be amused, happy, or concerned that you just don't see it." With that cryptic little remark, he brushed his fingers over Eli's and went back to his seat without another word. Eli slipped his glasses on and glanced down, scanning the note on the top.

This quote was one of my favorites.

My own dear boy: It's really absurd—I can't live without you. You are so dear, so wonderful—I think of you all day long, and miss your grace, your boyish beauty, the sword play of your wit, the delicate fancy of your genius, so surprising....

Dinger's tonight at 7?

"Okay, Nori," Eli said in a gentle voice as she gulped and turned pale, "it's your turn." He pondered Ash's note, sticking it in his pocket as Nori began her presentation.

ELI'S brows drew together in a frown as he neared his office door and saw that it was ajar. He was sure he'd locked it before he left. Security was one of the things that Britton kept harping on, and for once Eli agreed with him. He pushed open the door and felt like he'd been punched right in the gut as he stared in shock at the chaos within.

His bookshelves had been ransacked, some of the contents knocked onto the floor, the shelves pulled away from the wall. And the violation didn't stop there. Admittedly his office wasn't the neatest, and he did have a tendency to let books and papers pile up, but even at its worst the place had never looked like this.

All thoughts about whether or not he'd take Ash up on his dinner invitation disappeared. "What the fuck?" Eli growled, righting his chair and dropping his bag onto the seat. Who the hell would do something like this? Torn between disbelief and outrage, and feeling distinctly ill, Eli ventured the rest of the way into his office and slammed the door behind him.

His desk drawers were unlocked, the contents spilling out, and the broken lock on his file cabinets hung from the hasp. When Eli checked, folders were out of place there as well, as if someone had systemically gone through every one and just stuffed them back in whichever way they wanted. It would take hours to reorganize everything and check to see if any records or papers were missing.

Eli grabbed the phone off the floor and dialed campus security. His fingers drummed agitated patterns onto the desk throughout the short conversation. Afterward, he paced the floor as he waited, his fingers itching to start straightening up. Then his gaze fell to the floor and his resolve broke at the sight of his vintage Thoreau open and half buried under papers.

Eli crouched down and gently lifted it free, his teeth clenching as he found several of the pages split from the pressure on the aged paper. The corner of the hardback had been bent as well, but at least the spine was intact.

As he carefully placed the book in the center of his desk the sound of the door opening had his head jerking up. Britton glowered at him, his brows drawn together in one fierce line. "You've really done it this time, boy."

It was the "boy," so reminiscent of his father when he'd been in trouble as a kid, and the derisive note in Britton's tone that broke the leash on Eli's temper.

"You," Eli snarled, stabbing a finger in Britton's direction and unleashing years of frustration. "What the hell did you think you were doing by all of this?" Eli swept an arm out to encompass his destroyed office. He stalked toward Britton, whose eyes had widened as he stepped back. Eli's hands balled into fists, and he had to force himself to unclench them.

"What? What are you talking about? I didn't do this!"

"Only the departmental secretary, me, and the cleaning crew have keys to this office, Britton. Only you'd be able to get those keys from her. It was unlocked when I got back, not broken into, unlike my file cabinets, which you don't have keys for!"

Eli's hands shook with the strength of his fury. He was never going to be able to find another Thoreau like that one. Screwing with his files he could forgive, breaking into his space the same, but harming one of his rare books… that went over the line. Not to mention fucking with his career.

Britton charged past him, and Eli resisted the urge to grab the back of his suit jacket and drag the man back out of his office. He needed to get a grip on himself before they ended up brawling like teenagers. They'd both be in big trouble then. "How could you be so careless?" Britton's eyes bulged and his face turned red as he saw the ransacked files.

"I knew it. It's a damn setup that you thought up," Eli accused. "I cannot believe you've stooped so low. Were you getting tired of waiting for me to fuck up on my own? Is that it? What the hell would going through my files prove?"

Britton's mouth dropped open, and then his face reddened even more as the vein at his temple began to throb. "Who do you think you're speaking to like that?" he snapped. "I am the head of this department, and you are an insignificant worm trying to undermine the integrity of this college. I won't have it. This is confidential student information you've let leak. I'll be speaking with the dean about this, Hollister, you can count on it."

"Very poetic. But I'd pick a different metaphor. Worms are good for the soil. If you want a burrowing, destructive animal, compare me to a mole next time," Eli called to Britton as he stormed out. "Go ahead and talk to him. I have a few things to say to him myself."

He growled, kicking the leg of his desk and dragging a hand through his hair. "Fuck me." As satisfying as it would have been to plant a punch on Britton's jaw, that definitely would've ended his career at Amwich, friends with the dean or not. Dean Newton wasn't going to be happy that he went off on Britton. He didn't know if he was more irked with Britton or himself.

Eli shouldn't have let his temper get away from him. Britton didn't have the acting skills to pull off a scene like that. There had been genuine horror in his face when he'd seen the files. And he probably wouldn't have been able to bring himself to destroy them, or a rare book, no matter how much he hated Eli. And now he'd just given Britton another reason to hate his guts and deny him tenure.

CHAPTER 8

ASH'S eyes widened in surprise as Eli pushed his way through the crowd at Dingers. In all the times he'd seen Eli, he'd never been in a mood like this. Eli didn't pause to talk to those who greeted him; instead he nodded curtly, his mouth set in a grim line and his brow furrowed as he passed them by without even a hello. He was nothing at all like the smiling man Ash had left that afternoon, and the abrupt change worried him. He hoped that he hadn't given Eli that new tension with his teasing during class. Maybe he'd carried it too far.

Eli reached the table and yanked out a chair, his blue-gray eyes hot with suppressed anger. "What happened?" Ash demanded.

"My office was broken into sometime this afternoon, and whoever did it left it in a goddamned mess." Eli's mouth was set in a hard line and his lean body was tense as he sat down. "Then I got into it with Britton over the break-in and had to go explain myself to Dean Newton afterward."

Questions leapt to Ash's tongue, but then Lu came up and slipped her arm around Eli's shoulders before he could ask them. "I heard the news. How are you doing, hon?"

Eli cast Lu a surly glance and then squeezed her hand on his shoulder with an attempt at a smile. "Right now, I'm moody and reckless, a dangerous combination. But I'll be fine. I just need to work the mad out of my system."

"Was anything taken?" Ash asked as he took a sip of his beer. He found the steely glint in Eli's eyes to be a little arousing, despite the circumstances. Eli was so laid-back Ash had never thought he'd see him fired up like this. And oh, all the ways that fire could be used in bed. He wanted Eli to be under him the next time he saw him like this, those long-fingered hands hard on his body as Eli whispered hot words in Ash's ear. The thoughts made his heart pick up.

Get a grip, Ash. The last thing Eli needed right now was Ash making fuck me eyes at him.

"No, not that I could tell. And I also got reamed out by Sheriff Cooper for moving things about before he got there." A mutinous look crossed Eli's expressive face. "But I just couldn't leave some of those books on the floor. He didn't understand."

Neither did Ash, for that matter, but he kept his mouth shut. He was pretty sure that the sheriff had already told Eli plenty about the information that could be gathered from an untouched crime scene. No sense in rubbing Eli's nose in it and having that fierce gaze snap glares at him.

"You and those books." Lu shook her head and patted Eli's shoulder. "Just sit here and I'll fix you right up."

"Lu seems to think that a good meal and a shot of something strong cures everything," Eli said as she walked away.

"It doesn't?" Ash teased, trying to make Eli smile. "I thought the way into your heart was your stomach. At least that's what I've heard from certain people."

Eli leaned closer to him across the small table, his eyes intent on Ash in a way that brought a flutter of excitement. "Personally, I prefer a hard, dirty fuck when I'm in this mood."

Ash's mouth went dry and heat poured through him as Eli's words struck him. All thoughts of good intentions and waiting until the end of the semester immediately fled. "You've got my interest, Eli, though I should be the voice of reason and suggest we stay and behave."

He didn't want to. Damn, he wanted to take advantage of Eli's temper and discover exactly what he was like in bed when he was in such a mood. Over the past month, Eli had become more than the man Ash wanted to screw: he'd become a friend. A friend who wasn't thinking things through at the moment, and Ash had no damn wish to be a regret after Eli calmed down.

A catlike grin crossed Eli's lips. "But you won't. I don't believe it. Not after your little presentation today and all those letters about meeting up outside of town."

"I thought you'd pick up on that." Ash grinned, reminded of the whole reason why he'd wanted to speak to Eli tonight. This would cheer him up. "I wondered what it would take to lure you out to Boston with me."

"Boston?" Eli's dark-reddish brows lifted in question. "I don't normally choose to go to the city for a getaway, but I could be persuaded to if you're there."

"I happen to have in my possession two tickcts to game three of the ALCS at Fenway."

Astonishment lit Eli's face, chasing away the aggravated lines, and his eyes lit up with glee. "Hot damn, how did you manage that magic trick?"

Ash grinned to see Eli's mood change for the better. "One of the guys at drill had tickets. He's going to have to go out of town that week and he can't get out of it. So he offered them up for sale."

"There had to be quite a few people who'd want them. How much did you pay?" Eli's eyes narrowed. "They didn't cost you a lot did they?"

Ash waved him silent before Eli could offer to reimburse him. "Nope, I just gave him what he'd already paid. Since there were a bunch of other guys who wanted in, he decided to let us fight it out."

"Fight?"

Ash laughed at Eli's shocked expression and shook his head. "Not a real fight. I won them in a poker game."

"I could kiss you," Eli breathed with such a stunned, happy smile that Ash laughed again.

"I'll hold you to that sometime very soon." Maybe even after dinner, if Eli kept looking at him the way he was. Ash's cock stirred, reminding him that it had been a very long month since he'd been naked with this man and it wanted attention.

"And here I thought you got worked to death on those weekends. I was feeling all sorry for you, coming home sore and worn out," Eli teased.

"Liar," Ash replied under his breath as Lu approached. "You're just thinking of excuses to get me naked so you can massage me again." Then he raised his voice as Eli's cousin approached. "Once in awhile we have a little downtime at drill. This happened to be one of those times."

Lu set down bowls of corn chowder and what smelled like fresh-baked bread, a beer for Ash, and a squat glass of dark-amber liquid for Eli. "I was thinking of you earlier and whipped up a little something to bring just in case you showed up tonight."

"You're the best, Lu," Eli said with a grateful smile. "I don't know what I'd do without you."

"No need to cozy up to me. I just like seeing a smile on your face again." With that Lu disappeared into the swirl of customers.

"Me too." Ash broke off a piece of the steaming bread and slathered it with butter. "And seeing you all fired up was quite a turn-on."

"How the hell am I supposed to stay mad between you offering Red Sox tickets and her chowder? It's just not possible."

Ash dunked his bread in the chowder and took a bite, gauging Eli's mood. He didn't want to set him off again, but he did want to find out more about the break-in. Especially since it was just another one of those unexplained mysteries that seemed to surround Eli. Eli had told him of coming home to find Jabbers in rooms he'd sworn he'd left closed, and one time the dog had been outside. It was past time that he voiced his suspicions to Eli. Either Jabbers had learned to open doors, or Wayne was still going into Eli's house without telling him.

Just like he had to get his glove, but that didn't explain why he'd been there in the first place. Maybe it was coincidence. But Ash didn't really believe that. And every time he saw Wayne, the man wouldn't meet his eyes.

"So tell me what happened."

Eli set his spoon down, his brows furrowing and took a sip from his glass. "Not much to tell, really. Whoever tore apart my office had a key. Just between us, they had to have been looking for something, but it didn't seem to be any of the student records. Even though they'd been rifled through, they were intact. Sheriff Cooper wants me keep it quiet until he's done with his investigation. So don't say anything or he's going to bitch at me all over again."

"What else did you have in the office? Anything valuable?"

Eli's expression darkened and he took another sip of his drink. "Yeah, but it wasn't stolen, just roughed up a bit. I'd almost rather it have been stolen. I had some rare books, and one of them took some damage to the pages. If they had been after money, they wouldn't have done that."

From the look on Eli's face, the damaged book was what had gotten him so pissed off. Ash didn't get it. It was a book. Surely Eli could get another copy, even if it was rare. And then he felt bad for thinking that, because it had to have meant something to him to get Eli so worked up. He'd never met anyone who owned as many books as Eli had in his house.

"I'm sorry," Ash murmured. "How bad was the damage? Can the book be fixed?"

"Not really. And what really pisses me off is I can't figure out a reason why anybody would need or want anything from my office other than to harass me or make me look bad."

Ash closed his eyes and shook his head. He had a feeling he knew where Eli had gone with that theory. "Let me guess. You went off on Britton?"

Eli looked away and shrugged, an uncomfortable look crossing his face. "I may have accused him of being behind the break-in. It made sense then, even if it seems too extreme for him now. He had the unfortunate timing of showing up right after I discovered my damaged book. I'm supposed to apologize to him tomorrow."

Ash couldn't see that happening anytime soon. "Are you?"

"I haven't decided yet." Eli took a sip of his drink and a wicked smile crossed his lips. "If I can come up with a way to make my apology even more awkward for him than me, I just might do it."

Ash burst out laughing, and Eli's smiled turned a bit sheepish. "I'm not helping my situation out any with my attitude, am I?"

"The bastard deserves it. I heard the way he talks to you and I can understand you not wanting to apologize." Ash thought over the situation for a moment until the perfect idea came to him. "Didn't you say it irks him when he can't get under your skin?"

"Makes him nuttier than a cat in heat. And some days knowing that is the only reason why I manage to keep my cool."

"I'd suggest going to him with sincerity. Think you can fake that? It would piss him the fuck off."

"It would, wouldn't it?" Eli said with malicious glee. "I shouldn't be this excited over the chance to see the vein in his temple throbbing again, but I am. I don't know what it is about this semester, but he's more vitriolic than ever before. And as long as I apologize, sincere or not, the dean will be happy. He gets far more grief from Britton than he does from me."

"Hey, Eli, I heard what happened at your office." They both looked up at Wayne, who stood next to their table crushing his cap in his hand. "I'm really sorry about it. Can I do anything to help you?"

Ash felt a momentary stab of sympathy for Sheriff Cooper. How the hell he conducted investigations when everybody in town heard about things as soon as they happened, Ash didn't know.

Eli was friendly with just about everybody in this town and it never bothered Ash one bit. So why was it that he got irritated when Eli gave Wayne a warm smile? He knew there wasn't that kind of a vibe between them, but it still irked him.

"Thanks, Wayne. There's really nothing to do. I've already picked up and straightened everything I could. And except for the ruined book, nothing was destroyed. I don't know what to make of the whole thing. How's your dad doing? I hear he's getting stronger."

For a moment, Wayne looked stricken before he smoothed his expression. "The rehab is going slow, but he's making progress. I suppose little steps are better than nothing."

"It sounds encouraging," Ash cut in. "Steady progress, even in little steps, is a good sign." Mentally, he told the guy to go away, but Wayne didn't listen.

"I can replace the broken locks on your file cabinets," Wayne said, ignoring him. "Free of charge."

Eli's brows lifted in surprise. "You don't have to do that, Wayne."

"I want to, please. It won't take but an hour, tops. I can be there tomorrow morning."

"If you really want to, but I insist on you letting me pay. You've got your dad to consider."

"Free of charge," Wayne insisted with a stubborn tilt to his chin.

"Fine." Eli gave up. "I'm paying for the locks, if you won't let me pay for labor. Don't worry, the school will reimburse me."

Wayne hesitated and then nodded. "Deal. I'll see you in the morning." He cast a quick glance at Ash, mumbling something that could've been an acknowledgment before turning into the crowd.

"Think I'll be able to talk him into a check?" Eli asked, turning back to Ash.

Ash hesitated and then decided he couldn't hold back his concerns anymore. "Do you want my honest opinion?"

Eli's brows drew together. "How come I get the feeling I'm not going to like what you're about to say?"

"Because you're probably not. I don't know how close you are to the guy, but I'd watch out for Wayne. You think he's your friend, but I'm not so sure about that. And there have been a lot of weird things going on in your life right now."

Eli's eyes widened. "You're kidding me. You think Wayne's behind it? Get real, Ash, he's got enough going on with his dad and holding their business together with the way I hear he's mismanaging it. Why the hell would he be screwing with me?"

Now, that, Ash hadn't figured out yet. But someone was harassing Eli, and once he figured out why, and why now, he'd know who it was. "I don't know," he admitted. "But there's something about him that I don't trust. I mean he went into your house without you knowing about it."

Truthfully, it made him want to punch Wayne in the mouth, but he didn't think telling Eli that was such a good idea. He was already looking at him like he was crazy.

"He was just getting his glove. Jabbers has a tendency to swipe things, everybody knows that."

"Where I come from people just don't walk into somebody else's house when they're not home, unless they're expected, friend or not." Ash looked around the bar at the people who'd known each other so long they might as well be family. "I can't imagine that everybody here would be cool with that, no matter how relaxed things are in this town."

"Look, I've known Wayne for years. He's never gotten into any trouble like that. What makes you think he has anything to do with it?"

"Instinct and training." And the way Wayne always seemed to be around Eli, yet rarely ever met his eyes. Only Ash was sure pointing that out would only get him accused of jealousy. He folded his arms on the table and leaned forward. "Other than Cooper, you, me, and possibly Britton, who else knows what was disturbed in your office and what wasn't? Did you tell anyone else?"

"Of course not."

"Then how does Wayne know that you need the locks replaced on your file cabinets? I didn't even know that until he said something. You only said that your files were searched and your book was ruined. That's the kind of important detail that Sheriff Cooper wouldn't want leaked out. That's the kind of detail that the intruder would know."

Eli sat back and cast a look in the direction Wayne had gone. If he was still in the bar, Ash couldn't see him. At least Eli seemed to be considering the thought instead of just dismissing it as Ash had feared he would. Ash didn't like that the happy light had left his eyes, but it would've been worse if Eli had just dismissed his reasoning.

"Britton or the dean could've told him." His voice didn't sound certain, though.

"Maybe. Wayne has both motive—he needs money bad—and opportunity." He also had the skill set and tools to both break into Eli's office and to create a new key.

"Those rare books were worth a lot of money and none of them were taken," Eli pointed out.

Ash shrugged and drained the rest of his beer. Wayne probably wouldn't have known their worth any more than Ash would, but he'd said enough for now. "I just wanted you to think about it. First you had odd stuff going on at home, and now there's been an even more intrusive invasion at work. Whoever this is, be it Wayne or someone else, they're not going to stop until they've found what they're looking for."

"It might just be Britton looking for a reason to get me sacked."

Ash didn't think so, and he was pretty damn sure Eli didn't believe it, either, but he decided it was time to drop the subject. All those classes he'd been taking in criminology told him that this wasn't over with by a long shot. He'd just have to keep an eye on Wayne himself.

"So the Sox game is scheduled for a school night. Do you think you're up to being out late, Dr. Hollister?"

Eli's eyes gleamed with wicked laughter as he leaned in close. "Don't you worry about me, Ashley Gallagher. I can hold my own."

Ash's cock twitched, and he promised himself that somehow he was going to get a kiss from Eli before the night was over. He didn't know where or how, without half the town seeing them and commenting. Or how he'd find the willpower to leave it to just a kiss, but he was going to get one.

"I think an occasion like that calls for another bet," Eli continued in a low voice.

"Words that I've been waiting weeks to hear." Warning bells leapt in Ash's brain, and he cheerfully kicked them aside. What was the point of life if he didn't play with a little danger now and then? "I'm assuming from your smile that you already have something in mind."

"Damn right I do." Eli waved to Lu and laid some money on the table. "Did you walk or drive here?"

"Walked. Seems ridiculous to drive such a short distance." Eli walking him home was a bad idea, even if it would give Ash the opportunity to pull him aside for a kiss. Still, it wasn't going to stop Ash. He pulled some money out for his half of the meal and tip. "You can tell me on the way there."

The air outside had cooled considerably after the sun had set and it held the nip of winter to come. Ash dug his hands in his jacket pockets, grateful for the nearly deserted streets as they turned in the direction of his apartment. "So what's going through your devious mind?"

"If my boys win, I get to investigate the contents of that kink drawer of yours and use them on you."

Ash paused in the middle of the sidewalk and turned to face the man next to him, his heart racing. Eli's proposition filled his head with all kinds of ideas, only with their positions reversed. "You really are in a reckless mood, aren't you? Why don't we completely throw caution away, skip the bet, and head upstairs? I'll show you everything in there."

Eli cocked his head, his lips pursed in thought in a way that made Ash's cock jump. "Anticipation," he finally said, "makes everything sweeter in the end. Besides, I'm on a roll. I won the last bet."

"Winning one bet does not qualify as being on a roll," Ash said as they continued walking. "I'm due for a win of my own."

"If this were a poker game, you might stand a chance. Save your winnings for that game. From what I hear, it sounds like you're good at it."

"And if you do win, do you want to do your investigating right away? Or am I going to have to wait till the end of the semester, anticipating?"

"Anticipation is good for the soul." Eli chuckled and nudged Ash with his hip. "I can't let it be said that I'm a bad influence on the student body."

"You've got a good influence on my body." A smile tugged at Ash's lips, and he had to resist the urge to slide his arm around Eli's shoulders and to kiss his temple. It seemed he'd been spending all of his adult life resisting such things, and he was sick and tired of it. "Sounds like you're in a far better mood, Doc."

It would be a very good idea to remind himself just what was at stake if they got caught. It wasn't his career on the line this time.

"I am, thanks to you, and not just because of the tickets." They turned into the darkened shadows of the driveway behind Ash's apartment. His downstairs neighbor had forgotten to leave his kitchen light on, and the stars were faint. "So, you never said what your half of the bet would be on the very slim chance that you actually win."

Ash caught Eli's arm before he started to climb the stairs and tugged him deeper into the shadows of the building. "I never thought I'd have a professor who was such a tease," he said, trapping Eli between himself and the brick wall.

"Me? I'm not the one who was talking about secret getaways in the middle of class today. That was all you, Georgia."

"My motives were pure."

"Liar." Eli chuckled, snagging his fingers around Ash's belt to tug him closer. "Behaving is proving to be a lot harder than I thought it would be."

"You sure as hell don't make it easy," Ash replied, wrapping Eli's ponytail around his hand. "I've been thinking about doing this all throughout dinner."

Ash thought he was prepared for the sizzle of desire when he kissed Eli, but he'd been sorely mistaken. For the past several weeks, he'd been thinking about touching Eli again, tasting him, and now the feel of Eli's body against him, the heat of his eager mouth, was as potent as the smooth whiskey on Eli's tongue.

Eli made a small, urgent sound in the back of his throat and pressed himself closer. Ash's cock throbbed to life, aching inside his jeans as he pinned Eli against the brick. Ash felt like a fucking teenager again, stealing a kiss behind the school with the realization and spice of knowing they could be caught at any minute.

Ash slid his lips down Eli's throat and turned his head to rub the day's worth of stubble against the other man's smooth skin. Eli's hands fisted in his shirt, his breath coming quicker as his thighs parted. Ash bit back a curse as his cock ground against Eli's hip and Eli did the same to him in return.

This was really getting out of hand. They should stop. His neighbor was going to turn on that kitchen light any moment, and damned if that wouldn't kill the mood. Ash's body had something else to say about it, and he found himself nudging Eli's legs open a little wider so he could step between his thighs.

"Yeah," Eli breathed against his ear, circling his hips against Ash's. "Just like that. I had almost this exact fantasy, only it was against my office door."

Ash closed his eyes and shuddered as that image hit his brain. He nipped Eli's jaw, grateful for the cold, early October night air against his skin because the rest of him was on fire. Every time Eli's cock throbbed, his own answered. Searching lips found Eli's mouth, and Ash kissed him deep, muffling their groans.

A good portion of his fantasies had involved Eli's office and that gorgeous hardwood desk. It would look even better with a naked professor sprawled on it with his hair unbound around his shoulders. Bound. Yeah, a naked Eli with his hands tied over his head. Fuck, Ash wasn't going to make it through another class.

Ash slid his hands down to cup Eli's ass through his worn jeans. The soft material clung to him, letting Ash feel every ripple of muscle as they moved together. Eli pulled back, nipping Ash's jaw. Their breath steamed in the night air.

"You're going to have me coming in my damned jeans." Eli didn't ask him to take it upstairs, and Ash was enjoying the illicit thrill of this moment too much to suggest it himself.

Ash licked the pulse at Eli's throat as he laid his head back against the brick. "Do you want me to stop?" Ash rasped.

"Oh, fuck no," Eli whispered back. "Don't you dare."

Ash shuddered and gripped Eli's ass tighter, half lifting him as his hips began to work in a deliberate pattern. He felt the vibration of Eli's almost silent groan against his lips. The heat from Eli's cock seared against his own as their dicks ground together. Eli's hands slid under his shirt, and Ash flinched from the chill of his fingertips against his skin. Eli laughed softly, his breath sounding a little ragged.

"Evil," Ash said, retaliating by sucking on his throat, biting and nipping. He'd see his mark on Eli the next time they were in class, and the thought filled him with the primitive urge to see Eli marked as his. At least for the time being.

Neither one of them were kidding themselves. As much as he felt a connection to Eli, this wasn't going to last past graduation. Eli had a home here and Ash was moving on. It didn't mean they couldn't enjoy each other until then.

Ash kept an ear out for the sound of anyone approaching as his heart raced. Their hips rocked faster, and Eli's breath panted against his cheek. The urge to turn Eli around, work those worn jeans down around his thighs so Ash could sink his cock into his welcoming heat, was almost overwhelming. Then Eli dug his fingers into his sides, and Ash kissed him hard before Eli could cry out.

Electricity zinged through him and his entire body tensed as Eli came, shuddering in his arms. He bucked against Ash, fingers digging even harder into his skin. Ash felt Eli trembling as he made little, urgent, desperate sounds in his throat. It had to be the fucking sexiest sound he'd ever heard and was more than enough to send him right over the edge.

He broke his mouth away from Eli's, panting hard, shivers racing down his spine as his orgasm tore through him. "Goddamn, Eli," Ash groaned softly against his ear. He'd only meant to kiss the man, not have his way with him outdoors, against a wall.

He felt Eli's body shake he laughed silently. "Is that a good goddamn or a bad one?"

"Good. You tempt me, Dr. Elijah Hollister." Ash kissed the corner of his mouth. "I'll take your bet, but if I win, you have to wear something for me for the rest of the semester."

Eli drew his head back to study his face. Ash's eyes had adjusted enough to the dim light to be able to see the mingled curiosity and wariness in Eli's expression. "What? Not a rival team's gear, is it?"

Ash shook his head. "Nope, something in keeping with the spirit of your bet. Something from my 'kink drawer', as you call it. Something that should remind you to behave, and if you don't behave there will be consequences."

"Consequences, huh? Well, now you have my complete attention. What is it?"

Ash gave Eli a wicked grin as he pulled back. "I think it'll be more interesting if I don't tell you. Anticipation and all that, like you said."

"Throwing my own words back at me, huh." Eli straightened, narrowing his eyes at Ash. For a moment, Ash wondered if he'd back out on the bet, but he should've known better. Eli wasn't one to back down from a challenge. "Either way, the kink drawer gets used. As long as you don't dress me in women's underwear or Yankee gear, I agree."

"How can you even equate the two?"

Eli shrugged, grimacing as he took a step away from the wall. Ash sympathized. He had the same uncomfortable wet spot in his jeans. At least his apartment was right up the stairs. "You're right, the Yankee gear would be worse."

WAYNE'S hands shook, forcing him to set down the plane before he made a mistake and ruined the piece. He ran his hands along the grain of the wood, checking for splinters as he tried to calm his nerves. For once his favorite pastime wasn't calming him down at all.

He kept piling on mistake after mistake. First, that hurried search of Eli's office, where terror of being caught and frustration had made him so damn careless. He'd torn through that office as if a bear had been nipping at his heels. Every time he thought about that god-awful mess he'd left behind, he felt a little more ashamed of himself. He should've taken it in sections over several days instead of marauding through there like a maniac. The thought of breaking into a public building again had him breaking out in sweats.

And then, to make matters worse, he'd allowed himself to be guilted into trying to make it up to Eli. He should've walked away when he saw that he was sitting with Ash. That man saw right through him. Wayne just knew it.

He gave up for the night, carefully put away his tools, and cleaned up before heading from the woodshop into the house. His dad's nurse, Ms. Parisot, had gone shopping for groceries, but she'd left dinner warming on the stove.

Wayne washed his hands and went to go check on his dad. He sat in his wheelchair in front of the TV, watching a baseball game and toying with an envelope. He turned his head as Wayne came into the room and slipped the envelope into his dressing robe pocket. The side of his face always seemed to drag down more when he was tired, and it sagged tonight.

It was all Wayne could do not to show how much it upset him. It was considerate of Eli to keep asking about him, but it would be even nicer if he'd do what was right and hand over the card. "Hey, Dad. Did you already eat?"

His dad grunted and nodded. He didn't talk much at the end of the day. Wayne thought that he must be embarrassed by how slow the words came, or how they slurred together. Wayne just wanted to see him stop having to struggle for everything. His dad pointed to the TV. "Watch... with... m-me?"

"Sure. Just let me get a plate. I'll be right there." The corner of his dad's mouth lifted in a tired smile. Wayne's resolve hardened as he returned to the kitchen. He couldn't back down now. Since going through Eli's things wasn't working, clearly he was going to have to take other steps.

CHAPTER 9

ELI tucked his cell phone back into his pocket and adjusted his baseball cap with a grin. It was a freezing night to be going to a game. His ass would be numb before the end of the night, his fingers stiff with cold, and knowing him, he wouldn't even notice until the last out.

If only it wasn't a school night. He didn't get down to Boston that much, and it would've been nice if the game had fallen on a weekend. He would've talked Ash into staying the entire time. Even if he preferred going up to his camp, he would've liked the chance to experience the city with Ash.

"What's this place?" Eli asked as he met Ash in front of a neon sign emblazoned "Grady's." "I don't think I'd ever been here before."

"I've been dying for some good ole southern soul food." Ash opened the door for him, and Eli was struck by a wave of warm air redolent with the aroma of cornbread, greens, and fried chicken. Small tables crowded together with red-and-white checkered cloths over them, and the exposed brick walls were lined with pictures of blues singers. "Especially now that it's getting so much colder. You don't mind?"

"Hell no, I haven't had any since this summer. My mother's from Tennessee, and my cousins really know how to barbeque." They pulled out chairs, and Ash reached over, tugging the tie from Eli's hair.

"It's a damn shame to keep doing that," Ash said as he sat down and picked up one of the plastic menus. "I like your hair down."

"You have more to say on how I dress and keep my hair than certain other people who will not be named tonight," Eli said with a chuckle. Ash had pitched a fit when he'd shown up at class with a turtleneck on after the stunt they'd pulled outside his apartment. And the hot eyes Ash had kept giving him made it very difficult to remember that he was supposed to act professionally in return.

"I'll have even more to say when you lose the bet," Ash said, snickering. "And just so you know, I have my prize on me right now."

"Really?" Eli set down the menu and eyed the man across from him. It wasn't anything big, then, not like a body harness. He wouldn't put it past Ash to want him to wear a getup like that under his clothes during class. He definitely wouldn't be able to concentrate then. His mind had run the gamut between benign and downright naughty ever since the bet had been placed. And he still didn't have any clue as to what it could be.

"Oh, you know it. I wanted to be prepared, just in case, especially after you cheated me out of getting to see my mark on your throat," Ash added in an undertone as the waitress approached.

She set down a bowl of yeast rolls and cornbread with honey butter and took their orders. As soon as she left, Eli leaned across the table. "Bullshit. You accosted me in my office so you could get a look at it."

"Not the same as ogling it in class and knowing I put it there."

Eli narrowed his eyes and crossed the cock ring off his mental list. No, Ash would've picked something he could see, most likely something discreet. Damn, now he really had no clue about what it could be. Though there was no real sense in obsessing over it since Ash was going to lose.

Sixty-one more days until the end of the semester. After all the final exams were taken and all the grades turned in, then Eli would call in his bet. Now he just had to last another two months with blue balls. He'd almost had it under control until Ash had pinned him against that wall and driven him insane. He'd never been with a guy before who could get him so damn worked up when they hadn't even screwed yet.

"So, you ever think about moving down to Tennessee, where the weather is much less evil this time of year?" Ash asked, cutting into Eli's thoughts, just as his cock started to ache.

"Come on, it's not that bad. It's not even November yet." Eli cut open a steaming yeast roll and slathered it with butter.

"Don't remind me that I have at least another five or six months before I'm brought out of my misery." Ash drank half of his sweet tea in one go and sighed happily.

"I take it that means there's going to be no more hikes after the first snowfall hits?" Eli wagged his brows and continued in a wheedling voice, "I have extra snowshoes."

Ash gave him a mournful look. "You're just a glutton for punishment. No, I'll go. It'll keep me in shape. Then cold-weather training midwinter won't be such a shock to my system."

Neither said it, that the hiking gave them just another excuse to be in each others' presence. They'd migrated from seeing each other in class twice a week, to Ash joining him on hikes some weekends, to having dinner at Dingers on Wednesday nights. Though they rarely dined alone. They were often joined by most of the other kids in their class, who had somehow heard of the spot and joined them to do homework and hang out.

Thank God Britton never got wind of that. And the kids provided a good buffer. How they never picked up on the sexual tension, Eli didn't know. He felt like he was on fire every time he was around Ash and consumed with thoughts of him when he wasn't.

And it wasn't just the sex, even if Eli tried to kid himself that it was. He really liked Ash. He hadn't felt a connection like this since… well, it was better not to dwell on Jeremy. It only made him think that his relationship with Ash was doomed to end just as Eli's other relationships had: as soon as he got good and attached.

"But no," Eli said, returning to Ash's original question. "I'll never settle down in Tennessee. Even if my cousin Gareth is one of my best friends and would love to have me there, my dad and I handle each other better when there are several states between us."

"What happened? Did you not ever get along or did it all go sour later on?"

"A little bit of both." Eli was in too good of a mood to let the memories spoil his night. "We never understood each other. I was always more interested in doing my own thing than following the status quo. Dad tried to overcompensate by regimenting everything to death, and I retaliated by rebelling just because."

"I can picture that without any difficulty at all." Ash sat back as the waitress set down the platter of smothered pork chops and sides of black-eyed peas, collards, and what looked like homemade macaroni and cheese instead of processed crap. Eli had to grin at the satisfied gleam in Ash's green eyes.

They sat for a few minutes in companionable silence as they ate. Ash was easy to talk to; Eli didn't share his childhood stories with just anyone.

"But the shit really hit hard the summer I turned fifteen. School had just ended, and I was head over heels for this guy who was a grade ahead of me. He was teaching me all kinds of fun things until we got caught by his dad not two weeks into our vacation." Ash winced in sympathy, though in truth the humiliation from that incident had ceased to sting years ago. "There was no hiding what we were doing or pretending it was something else. Not with the half naked lip-lock we had going on."

"What happened after that? Did the guy's dad hush it up or make a big stink?"

"Oh, he hushed it up, alright. The man who caught us was the commander of Dad's base. His response was to get Dad reassigned to Alaska." Eli shook his head as he dished himself some more greens. "It wasn't like Alaska hadn't been a possibility before. My parents had been happy to get Georgia instead, and according to my dad, I ruined it for them. Even shipping me off to my grandparents up here didn't help. He was still furious when I returned for school."

Eli's heart flipped as Ash just looked at him with empathy in his gaze. Jesus, he could really find himself falling for Ash, with his boy next door looks and the sexy smattering of freckles on his nose and cheeks. Ash was a genuinely nice guy, one of the good ones that could be trusted. Someone who'd made it clear that he was looking to head out as soon as he graduated. Man, Eli could really pick them, couldn't he?

"Sometimes I forget how lucky I've been." Ash's gaze dropped to his plate. "At least with my family. They've never given me any grief over being gay."

"You still know what it feels like," Eli said quietly. "I've heard you talking about what it was like being in the Marines, how they were a family for you." And if Ash had let it be known he was gay, he would've been drummed out of there as quick as Eli had been booted out of his father's house. Like Eli, Ash had a few people in his group that he could trust to be himself with. And that was worth more than words could say.

"Look at us getting all self-pitying." Ash tossed his napkin down onto his empty plate. "There's a baseball game waiting for us, and I haven't been to a post-season game since I was in high school. Let's go make a ruckus."

"Well, when you put it like that, how can I say no?"

"There is a streak of romance in you that's unexpected," Eli teased as Ash opened the door for him as they walked out. "Surprising me with tickets and holding open doors."

"You wouldn't call me romantic if you knew what was in my pocket."

Eli shoved him with a laugh. "Good point. You're wicked to the core, Georgia."

"I just wish you hadn't felt the need to pay for the second ticket."

"I had to. Technically I'm a state employee, and there are laws about accepting gifts from students. That would get me fired in a heartbeat." He was walking the line enough. "Still, I thank you for the sentiment."

"You know you're really sexy when you get all ethical on me." Ash grinned and leered mockingly at him.

They continued to joke as they walked down Yawkey Way and lined up outside the entrance. Eli stuffed his hands in his pockets, finding it hard to keep still in his excitement, until Ash leaned over with a snicker. "You know you do that in class too, sometimes, when you get all worked up on a subject."

"Do what?" Eli asked, cocking his head in curiosity.

"Bounce on your toes."

"I do not." Eli's mouth dropped open and then his eyes narrowed as Ash snickered again. "You're making that up."

"Ha, you don't remember that day when Bron and Hannah got into the debate over Ben Franklin's letters and Nori forgot her shyness enough to join in? You did it then. I thought Isaac and Elsa were gonna bust a gut trying not to laugh, and Whitney was making calf eyes at you over it."

Eli tried to picture it, but all he could remember was elation because Nori had opened her mouth without prompting and irritation because Whitney had been late again. "If you say so." He shrugged and mock glared at Ash. "And were you snickering too?"

"Nah, I was too busy trying to tame all the indecent thoughts I was having about you." They handed their tickets to the attendant and crossed through the turnstiles. "Let me tell you, this is the first English class I've had where I didn't fall asleep once."

Eli shook his head as he led Ash toward the seats along the first-base line. "Thank you for the stroke to my ego, but I could wish that a part of your interest was because of the content and not just because you know what I look like naked."

"Spoken like a true professor," Ash said, touching his hand to the small of Eli's back before letting it fall away. "I will admit, other than the sexual tension the class is pretty cool. I'm enjoying it."

Eli leaned forward in his seat, watching all of the activity on the field as the players warmed up before the game. "Man, I don't know I'm ever going to thank you for thinking of me. Do you have any idea how hard it is to get post-season tickets at Fenway? You're one lucky bastard."

"What can I say? I lead a semi-charmed kind of life."

Eli warmed inside as their knees brushed up against each other. It would be nice to be able to hold hands or snuggle up together like the couple down the row in front of them. Not being able to definitely made the little touches mean more.

"You know it's going to be a tough game," Ash said with a quick, teasing sidelong glance as the seats filled. "You've won one and they've won one. Are you sure you can handle the pressure?"

"Those are the best type of games." Eli shifted, too restless to give in to Ash's attempts to bait him. Of course that only led to renewed curiosity over what was in his blasted pockets... probably Ash's intent all along.

They continued to talk as the clock wound down toward the game, exchanging stories of past baseball games they had been to and the memorabilia they'd collected over the years. "My dad used to have this baseball card collection when he was a teenager. Grumpy told me about it. I'd've loved to have had a chance to go through it and see what he'd gotten."

It was too damned bad his dad never shared them with him. His dad had once loved baseball too, but somehow had lost that love long ago. Eli never could understand that.

"Have you been having any more problems with break-ins? Or weird stuff going on at your place?"

Now, those unsolved mysteries had led to a few nights where Eli had found it difficult to fall asleep over wondering who it could be. He found himself locking his doors before he left his house now, something he'd never done before, and he hated feeling like he had to. He doubly hated the idea that anyone he knew or respected might be behind it. Especially since he couldn't come up with one single reason why anyone would target him.

"Not one thing. Maybe whoever it was came to the conclusion that I have nothing they want."

Eli could certainly hope so. At least whoever it was had the decency to only come in during the day. Probably because he knew Jabbers would raise a holy racket if anyone came sniffing around in the middle of the night. Which meant they also knew that Eli had a shotgun, even if the thought of pointing it at another human being made him sick inside. All thoughts that led back to it having to be someone who knew him.

Ash rose as the players took the field. "Sheriff Cooper have any suspects?"

"Nope. He thinks it was a passing thing, probably a student pulling a prank or trying to get at some records." Eli didn't believe that. His students were all good kids, and he only had one who was doing poorly in his classes this semester. Somehow, he couldn't see Whitney risking breaking a nail on his file cabinets.

"How's Kurtis doing?"

Ash sucked in a breath with a slight shake of his head. "Eager to be home. It's been a long tour."

They pulled off their caps as the national anthem started. It never failed to send a shiver through Eli. There were just some things that being a military brat instilled in a person. He cast a quick glance at Ash, who stood rock still, saluting the flag. His face was impassive, but Eli couldn't miss the emotion in his eyes.

It gave him another shiver as he wondered just what Ash thought of at moments like this. What memories haunted him? Because as much pride as he saw in Ash's gaze, there were bad memories there too. It made him want to soothe them away. Eli turned his eyes back on the flag with an ache in his throat as the music swelled to a crescendo.

"OH MAN, I think you jinxed me." Eli shot a mournful look at Ash. "I cannot believe we lost like that."

"Don't say that. Then I'll never be able to talk you into going to another game with me. I wouldn't be able to compete with a baseball superstition." Ash wrapped his arm around Eli's shoulders and squeezed his bicep before letting him go. He was finding more and more excuses to touch him. Eli invited caresses from his tumbled, tousled hair to his long, lean body.

"I don't think you'd have a problem," Eli said with a smile. "Even if we did lose, I had a great time."

It was late, and except for the flock of disappointed fans leaving Fenway Park, the streets were mostly empty. If they didn't have such a long drive home, Ash would've cajoled Eli into staying a little longer, maybe even finding a hotel for a few hours. He had a hankering to see Eli naked with nothing on but the little present that was currently burning a hole in his pocket.

"You might hate me, but I can't say that I'm unhappy the Red Sox lost. Not tonight."

"That's only because you won the bet." Eli eyed him curiously as they turned toward the nearby parking lot, where Eli had left his Jeep. "So how long am I supposed to wear this thing?"

"At least every Monday and Wednesday for the rest of the semester. Hell, while we're at it, why not on the nights we meet at Dingers and the days we go hiking?"

"So pretty much every time I see you. And it's supposed to remind me to behave?" The crowd around them dwindled as people found their cars and began to drive off. Traffic had slowed to a crawl, and the cars seeking to exit piled up. "Don't you think you should be the one wearing it? After all, you're the one who pinned me against the wall outside of your apartment and—"

"After you gave me the sex eyes and told me you liked to fuck when you were in that kind of a mood. I only have so much willpower, and you pretty much destroyed it with that statement. I was ready to drag you out by your hair right there."

And damned if that didn't put an image in his head that Ash did not need. This waiting and buildup ate away at his patience. So what if they were only going to get a few hours sleep as it was by the time they got back to Amwich. Ash knew he was going to find it hard not to stake a claim on Eli once he gave him his present.

Ash rubbed his hand along his arm. His scars always seemed to ache more in the extreme hot or cold. Eli unlocked his Jeep and motioned for Ash to go around the other side. "Hop on in. We can wait till the clusterfuck eases up a bit, then I can drive you to your truck."

Ash was not about to argue against the chance to warm his hands and spend some more time in Eli's company. Whichever way, he was going to end up waiting, and he'd rather wait with Eli.

He slid in and held his hands up to the vent as Eli turned on the Jeep and cranked up the heat. "I hadn't realized I'd gotten so damned numb. That game was damn close right down to the last out."

"Don't remind me. Next time I say I like tense games, remind me of tonight. I think my blood pressure rose into dangerous territory."

Eli turned in his seat and took Ash's hand, chafing it until it was warm before moving on to the other one. "You don't have to do that," Ash said.

Eli smiled at him, palms and long fingers still rubbing. "I'm more used to the cold than you are and I don't mind."

Ash knew he could feel the scars where they ended at his wrist, but Eli didn't comment on them. He never tried to make much of them like some others had, fussing over him like he was some kind of hero, which he wasn't. He preferred to just not think of them, and Eli had respected that from the first night. He also didn't ask Ash a bunch of stupid, thoughtless questions about what it was like to be on the battlefront, or to be shot at, or if he'd killed anyone.

Questions like that had turned Ash off dating anyone for awhile. Eli wasn't like that. It had surprised him earlier when Eli had opened up about his dad. That wasn't something he had planned on pressing Eli about. Not with the underlying, lingering hurt he'd sensed in Eli.

It made him want to give Eli something just as personal in return.

"I think I've lost you," Eli said with a little laugh as he let go of Ash's hand. "What's got your mind wandering?"

"You."

Eli cocked his head, looking at Ash in the dim light, and the teasing smile on his lips faded as his expression became more serious. "What about me?"

"I was just thinking how you don't press me for any more than I want to give."

Eli shrugged and combed his hair back with his fingers. "I could say the same about you with me."

Ash hesitated, searching for the right words, but they all sounded pretty damned awkward to him. "I'm sorry you went through all that with your dad. I was one of the lucky ones. My parents worried about me being gay, but they didn't use it to guilt me into trying to change."

"It fucking sucked, I'm not going to lie, but my grandparents and Lu more than made up for my parents." Ash reached for Eli's hand again, tangling their fingers together. "And I do have to give my Dad some credit. He has been trying ever since I left for college. We have a tentative truce. And that's better than what a lot of other people have."

Very true, but still it didn't dismiss the pain. That much Ash did know. Eli didn't seem like the type to let it embitter him. He lived in the moment far more than he lived in the past. And right now Ash didn't feel like reliving the past himself. He didn't want to talk about deceit and bombs, or of the terror that had struck him right before the pain when he'd gotten hurt anymore than Eli wanted to talk about how his parents had let him down when they were supposed to be his haven.

The cars started to thin out, so Ash dug in his pocket and pulled out two flexible leather wrist cuffs with a buckle on one side and a small D ring on the other. He twirled one of them on his finger and caught Eli's amused glance. "It is time, my friend, for you to make good on your bet."

"You do realize there is quite enough talk about me on campus already without me wearing those."

"Anybody who would recognize them wouldn't care what you do on your off time, and Britton wouldn't know what these were if he were slapped in the face with them," Ash countered.

Eli laughed and held out one lean wrist. "Good point, and if he were given a demonstration he'd run screaming in the other direction. You just want to find some way to stamp 'Ashley Brandon Gallagher was here' on me. And I think you succeeded."

"Well, not entirely, but it's a start." Ash secured the first cuff around Eli's wrist, tightening it enough so that it couldn't slip off his hand, but not so much that it would chafe him. It made him feel funny inside to see it there, and he wondered just what kind of a game they were playing. He wasn't sure that it was just about waiting for the sex anymore.

Eli examined it as Ash secured the second cuff. "And just what do you plan on doing if I don't behave? Call me crazy, but tying me up is not behaving yourself either."

"Touché." Ash hooked his finger through the rings, binding Eli's wrists together. "What are we going to do about this thing between us, Elijah?"

"Well, if it hasn't burned out by now, I don't think it's going to, even if we do wait till the end of the semester." Eli wet his lips and slowly leaned closer as the air in the Jeep seemed to sizzle. "Honestly, after last week, I'm not all that keen on waiting."

Ash slid his other hand into the weight of Eli's hair. "Kissing you would be a very bad idea."

"Don't let that stop you." A quick grin flicked across Eli's lips, and then he took matters into his own hands and leaned the last few inches in to kiss Ash instead.

Ash's breath caught, and he groaned deep in his throat as his hand tightened in Eli's hair. The kiss was slow and drugging, no less intense than when Eli's body had been trapped between Ash and the wall. Ash released Eli's wrists and twisted his body in the seat to get closer, mentally cursing the seats and the stick shift between them.

The glare of headlights broke them apart, and Eli turned away with a shaky laugh. "Come on, I'll drive you to your truck."

Ash shifted in his seat, trying to ease the throbbing ache in his groin, without much success. There was a strange note in Eli's voice, almost as if he was distancing himself, but that didn't make much sense. Ash was just letting his frustrated cock do the thinking for him. Because there was no reason for Eli to pull back now. Not after initiating a kiss like that.

The corner of the lot where he'd parked his truck was encased in shadows, and damn if it didn't tempt Ash. "Any chance I could lure you over to my truck?" Where he had a long bench seat and room to stretch Eli out. He grinned and glanced at Eli to see the impact of his next words. "I've been thinking about cuffing you to the oh-shit handle and going down on you."

"Dammit, Ash, that image is going to keep me awake the entire way home," Eli said with a groan.

"That was kinda the idea. I like knowing I'm haunting your thoughts."

A cop car rolled on by, moving slow enough to get a good look at them, and Eli sighed. "They're going to be patrolling until most of the crowd is gone. There are going to be some drunk, angry people out tonight."

"Enough said." Ash had spent too many years hiding who he really was, and there were times when he'd been more than ready to explode from the pressure and frustration, but it would just be stupid to throw it all away when he'd be opting out and discharged this summer with his reputation intact.

They'd already played fast and loose once and managed to not get caught. At least that had been in Amwich, so they probably wouldn't have been arrested, though Eli didn't need that kind of notoriety if the gossips got going.

Ash leaned forward and caught Eli's lips in a hungry kiss. "I'll see you in the afternoon, Doc."

CHAPTER 10

THERE was something odd going on with Eli. At first Ash thought it might be because they were both tired. They'd both had big days today, and Ash didn't even want to remember how late it had been before he'd finally crashed last night. Still, that didn't explain the air of reserve that hung around Eli today.

Every once in a while, Eli would tug on one of the leather cuffs, toying with the D ring, and it made Ash crazy with desire each and every time. Then Eli seemed to realize what he was doing and he would pull his shirt back down over them.

Ash wasn't sure of what to make of it all. But he damn well did like the sight of the cuffs on him. And he was too tired to concentrate on much else. At least this would be a short class. They were just going over what topic they'd chosen for their upcoming papers. He was actually rather proud of his. He'd put quite a bit of thought into it and picked a subject that suited him, just as Eli had suggested. That had to be a first for English class.

"Well, Ash, what day did you want to meet to go over the outline for your paper?" Eli glanced up from the appointment book balanced on his knees, and the firelight glinted off the frames of his glasses. He looked so serious that Ash wanted to grin.

"Do you have the last hour free on that Thursday?"

Eli glanced down at his book then gave him a wary glance. Ash wasn't sure if he was going to hedge or not. What had gotten into him? There hadn't been one naughty glint in his eyes yet. When Eli actually met his eyes.

"As a matter of fact, I do."

"Then put me down for that." Ash planned on using all of his charm to get Eli to meet him someplace over the weekend. They could do whatever Eli wanted, he didn't much care what. Eli had a camp out of town where he went sometimes. It might be a perfect place to hole up just the two of them.

"Be sure to have your outline with you," Eli said absently as he noted it down. There were shadows under his eyes from the late night, and Ash was struck with the urge to pull Eli into his arms to kiss those shadows away. The man was turning him into a sap. This was the first fantasy he'd had that involved cuddling.

"Not a problem, Doc," Ash drawled and was rewarded with another glance, this one finally with a heat that warmed those oh so cool blue-gray eyes. Was he shameless for using his accent like that when he knew how much it got to Eli? Maybe; he didn't much care.

Eli tucked his schedule book into his overstuffed satchel and leaned back into the cushions of the chair. It was a cozy setting for a chilly day, and honestly, Ash could look at Eli in the firelight for hours on end. He twirled his pen between his fingers and met Ash's gaze. "Okay, you're the last one, and then we all can go a little early today. Do you have a topic for your paper yet?"

This time Ash did grin, because Eli had tried without success to get that information out of him on several occasions. "I have given it some thought."

"Ooohh, you should do it on Oscar Wilde and his lover," Kerry burst out. "That was so tragic."

Ash smiled at her. She was such a hopeless romantic. Talk about somebody who would be on their side if the news ever got out... her and Nori both. "That would be fun, but cheating, I think. I covered most of the points during my presentation, and the story didn't get any happier after that. I was actually wondering if I could do a paper on a broader scale. Everyone else seems to have picked letters between two people but me."

"That shouldn't be a problem. Isaac's doing his on Ronald Reagan's letters, and those aren't specific to one person." Eli tucked his foot under his knee, his gaze curious. Ash liked how he did that, how he made each and every student there feel like all of his attention was on them when they spoke, without it being judging. More like he was genuinely interested in their opinions. "What do you have in mind?"

"I wanted to do my paper on the Victory mail from World War II."

Eli's brows furrowed as he tapped his pen against his jaw. "That's something I haven't heard of before."

"It was pretty neat. The Brits developed it to save space on shipping war materials while still allowing for servicemen to get letters from home." Ash leaned forward, elbows on his knees as he warmed up to his subject. "They'd basically take these one-page letters, reduce them down to microfilm, and ship off the film instead of bags and bags of letters. Then when it got to the post, they'd blow it back up again and deliver the letters."

"Sounds like you picked the perfect topic, and it ties right back in to why you took the class." Eli gave him his first real smile of the day and Ash found himself warming under that more than the fire. God, the man really did turn him into such a sap inside. At this rate he'd end up just like Kerry, sighing over the corniest things.

Ash waited as Eli dismissed the rest of the class. He tried not to stay behind too often. And damn, all this worry over people talking was starting to get to him, but he wanted to know what was bugging Eli.

"Can I walk with you back to your office?" Ash asked out of reflex and was surprised when Eli paused.

"Sure," Eli replied, grabbing his satchel, his face turned away to hide his expression. Ash kept silent until they were outside. The bright sunshine did nothing to dispel the bitter, raw cold. Eli lifted his face to the sun. "It's probably going to snow tonight."

"Oh, well. If my nuts are going to freeze off, I might as well have something to enjoy about it. That first snow is like magic to this Savannah boy." Ash waited until they reached one of the many copses that dotted the campus before taking Eli's elbow and tugging him to a stop. They were on the bridge over the stream near where they used to sit outside for class. They'd be able to hear anyone before they got close. "Is everything okay?"

"Yeah, just got a lot on my mind and little sleep." Eli leaned his hip against the bridge rail and looked out over the trickle of water. "I'm surprised you're as awake as you are."

"I'm used to running around on no sleep." A flash of light gleamed from the trees, stabbing at his eyes. Ash hesitated, not sure whether to pursue Eli's distraction or not, when that flash of light came again.

A cold sensation settled in the pit of his stomach, and Ash narrowed his eyes, staring hard at the trees where the light had come from. He'd seen a very similar gleam one too many times while on tour—the glint of sunlight off binoculars. Overseas, he'd be thinking ambush and he wasn't sure if it wasn't too different here.

Was someone looking to hurt Eli, or get some dirt on him, or were they just keeping tabs on him? Ash didn't like any of those thoughts. He quickly judged which course of action to take, and it was the bright sunshine and middle of the day that decided him. Eli should be pretty safe getting back to his own office, and Ash dearly wanted to get a glimpse of whoever their watcher was.

"I'll talk to you later, Doc," he said, clapping Eli on the arm. He gave him a startled look followed quickly by what Ash would've sworn was relief. Ash stamped down the irritation and nip of hurt. It was just another damn mystery and one Ash would track down as soon as he finished this hunt.

ELI'S insides stirred up a mess in his gut as he watched Ash veer off the path and disappear into the trees. He was doing it again: falling hard for a man who wasn't going to stick around. Ash would be number four, and Eli wasn't sure he really wanted to go through all that again, no matter how hot the sex or how comfortable the companionship.

Only he didn't think holding Ash at a distance would be his wisest decision. He got the impression that Ash would be as tenacious as Jabbers when he got hold of something he really wanted. There was no getting it away from him.

The walk back to his office soothed him some, and Eli looked forward to burying himself in grading essays so he could stop obsessing over Ash for awhile. He wasn't going to get any answers by going over the same thing in his mind and blowing it all out of proportion. The peace he was searching for shattered the moment he turned down his hallway and saw Whitney Grenier waiting outside his door.

Eli bit back a sigh and wondered what sob story she was going to come up with to explain missing class today. Maybe if he turned around and sneaked back down the stairs quietly she wouldn't spot him.

"Dr. Hollister!"

Eli groaned inside as a slow smile crossed Whitney's face. "I'm so glad I caught you. I know this isn't your normal office hours but I was wondering if we could talk."

"Of course." Eli fumbled for the keys in his pocket and opened the door for her. He might as well lay it on the line for her now. They'd almost reached the midpoint of the semester, and if she didn't change her ways now she was going to fail the class. "Why'd you miss class today?"

A plain white envelope on his chair distracted him from the faint sound of the lock sliding into place on the door. He picked the envelope up and turned it over to see his name scrawled across the front.

"Actually, I came to talk about something else."

Eli pressed his lips together at that response and looked up from unsealing the envelope. "Sit down." He stabbed a finger toward the chair. "That is what we're going to talk about, and afterward, if there is something else you want to address, we can do that as well."

Whitney swallowed hard and sank down on the chair. Her coat rode up, revealing a surprising amount of bare thigh. It was a wonder that the girl hadn't gotten frostbitten last winter if she'd run around like that.

"Please, Dr. Hollister, I don't want to fail." Nervous fingers fiddled with the top button of her coat. She drew in a deep breath and seemed to collect herself. The look she cast Eli through her lashes gave him an odd sense of foreboding. "I'll do anything," she said in a breathy kind of voice.

"Anything?" Eli leaned back against his desk and crossed his arms.

A little smile crossed Whitney's lips and she rose, walking toward him in a slow kind of strut. She stopped in front of him, standing too close for comfort. It felt like more than an invasion of his personal space. "Anything, I swear it." She looked up at him through her lashes and ran a hand up his arm.

"Okay, I have an idea." Eli captured her hand and gave her a hard look. "Why don't you try coming to class, on time, ready to discuss the material?" Whitney's eyes widened with incredulity as Eli continued on. "I'm not into playing games, and I give everyone the grade they deserve. Unless you buckle down, attend the rest of the classes, ace that paper that's coming up and the final exam, you will fail."

"But—"

"There are no buts. There is no room for discussion. You're a bright girl, Whitney, if an unobservant one. Looks and charm and skimpy clothes are only going to get you so far. You can do better than that."

Whitney took a step back, looking thoroughly confused. "I don't understand."

Eli sighed and turned to toss the letter on his chair instead of onto the mess of his desk. "I thought I said it pretty clearly. I don't know how else I can say it."

"I've seen the way you look at me. You're always looking at my legs."

Eli should've kicked her out of his office. She had this idea stuck in her head, and it didn't even seem like she was considering actually doing what she was supposed to. But if he did that, she probably would never show up for class again and would fail for sure. Damn, he wanted a drink and his camp up north.

Eli tried to think of a polite way to phrase the biting remarks that were on the tip of his tongue. He turned back around to see Whitney sliding out of her coat. The girl stood there; completely unashamed in some pale-blue, silky, fluttery scrap of nothing that barely brushed the top of her thighs.

Pure shock lanced through Eli, followed by a spurt of panic. "What in God's name do you think you're doing?"

The only thing that would make the situation worse would be if Britton decided to show up to bellow at him. The man had amazing timing. He was going to pick this very fucking moment to harass him about something. And there was no defense he could come up with for this.

"I've seen the look in your eyes during class and I wanted to tell you that I feel the same way about you too, Elijah."

He took a startled step back and collided right into his desk. The next thing he knew, Whitney had closed the distance between them and flung her arms around his neck. How the hell could she move so fast in those heels? It wasn't natural. Holy fuck, there were jiggly bits pressed against him. Oh, dear God, the irony.

Eli pried her arms from around his neck as he tried to get his panicked thoughts working again. Because repeating "holy fuck" in his head wasn't going to cut it in this situation. "Whitney, there has been some kind of a misunderstanding." He pushed her back and retreated a few steps before forcing himself to stop. He was not going to be trapped in his own office playing race around the desk with a student.

She leaned on her hands over the desk and her breasts threatened to spill out of her indecent negligee. Eli looked away, grinding his teeth together so hard his temples began to throb.

"It's okay, no one has to know you think about me the way I think about you. It'll be our little secret."

"You are out of your mind." Eli caught Whitney by the shoulders as she advanced on him again and glared at her. Whitney's eyes widened as Eli pushed her back and sat her unceremoniously down in the chair. "Young lady, you and I need to have a very serious conversation."

"Eli."

"It's Dr. Hollister. You have no business calling me Eli." He scooped up her coat and handed it to her, keeping his eyes averted. "Now put this on."

He circled back behind his desk, and when he looked at Whitney she was sitting there with a stunned and confused expression on her face with the coat still in her hands. "That wasn't a request, Miss Grenier." Eli gave her a hard look. "Put it on now and have the decency to cover yourself."

Whitney flushed a dark red and tugged her coat on. She sat awkwardly in her chair, hugging her arms around her chest. And if Eli hadn't been so infuriated, he would've felt sorry for her. This clearly wasn't the reception she had been expecting, and she looked humiliated. Well, she chose to do this, not him, and in the process she had risked Eli's career, all so she could manipulate him instead of doing her own damn work. So her humiliation and embarrassment were on her.

"Thank you," Eli said, softening his voice just a bit. "As I tried telling you, there has been a misunderstanding on your part. I don't have...." Damn, he couldn't really say he didn't carry on with students since he was throat deep in one whether they were screwing or not.

"I don't have the feelings for you that you seem to think I do. I'm already in a relationship."

Whitney's mouth fell open and she flushed again. She rose, clutching her coat to her. "Excuse me."

"Sit right back down, young woman." Eli stabbed a stern finger toward her chair. "I'm not done talking."

Whitney sank back down, tears welling in her eyes, and Eli prayed that she wouldn't start crying on him. "But I saw the way you were looking at me."

"I think you saw what you wanted to see, or perhaps what other professors had given you. I don't know, but you didn't see it from me." Eli started throwing his weekend work into his satchel. He was anxious to get off campus and find some balance in his life. First, Ash and all those feelings Eli needed to come to terms with that were growing too strong, too fast. And now this bullshit from Whitney. "I'm surprised you haven't heard the rumors on campus, but I'm gay."

"No way." Whitney's eyes widened with shock.

"Yes way. Now, are you ready to come to class and actually work?"

"You still want to see me in your class?" Whitney asked, her tears drying up.

"I want to see you pass my class the right way." Eli sighed and made a shooing motion toward the door. "Go home, put some clothes on, and I'll see you Monday afternoon."

Whitney rose and took a few steps toward the door before pausing and looking back at him uncertainly. Eli grabbed his belongings before he opened the door, giving her a pointed look. "Good day, Miss Grenier."

Eli left her in the middle of the hallway and headed out. Tomorrow was supposed to be his research day, but all he wanted was to get out of town for a few days to think. He'd leave a message with Lu, collect Jabbers, and he could be up at camp before bedtime.

Some of the tension left his shoulders as he made the decision. Now if he could only make one about Ash.

ASH knocked on the door to Eli's office and then tried the doorknob when he didn't answer. It was unlocked and the office empty, so he must have been planning on coming back sometime soon. Ash figured he'd just take a seat and wait him out. Only when he entered did he realize that Eli's satchel and coat were gone.

So the question was, did he leave it unlocked or did someone else come by afterward and break in again? After spending the past hour knocking around in the woods, looking for whoever had been watching them, Ash's paranoia was running high. He hadn't been able to find the guy, but he sure as hell heard him running off.

Ash examined the lock with a frown. It didn't look as if it had been tampered with and Eli had mentioned that the locks had been changed. Maybe Eli had forgotten about it and left for the day. What the hell was he going to do with Eli? One glance at the bookshelves was enough to see that those books Eli prized so much were still there. How could he be so careless?

"Dammit, Eli, you need a keeper," Ash muttered.

He was going to have to find a way to talk Eli out of his daily hikes. No matter how bad the weather was, Eli was out there with Jabbers. Anyone who knew him at all could set up an ambush. An ambush. Fuck, he did sound paranoid.

Ash was about to leave when a slightly rumpled envelope on the floor caught his eye. He picked it up, noting Eli's name on the front. It looked as if someone had started to open it. Ash debated for a few seconds. Eli would rightfully be pissed if he peeked, and it might not be anything to worry about. Ash's instincts said there had been something off the entire day. He held the envelope carefully by the edges and used Eli's letter opener to slit the top.

A quick look, and then he could confess to Eli and they could have a good laugh over the way Ash's mind was screwing with him. If Eli didn't lose his temper.

He tugged the brief note out by the corner, and his insides turned to ice.

> *I know you're carrying on with one of your students. I have proof. If you don't want anyone else to know get together $15,000. I'll contact you another time and let you know when and where to leave it.*

"Son of a fucking bitch." Ash stuffed the note back into the envelope as he heard someone at the door. He dropped it into his book bag and turned as Britton entered the office.

The other man blinked in surprise before his heavy brows drew together in an aggravated frown. "Just who are you?"

"I'm one of Doc's students. I was waiting for him to get back," Ash said smoothly. Britton would blow a fucking gasket if he knew Eli had left his office unlocked. Hell, Ash was tempted to give him an earful as well.

"Well, get out and wait in the hallway. You have no business being in here without him." The old man turned around, grumbling under his breath. "And if you do see him, tell him I expect him in my office before I leave today."

Ash bit his tongue and waited for a minute after the old windbag left. "Asshole," he muttered under his breath. At least his classes were over for the day. He should be able to catch Eli on his way back from his hike. They had some serious things to discuss.

CHAPTER 11

ASH'S truck moved down the road slower than he would've liked. This drive was taking forever and wearing down his patience in the meantime. But he'd already startled more than one critter on the road and Lu had called this stretch of road Moose Alley. The last thing he needed was a run-in with a beast that size. It seemed like he'd reached the end of the last bit of civilization at least half an hour ago and he still hadn't seen the turn off.

His hands tightened on the wheel. Lu had assured him that Eli was at the camp, only there was no way to check without actually going himself. She hadn't been kidding when she said there was no cell phone service and there wasn't a landline there, either. She hadn't seemed at all worried because Eli often disappeared for days at a time.

Ash hadn't wanted to scare her. If Eli hadn't seen fit to tell her about the break-ins and stalkers and blackmail notes, Ash wasn't about to. At least not yet. It did make him wonder if there had been other notes that Eli hadn't bothered to mention to him. And that just made him want to grind his teeth in frustration.

If he found out that Eli was holding out on him, he'd…. He'd what? What kind of claim did he really have on Eli? They weren't lovers, yet. Eli wasn't his boyfriend. Ash wasn't looking to settle into a long-term relationship at this stage of his life. At least, that had been the plan. They were more than professor and student, that was for sure. Eli was his friend, and that, at least, gave Ash more than enough reason to show his concern.

The headlights picked out a small break in the trees, and somewhere up the mountain a solitary light gleamed. "That had better be you," Ash muttered as he turned down the rutted, narrow dirt road.

From time to time the light provided a beacon through the pitch black of the woods.

When the trees finally opened up, Ash breathed a sigh of relief. Eli's Jeep was parked outside a small cabin that had windows ablaze with light. Jabbers barked excitedly as he got out, and the screen door on the porch creaked when Eli stepped outside. "What the hell are you doing here?"

The combination of Eli's irritated tone and the hours of worry lit the spark of Ash's smoldering temper. He slammed his truck door shut and stalked toward Eli. "No hello? Or concern? 'Cause clearly something must be wrong if I followed you all the way out here. I'm here because you scared the hell out of me, jackass. So you can drop the attitude."

As he got closer, Eli turned so the light fell across his face instead of silhouetting him, and his lips and jaw were set with a stubborn tilt. He'd let his hair down and it fell in a tangled cloud around his shoulders, and despite the cold, his feet were bare. Ash should not find the combination sexy, not when he was angry over his reception.

"Lu knew where I was, and since you're here I'm assuming you talked to her and she told you." Eli's cool tone set Ash aback. He'd seen Eli run hot many times, but never cold. What the hell was going on with him? "Now that you've seen for yourself that I'm okay, you can go."

Ash gaped as Eli turned away and walked back into the cabin. Ash seized the door and followed, itching to grab Eli and shake some sense into him or to kiss him. He wasn't sure which urge was greater. "I'm not leaving until we've had this out. Are you out of your goddamn mind?" Okay, maybe that wasn't fair. Eli probably hadn't known about the blackmail note, and Ash was just letting the long hours of frustration and worry get to him.

"Me? What bug has crawled up your ass and died? I don't answer to you."

Damn Eli and his overdeveloped sense of independence. A mournful whine had them both looking down to see Jabbers sitting between them with big, sad eyes. "It's okay, Jabbers. I'm just having it out with Ash."

Ash attempted to moderate his voice, but despite his best efforts it came out as a growl. "It didn't occur to you at all that I would be worried? You've had both your home and your office broken into. You have somebody following you around on campus and then you fucking disappeared, left your office unlocked and—"

"I needed time to think, dammit, and right now, you're fucking that up!" Eli snapped, his blue-gray eyes hot with anger now. At least the cool distance was gone. Ash could handle this side of Eli. "I didn't mean to worry you, but I wanted some time to myself, is that too much to ask for? Who was following me?"

"I don't know."

Jabbers bayed, the sound cutting through their rising voices. "Dammit, give me a minute." Eli knelt down and rubbed Jabbers's ears and body until the dog's tail wagged. "Jabbers, loft," he said firmly, pointing up the narrow staircase. The beagle whined, but when Eli repeated the order, he disappeared to the sound of nails scrabbling on wood.

Needed time to think? What did he mean by that? Needed time to think about him? Ash didn't like that thought at all, or the little slice of hurt that came with it. Then Eli turned back around, and Ash could just see him gathering himself to put that cool wall up again. Ash's heart sank. He was not ready for Eli to end them. And that reserve? Oh, fuck that. Ash preferred Eli standing toe to toe with him instead of hiding behind a detachment that didn't suit him at all.

"What are you afraid of? It's not like you to run off and hide." Ash closed the distance between them, and for a second he thought Eli would back off, but then those blue-gray eyes flashed as he drew himself up.

"I'm not hiding, now will you leave?"

"I'm not going anywhere. Besides the fact that I'm not sure I could find a place to crash at this time of night in the middle of bumfuck nowhere, you forget that there's someone stalking you."

"One confirmed break-in does not mean I have a stalker," Eli snapped, getting in his face. "What has gotten into you?"

Ash grabbed Eli's shoulders, but touching him proved to be a mistake. His heart flipped and pure desire rushed straight to his cock.

Dammit, Eli couldn't just walk away from the sizzling chemistry they had.

Ash wasn't sure who moved first or who kissed whom. All he knew was that Eli's hands had fisted in Ash's shirt at the small of his back, pulling him closer in a hard grip. Ash's hands were buried in the softness of Eli's hair as tongues tangled and mouths bruised. Ash growled, pushing Eli as he kissed him until Eli's back thudded against a wall.

"Are you in that mood, Eli?" Ash rasped, pulling his mouth away, their breaths ragged on each other's lips. "You want a hard, dirty fucking?"

Eli dragged his mouth down to Ash's throat and bit him hard enough to mark, followed by a flick of his tongue. "What do you think?"

Ash dragged his scattered thoughts together enough to focus on what they needed to give in to their bodies' demands. "Thank fucking God, I have condoms in my wallet." Fire seethed in his brain and heated up his body as he yanked Eli's hoodie off of him only to find a T-shirt underneath. "I hope you have lube."

"I've never brought a lover here. So lube is rather scarce." Eli's eyes narrowed, saying without words that Ash hadn't been invited, and the reaction made Ash crazy. He was happy that Eli wasn't in the habit of using this camp for trysts. Then irked because Eli seemed to be lumping him along with all the other men who hadn't earned an invitation here. Both emotions had him craving to make a mark on Eli here, in his sanctuary, so that whenever he returned he'd be thinking of Ash.

"We'll have to be creative, then." Ash tugged off Eli's T-shirt as well. He slid a hand down Eli's long, lean torso. His clothes sometimes masked the whipcord strength Eli had. His abs were tight and smooth muscle covered his chest and arms. Ash circled a thumb around one flat nipple as Eli attacked his throat again.

Dizzying heat rushed through Ash. At least Eli wasn't going to let the lack of an invitation get in the way of the heat between them. He groaned as Eli's teeth raked his throat again, and Ash tweaked the other man's nipple in response.

His cock throbbed in his jeans, demanding to be set free, and damned if he didn't want to strip, but the wide bank of curtainless windows stopped him. Logically, he knew they were in the middle of nowhere. Jabbers would bark his head off if anyone approached, but still, the bare windows made him feel exposed.

"Do you have a bedroom?" Ash asked and then groaned as Eli palmed his cock through his jeans.

"What? You're not going to take me against the wall like you were thinking of doing not so long ago?"

"Not tonight." Though the idea definitely had appeal. One Ash would linger over later. "If you must know, I fought myself to keep from dragging you upstairs and tying you to my bed that night."

"This is the second time you've mentioned tying me up." Eli snagged his fingers in Ash's belt loops and started pulling him toward the back of the cabin. Ash had a vague impression of the living room leading right into a tiny kitchen. "Are you sure you're going to be able to handle those base instincts of yours when you get your badge, gun, and handcuffs?"

"If you're around to set me off, definitely not." In fact, Ash didn't really want to think about some distant future when he had a half-naked Eli right in front of him.

Eli pushed open a door and yanked him into the dark of a bedroom. The bed was right there, they practically tripped over it and half fell in a tangle on the mattress. It didn't seem to be that big, maybe a little bigger than a twin, but not by much. Big enough for Ash's purposes, and if they ended up all over each other all night, then that worked too.

Ash pinned Eli under him with a hungry groan. Fuck. He'd been thinking of just this for weeks. Eli under him, naked... well, almost naked. Ash needed to rectify that situation. Eli must've had the same idea because he began assaulting Ash's jeans, popping open the button and sliding down the fly.

They undressed each other, fumbling in the dark with impatient hands and muttered curses. The sensation of hot, naked skin against hot, naked skin seared into Ash's brain. The cool of the sheets and the air in the bedroom did nothing to ease the fever raging between them.

Fuck, he'd been fantasizing about this for too long. His cock felt like it was going to explode as they ground against each other. Eli dug his fingers into Ash's back, rocking his hips urgently. Ash wanted to get under Eli's skin, get into his blood, and stay there.

"Go slow another time. Where are those damn condoms?"

Ash broke his mouth away from Eli's skin and tried to remember where his jeans had disappeared to. "Give me a sec." He leaned over the side of the bed, searching in the dark. The mattress shifted as Eli stood up. "Where ya going?"

"I think there might be some oil in the kitchen." Eli walked out the door stark naked. Damn that tight, muscled ass was a gorgeous sight, even if Ash didn't like the idea of the man parading himself in front of the windows like that.

"You could've put on a robe, you know," he said a few moments later when Eli returned.

"Why, so I wouldn't offend a deer's sensibilities?" There was amusement in Eli's voice and something clinked as he set it down on the table. "Is that why we're in here, Ash? You got shy?"

Ash found his hand in the dark and yanked Eli down on the bed. Rolling, he pinned Eli under him and reached for the bedside lamp, fumbling until he found the switch. Golden light spilled across the bed and lit the highlights in Eli's hair, turning it a deep, burnished red against the white of the pillows.

The man was such an enigma. One part rebel, one part hellcat, and one part confident, intelligent man. Ash was fascinated at how Eli could go from being stubborn one minute to caring the next. He could never predict how Eli's contrary mind worked. He was amusing and exasperating, and he drove Ash crazy with longing.

One slim brow rose in query, and Eli slid his hands down Ash's shoulders. "Why're you looking at me like that?"

"I'm trying to decide whether I want to fuck you or strangle you."

Laughter lit up Eli's eyes, banishing the last of the irritation that lingered there. "Damn you for making me laugh, Ashley Gallagher. I was still irked with you."

There went that quicksilver change of moods again. Ash shook his head and pinned Eli's hands to either side of his head. He rocked his hips, his cock rubbing slick and hard against Eli's. "That makes two of us. I'm still pissed." It was really hard to remember why, though. It was hard to think, period.

"Let me take care of that." Eli lifted his head and kissed him, and those lingering thoughts scattered and disappeared under the heat of his mouth. Ash groaned and let go of Eli's wrists in favor of burying his hands in Eli's hair.

Eli's tongue drove into his mouth, demanding more, making Ash dizzy. His long, limber body moved under Ash, twisting and arching for more contact. His hands slid over Ash's body, exploring him with a possessive touch from the back of his neck down to the tops of his thighs. He didn't flinch from Ash's scars, neither the burn on his arm nor the marks on his side. He touched them with the same need in his hands as he touched every other part of Ash's body.

That too drove Ash crazy.

He lifted his head long enough to grab the bottle of lube off the nightstand. "I thought you said you didn't have any."

"I found some in the bathroom. I'm not going to ask any of my cousins why it was there, and they aren't going to ask me why it's missing." Eli kissed his way down to Ash's chest. "We're all happier that way."

"We're not going to have anyone barge in on us, are we?"

"Nope, it's moose hunting season and none of them won the permit lottery. We'll have the place to ourselves all weekend long."

Before Ash could ponder the implications of that statement, Eli was kissing him again. Fuck, he wanted that hungry mouth on his cock. As soon as the thought hit him, the want became need. He shifted on the bed, trying to turn them both over without tumbling them on the floor. "Turn around, sexy," he groaned.

Eli leaned over him, bracing his hands on both sides of Ash, and his hair fell around his face, framing it in a curtain of heat. "Nope, you promised me a fucking, hard and rough. Do I have to piss you off again to get it? Because I'm sure I could come up with something."

Ash popped the cap on the lube and watched Eli's eyes darken when he pushed two slick fingers into him. "Like leaving your office door unlocked after it had already been broken into once?"

Eli groaned and twisted his hips back. "Okay, I can see how that might be mildly annoying."

"That's it," Ash growled. He sat up and dumped Eli on the bed.

"What are you doing?" Eli asked as Ash leaned over the bed and began to tug one of the shoelaces off his sneakers.

"Giving you back just a little bit of the torment I went through today."

Eli snickered as Ash turned around with the shoestring in his hand. "Formidable. What are you going to do? Strangle me with it?"

"Oh, no, I'm trying to keep you safe, not hurt you. And if I have to tie you up to make you see it, then I will." Eli twisted like a cat and rolled out of the way as Ash lunged for him. Ash snagged him around his lean waist and hauled him back. They wrestled on the bed, Ash trying to bind Eli's wrists together and Eli doing everything he could to stop him, his laughter hampering his efforts to hold Ash off.

It didn't take too long before Ash managed to tie the D rings together with the shoelace behind one of the slats on the headboard. He sat back on his heels, admiring his handiwork. He'd like to see Eli get out of that one. He had to admit, Eli had given him more of a fight than he'd expected.

"Okay," Eli panted, blowing his hair out of his face. "What did that solve? Dammit, Ash, why did you come?"

"We can talk about that later. After I've driven you out of your mind."

Ash looked down at Eli, his heartbeat picking up. Damn, he was never going to get that sight out of his mind. Eli glared at him, his eyes like granite. The muscles in his arms strained as he fought the ties around his wrists. Ash slid a finger down his chest, following the reddish-brown light smattering of hair that led all the way to Eli's cock.

Eli's chest rose and fell with his quick breaths. "You did that a long time ago. Now let me go."

Ash circled his fingertip around one of Eli's nipples and watched it peak and harden. "It really drives you nuts to be caged, doesn't it?" He leaned over him, and his dog tags brushed Eli's chest. "Trust me, Eli, you're in good hands."

"I do trust you," Eli said between clenched teeth. "Doesn't mean that I don't want to kick your ass right now."

"I thought you wanted to fuck." Ash slid his hands along Eli's long, lean thighs.

Eli shuddered, his eyes going hot as Ash cupped his balls. They were heavy in his hand, and Eli's lips parted on a moan. "I do, but you're taking your sweet ass time getting around to it."

"The last time I had you naked, you had the chance to get your hands all over me. Now it's my turn."

One leg snaked around Ash's waist, tugging him closer. As much as he wanted to fuck with Eli until he surrendered, he didn't think that tactic would ever work with his lover. Eli needed to be wooed and seduced, not coerced. And the look on Eli's face had him mesmerized. He might be the one tied up, but he had all the damn power.

"Fuck me," Eli said in a low, compelling voice, arching up against Ash.

"Damn, you make it hard to think."

"Thinking's overrated right now." Eli wrapped his other leg around Ash's waist. "Fuck me."

Ash rubbed a fingertip against Eli's entrance, still slick with the lube, and Ash's cock leapt. "I'm considering—" He broke off with a gasp as Eli's legs suddenly tightened around his ribs, cutting off his air.

Eli lifted his head as he gave Ash a wicked grin. "You were saying?"

Ash drew in a shuddering breath as Eli released him. "God, you're a wicked bitch." He couldn't figure out how the hell the man had still been single by the time Ash had come into town. Someone should've snatched him up a long time ago, and he was very grateful that they hadn't.

"Language," Eli tsked, flexing his thighs again in a not so subtle threat. "You know, I can squeeze until you pass out and when you wake up you'll be the one tied to the bed."

Ash reached for the condom on the bedside table. "You wouldn't know what to do with me if you did."

"Try me, Georgia. Just try me. You're not the only one with bondage fantasies. Trust me, having a Marine tied up and at my mercy is high on the list of things I want to do before I die."

Ash groaned and rolled the condom on with impatient fingers. He'd been anticipating this moment the last six weeks and he didn't want to wait anymore. Eli's eyes glazed over and a tremor went through him as Ash started to push into him. His thighs relaxed around Ash's waist, and his hands clung to the headboard. "Yes."

Ash watched him through half-lidded eyes, heat pouring through him. Damn, Eli was ready for him. There was no resistance, just a snug heat that gripped his cock as he sank into him. Ash thought about using Eli's distraction to break free of his legs, but now that he was inside of him he didn't want to leave.

Eli arched and clenched his inner muscles. "Fuck me, Georgia."

Who had whom captive?

"Anyone ever tell you that you're mouthy and demanding?"

Eli chuckled and lightly squeezed Ash's waist with this thighs. "No one else matters but you." He circled his hips in invitation and drew himself up to kiss Ash. It was like the man had somehow seized hold of his will. Ash drew slowly out of him only to surge back hard. Fuck, he'd been thinking of just this for too long.

"Yes," Eli groaned against his mouth and lightly bit Ash's lower lip. "Harder."

Ash braced his hands on the bed and snapped his hips, staring down at the man who writhed so beautifully under him. Eli demanded, he begged, he teased, using both mouth and body to convey what he wanted. It was absolutely fucking breathtaking.

The bed squeaked as they rocked, Eli rising up to meet each of his thrusts. Ash dipped his head down to bury his face in Eli's exposed throat. He breathed in the scent of Eli's hair and the sweat on his body as he savored the feel of him.

Then arms came around his body, and Ash cursed, lifting his head to see that sure enough, somehow Eli had managed to get the buckles free. The cuffs dangled around the slat, still bound by the shoelace. Eli chuckled in his ear and slid hard hands over Ash's short hair. "The look on your face is priceless."

Ash sank his entire weight against him and burrowed his arms under Eli's shoulders. "You're impossible."

"I know," Eli breathed against his ear. "Now, harder. I'm almost there."

Ash thought he was about to explode himself. He reached between them and began stroking Eli's slick cock. "Hold on... just a little... bit... more."

Eli clenched around him hard enough to drag a ragged curse from him. "Like that?" Eli whispered in his ear.

For someone so nice everywhere else, Elijah Hollister was an evil man in bed. Before Ash could catch his breath Eli clenched again. Ash panted, stroking Eli faster because he couldn't hold himself back anymore. He tightened his hands on Eli's shoulders and kissed him as his orgasm hit him hard. Eli groaned desperately against his mouth, and then his cock jerked in Ash's hand, spilling and twitching, muscles clenching in rhythmic waves as Eli came too.

Panting, Ash dropped his head onto Eli's shoulder, groaning as his body shuddered with the last rumbles of his climax. "Damn, Eli, you win."

Eli chuckled and kissed Ash's temple. "Good, I love to win."

They didn't move for a few minutes, just held each other until Ash finally shifted off of him with a rough groan. When he came back from the bathroom, Jabbers was stretched across the foot of the bed, eyeballing him warily. "I don't think there's room for three of us," Ash said to him as Eli slipped from the bed.

Jabbers thumped his tail and answered with that odd throaty sound he made that sounded so much like conversation, but he didn't budge. "How's this, buddy, the next time I see you back home, I'll bring you a nice, big bone. Or maybe a piece of rawhide, would you like that?" Jabbers lifted his head and cocked it as if considering the bribe. "Okay, you drive a hard bargain, I'll bring both."

"Jabbers, down," Eli said in a firm voice as he returned.

With a whine, Jabbers jumped off the bed and slunk out the door with an air of total dejection. "See, now you've gone and broken his heart. We were coming to a deal," Ash said as he crawled under the blankets and held them open for Eli.

"He was playing you like a like a blackjack dealer in a stacked game. Don't worry about Jabbers, he actually prefers sprawling in front of the stove. The hearth stones are nice and warm."

"So he looked at me and saw a sucker?" Ash scooted over and held open the blanket, wondering if Eli was going to take him up on his unspoken invitation or start up the argument again. He did not feel like getting into it all over again, even if it had led to a naked Eli.

Eli chuckled and curled into him so they both could fit on the bed. He laid his head on Ash's shoulder, slid his arm around Ash's waist, and tangled their legs together. "Pretty much. A born sucker."

Ash reached over to shut off the lamp and closed his eyes. He rubbed Eli's shoulder, laying his cheek against Eli's hair. Why had they waited this long to spend the night together?

"What are you thinking?" Eli asked softly.

"I'm thinking I don't want to leave this cabin, ever." The thought of going to Amwich and pretending that they weren't a couple for the next two months was depressing. So Ash wasn't going to think about it.

"You don't have class tomorrow, do you?"

"I do, but they're all lectures, so I'll borrow the notes and since I haven't missed any days yet, I should be fine. My Fridays are free. I arranged my classes that way so I wouldn't have problems on drill weekends."

"Well, then, you don't have to worry about leaving. We have four whole days to ourselves." Eli trailed a suggestive hand down from Ash's hip to his thigh. "And I, for one, intend to make the most of it."

Ash's heart quickened. Eli wasn't going to try to kick him out in the morning. And no awkward conversation right now about why Eli had been so distant or why Ash had hunted him down. Damn, he had four days of just him and Eli and nobody questioning what in the hell they were doing. He tugged Eli over him and ran his hands down those long thighs. "I'm all yours, Doc."

CHAPTER 12

THE cabin smelled of the fish they'd caught earlier and fried for dinner. Between that, the potatoes Eli had roasted, and the fresh greens with mushrooms, Ash couldn't remember ever being so full. And he'd worked up quite an appetite being outdoors all day. He groaned and pushed his plate away. "You are a liar, Eli."

"How so?" Eli asked as he stacked the plates to take to the sink.

"All that bitchin' and moaning and it turns out you're a pretty damn good cook yourself."

"Don't you dare ever let those words pass your lips where Lu can hear them." Eli leveled a hard glare at him. "I hate cooking, but I put up with it when I don't have her around to make doe eyes at. If you ruin my meal ticket, you are done for."

"I hear you loud and clear, Doc." Ash rose and went to fill up the sink with hot water. "Since you cooked, I'll do KP duty."

This break had been just what he needed to recharge. So much so that yesterday he'd avoided bringing up what had sent him after Eli in the first place, and Eli hadn't pressed him on it. Seemed like neither one of them wanted to get into the complicated stuff. Real life would intrude soon enough. He washed the dishes, listening as Eli brought in more wood for the stove and Jabbers chased something out in the underbrush.

That didn't mean he'd forgotten about Eli's stalker problem, and he'd spent quite a bit of time figuring out how to convince Eli to take a harder look at Wayne. He had a feeling Eli would dig in his heels. Stubborn man.

"It's going to be a cold one tonight." Eli stoked the fire and closed the stove.

"I have no doubt we can keep each other warm." Ash looked over his shoulder and blatantly ogled Eli's ass as he stood up and went back outside for more wood. He still didn't understand how an ass could be that lush when the man hiked every day, and he didn't care why as long as he got to get his hands on it often.

Ash could get used to seeing a lot more of Eli. He'd never been in a position before where he could imagine living with a lover. He'd never even really wanted to. But these last two days of being with Eli, fishing and hiking, teaching him the finer points of poker, and trying to make the most of the small bed in the back, made him wonder just what he'd been missing when it came to long-term relationships.

It seemed rather pointless to consider anything lasting. Unless he was redeployed, he'd be graduating in the spring. He had a possible job offer through a friend of the family in Atlanta with the Defense Criminal Investigation Services. Both Melanie's and Kurtis's family were in Atlanta, so it was very tempting.

That wasn't his only option. If he applied for the FBI, the closest field office to Amwich was in Boston. There were plenty of really good universities and colleges around there, and he had no doubt that Eli could make a successful career at one of them. After this weekend, though, he couldn't picture Eli in a city. At least not for a long time. And who even knew what field office he'd get assigned to?

Good God, what had gotten into him? He'd spent one weekend with the man and now he was considering more than he'd ever sought from another lover. Eli belonged in Amwich. He thrived on his daily hikes and his getaway camp up here near Canada. Here, he could go rock climbing whenever he wanted, or camp, or take his Jeep off-road. He'd hate being in a city all year round, and Ash couldn't think of anything that would tempt Eli to do so. Time to focus on why he'd come to the camp in the first place instead of daydreaming about a future that wasn't going to happen.

"So why did you run out of town so fast?" Ash asked, stacking the frying pan on top of the drainer as Eli came back in.

"I don't even want to think about it. Next topic."

Ash pulled the plug on the sink and turned around, drying his hands on a towel. He couldn't tell if Eli wouldn't meet his eyes or if it was just a coincidence. "It wouldn't have anything to do with a blackmail note, would it?"

Eli turned toward him with a stunned expression on his face that rapidly turned to fury. "Whitney left a fucking blackmail note? That's it; I am reporting the incident to Dean Newton. I should've done it before I left."

"What the hell does Whitney have to do with it? What incident?" Ash asked, trying to figure out if they were having the same conversation or not. "I'm talking about the manhandled blackmail note I found on the floor in your office."

Eli looked blank for a moment before recognition dawned in his eyes. "Oh, yeah, there had been an envelope on my chair or was it my desk? I guess I lost track of it in my panic. I'm not sure how it got there."

"Okay, now I'm really getting curious. What happened? All I've got is Whitney, incident, and blackmail."

Eli looked away with an uncomfortable cough. "I really don't want to talk about it. Maybe when the semester's over with, but right now it just wouldn't be right."

Ash should let it drop, but he had a hard time when his curiosity had been roused. He put together everything Eli had and hadn't said, along with the way certain people had been acting all semester and started chuckling. "Whitney finally cornered you alone and batted her eyes, thinking to seduce you, didn't she?"

Eli groaned and shook his head. "More like she tried to take a club to my head so she could drag me off to her cave."

Eli glared as Ash began laughing in earnest. He could picture it all too clearly. Eli had never noticed the signals from her, but the rest of the class had, and it had been the subject of many whispered conversations. Eli was so damn clueless sometimes.

"I'm sorry," he managed to say, when Eli's eyes narrowed with dangerous intent. "I'd heard rumors from the girls in class that she had a thing going on with Professor Hayworth for about a year or so. I guess after he left, she picked you to be his replacement. You never heard about that, did you?"

"No, I didn't." Eli made an aggravated sound. "And I certainly didn't expect to be ambushed like that in my own office. I know you're worried that someone's been snooping around, but they aren't half as dangerous as she is. It's going to be a long semester if she stays in the class."

"She'll behave herself." Even if Ash had to pull her aside for a few pointed words. Eli had enough on his mind as it was, and Ash didn't even want to think about how Britton would react to rumors about her.

"She'd better," Eli muttered, as he turned red. "I've already threatened her with failing. I don't know what else I can do to make her keep her clothes on."

Ash's jaw dropped, and he began to chuckle as Eli flushed even darker.

"It's not fucking funny."

"Oh God, I can only imagine the look on your face. No wonder you bolted for your camp." Ash slipped his arm around Eli's waist and tugged him close for a quick kiss. "It is and isn't funny. Not so much now with the way Britton's been riding your ass, but years from now, you'll be laughing too."

"Maybe, I just want to get through this semester intact. She was not the student I wanted to trap me in my office with blatant come-ons." Eli slipped his arms around Ash's neck. "All of my fantasies involve someone older who knows how to make the most of an opportune moment and has a fetish for bets."

"Before we get distracted, we need to talk about that envelope that was left behind in your office. Give me a sec. I've got it out in the truck." Ash ignored Eli's baffled expression and steeled himself for the oncoming storm. Maybe he was making too much of it; Eli could be reasonable about the whole thing.

He handed the envelope to Eli, who turned it over in his hands with a thoughtful expression and raised one slim brow. "It's already been opened. I didn't leave it like that."

That was one of the things Ash liked about him. Eli didn't jump to conclusions and accuse Ash of snooping, even if in this instance he would be right. "Yeah, that would've been me." He held up his hand as those blue-gray eyes hardened. "Hear me out, and maybe you'll understand why I opened it, even if it was an invasion of your privacy."

"I'm listening."

"Remember when I disappeared after class even though I'd asked to talk to you?" Eli nodded and Ash continued on. "There was someone in the woods watching us."

A skeptical look crossed Eli's face. "What makes you think that? I didn't notice anything."

"Eli, you have the self-preservation instincts of a lemming. Not that I consider you a follower, but you just don't see the cliff in front of you until you're already over it."

"Has anyone ever told you that you have a suspicious nature?"

Ash shrugged, refusing to apologize for it. "Comes from the job I had before and what I'm training for now."

"Are you going to try to tell me it's Wayne again? That I don't really know the people who've been around me all my life?" Eli's eyes narrowed.

"I'm trying to say that unless a person openly attacks you, like Britton, you go out of your way to give them the benefit of the doubt. Take Whitney, for instance. A lot of other professors might not have been as patient with her track record for attending class. Not to mention that everyone in that class knew the girl was angling every way she could to get your attention."

Eli flushed again and looked away. "That doesn't explain what made you think someone was watching us."

"I saw the sun reflecting off of something, probably binoculars. I've seen it before." And each time it had preceded a disaster.

"Did you catch the guy?"

"No, not this time. He knew the woods around there better than me." A situation Ash intended to rectify. If he was going to hike around Amwich, it wouldn't hurt to get to know the area around the college. "Then, when I got to your office and it was unlocked, and Britton said you'd hightailed it out of there, I got worried. I saw the envelope and my instincts said it was important."

"I noticed there wasn't an apology in there," Eli said, and Ash searched his face, unable to read if he was pissed or not. Probably not, Eli wasn't very good at hiding his anger. His lips would press together and lines would appear between his eyebrows. Neither of those warning signs appeared.

"You're right, there wasn't." Ash tapped the envelope in Eli's hand. "I know I overstepped, but I'm glad I did. What's in there is too important to have been accidentally tossed when the cleaning crew hits your office."

"How bad can it be?" Eli fished out his glasses and then pulled out the slip of paper. His brows snapped together in a fierce frown. "Is this a joke?"

"I think it's very serious. Someone's been snooping around your house and office, obviously looking for something. And since they haven't been able to find it, they plan on getting what they feel is owed to them in money instead."

"It doesn't make any sense. If they had stolen all of my rare books and sold them, it might come to around that amount, but the person who broke into my office had no idea what that book they ruined was worth or they wouldn't have tossed it on the floor. What else could I possibly have that could in any way be valuable?"

"Is there anything else in your house that could be worth a lot of money?" Ash tugged out a chair at the table and sat down. "Something that might've been tucked away. It's an old house, are there any antiques?"

Eli sat down as well and tossed the note down in front of him. "There are, but they're right out in the open, and *if* someone broke into my house, they didn't touch those."

The *if* irked Ash. There was no doubt in his mind that someone had been in Eli's house. "Have there been any other unexplained things, like doors being open that you swore you left closed, something out of place from where it belonged? Anything you haven't told me because you dismissed it or because you didn't want me arguing with you?"

"As you've pointed out, I'm not always the most observant unless I'm actually looking for something, like when I'm hiking." Eli hesitated and glanced toward Jabbers who was snuffling around the woodpile. "I wouldn't notice anything weird about the house itself unless someone left it a mess, but there were two things with Jabbers in the last couple months that struck me as odd even if he does have a habit of getting into things that he shouldn't."

"Tell me, Eli, it might be another piece to the puzzle, it might not."

"Once, before the break-in at my office, I came home and Jabbers met me at my bike." The beagle came over at the sound of his name and laid his paws on Eli's thigh, making an inquiring sound in the back of his throat. "He was quite the escape artist as a puppy. I had to be very careful not to leave windows open more than a couple inches or he'd destroy the screen and get out. Or he'd slip out on my heels and sneak around the corner and hide until I was gone. He hasn't done that in a long time, but every once in a while he'll pull a trick like that again."

Eli glanced at Ash with a troubled expression. "What was the other thing?"

"Jabbers had a rawhide bone that I know I didn't give him. Still, he's a champion thief and I do have a bag of them stored in the mudroom. He could've gotten into them and stashed a few."

Ash nudged the blackmail note, drawing Eli's attention to it. "I don't think this guy is playing games. There is going to be another note. I'm not sure if he's bluffing about proof or not, but it's better to err on the side of caution."

Eli rubbed Jabbers's ears as he stared at the piece of paper. Ash wished he could figure out what Eli was thinking. Eli didn't like being cornered, and a blackmail note had to have him feeling like that. On the other hand, he had quite a bit riding on his reputation, and Ash would hate to see him cave in to this bastard's demands. He would find another way if that's what it took.

Ash couldn't say why he was so invested in this. Yeah, he would do the same probably for any friend. But with Eli it was more than just friendship that made him push it. Hell, maybe it was even more than sex too. He wasn't sure if he was ready to talk relationship so he pulled back from those thoughts.

"Well, he can go fuck himself if he thinks I'm handing over my savings." Eli sighed and stuffed the note back into the envelope. "And thank you for not trying to convince me it was Wayne. He wouldn't do something like this. Maybe I could see break-ins if he thought I had something of his, but not blackmail."

"Not even if it would pay for his dad's medical expenses, make him more comfortable, keep their business and house intact? What about then?" Ash asked softly and was gratified to see the sudden doubt in Eli's eyes. "This is personal, Eli. Has anyone ever given you any indication that they feel you owe them something?"

Eli was silent as he considered it and finally he sighed in frustration. "No."

"You need to show that note to Sheriff Cooper."

Eli's head jerked up and his jaw hardened. "No. Not yet."

"Why the hell not?" Ash shoved his chair back and gave Eli a hard look. "I've gotten to know him pretty damn well. You can trust him to be discreet."

"And can I trust everyone he works with to be the same? If we tell Cooper, then we're telling the police department. And despite the college, Amwich has a small-town mentality. It'll be all over the place before the month is out."

Ash hated it, but what Eli said was true. "I think if you ask him not to say anything right away he would. He's a part of my poker crew, and I've been meeting with him for one of my criminal justice projects. He's a good guy, real clearheaded. I think we should go to him with all of our suspicions and get someone else's thoughts. Both of us are too close to it to really be objective. We need him."

Eli's chin had that stubborn tilt to it that Ash had learned to recognize. "No. I'll take care of it myself."

"The fuck you will." Ash got hold of himself as Eli's eyes flashed with temper. If they both went off in anger, nothing would get resolved. "In case you forgot, that note involves me now. Not just you. It's implicating our relationship, so I have a say in it as well."

"I hadn't thought of it that way," Eli admitted. "I still don't want to go to Cooper, though, so where does that leave us?"

Ash couldn't escape the feeling that Eli's reputation wasn't the real reason why he didn't want to talk to the cops, but he had no idea what it could be. This arguing around in circles was giving him a headache.

Time for a change in tactics, because butting heads with Eli would never work. Eli's brows rose as Ash stood up and took his hand, but he didn't comment and let Ash lead him over to the couch. "Have I ever said that I find you ridiculously sexy in those glasses?"

"Schmoozing me with compliments isn't going to work." Eli's lips curved as he let Ash tug him down on the couch. "But that doesn't mean you have to stop."

Ash nuzzled Eli's jaw, tracing a path with his lips to Eli's throat as he racked his brain, trying to come up with an argument that would make Eli see the danger he was in. "What's the real reason why you don't want to go to Cooper?"

Eli pulled away to give Ash a guarded look. "I told you the reason."

"I'm sure that's part of it, but it's not the whole one. You know what I think?" Eli tensed as Ash kissed his neck again, seeking out that sensitive spot he'd discovered.

"*I* think you should shut up and kiss me." Eli pushed Ash back on the cushions and straddled his thighs. His hands slid up Ash's chest as Eli leaned down, and when their lips met, Ash wasn't sure who was seducing whom anymore.

Eli slid his hand under Ash's T-shirt, his tongue teasing and playful as he kissed Ash. Ash groaned and sank his hands into Eli's hair, cradling his head as he kissed Eli back. He was going to damn well win this hot tug of war. He struggled to keep his mind on the problem at hand and not on the fact that his cock was stirring in his jeans as if he hadn't had Eli naked just that morning.

"I think you're afraid I'm right and you don't want to have proof that someone you consider a friend betrayed you," Ash said as their lips parted. Eli's eyes flashed and Ash cupped his jaw. "Has that happened to you before? Is that why you don't want to face it?"

"You aren't going to be able to get that out of me or seduce me into going to talk to Cooper."

"Are you so sure?" Ash rolled them both over and settled between Eli's thighs. They groaned as their cocks rubbed together through their jeans and hardened even more. Ash circled his hips, giving them more friction, and Eli arched against him, his fingers digging into Ash's back. "Betcha I can seduce you into going to Cooper."

ASH would not fucking drop it, and Eli was torn between irritation at his persistence and laughter at Ash's sure confidence. It was kind of sexy to have Ash's sole focus on him, bent on driving him crazy until he gave in.

"I bet you can't." Eli bit Ash's shoulder and tugged off his shirt. "We'll see who has who squirming and begging at the end of this."

"Oh that's how you want to play this game?" Ash shucked up Eli's shirt, and his lips ran a wandering path from Eli's stomach up to his nipple. Oh, that was just wrong, going straight for one of Eli's weak spots.

"You started it." Ash's tongue circled and flicked, filling Eli with anticipation as he squirmed under Ash. Such a damn tease. Finally, his lips closed around Eli's nipple with a rough tug. Eli drew his knees up to hug Ash's hips as he undid his lover's jeans.

"I'm going to finish it too." His hand found its way into Ash's jeans and caressed the hard length of Ash's cock. "Where'd we leave the condoms and lube?"

"I think… maybe the bathroom." Ash groaned as Eli squeezed his cock, and he rocked against Eli's palm. "Or the bedroom. Maybe we should take this back there."

"Hell no." Eli nipped Ash's earlobe and pushed him up. "Stay right here and don't you dare move. I'll be right back." He took off his shirt as he walked toward the back. "Prude."

Ash raised himself up on one elbow, and the setting sun gleamed through the bay window, gilding his skin. "There's more room back there," he called after Eli.

"Bullshit. I think the couch is actually wider than the bed." In the bathroom, Eli found the lube and condoms they'd bought when they'd gone to town for supplies. He stripped out of the rest of his clothes, grinning as he stuck his head back out into the short hallway. "You'd better be naked when I get back."

Eli emerged to find Ash kicking out of his jeans. "You do follow orders better than I do," he said as he crossed over to him.

"I think I'm just more sensible than you." Ash caught him around the waist and bore Eli back down to the couch as the lube and condoms dropped onto the floor. At least Ash didn't seem inclined to talk anymore.

"I can't argue with that." Eli laughed softly in Ash's ear as his weight settled over him again. Ash kissed him and heat shivered through him. His breath came faster as he moved his hands over Ash's body, exploring him from his broad shoulders down to his tight ass. Their moans mingled and then Ash broke away. Eli heard the pop of the bottle cap and impatience tugged at him. "Hurry."

Ash growled and nipped him on the jaw, but moments later Eli felt the sweet ache of being penetrated as Ash pushed a slick finger into him. "Oh yeah," Eli breathed, sliding his leg up and wrapping it around Ash's waist.

He fumbled for the box of condoms as Ash teased and stretched him. Ash kept nipping at his throat and jaw, making Eli dizzy with desire. His face was so close, Eli could see every gold fleck in his green eyes. He nuzzled Ash's cheek, kissed that freckle near his mouth that enchanted him so, and then grinned in triumph as his fingers finally closed on a foil packet.

Ash chuckled, brushing a hot openmouthed kiss over Eli's lips. "You should've seen the look on your face, positively gleeful."

"That sounds just about right." Eli slid his hand between their bodies and smiled as Ash's cock throbbed against his palm. It was so hot that it seemed to scorch his fingers. He stroked Ash and then gasped as Ash found his spot, sparking little flashes of pure sensation.

Somehow Eli managed to get the condom out of the wrapper, his fingers clumsy with his impatience, and onto Ash's cock. He gave it a squeeze that made his lover groan, and then Ash's fingers slipped out of him. Before Eli could register the loss, Ash had maneuvered them both over again, and his hands slid to Eli's hips. "I want to watch you ride me."

Eli wasn't about to argue with that. He grasped Ash's cock, his heart flipping as he sat back on it with a soft moan. Ash's fingers flexed on Eli's hip as he rocked up to meet him. Ash's lips parted on a sigh of pleasure. "You feel so fucking good."

Eli half-closed his eyes, his head tipping back, hair tumbling over his shoulders as he savored the sensation of Ash's cock stretching him to the fullest. "So do you."

Ash trailed his fingers along Eli's thigh. Their gazes met, challenge in Ash's, and Eli smiled as they began to move. Eli's pulse sped and heat rose to a fever pitch. He braced his hands on the couch and leaned low over Ash, wanting to be able to touch him as much as possible. Ash's rough hands cupped his ass, kneading the cheeks as Eli kissed across his chest.

Ash slid his fingers into Eli's hair again, tugging his head back so he could feast on Eli's throat. "Damn, your hair is such a turn-on," he murmured against his skin.

"I feel the same way about your freckles." Ash intoxicated him, from the way he smelled to the way he tasted. Desire and need raced in his blood, turning him inside and out. They moved faster, the thrusts becoming harder, and Eli moaned.

Ash's mouth heated his skin, and then his other hand tunneled in Eli's hair as he claimed his mouth in a torrid kiss. Eli groaned, his breath coming faster, his heart pounding wildly. He scratched his nails lightly over Ash's ribs and smiled as he shuddered and broke the kiss with a low growl.

Eli smiled into those gleaming green eyes and straightened, crying out softly as the motion seemed to settle Ash's cock deeper inside of him and it brushed against that spot that sparked pure sensation. "Oh fuck," he breathed, his head falling back as he rode Ash.

"You're so damn sexy," Ash murmured. He gripped Eli's hips, fingers flexing against his skin as he rocked up. "Faster, Eli."

Eli dragged his hand down Ash's chest, finding it hard to think and to remember what he was after. He circled his hips, twisting as each hard thrust hit his spot right on and pushed him closer to the edge. Sweat dampened their skin, harsh pants and groans filling the air.

"Let me watch ya stroke yourself, Doc," Ash said in a rough voice.

Eli shuddered as his fingers closed around his cock. He was so close already, and the new friction only added to it. Hot shivers raced through him as his balls tightened. "Dammit, Ash."

"Don't stop," Ash said, lifting himself up enough to steal a kiss. "You don't know how hot you look when you touch yourself."

Ash was making him come out of his skin. Then Ash's arms came around him, and Eli cried out as he found himself sprawled out on his back again. How the hell did he keep doing that?

Ash surged into him hard, and Eli arched against him with a ragged, strangled groan. His fingers dug into Ash's back as his legs wrapped around him, and with two more hard thrusts, Eli was lost. The tension in him shattered and his orgasm tore through him with stunning force as Ash murmured to him, brushing his lips across Eli's jaw.

Eli buried his face against Ash's neck, his breath coming in quick gasps as Ash continued to roll his hips, rocking faster. "Oh damn." He'd meant to drive Ash out of his mind, but Ash was doing a damn good job of driving him crazy instead.

Eli clenched around him, and Ash shuddered in response. "So close," he whispered against Eli's ear and kissed his temple.

Hot shivers raced through Eli as the last vestiges of his climax ended. Ash's cock throbbed inside him in a sweet torment. It was almost too much, though he didn't want it to end. He turned his head, found Ash's mouth, and kissed him hard as Ash's thrusts became more erratic. The muscles under Eli's fingers tensed, and Ash groaned against his lips as he came.

Eli stroked his back, long caresses from Ash's shoulders down to his taut ass, and slid his fingers along the scars on Ash's ribs. They kissed again, tongues tangling in a lazy dance as their breathing slowed, and Eli's heart gradually stopped pounding so hard.

"Seems like we have a draw," Ash murmured against his mouth, his arms settling around Eli.

Eli groaned and lifted his head. "What do you want to do about it, then?"

"How about another bet between us? If I win, we go to Cooper and tell him everything, even my suspicions about Wayne."

Eli frowned and sat up. He hated to even consider that, but he resigned himself to the fact that Ash was not going to let this drop. "And if I win, we hold off until I give the go-ahead."

"Damn hardheaded, softhearted...." Ash ground out the words as he shifted Eli to the side and sat up as well. "As for what we're betting on—"

"Not baseball," Eli cut in. "I want to enjoy the last games of the season without jinxing my team."

"Actually, I was going to suggest something far more interesting for both of us." Ash gave Eli a wicked grin and leaned over to steal a kiss. "I'm going to seduce you. As long as you hold out, we don't go to Cooper. When you give in we do."

"You cannot be serious. You want to gamble on something as important as that over sex?" That shouldn't be too hard—what they were doing up at camp was one thing, but when they went back home, all the reasons why they should stay apart were still there. That thought didn't have the conviction it should.

"What, you afraid you can't hold out against me?" Ash sat back on the couch and smirked at him. Smug bastard, he knew how easy it was to get Eli all worked up. "I promise not to knock you out and tie you to my bed. Does that make you feel better? Otherwise, gorgeous, all bets are off, and I get to try anything I want as long as it's not public."

Eli drummed his fingers on the couch arm, looking between Ash and the note on the table. It was only Friday, so he still had two whole nights and days he could be with Ash, unless he wanted to be an ass about that too. "Do we start now or on Monday?"

A look of regret crossed Ash's face as he glanced toward the back room they'd been sharing. Damn him. He didn't have to say anything for Eli to know his decision. "Now. And come Monday, you'd better not disappear on me. I promise not to come crawling into your bed at your house if you promise that we still meet at Dingers on our nights."

"Now? You drive a hard bargain."

Ash grinned as Eli glared at him. "What's the point in waiting?" Ash called after him as Eli stalked toward the back to retrieve his clothes.

"I was enjoying the weekend and I thought you were too." Eli came back out, buttoning his jeans, only to find Ash waiting for him in the hallway.

Ash took Eli's hand and gave him his most charming smile as he kissed the inside of Eli's wrist. "I was, I still am. But this is important and since your whole point is a delaying tactic—"

Eli snatched his hand back, feeling boxed-in and manipulated, right where Ash wanted him. Ash was probably thinking of course they could still screw over the weekend because it probably wouldn't take much for him to cave, and it frustrated the fuck out of him. "We wouldn't be going to Cooper until the day after tomorrow, anyway, unless you wanted to send him a smoke signal. In case you've forgotten, there's no phone here."

Ash's expression hardened as he glared right back at Eli. "I haven't forgotten at all. I seem to remember several worrisome hours trying to get a hold of you. What's got you so pissed?"

"Now there's going to be a conflict between us where there wasn't any before. And I came up here to get away from that shit."

"There doesn't have to be any conflict." Ash caught Eli's hand again and tugged him closer. "Giving in will only sting a little, and I'll make it up to you."

Eli pulled away with a growl of frustration and jerked on his shirt.

"Where are you going?" Ash asked as Eli stuffed his feet into his sneakers and stalked toward the door.

"To set up the pup tent. I had planned on doing an overnight hike but that changed when you arrived." Eli pulled open the door, and Jabbers scrambled toward him with a mournful whine. "Just so you know, there's only room for one man and a dog."

"Eli, don't be ridiculous."

Eli ignored him as he rummaged through his Jeep for his camping equipment while Jabbers pawed at his leg. "Want to go camping, Jabbers? That hardheaded man can have the cabin all to himself and I wish him joy of it."

CHAPTER 13

ASH got dressed and started to put away the dishes, telling himself that Eli would come to his senses. Sleeping in a tent, please, not when there was a cabin right here and the nights now dipped near freezing. Eli was just waiting for him to back down and apologize, to call off the bet so he could have his fun and still get his own way.

It wasn't fucking happening. The way he saw it, his way was a compromise. It wasn't like he was asking to have Wayne arrested. The door opened, and Ash turned around and made an aggravated sound when he saw that it was only Jabbers. The beagle let out a mournful howl and cast Ash an accusing glance. "Hey, don't look at me, buddy. Your dad is stubborn and prickly."

He peeked outside, watching as Eli systematically loaded a backpack with the ease of long practice. "He wouldn't really sleep outside all night when there's a perfectly comfortable bed in here, would he?"

Jabbers barked and then trotted off, using his paws to open the screen door. Ash looked around the now-empty cabin. Damn, maybe he'd miscalculated. By the time he finished cleaning up, the sounds outside had ceased and Ash sat down to wait for Eli to come back in. They'd talk and find a way to smooth things over.

As the darkness outside deepened into true night, the quiet started to worry him. For the life of him he could not picture Eli sitting in his tent, sulking. It was not his style, so what the hell was he still doing outdoors?

Ash drifted to the window and frowned when he didn't see Eli's tent in the yard. Moments later he had his boots on and a quick recon of the perimeter of the cabin confirmed his fears. The bastard had disappeared, and with his long legs he could cover a whole lot of ground. He could be fucking anywhere.

Swearing, Ash got some camping gear together for himself and set off after Eli. It took Ash over an hour to track him down, and it might've taken him even longer if Jabbers hadn't met him halfway. When they emerged into the little grove, Ash was cold, hungry, and very glad to see Eli sitting in front of a small campfire.

"Traitor," Eli muttered to Jabbers, but there was no real rancor behind it, and the look he gave Ash was more wary than angry. It robbed Ash of his own irritation. "I thought you weren't going to come crawling into my bed."

"I thought you said that tent was only big enough for you and a dog." Ash slung his pack down by the fire and dug out some beef jerky. "I brought my own sleeping bag, thank you."

"You didn't have to follow me." Eli reached for a small pot hanging over the fire and a moment later handed Ash a hot cup. "The tea's a little strong."

"Yes, I did. It would've been utterly ridiculous for me to stay behind in the cabin while you were out here." Ash wrapped his chilled hands around the mug and let the heat seep through.

"I didn't realize you had so much stiff-necked pride," Eli murmured.

"Are you trying to piss me off again?"

Eli poked at the fire with a stick, sending up sparks. "No. I'm sorry." He poured himself a cup of his own and stretched out his legs as he sat back against the log. "Tell me you didn't come out here to argue again."

Ash took a sip of the bitter, unsweetened tea. It tasted like crap, but Ash welcomed the spreading warmth in his stomach. "No, I didn't. Thanks for the tea."

They sat in silence, drinking, as Eli petted Jabbers. Ash yawned, feeling more comfortable now that there was something in his stomach and he was beginning to feel less numb. Without a word, Eli doused the fire, making sure he had every last ember out. "You'd be much warmer if you went back to the cabin."

"Drop it, Doc. If you can rough it, so can I." Ash followed Eli into the small tent and laid out his sleeping bag. They rustled around in the dark, shifting for space that wasn't really there while Jabbers lay in a contented ball at their feet. Ash brooded up at the canvas ceiling, only a few inches away from his nose, and listened to the sound of Eli's even breathing. How the hell was he supposed to bridge this new distance between them when Eli was so damn cool and remote? Anything he did would make it seem like he was trying to push the bet, which would only drive Eli further away.

He was on the verge of calling off the bet and figuring out another way of getting Eli to go to Cooper when Eli turned around and brushed his lips over Ash's face. "That was an apology, not an invitation," he murmured.

Ash grinned and curled his arm around Eli's waist, hauling him closer, sleeping bag and all. "This is an apology too, not a come-on." He kissed the side of Eli's neck and drifted off to sleep. When he woke up in the morning, the tent was empty and he could hear Eli moving about outside. His tendency to wake up at the buttcrack of dawn was a serious abnormality.

He stuck his head out of the tent with a groan and met Eli's solemn gaze. "You couldn't have stayed snug and warm for another couple hours?"

"I'm heading back to Amwich. You're welcome to use the tent or the cabin if you want to stay."

"Eli, we have another night before we have to head home." Ash dug out his boots. "I thought we apologized last night."

"That was for my snide remark, and maybe because I might've worried you again when I left." Eli checked over his gear and then slung the pack over his back. "It wasn't me giving in, unless you want to drop the bet."

"Would you go to Cooper without it?" Ash laced up the boots, sparing a glance for Eli, who looked away. "Thought not."

"If you're going to back me into a corner like that, then you have to work to win that damn bet. I'm not going to make it easy for you." Eli tied his sleeping bag into a tight roll and attached it to the bottom of his pack. "I'll see you in class on Monday."

EVERY sound seemed amplified a thousand times in the middle of the night. Wayne pulled his truck to a stop in front of Eli's house, and the crunch of tires on gravel made him wince. He had to get that damn note. What had he been thinking? He was asking to get into real trouble now.

Eli had to have read it. That's why Wayne hadn't been able to find the damned thing in his office yesterday. He'd waited till the weekend so he could do a thorough search without worrying that someone would catch him. Wayne prayed that Eli had left it at his house before heading off to his camp. He'd be able to search all night.

Once he found that note he'd burn it and then it would be over. Eli would wonder for a while, until no new demands came, and then eventually he'd forget about the whole incident.

Wayne fished the keys he'd made out of his pocket and gingerly stepped out of the truck. The house was dark and quiet. The light that Eli usually left on in the kitchen while he was gone must've burnt out. A light wind rustled through the trees and through piles of dry leaves, mocking his nerve. He wiped a hand across his sweaty brow and stuck the key into the lock.

The door swung open, and Wayne paused in the open doorway to allow his eyes to adjust to the darkness within. A skittering of claws on the floor and a happy little bark of welcome was the only warning he had. A black, brown, and white blur barreled through his legs, almost knocking Wayne down. "Oh no!"

Wayne's heart skipped several beats as his insides seized up with ice. Oh, for fuck's sake, couldn't something go right just once? His heart began slamming in his chest as he eased the front door closed again. Eli had come back early. He never came back early. Any second now Eli was going to come charging down those stairs, and he'd be caught.

He ran to his truck, shoulders hunched, as if to make himself smaller. Jabbers was nowhere in sight. Damn fool dog. Eli would get him. Jabbers always listened to him. Wayne tore back down the mountain and didn't start to feel safe again until he'd reached his own home. It was seriously time to give up this criminal bullshit.

ELI jerked out of sleep from the combined racket of something screaming with an unholy shriek and Jabbers baying his head off. For a moment he was disoriented and it took him a minute to remember that he wasn't at the camp anymore, nor crammed in his tent with Jabbers. He was back home in the dead of night.

"Jabbers?"

Eli tossed back the blankets as the scream intensified, and his heart pounded until he realized that the racket came from outside. How the hell had that dog gotten out again? He ran downstairs and grabbed the shotgun out of the cabinet before flipping on the outside light and heading out the back door.

The cold slapped him hard, reminding him that he wasn't wearing anything more than a pair of thin sleep pants, and the frigid ground bit into his bare feet. Jabbers barks changed to high-pitched yelps of pain, and Eli followed the sound, dashing toward the shed. The door stood ajar, and Eli clearly heard the sounds of a scuffle, paws skittering on concrete, the scream of a fisher cat, and Jabbers's growls.

Eli kicked the door open wider so some of the light spilled into the shed as he raised the shotgun. He whistled sharply, his eyes intent on the glittering eyes in the corner. "Jabbers, come."

Jabbers must have decided he'd had enough of this battle because for once he immediately turned tail and bolted. The fisher cat scuttled forward a few feet, mouth open and sharp teeth bared. Its little eyes didn't look rabid, but Eli decided not to take the chance. He slid the shed door closed as the animal screamed again.

Eli ignored the fisher cat's shrieks as he knelt down on the ground and set his shotgun aside. Jabbers whimpered, his big eyes sad and filled with pain. "Come 'ere, buddy. Where did it get you? What were you doing outside, huh?"

His heart raced with fear. Fisher cats could be vicious, and their jaws were strong. He'd have to call the game warden and have him come out to make sure this one wasn't rabid. God, please, not that. There would be no telling how injured his dog was if that was the case. Jabbers limped over to him, and Eli ran careful hands over his body. His stomach clenched as he felt the warm blood slicking the beagle's fur from scratches and bites.

He continued to speak to Jabbers in a soothing croon as he carefully picked him up. Soon Jabbers was wrapped up in a warm towel, nestled in the front of Eli's Jeep with his favorite toy under one paw. "Dr. Gemma is expecting you and she's going to yell at me for not taking better care of you. Want to go see Dr. Gemma?"

Jabbers lifted one ear at the familiar name, though all he did was whimper. He loved the vet because she always made much of him every time she saw him. He tolerated the shots and the examinations for her lavish affection afterward.

Jabbers couldn't have broken out of the house on his own in the middle of the night. He'd always saved such escapades for when Eli wasn't paying attention. He'd dash through his legs to go tearing off through the woods. He loved it and wouldn't stop unless he was exhausted or until Eli called him off. But he'd never gotten outside in the middle of the night.

So the only way Jabbers could have gotten out was if someone had let him out. No matter how clever the beagle was, he didn't have the ability to unlock a deadbolt, and all the windows were shut tight. A midnight intruder didn't make any sense either. Jabbers should've bayed his head off. Unless he knew the intruder, especially if the intruder was in the habit of bringing treats. Jabbers was smart, he'd stay quiet for treats if asked to by someone he trusted.

Eli scowled, hating the direction of his thoughts as he headed down the mountain. He hated the sound of those pain-filled whimpers even more. Ash was right: it did all point to Wayne. He had the ability to make a new key for the lock. And if it was money he was after, he certainly had the motivation, even if Eli couldn't figure out what the man wanted from him. A sick sense of betrayal mingled with his fury.

What Eli didn't understand was, why him? He hadn't heard of anyone else in town plagued by break-ins. And there were plenty of other people with more money than he had. One thing was for certain: it was past time he sat down and had a long talk with Wayne Grayson. And the man had better hope that Jabbers would be okay.

ELI walked into Dingers the following night and was enveloped by the scent of damp wool, stale beer, and wood smoke. He really loved this time of year. Actually, he enjoyed all of the seasons, except for the middle of spring when everything was cold and muddy, and winter didn't seem like it would ever ease its grip. By then he was ready to run off to a place where it was ridiculously hot and dry.

Right now those scents were a comfort. They were familiar and warming after his long, exhausting night. Jabbers would have to remain with Dr. Gemma until tomorrow. He looked ridiculous with one ear shaved and stitched up, a cone around his head. He'd had a deep bite on his backside too; one that she wanted to keep a close eye on to make sure infection didn't set in. Every time he thought of it, his fists clenched again.

At least the fisher cat hadn't been rabid. Finding that out had been a relief, and it was the only thing that kept Eli from going to Cooper like Ash wanted him to. He'd invited Wayne to meet him for dinner to give the man a chance to spill his guts. If he didn't confess, then Eli would go to Cooper and not feel one damn bit of guilt for the situation that Wayne was in. Asshole. Coming after him was one thing. Last night had been something else altogether.

"Hey, Eli. Sorry about Jabbers." Neil waved him over from the bar. "Ash joining you tonight? I wanted to see if we could have poker night at his place instead of mine this week."

"What's wrong with your place? You'd have to clean up?" Eli followed the direction of Neil's gaze to his cousin, and when he looked back at Neil, the bartender was polishing and examining a beer mug, his attention entirely fixated on it. "Or you don't want the others to know that you're shacking up with Lu?"

"You don't comment on that, and I'm not going to comment on what you were doing over the weekend and who you were doing it with." Neil gave him a level look that brought to mind memories of past transgressions as a teenager.

"I'll keep my mouth shut and go sit in my usual seat." Eli started to turn away before looking back at him, unable to help himself from teasing. "Except to say about damn time, and as her closest male relative, I approve."

"You just wait until you fall for someone, Eli," Neil growled, shaking a bar towel in his direction. "Just wait. I'm going to give you so much shit about it."

"You give me shit anyway, my friend. Ash isn't joining me tonight, but I can pass along a message in class tomorrow." Though the thought of seeing Ash tomorrow gave him mixed emotions.

It didn't help that he felt guilty for not telling Ash what had happened with Jabbers. Only he knew exactly what Ash would've done if he had. Ash would've gone to Cooper immediately, without knowing for sure whether or not Wayne was behind it or why. Ash would also be pissed if he found out that Eli planned on confronting Wayne without him, which was why he'd decided to do it here instead of someplace private. That ought to cool Ash's overprotective temper.

"How's Jabbers?" Lu asked, coming up and plunking a bowl of popcorn down on the table. "That dog doesn't have the sense God gave a gnat."

"I think I can say he's lost his fascination with fisher cats. He'll be okay. He's a fast healer." Eli dug in the bowl and pulled out a chair for his cousin. "Sit with me for a little bit?"

"Maybe later. If I sit now, I might not get up again. Let me get you a glass of wine. You can bring the rascal to my place while you're at work if you want to."

"Thanks, I just might do that. I was thinking of setting up a doggie bed in my office, but your place would be better." Eli squeezed Lu's hand. "And no wine, please, I'd probably pass out. I didn't get any real sleep last night."

She sat down next to him. "On second thought, I need a break. So tell me what's going on with you and Ash? I like that one, Eli. He makes you smile."

"Neil makes you smile too, when he's not driving you crazy."

"What are you trying to say? That Ash drives you crazy or that I should start dating Neil?"

"Start?" Eli teased, casting Neil a quick glance. The man stood behind the bar, absently drying a mug with a towel, and his eyes were all for Lu. "You can't fool me, cousin mine."

"Oh, you're impossible." Lu rose to her feet with a huff. She leaned down and wrapped her arms around Eli's shoulders, giving him a hug. "I know why you're playing it quiet, but I wanted you to know that I approve of that one."

"I said something just like that only a few minutes ago, but Neil growled at me."

"I wasn't talking about me, Elijah. Stop changing the subject." Eli smiled as she walked off. It wasn't easy to impress Lu, especially when it came to him. She'd only liked one of the men he'd dated. Too bad Ash wasn't going to be sticking around.

His thoughts continued to whirl between Jabbers, the situation with Wayne, and what he was going to do about Ash, until he saw Wayne come through the door. Their eyes met, and Eli's heart sank when the other man jerked his eyes away, as if he couldn't look right at him. Oh, man, he really hadn't wanted to believe that Wayne could be capable of anything like this.

"Wayne, please, sit down," Eli said as the other man reached him. "We really need to talk."

"How's the dog?" Wayne mumbled as he dragged out a chair.

"Jabbers," Eli said, stressing his name and getting angry all over again, "will survive, but he'll always have scars."

Wayne flinched and clasped his hands together on the table. "I'm really sorry about that. To hear that, I mean."

Eli pressed his lips together as Lu dropped off his tea and took Wayne's order. Maybe he should've gone elsewhere. His cousin liked to insert herself in most conversations, and he didn't want her to get involved with this one. "How's your dad's rehab going?"

"Slowly, but he seems determined to get back on his feet and his speech is better."

"Must be rough." Eli studied him for a minute, and Wayne's nervousness only seemed to increase. He tempered his anger and leaned forward. "I can't imagine what you're going through. And not just the worry over him recovering, I know money's been scarce."

Wayne's face tightened as he nodded. "Yeah, but I think it'll be looking up soon."

Eli went through all the conversations they'd had since the stroke. There weren't that many. To his surprise, Eli realized that Wayne had distanced himself. He'd been too caught up in the craziness of his own life to notice. Then he remembered the question that had seemed to come out of nowhere.

"You once asked me to show you the baseball cards our dads collected."

For the first time since Wayne sat down, he met Eli's gaze directly and he couldn't hide the desperation in his eyes. "You said you didn't have them. Did you find them?"

"I'm curious about the way you phrased it. If they both collected them, then why would my dad or I have them all?"

Anger flashed in Wayne's eyes and his nostrils flared.

"Wouldn't your dad have half of them?"

"He should," Wayne snapped bitterly. "But your dad cheated him out of them. One of those cards was worth $12,000."

Eli frowned, holding onto his temper with an effort. He might have issues with his dad, but he'd always known him to be an honest man. "How did he cheat him?"

"They had a bet going, and your dad rigged it because he wanted that card. And when my dad called him out, the bastard refused to give it back. I could've sold that card and used the money to save the business. I wouldn't have to worry about taking care of Dad. We'd be set."

For a little while at least, but even if the card was worth that much, with Mr. Grayson's medical expenses it wouldn't go far. It wasn't Eli's fault that Mr. Grayson hadn't had medical insurance or that Wayne was having a hard time holding the store together.

One thing he did know: his dad wouldn't cheat. He also wouldn't give something back if another man foolishly bet it away. In his head a deal was a deal, even if it killed a friendship.

"So you think that gives you the right to break into my house and office and destroy my belongings?" Eli snarled low enough that only Wayne would hear him. "You think it gives you the right to put Jabbers in danger by letting him out in the middle of the night?"

Wayne's mouth dropped open, and he half shook his head. "Wha— I don't know what you're saying."

"You broke into my house looking for those cards, and when you didn't find them you sent that blackmail note." Eli wanted to grab Wayne by his shirt and shake him. "That book you threw on the ground was worth a nice amount. So it seems to me like you're the one who owes me money, not the other way around. Not to mention Jabbers's vet bill."

"You're crazy," Wayne burst out, jumping to his feet, his face red. "I don't have to take this from you."

Eli rose as well, as Neil came around the bar with a look of alarm on his normally dour face. "Jabbers could've gotten killed. What the hell possessed you to come snooping around last night?"

"I don't have to answer these ridiculous accusations." Wayne looked around wildly. "You stay away from me."

"One more incident and I'm going to Sheriff Cooper," Eli snarled.

Neil jumped between them as Eli took a step toward Wayne, and the bartender shoved them both back with a hand to their chests. "I haven't had a brawl in two years and I'm not about to allow one now. Both of you calm down."

"That's okay, I'm leaving." Wayne turned tail to run before Eli could reach him.

"No you don't," Neil growled, grabbing a hold of Eli's arm. "You're not going after him until you've gotten a hold of your temper again."

"My temper is just fine, thank you." Eli jerked his arm away. Dammit, he'd fucked up that confrontation from the start. The sight of Lu standing near the bar with her hand over her mouth and worry in her eyes made him a little ashamed of himself. He really could've handled that better.

At least Dingers wasn't that crowded, though he was sure the story of him making a fool of himself would spread before morning. "Why don't you come sit in the kitchen and have a bite to eat, and we can talk?" Neil took his arm again.

"No. I need to get home and call Dad."

Neil's eyes flashed as he steered Eli toward the kitchen. "You put tears in Lu's eyes, you're damn well going to give her an explanation."

Eli gave in to Neil's manhandling and let himself be led to the warm kitchen. At least it was out of the way of prying eyes. Neil gave a few snapped orders, and Eli found himself sequestered in the man's tiny office feeling even more like a fool until Lu rushed in. Dear God, it was like the few times he'd managed to fuck up enough to get these two mad at him as a teenager.

"Okay, before you start in on me, hold up. I know the argument between Wayne and me seems to have come out of nowhere, but I have my reasons for what I said to him." He looked between their worried faces and decided that he couldn't give them the whole story. Not until it was resolved, or else they'd really fret, especially Lu.

"We're listening," Neil said, rubbing Lu's shoulder with his large hand.

"Lu, do you remember the fight my dad got into with Wayne's dad?"

She blinked in surprise and then frowned. "Good God, Eli, that was a long time ago. They were in high school then. What does that have to do with Wayne getting Jabbers hurt or you going to Sheriff Cooper?"

He hadn't realized he'd said that part loud enough for anyone else to hear. "He's been snooping around my place looking for Dad's baseball cards so he could sell them to pay the medical bills. I guess he thought I was still out of town last night, and when he broke in, Jabbers took the opportunity to streak outside. You know how he is."

"Son of a bitch," Neil muttered and then cursed again when Lu elbowed him in his ribs. "I'd known your office was broken into but you didn't say anything about your house too."

"Because I didn't know for certain anyone had broken into the house. Ash thought so, and I thought he was just being paranoid. But there's no other way Jabbers could've gotten out last night. Wayne must think Dad left the cards behind when he went to college and they're stored in the house, or that he gave them to me or something asinine like that."

"The only thing your dad ever gave you was criticism, stupid fool." Lu patted Eli's shoulder. "You should've come to us sooner."

"I just started believing it myself. I'm going to talk to Dad and find out what happened to them so this can stop. I swear, it's absolute idiocy to lose a friendship over a bet. Even if they are worth what Wayne claims, Dad doesn't need the money and Mr. Grayson does."

"Good luck with that," Neil muttered. "Well, now that you've cornered Wayne and let it be known you're onto him, he'll probably drop it. He hates confrontation."

"That was my thought, but I could've handled it better. Ash wants me to go to Cooper, but things are rough enough for Wayne without adding police trouble. I'm just hoping this has knocked some sense into him."

"It'd better. Or I'll have a talk with him," Neil said.

"Forget that," Lu cut in. "I'll go to Cooper myself. You hear me, Eli?"

"Yes, ma'am." Eli didn't know how much longer he could hold Ash off, not to mention resist him. Yesterday had been hard enough, waking up next to him, with Ash looking so damn sexy without even trying. Tomorrow was going to be even harder, sitting across from him in class with the memory of the weekend vivid in his head. Ash wouldn't even have to make eyes at him for Eli to feel the heat.

"Thanks for the talk. I'm going to go check on Jabbers and call Dad. 'Night." Eli kissed Lu's cheek and got out of there before she recovered enough from her surprise over Wayne to remember how Eli had made her worry, and even worse, kept things from her.

"ELI? Is something wrong?"

Eli winced at the faint note of concern in his dad's voice. Did he really only call if something was wrong or to plan those brief visits in the summer? He needed to do better than that. "Actually, no, everything is good here. We're expecting our first snow this week."

"Ah." A strained silence fell across the line for a moment, and Eli wished he had come up with something better to say than inane chat about the snow. "Are you coming down for Thanksgiving?"

"I don't think so. I don't like traveling mid-semester; things get crazy enough as it is." Eli hated this awkwardness between them, only he didn't know how to fix it after all this time. And he sure as hell didn't want to call a truce if it would be shoved back in his face.

"Your mom will be disappointed."

Yeah, but what about you, Dad? Eli held his tongue, though. He had to stop feeling like the little boy wishing for things he was never going to get. Was it too much to ask that his dad be disappointed too? "Maybe Christmas, we'll see how the rest of the semester goes."

"Is that man still giving you a hard time? You know he might go a little easier on you if you cut your hair."

"Cutting my hair won't help, Dad. Britton is one of those men where once he's decided to dislike someone, he dislikes them for life. I could win a Nobel Prize and he'd still think I wasn't worthy."

"Don't let him get to you. Then he wins."

Eli chuckled softly and relaxed a bit. He really should call more often, they were never going to get beyond this if they didn't both make an effort. "I try. Usually it works."

"So did you just call to chitchat? I can get your mom."

Eli's heart sank. It would help if he got the impression his dad wanted to put forth an effort too. "Actually, I called because I had a question I wanted to ask you. Whatever happened to your old baseball card collection?"

"I got rid of most of them in college. They didn't hold any appeal for me anymore," his dad said gruffly. "Why do you want to know?"

"Wayne's been asking about it," Eli replied, trying to decide how far to press the questions. He could already hear the withdrawal in his dad's voice. There was nothing else he could say without sounding accusing, and that was not how he wanted to end their conversation.

"You tell Wayne Grayson to talk to his dad," Dad said in a tone that Eli recognized all too well, a tone that said he would speak no further on the subject.

"I'm sure he has." As much as he tried to keep the barb out of his voice, Eli didn't entirely succeed. "Maybe you'll recall that he's still recovering from his stroke."

"Gareth's here, perhaps you want to talk to him instead." And with that, Eli's dad was off the phone. Eli didn't know whether he wanted to snarl or sigh. Just once, he'd like to have a conversation with him that didn't end with his insides tied up in knots.

Stupid fool. Only Eli wasn't sure if he was referring to himself for hoping or to his dad.

"What did you say? Did you tell him you were bringing a handsome hunk home for the break?" Gareth said with a laugh in his voice as he picked up. Eli certainly didn't mind talking to his cousin. Gareth was his age and one of his closest friends growing up, but dammit, his dad frustrated the hell out of him.

"I think his hair would've fallen out on the spot. I haven't even told Dad that I'm seeing someone, much less that he has a military background too." His dad would probably accuse him of corruption or something stupid like that. If he found out Ash was his student, too, Eli didn't even want to think about his reaction. "I haven't figured out how to break it to him."

That was a conversation for another day. There was no way Eli would put Ash in the awkward situation of being sprung on his family. At least he had one absolute ally in Tennessee. It shouldn't ache so much that his dad never had a problem accepting Gareth's gayness. It wasn't fair, but then Gareth wasn't his son, and that made all the difference.

CHAPTER 14

ASH smiled as he reached Eli's office. The man had gone out of his way to avoid him this week. There had been no more lingering after class so they could have a few words together before parting, and Eli certainly hadn't extended an invitation to join him on one of his afternoon hikes. But Eli couldn't avoid the one-on-one meeting to talk about Ash's paper, and he wasn't allowed to avoid dinner tonight. Ash intended to make the most of both opportunities.

He knocked on Eli's door and peered in, grinning anew at his lover's wary gaze. "Hey there, Doc."

"Any chance I can count on you to behave this afternoon?" Eli asked as Ash came in and locked the door. "Never mind, I take that as a resounding no. A man's office should be sacred."

"Don't worry, Eli. I don't plan on molesting you." Ash paused and blatantly ogled Eli. "Yet. Paper first."

"It's the 'yet' that concerns me. Just as long as I don't turn around and find you next to naked, we'll be fine." Eli sat back in his chair and propped his feet up on his desk as he watched Ash take a seat. "How have you been?"

"You'd know if you hadn't tried avoiding me this week. I didn't realize you were that worried about my seduction techniques."

Eli shot him a withering glance at his teasing. "I was still irked with you. I wanted the chance to calm down before you pissed me off again."

"You know, every time I think I have you figured out you surprise me again."

"What's that supposed to mean?"

Ash pulled off his gloves and started to unbutton his coat. "I never would've taken you as a man who held grudges."

"It's not a grudge. Sometimes it takes me a while to calm down, especially when people keep provok—" His mouth dropped open as Ash took his coat off and tossed it onto the other chair. Then Eli's eyes heated, and he abandoned his casual pose to sit up and lean forward. "You are an evil man, Ashley Gallagher."

"If you say so." Ash glanced down at his T-shirt, emblazoned with the words *I have no gag reflex*, and grinned at Eli. "Bring back memories, gorgeous? I can demonstrate if you like."

"Now that you've fried my brain, did you bring your outline?"

Ash laughed and dug in his book bag for the paper. "You're right, let's get business out of the way first; gives us more time to play after." He captured Eli's wrist as he reached out to take the document. "You're still wearing your cuffs. I thought you'd gotten rid of them after last weekend."

"I didn't mind being tied up that much." Faint spots of color appeared on Eli's cheeks. "And just because I left camp mad doesn't mean I didn't like the sentiment behind you giving them to me. Besides, a bet is a bet."

Ash released him and sat back, trying to figure out what Eli meant by that statement. Was that an invitation to tie him up again? Maybe. Because if Eli was bound, he could claim he wasn't responsible for what happened between them. Clever bastard. Then he'd get the sex and still wiggle around the bet.

Maybe that was part of it, but Ash didn't think that was the only thing Eli meant. He watched Eli dig out his glasses, his face turning serious as he looked over Ash's outline. That expression hit him like a fist to the gut. Eli's good opinion mattered to him. More than anyone's had in a long time, ever since he'd left the Marines and those he'd considered family far behind.

Holy shit. Wait till Kurtis got a load of this. Ash might be falling for someone.

"Well done," Eli said, looking up to smile at him. "It sounds like it's going to be a good paper. Have you started it yet?"

Ash's heart flipped at that warm, genuine smile. If he didn't get it together he was a goner, and he *couldn't* fall for Eli. That wasn't in the plans he had for his life, even if daydreams of future possibilities kept intruding on his thoughts. "Not yet. I've been working on another project for my criminal justice class. I went off my schedule last weekend."

"Life has a way of doing that to us sometimes." Eli handed the outline back to him. "As much as I would like to stall and nitpick, I can't. You've got a solid start."

"Thanks. I have to say, I'm impressed. I don't know what you said to Whitney, but she's a changed lady." Whitney had shown up on time all week, dressed demurely by Whitney standards.

"I just laid out her options."

"Uh huh. I'm sure that was it." Probably with a little bit of that disapproving look Eli wielded so well in class. Eli also had a pointed way with words when he didn't let his emotions get the better of him. Ash tucked his outline away, and when he turned back, he had the pleasure of seeing that wary look on Eli's face again. Damned if it didn't just make him want Eli more.

"Now for the second reason why I'm here."

"Ash, you stay right there in your seat," Eli snapped as Ash rose. He started to take off his glasses, but Ash stopped him with a quick shake of his head.

"Leave them on. You have no idea how sexy they are on you."

Eli's hand fell away. It looked as if he wanted to get up and bolt, but his own stubborn nature held him in the chair as Ash approached. "I am not giving in to your fantasies of seducing a professor in his office."

"I never had such a fantasy until I met you." Ash came around the desk and leaned his hip against it. Eli was sitting properly in his chair, with it scooted close instead of sprawling out, one foot propped up on his desk as usual. It made Ash wonder what he was trying to hide. He smiled and used his foot to roll the chair back.

"You know how much I love a man with pride?" he asked as Eli's hands twitched, but he didn't cling to the desk to stop the chair from moving. Eli glared up at him, two spots of color dark on his cheeks as his obvious arousal pressed against his jeans. It made Ash's cock throb as well.

"Is that hard-on because you've been thinking of me deepthroating you? Or because I locked you in here with me?"

"A little of both."

Ash eyed Eli's groin. He could almost taste him in his mouth already. "Are you going to stop me?" Ash didn't wait for his answer. He swiveled Eli's chair around and sank to his knees in front of him.

"Wait." Eli caught Ash's hands as he slid them up his thighs. "Fuck, you make it hard to think."

"That's the point." Ash laughed. "I don't want you thinking, unless it's of my mouth on you."

He watched Eli's Adam's apple bob as he swallowed. "You know, I have been waiting all week for you to make your move, and you behaved. I got myself all worked up, steeled myself, and you had my own mind working against me."

"If you hadn't run so fast out of class all week, I might've had a chance to misbehave." Ash rubbed his fingers in circles on Eli's thighs since the man hadn't released his hands yet. "I don't see why you're putting up such a fight. You want me as much as I want you."

Eli groaned, a shiver going through him, faint, but Ash could feel it in his grip. God, the man was addicting.

"And all the reasons for keeping our hands off each other haven't changed despite our bet."

"A convenient excuse. That didn't stop you from indulging in exactly what you wanted last weekend."

"Those were special circumstances. If anyone had found out you'd followed me, they'd never believe we behaved. If I'm going to be damned for something, especially something I want, then I'll take it." Eli pulled Ash's hands off his thighs though he didn't try to retreat more than that. "Besides, you stormed in there all pissed off and I was already fired up. It just added fuel. How could a man resist that?"

The man could trap him up with words all afternoon long, and Ash still wouldn't be able to outargue him. Eli would talk until Ash's knees were stiff, so he did what was more natural to him and took action. He leaned forward and planted his lips right on the delicious bulge pressing against Eli's jeans.

Eli gasped and jerked back. Fuck, Ash was going to make this really hard. He couldn't really feel Ash's lips through the thick denim, but that didn't stop his cock from reacting to the kiss. A wave of electricity zinged through him as his cock ached in a demand to be released.

"Dammit, Ash."

Eli jumped to his feet, all of his arguments skittering right out of his thoughts. It was hard to remember them, especially considering most of them no longer had any validity. The bet was all but over now that he'd confronted Wayne. There wouldn't be any more threats, so there was no need to go to the police. Wayne wasn't going to risk going to jail and abandoning his father, and he now knew that Eli was willing to go to Sheriff Cooper if he was pushed further.

He didn't think Ash would be happy when he found out.

Ash gave him an amused smile that did nothing to mask the hungry light in his eyes. Damned if the man didn't make him weak inside. And the kicker was, Eli wanted to give in to him and not because of the allure of illicit sex in his office, as powerful as that was at the moment.

He wanted to give in to Ash all the way. He wanted to let Ash into his heart like he hadn't let anyone in for a long time. Conversely enough, because of that need, Eli pushed him away even harder and hid behind his genuine need to keep the affair private for now.

Ash rose to his feet and circled behind Eli. The hair on the back of Eli's neck stirred as warm fingers brushed aside his ponytail to expose the nape. "You're right, foreplay can wait."

"Ash." Eli shivered as warm breath ghosted over his neck. Ash kissed him there, a simple touch that made his heart race and had Eli wanting to lean back into his arms.

"Eli." Ash slid his arms around Eli's waist, tugging him back. Eli half-closed his eyes, his head tipping to the side as Ash's lips wandered down to his throat. "I've missed you this week. You've been so distant. I don't like it when you put up that wall."

Eli turned his head to reply, and the words were lost as Ash kissed him. His hand came up to cup the back of Ash's neck as his lips parted. He'd missed Ash too; he hadn't realized how much until Ash had showed up for their meeting. He'd missed his companionship and the way Ash challenged him more than he'd missed the sex. And kissing him now was like finding a little piece of himself that had been missing.

Ash groaned and slid his hand down to Eli's cock, squeezing it through his jeans. Eli jolted, his knees weakening from the rush of pure heat. He hadn't realized Ash was moving them until Eli's thighs touched the desk. Ash had told him of this particular fantasy a number of times, how he thought of bending Eli over his desk or laying him back on it. And damned if Eli couldn't picture it in intimate, glorious detail.

Eli broke the kiss and turned his head before Ash could capture his lips again. "Are you doing this because you want to seduce me or because you want to win the bet?"

"Can't I want both?"

Disappointment left a sour taste in Eli's mouth. What were the odds of him having two students come on to him in his office during the same semester? Hell, within a week, even. Even if the circumstances were completely different. Ash had him wanting to melt through his desk, while Whitney had had him contemplating hiding behind it. But they both did it because they wanted something from him, whether it was improved grades or to win a bet.

"Not if you were looking to score today." Eli broke free of Ash's embrace and turned to face him. "And even if you weren't looking for that, and as hot as I would find it to fuck in my office, you're still my student and here on class business."

"You're even hot when your mouth gets that little prim line." Ash leaned his hip against the desk and crossed his arms. He didn't have to look so damned amused. "You have to admit the forbidden is part of the attraction."

Eli ignored the quick slice of hurt and started to gather the books he wanted for the weekend. What did that mean for them? Dammit, why did he always seem to want more than what he was given?

"You're doing that again, pulling away." Eli glanced over and saw the concern in Ash's green eyes.

"I'm gay. I've had my fill of wanting the forbidden, Ash. I'd think you'd be tired of it too." He wanted stability and comfort. He just wanted to find somebody he could grow old with. He didn't know when that want had crept up, but it had sunk its claws into him with a vengeance.

"What's that supposed to mean? You can't change who you are."

"That's not what I meant." Eli broke off, his arguments and reasons getting tangled up inside. All he knew was that he was frustrated with the entire situation, with Ash and with himself. It wasn't even Ash's fault. He hadn't been anything but honest with Eli about what he was looking for. It was Eli's problem that he wanted more.

"What's going on with you?" Irritation laced Ash's voice now. "I don't get you sometimes. One minute you're hot, the next you're cold. What aren't you telling me?"

The way Ash phrased it made Eli think of Wayne, and he winced. Unfortunately, Ash noticed. "Okay, out with it."

"You really don't want to know." Eli began stuffing his books in his satchel, but Ash put a hand on his, stopping him.

"You got another blackmail note."

"Christ, no, and I won't be getting another one." Eli met Ash's gaze. "I spoke with Wayne several nights ago. It's over with."

Ash's brows leapt up. "You confronted a man you suspected of breaking into your house by yourself? I know you think he's your friend, but friends don't do what he did."

"I'm only half an imbecile, not a complete one. I met with him at Dingers."

Ash gave him an exasperated look, and Eli waited for him to go off on him, but instead Ash rubbed a hand over his short hair as if he were trying not to strangle him instead. "Okay, I'll give you that. I know I'm coming across as overbearing, but I've learned too much about people not being what they seemed. It comes back to bite you in the ass."

Eli relaxed. He hadn't liked keeping that from Ash; it had just seemed wrong to him. "You were right; he was behind it. He didn't come out and admit it, but he made it clear that he feels my family owes his family. And since he couldn't go after who he really wanted to go after, I was the next logical target."

He explained the whole fucked-up situation, from the bet their dads had made to his confrontation with his dad on the phone, as Ash listened with his arms crossed and his eyes narrowed. At least he didn't try to rub it in Eli's face that he'd been right.

"I thought you were dead set against him being guilty. What made you decide to confront him?"

"I started giving it a lot of thought when you pointed out how desperate his situation was and how he'd have the skills and opportunity." Eli had to admit Ash had been patient with him when he'd been so hardheaded about the whole thing. "Then, after the bet, I wanted to give him a chance to tell me before you ended up going to the sheriff, so I had planned on talking with him anyway."

"You're still leaving something out."

"You know, you're really good at that. God help whoever faces you across the interrogating table." Ash would make a good federal agent. He certainly had all the right instincts.

"God help me if they're as stubborn as you. Now stop avoiding the question."

"Wayne pissed me off. So the confrontation didn't go as smoothly I wanted." Eli hesitated and then decided to come out with the whole story. Keeping things from Ash was uncomfortable, and Eli was surprised he hadn't already heard. "Wayne broke in again Saturday night. I guess he thought I was still out of town. Jabbers took advantage of that and ran outside and ended up getting hurt pretty bad."

"Is he okay?" Ash's face darkened.

"He's bouncing back faster than I am." Eli sighed and stuffed the rest of his books away. "I could've handled it better than I did. And maybe I should've come to you before confronting him. I admit, I let my pride get in the way. The whole bet really did piss me off."

"And Wayne is a friend and I'm an outsider you just met a couple months ago. I get it."

"Wayne was a friend. I don't consider him one anymore." Eli turned to Ash, frustrated by his inability to read Ash's tight expression when he seemed to read Eli's face just fine. "And you're far more than an outsider. That's not why it pissed me off."

Whatever Ash was going to say to that was lost at the sound of someone trying the knob on Eli's office door. They both tensed as Eli wondered if they'd be catching Wayne in the act, but then there came a firm knock and the sound of Britton's testy voice. "Hollister, you'd better be in there."

Eli stifled a groan as Ash moved to snatch up his coat. A dozen things he could say came to his lips and not one of them was appropriate. Britton couldn't have decided to show his ugly face at a worse time. Unless, of course, Ash had gotten his way and they'd been half naked blowing each others' minds like Eli wanted.

"I'm meeting with a student." *Now go the fuck away.* Eli still had things that he needed to say to Ash.

"With the door locked?"

Eli winced, but before he could respond, Ash opened it up. "That was my fault, sir. My hand must've slipped when I shut it."

"Probably a good thing, since people have a tendency to walk right in when I'm conducting meetings," Eli said, with a hard look at Britton.

"I thought your office hours were on Wednesdays?"

Eli really fucking hated how the other man questioned everything he did. Especially since it wasn't at all out of the ordinary for any professor to schedule student meetings outside of their regular office hours. "My hearing is perfectly fine, thank you. There's no need to have everything you say come out in a bull roar."

Ash shot him an incredulous look, and Eli supposed that Ash had never been stupid enough to mouth off to a superior officer. Britton seemed entirely too pleased to take offense; there was a faint, supercilious smile tugging on the corners of his mouth. "I received a complaint about you, Hollister."

Eli's insides turned to ice. Please not Whitney, not after he gave her another chance. He really was a trusting fool. And what the hell did Britton think he was doing, bringing up a complaint about him in front of Ash, or any other student, for that matter?

"What kind of a complaint?" Ash demanded, and Britton turned to him, his eyes widening as if he'd forgotten Ash was there. "Sir."

"Who are you again?" His bushy brows came together in a fierce frown. "Are you a friend of Hollister's or are you on the janitorial crew?"

Eli bristled. Britton's grasp of politeness got worse every year. And the younger a person was compared to him, the worse his rudeness. Eli pitied his students. One thing was for sure, he wasn't going to sit back and let Britton belittle Ash.

"Sergeant Gallagher served in the Marines and was wounded in action. He joined the Reserves and enrolled at Amwich only to have his studies interrupted when his unit was activated. He returned and continued with his studies and will be graduating in the spring. And if you'll recall, I told you when you came in that I was meeting with a student."

"Please, Doc, don't make me out to be some kind of hero. I was just doing my duty. We've met once before, sir," Ash said with a slight edge to his voice. Eli could've told him that Britton wouldn't have remembered. Unless Ash was a troublemaker in his class or a rare prized student, Britton didn't remember most of the students who came through the department.

"He is in my Historic Letters class, and we're discussing his paper. So, as you can see, he has every right to be here. Ash, would you mind stepping outside for a minute? I apologize for the interruption."

"Sure, Doc." Ash gave Britton a hard look. "I'll be right outside if you need me."

Eli waited until the door shut before turning on Britton. "You shouldn't have brought that up in front of a student. What is the complaint about?" Eli asked, unable to bear the suspense any longer.

"Favoritism, in your freshman comp class. A young man claims you're not grading him fairly."

Eli bit back a sigh of relief. He'd gotten bullshit complaints like that on occasion. Almost all of the professors did, and Britton usually didn't take it seriously. There always seemed to be one student who resented having to take the requirement or who was entitlement happy and shocked to realize that college was a whole different ball game from high school.

Britton's behavior completely confused him. It was almost as if he'd forgotten all the departmental rules and procedures. And Britton was an absolute stickler for rules. Eli frowned and looked closer at him. He didn't seem like he had a head cold or any other illness that would impair his judgment.

"I'm sorry that a student took a complaint directly to you. Did you suggest that he come speak to me so we could work this out?"

"No, I told him to come back to me with the papers in question." Britton couldn't hide his pleasure at that statement. Eli counted to ten in his head and told himself that losing his temper again wouldn't solve anything.

"Fine, if that's the way you want to do it, go ahead." At least it wasn't Whitney trying to claim that he'd come on to her. Let Britton do the extra work if he wanted. Eli knew he graded fairly, and soon the other man would realize it too.

Britton left, leaving Eli staring after him in confusion and exasperation. Ash popped back into the room and shut the door behind him. "He's going to try to nail you to the wall with that complaint."

"Trying is not succeeding, my friend. I stand by everything I've graded, and even though Britton has an asinine attitude, he tends to stick by the professors in situations like this. He hates students that try to take the easy route or who whine even more than he hates me."

"Eli, he despises you," Ash said bluntly. "A student he can put out of his mind, you he faces every day, and it's eating him alive."

"Well, I'm definitely not one of his ass kissers, that's for sure." Eli met Ash's worried gaze. "I've got enough going on right now to waste time worrying about him. As much as Britton would love to pin any wrongdoing on me so he can justify to the dean why he fired me, he can't. I haven't done anything wrong, and no amount of digging through my work is going to change that." The concern in Ash's eyes touched him even as it made him wonder what Ash was going to do next. "Are you going to try to fight all of my battles for me?"

"I'd rather fight your battles with you."

Those words tore down all of Eli's walls as his heart lurched. Dammit, Ash made it so easy to fall in love with him. How could Eli summon up any kind of a defense against that? "I...." Eli stopped himself before those words could fall from his lips and change everything. That's what happened the last time he'd admitted to being in love. "Thank you, Ash."

Some of the tension left Ash as he grinned. "I was half afraid you were going to get defensive and tell me that you can take care of yourself."

"I can, but I guess that's not the point." Eli came around the desk and cupped Ash's face in his hands. "You are amazing."

"One of these days I'm going to predict what you're going to do correctly."

Eli laughed and kissed him. "Maybe, but where's the fun in that?"

CHAPTER 15

"I SEE you're still looking as ugly as usual, Kurtis," Ash said to the image of his friend on the screen. In truth, Kurtis was looking better. The lines of exhaustion remained on his face, but Ash was pleased to see the light had returned to his eyes. Two more weeks, and Kurtis would be reunited with his wife and twins.

"You're one to talk, did you make any boys cry today?"

"Very funny. How's the rest of the crew?" Ash could see them over Kurtis's shoulder, the other men who had made up their little family when he'd still been with the battalion. Lewis and Mike were sitting on the ground in front of a TV, looking like they were playing video games. Knowing Jamison, he was probably off somewhere reading or napping.

There were times when he really missed those guys. There were so many things soldiers didn't talk about, the fear, the homesickness, but they still shared those emotions even if they remained unspoken.

"They haven't changed. Jamison still sucks at poker, Mike's still a geek, and all Lewis talks about is getting laid."

Ash grinned. Boy, did that bring back memories. "Speaking of poker, I've got a new group going."

"You do, huh?" Kurtis leaned back away from the screen and took a swig from a bottle of water.

"It's an interesting group of characters. You'd like them. That's what's cool about small towns, you hear the best stories about everybody. Cooper is the sheriff, Neil owns a bar, and Robert has worked at the so-called adult store for the last thirty years. My campus tales cannot compare."

"You gossip worse than a girl."

"Not half as much as some of the people in this town. How about you, big guy, pull any good pranks lately?"

"Hell no. I'm just counting down the days, man. Going home cannot come soon enough. So, I thought you weren't looking to settle down?" Kurtis leaned toward the screen with a glint of amusement in his eyes. "I thought the whole plan was to remain unattached when you moved to Amwich. Starting a poker group sounds like you're disobeying your own rules. And this is after you got an apartment there. Are you looking at possibly sticking around after graduation?"

"Maybe, maybe not. The year's not over with yet."

"Good God, who would've thought you would've found a home in a little podunk town in New Hampshire? Wait till I tell Jamie."

"You do and I'll kill you myself. Jamie will tell Melanie, who'll call Mom and Katie, and next thing I know the phone will be ringing nonstop." His sisters would be the worst, but they all were angling for him to come back to Georgia. Katie might even feel justified in popping up for a visit since she was the closest, just to snoop.

"I thought Dennis was looking to get you a position at DCIS?"

"I know. I haven't taken that off the table. I still have time to decide. To be honest, I really like it here." Something about this town had quieted that restlessness inside Ash.

"So the FBI isn't your number one choice anymore? Amwich is a little far from Boston. How are you going to be a big super-agent in a small town like that?"

Ash had given it a lot of thought lately. He could drive down to Durham and take the train, but that was one hell of a commute and he wasn't all that fond of the idea. It just seemed like too much wasted time. He could move closer to Boston, but he'd gotten rather attached to this town and most of the people in it during the past six months. It had been easy to leave Concord, but it would be much harder to leave Amwich.

"With my luck, I wouldn't get Boston. I'd probably end up in the Midwest somewhere. Besides, I've bumped up another job option to the number one spot."

A knowing smile crossed Kurtis's lips, almost a smirk, and if he didn't wipe it off his face Ash would find a way to make him squirm come Thanksgiving. "Uh huh, okay, you've intrigued me. What's this other career you've planned, Fish and Game Warden? Hey, guys, Ash is turning into a tree hugger on us."

"Fuck all of you," Ash said, laughing as the others joined in ragging on him. "Seriously, Cooper has been talking to me about joining the State Police when I graduate. He's got some good selling points." One of them was being able to stay put in Amwich. Another one was that he'd really feel like he was working for a community, in a place he loved, even if it was on a state level.

"And this decision to stay would have nothing to do with one of your professors, would it?" Kurtis asked, lowering his voice as he leaned closer to the screen.

"He is definitely a factor. I'm not sure how much of one, but I'd be lying if I didn't say so. Still, Kurtis, you should come up and visit, bring Jamie and the twins. I think you'd like it up here too."

"Don't even think you're going to be able to convince me to stay. I've heard you bitch about the winter."

"No more than you've heard me bitch about the heat. And you bitch even louder than I do," Ash said with a laugh.

"Maybe I'll be able to convince Jamie to come up to go skiing, or maybe in the summer. We could use a family vacation." For a brief moment those shadows once again flickered in Kurtis's eyes, and Ash vowed that he would get Kurtis and his family up to Amwich for the most relaxing trip they'd ever had.

"I don't think it would be too hard to convince Jamie if Melanie and Bruce come. We can have a reunion."

"I do like the sound of that," Kurtis said with a sigh, before a grin broke out on his face. "Even if I would have to put up with your ugly face making gaga eyes."

"I do not make gaga eyes. I may occasionally leer. I've been accused of ogling, but never gaga eyes."

"Yeah, I'll believe it when I see you. Hey, why don't you bring your professor down for Thanksgiving?" Kurtis's grin widened. "I know you haven't told me half the stories you could have. I want to meet this guy."

Tempting. Very tempting, but Ash was sure Eli wouldn't agree to another trip during the semester. "I don't think so. Things are a little tricky right now, but who knows if things keep going maybe you'll get your chance."

"Tricky?"

"Mostly just the whole professor/student thing. To be honest, I did piss him off when I told him that the bet was still on. The one I told you about the last time we talked."

Kurtis's brows furrowed, and he glanced over his shoulder at the others in the room, but no one was paying any attention. "Have there been any more blackmail attempts?"

"Nope." Ash tugged on his earlobe. "Still I don't know if Eli would tell me right away if there had been. Maybe it is over with, but all of Wayne's reasons for blackmailing him in the first place still remain, and if he does have the proof he claimed in the note, then he could be tempted. He could destroy Eli's career with even a hint of it to his department head."

"I don't envy you that balancing act you're playing. How pissed was he when you told him the bet was still on?"

Ash thought back to their dinner the other night and the expression on Eli's face. "He's got a temper, that's for sure. It catches you by surprise because normally he's so easygoing." At least Eli didn't usually stay mad long. Ash was sure that Jabber's injuries and his confrontation with Wayne had played a part in Eli being so distant last week. "Blackmail is a felony, and Wayne's given no indication that he plans to stop, even if Eli confronted him. If there had been an apology or admission of guilt, then I'd be more inclined to drop the bet. I don't think it's over with and someone's already been hurt."

"You could go to Cooper yourself. As you said, it involves you now. You'd be within your rights."

Ash scrubbed a hand over his hair and shook his head. "Believe me, the thought did cross my mind. But I think it just might kill whatever it is I've got going on with Eli. It's bad enough that I've cornered him, he'd see that as a betrayal on top of it."

"Good luck."

"You too, buddy." Ash smiled at Kurtis. He felt like he had too many sisters sometimes and Kurtis was like the brother he'd never had. "I'll see you soon."

ELI was going to find a way to finish this damned bet once and for all without letting Ash win. Unless Wayne pushed him again, in which case he'd happily let Ash do whatever he wanted. And Ash was thirsting to take Wayne down. He hadn't seen Wayne around town since Eli had confronted him, but he was pretty sure there hadn't been any more break-ins. So that was one mark in Wayne's favor. A small one.

He was running out of time. Sooner or later, either Ash or Wayne would lose their patience. He couldn't picture either one just dropping the whole matter, so he needed to find that damn baseball card, without alienating his dad any more than he already had. Eli wasn't quite sure what he'd do with it once he had it, but it would at least give him some leverage to make Wayne see sense before he truly lost everything and ended up in jail.

Wayne's truck wasn't outside the house he shared with his dad. Good, he didn't think Wayne would let Eli speak to him. Mr. Grayson's nurse, an older woman with graying hair opened the door at his knock, and Eli smiled at her. "How are you doing, Ms. Parisot? Is Mr. Grayson in?"

"Of course, Eli. He'll be glad for some company." The nurse stepped back to let him in. "I was just heating some water for tea, would you like some?"

"If it wouldn't be any trouble." Eli felt a little twinge of guilt. He hadn't been by to visit Mr. Grayson since he'd been in the hospital. A busy, crazy semester didn't excuse him.

"No trouble at all." She pointed down the hallway and then made a shooing motion. "He's in the sitting room. Go on, I'll be along in a bit."

Mr. Grayson sat by the windows in the sun. It was strange to see him in a wheelchair. Until his stroke, Mr. Grayson had worked twice as hard as younger men. He turned toward Eli as he entered the room, and one corner of his mouth lifted in a smile. The other side of his face remained slack, the muscles dragging down.

The room showed all of Mr. Grayson's attention to detail. One wall had been taken out and replaced with floor-to-ceiling windows that looked out on the back garden. Handmade shelves lined the walls, loaded with pictures and plants. A stand with more plants sat under the window, getting plenty of sun. They obviously flourished, a talent that Eli was a trifle envious of. He couldn't keep anything green alive in his house.

"How's it going, Mr. Grayson? Wayne tells me you've been making good progress."

Mr. Grayson grunted, his hands twitching on his lap. "Too slow," he slurred. "Body's... taking advantage... ha... needed a vacation...."

"True, I'm sure it's frustrating." Eli watched him attempt to straighten in his chair, pride still evident in every line in his body. "Still, you're the one who taught me that the things that matter take time and to do a good job you need to take little steps."

The corner of Mr. Grayson's mouth twitched and his eyes glinted with humor. "Don't throw... words back at me... boy."

"Yes, sir." Eli laughed, Mr. Grayson was going to be just fine, he was sure. He still had plenty of fight in him. Maybe Wayne couldn't see that. And for as rocky as Mr. Grayson's relationship might have been with Eli's dad, the man had never treated Eli wrongly for it, and that counted for quite a bit in Eli's opinion. If anyone deserved the baseball card, it was Mr. Grayson, not Wayne.

"Look, I needed to ask you about something. Wayne told me about your and Dad's falling out in high school." Eli waited for Mr. Grayson's nod to continue. He seemed more curious than upset at the change in topic. "He thinks that Dad wrongfully kept the baseball card you guys betted over, and I'm not here to argue that. I wasn't there and I'm not about to pass judgment on anybody. But Wayne is pretty upset over it. He seems to feel like Dad owes you, and when I asked my dad about the card for Wayne, he told me to talk to you."

Mr. Grayson furrowed one brow in concentration. "Teenagers are stu-stupid.... We were stu-stupider... to let it... get between us." He held up a finger as Eli started to reply and grunted again. "Took me... long time... to realize."

Ms. Parisot came in carrying a tray as Eli pondered that statement. On the one hand, he was glad that Dad and Mr. Grayson seemed inclined to unbend and make up, but it didn't get him any closer to finding the card. He remained silent, giving Mr. Grayson a chance to rest, as Ms. Parisot set everything out before disappearing again to finish lunch.

"Woman can c-cook. I'd fall in love... if she'd... quit poking me."

Eli chuckled. "I know it eases Wayne's mind to have her here with you during the day."

Mr. Grayson grunted and fumbled with his mug of tea before responding. "Wayne worries... too much. We'll... be fine."

"Mr. Grayson, if you don't mind me asking, whatever happened to that baseball card you and my dad argued over?"

The older man's brow furrowed so fiercely at him that Eli wasn't sure he would answer. Finally, he grunted, his expression easing. "I... have it."

"That's great news," Eli said after a moment of stunned silence, as relief swept through him. He really owed his dad an apology for the way he'd spoken to him. "If you could just let Wayne know I'd—"

"Don't!" He cut off as Mr. Grayson shook his head. "Tell him! Please... don't."

"Why?" Eli stared at him in disbelief as the old man continued to glare at him, and then he realized what had upset Mr. Grayson. "He'd sell it and you don't want him to."

Mr. Grayson nodded and his hands trembled. "Just got it... back. Waited too... damn long... to sell." He pulled out a smudged envelope from a pocket in his robe, the corners bent and handed it to Eli.

He recognized that envelope. He'd brought it to Mr. Grayson from his dad when he'd visited him in the hospital just after his stroke. Eli drew out a letter folded around the baseball card laid in a protective plastic sleeve and backed by stiff cardboard. He let out a low whistle, his stomach jumping with excitement. It was in beautiful condition, with no tears or bends. "Wow, Mr. Grayson, that's just amazing. A genuine Ted Williams card." He'd never even dreamed of holding a card like that.

A quick glance at the letter showed his dad's handwriting, but Eli didn't read it. That was private business between the two of them. "How'd you get the card in the first place? It had to have been worth some money even when you were a teenager."

"Grandfather... collected. Got it... when it came out... saved for me."

And then he'd gone on to gamble something so precious away and Eli's dad had let him, knowing what it had meant to his friend. It was senseless on both sides. Eli stared down at the card, weighing his options now until another grunt from Mr. Grayson drew his attention.

"Don't tell! Please."

Eli nodded slowly. Wayne would sell it. He had been hell-bent on that idea from the first, and Eli could understand Mr. Grayson's reluctance to part with the card.

"I understand, Mr. Grayson." Eli couldn't promise that he wouldn't tell, but he could hold off for a little bit. Maybe Wayne would find another way to raise the money if he tried as hard to get it legally as he was trying to get it illegally.

"It's time for your medication," Ms. Parisot said as she came back in with a glass of water and a small container that rattled with pills. "Now don't give me that glare. It's not like you didn't know it was coming."

"I'm... talking... woman."

"I think I need to head out, anyway. Thank you for your time, Mr. Grayson." Eli did not want to get between Ms. Parisot and her patient. Besides, he needed to think about his next move and he wanted to talk to Ash about it too. "It's good to see that you're doing better than what the rumors have been saying."

Mr. Grayson's eyes gleamed, and he shrugged one shoulder. "What... do they... know? Just need a little rest. Be fine... you'll see."

"Of course you will. You're too hardheaded to not be fine." Ms. Parisot gently placed the baseball card back in its envelope and returned it to Mr. Grayson's pocket. His hand settled over it protectively as she turned his chair toward the window. "Now, relax while I walk Eli out. You've talked yourself out."

Ms. Parisot flipped her hand at him, and Eli took the hint and walked back to the kitchen door. "You tell your dad that it was really nice of him to send that card. I think it's made a difference."

"I will, I promise." Eli hesitated as Ms. Parisot opened the door. "How's Wayne been doing?"

"Brooding. So busy concentrating on the fact that his dad's in a chair that he can't see the improvements he's been making. I think it's a source of frustration for them both."

"Well, they'll figure it out. Thanks again, Ms. Parisot." Eli paused and then looked back at her. Maybe he'd be able to cajole her into a bit of gossip. "You wouldn't mind answering one or two questions, would you?"

ELI smiled as he hung up the phone. That had to have been one of the better conversations he'd had with his dad in a long time. Even if his dad hadn't wanted to hear anybody's thanks over the card, he'd still been happy to know that Mr. Grayson was improving.

The click of claws on the wooden floor alerted him before Jabbers trotted around the corner with a questioning bark. He went to the window and looked out over the snow-covered ground with a little whine.

"Yeah, I agree. It's awfully quiet in this old house with just the two of us, isn't it?" Eli sat beside him on the couch so he could rub Jabbers's ears. "Would you like some company?"

Jabbers wagged his tail and answered with his little rumble. It was good to see him with that stupid cone off of his head. The beagle had been humiliated by it and moped about like it had been a personal affront to his dignity. It would take longer for the shaved hair on his haunch and ear to grow back completely.

"Maybe we could invite Ash over." Jabbers's ears perked at the sound of the familiar name. "You'd like that, wouldn't you? To see your buddy again."

Lu had given Eli so much food for dinner that he would have no problem setting a table for two. And if he recalled correctly, Ash didn't have drill this weekend. If he called Ash, he'd have to deal with that stupid bet. He really must be a masochist. He wasn't sure that he could handle all that sexual tension just for a bit of Ash's company in return.

And did he really want to risk his heart even more than he already was? He was afraid that the answer was a resounding yes. "Yep, masochist. That's me."

CHAPTER 16

THE HERMITAGE looked pretty all lit up in the dark, with snow clinging to the shingles and mantling the sloped roof. Ash could picture it all decorated up for Christmas, with candles in the windows that held old-fashioned wreaths. Eli came to the door as Ash pulled his truck up in front of the house, and Ash warmed inside despite the frigid cold outside. He could get used to Eli turning him into an utter sap.

Jabbers burst out the front door, snow spraying up as he bounded toward Ash. Wet paws plopped on his thigh, and the beagle licked his hand in between excited barks. "Opportunist," said Ash, chuckling. "Yes, I brought you presents. We can share war stories and scars later."

Ash grinned at Eli as he nudged Jabbers off of him. "Do I get the same enthusiastic greeting from you?"

"I'm considering it," Eli said with one of his slow smiles. "But I promise not to lick your hand or paw your leg to death."

"Doc, you can lick and paw me any damn time you please." Ash tossed a rawhide bone to Jabbers then picked up a bouquet of flowers off the truck seat. He held them up as he walked toward Eli. "Ms. Beauchamp at the florist says that you'd better keep me. I swear I didn't tell her who they were for."

"Ash, if there is anybody on the north side of town who doesn't know we're keeping company, they're either dead or have their head buried so damn deep in the ground they'll hit lava before they decide to emerge." Eli smiled and slid warm fingers around the nape of Ash's neck. "Did Ms. Beauchamp tell you I liked irises in the house?"

"She might've mentioned that your grandmother always kept them around." She'd actually had quite a bit to say about Eli and had held Ash captive for twenty minutes before he managed to escape. He leaned in and brushed his mouth over Eli's. "Are you going to let me in or make me freeze out here?"

"I suppose I could find it in my heart to let you in," Eli said and stepped back, opening the door for him. "Watch out for Jabbers because here he comes."

Ash had no idea why Eli had invited him over for the evening. He hadn't mentioned the bet at all, and Ash didn't really want to bring it up himself. It had been too long since their weekend at camp, and he didn't want to start the evening out with an argument or worry about everything going on outside Eli's little antique house. There was a fire crackling on the hearth, and the wood-paneled room with its throw rugs was much cozier than Ash's apartment.

"Seriously, Eli, I love your place. People don't build homes like this anymore."

Eli took his coat and hat and hung them near the door. He wrapped his arms around Ash's waist, pressing against his back. "I love seeing you in my place. And thank you for the flowers. I can honestly say I have never gotten any before." He kissed the back of Ash's neck.

"Well, I did piss you off on purpose a couple of times. That does call for an apology of some sort." Ash twisted around to smile at Eli over his shoulder. "I thought you'd get a kick out of them."

Eli smiled and laid another kiss on Ash's jaw before plucking the flowers out of his hand. "Your instincts were correct," he said as he headed toward the kitchen. "Do you want a beer before dinner?"

Ash followed him into the kitchen as Jabbers sprawled in his doggie bed in front of the pot-bellied stove with his new bone clutched protectively between his paws. Ash could smell the stew simmering on the burner and something warm and yeasty coming from the oven. Even if he hadn't really come because of Eli's promise of dinner, his stomach still rumbled.

"I'll take one." Ash popped open the beer Eli handed him, curiosity getting the better of him. "So why did you invite me?"

Eli set the irises in a vase on the table and poured himself a glass of red wine before fiddling with the oven and stove. "I wanted your company."

"Are you going to ask me to behave myself?" Ash asked as they went back to the living room. Eli's eyes twinkled, and he leaned against him on the couch as he took a sip of the wine.

"Where would the fun be in that? Besides, wouldn't asking you to behave be cheating?"

Ash stroked his hand through Eli's hair, admiring the way the fire brought out every bit of red. He didn't know where that wall of Eli's had disappeared to and he didn't care, as long as it stayed gone. He wasn't sure who had the upper hand in this bet anymore, because not getting the chance to have Eli naked was driving him mad. "That's good to know."

He sank his hand deeper into Eli's hair and kissed him. He tasted like wine and an indescribable something that kept Ash wanting more every time. Eli didn't resist him or hold back this time. Ash heard the clink of Eli's glass being set down and then his beer was taken out of his hand. Eli kissed him again, his mouth hungry and hot as he pressed Ash back into the cushions of the couch.

"Who's supposed to be tempting who?" Ash asked, his hand sliding down Eli's back. "You've got me all turned around."

Eli cupped Ash's cock through his jeans and laughed softly. "And turned on too, I can tell," he said, giving Ash's cock a rough squeeze that had him groaning.

"Jeezus," Ash groaned. "Fucking cocktease. C'mere."

"Me?" Eli lifted a brow as he straddled Ash's lap. "Me? Oh no, buddy, if anyone is the cocktease, it's you with that damn bet."

Ash cupped Eli's ass in his hands and pulled him closer. He hadn't actually come to seduce Eli, at least not right away. Ash had just been looking forward to spending some time with him, but he sure as hell wasn't going to shove him off his lap if Eli was offering. If anything, their weekend together had fueled his fantasies even more. "This is a dangerous game you're playing, Doc."

"For who?" Eli leaned over him and grazed his lips across Ash's jaw and down to his throat. "You or me?"

"Fuck if I can remember anymore." Ash slid his hands under Eli's shirt, his brain short-circuiting as he touched Eli's skin. There had been a whole argument power play somewhere in there, but he'd lost track of it. With a groan, he turned them both, tumbling Eli onto his back on the couch. "What made you change your mind and save me from blue ball hell?"

"I was there with you." Eli lightly bit Ash's throat. "And I sure as hell wasn't planning on letting you win any bets when you came over."

"Was it the flowers?" Ash had meant them as kind of a joke, but if this was the reaction he got, he'd buy a whole damn hothouse of them.

Eli's laughter vibrated against his throat, and when he lifted his head to look at him, his eyes were lit up. "No. They're nice, but definitely not worthy of just handing you a win on a bet."

"Then what?"

Eli cupped Ash's face between his hands as he lifted up to kiss him again, a quick, heated taste. "Because you matter far more than he does."

Ash stared back at him, stunned. His brain was still whirling when Eli tugged him down for another kiss. He might have won, but somehow it felt more like Eli had. Only he wasn't quite sure what Eli had won and he really couldn't bring himself to examine it more closely with Eli's tongue tangling with his own.

"Oh," he said as their lips parted and Eli laughed again. "Okay, then." One idea sneaked past everything else crowding his brain. He could have Eli naked again. "Hot damn."

He knelt up to tug off Eli's shirt and his own, tossing them over the arm of the couch. He leaned over Eli, sliding a hand over his long, lean torso and side. "You make me crazy. So fucking out-of-my-mind crazy."

Nails scraped lightly on Ash's skin, and Eli sat up, pressing a kiss to his dog tags. "The feeling is mutual. Come on, I've wanted you in my bed for months now. As much as we like to get started on couches, I want room to play." He rose and grabbed Ash's hand, leading him toward the stairs.

Ash had to be fucking dreaming. This was another midnight fantasy, and he was going to wake up with a wicked boner and aching balls. The air upstairs was cool enough to raise goose bumps on his skin as he followed Eli down the hallway to his bedroom. No sooner had they crossed the threshold than Ash tugged Eli back against him. "No more games, Eli. Not from you or me, okay? No more waiting and hedging. We can still keep it a secret at school, but from now on, you are mine."

A shiver ran through Eli, and his hands came down to clasp Ash's arms at his waist as he leaned back into him. "You swear that, Georgia?"

There was a little catch in Eli's voice, barely there, that had Ash wondering about what he had told him once. How Eli always seemed to find the right guy at the wrong time. Had he had his heart broken before? Was that why he kept distancing himself? Ash kissed the side of Eli's neck, his arms wrapping around him more securely. "I swear it, Eli."

He responded by tugging Ash toward the bed. The moon shone through the frost-edged windows, bathing the room in a cool, blue tinge. Ash's heart beat faster as Eli undid his belt. He kissed Ash's chest, then knelt in front of him, kissing his stomach as he undid his jeans. Ash threaded his fingers through the weight of Eli's hair with a soft groan as he felt warm breath brush over the head of his cock.

Eli slid his mouth down, and as Ash's cock sank into Eli's hot mouth, Ash decided that his fantasies had nothing on the reality. Eli's tongue teased his shaft, rubbing wantonly, sinking a little lower with each rock of his head until he'd taken Ash the all way in. Ash groaned, his fingers flexing in Eli's hair. "Damn, Eli, you've got a beautiful mouth."

Eli responded with a little hum that vibrated through him before he began bobbing his head with a suction that made Ash's knees weak. Fingers slid between his thighs to chafe his balls, and then Ash gasped as one wicked finger slid back, searching until it found his entrance. "Fuck, gorgeous, are you looking to pitch tonight?"

Cool air touched his cock as Eli drew off of him. He gave Ash a little push toward the bed, and Eli's teeth flashed in the dark with his grin. "Lie down before your knees give out on you."

"Yes, sir," Ash murmured, watching Eli stand up as he lay back on the bed. The cool comforter felt good against his skin, because his body was on fire. Eli quickly got rid of the rest of Ash's clothes, stripping him bare before kicking off his own jeans and joining him on the bed. A drawer rattled next to the bed, and Ash shivered as a cold bottle rolled against his leg.

"Sorry about that." Eli snatched up the lube again and poured some into his hand and then rubbed his palms to warm it, all the while staring at Ash in a way that had his heart racing. He wanted to touch Eli all over, press lingering kisses against all his favorite spots and savor the anticipation building between them.

Ash smiled and reached for him. "You can come down here and warm me up again."

"Oh no, troublemaker, I'm calling the shots now." Oh, the wicked promise that was in Eli's smile. Ash's cock surged as Eli moved out of immediate reach of his hands. "I'm going to set you on fire, Georgia."

"I think you already have."

Eli stretched out between Ash's thighs and took his cock deep into his mouth again. Damn, the man wasn't kidding. Ash hadn't even had a chance to get accustomed to the perfect heat of Eli's mouth when a warm, slick finger circled his entrance.

Ash's heart skipped a beat. It had been a long time since anyone had fingered him. He groaned as Eli's finger pushed inside. He'd forgotten how good it could feel. The dual sensation of the hot suction on his cock and the slow thrust inside him soon had his cock jumping and aching for more. Ash raised his knees, bracing his heels on the bed so he could rock his hips and move with Eli.

Eli's hair swept across his skin and tickled his thighs. With a low groan, Ash tunneled his fingers in it again. "I swear, don't you ever let any of them talk you into chopping your hair off." He loved the way it looked in the light and the heavy, silken weight of it that begged to be touched. He loved how it represented Eli's rampant individuality and stubbornness.

Eli lifted his head and kissed Ash's thigh. "I think I would be in more trouble with you if I did cut it than I would be with anyone else for keeping it long."

Before Ash could respond, Eli's mouth enveloped him again. A second finger pushed into him, increasing the ache. It had been a long time since he'd been fucked. But instead of scissoring and stretching as he'd expected, Eli seemed content to finger him. His head started to bob faster on Ash's cock. Ash's hands tightened in Eli's hair as it became harder to think. "Oh fuck, Eli."

Ash's hips jerked as fingers nudged his spot and Eli swallowed around him. Ash's balls tightened as the tension rose in his body. Curses fell from his lips while Eli played him inside and out. Fingers twisted, manipulating his spot ruthlessly between thrusts that got increasingly harder and faster.

Ash's heart pounded, his breath broken by moans and pants. Fucking him wasn't what Eli had in mind. That thought seared into his brain and threatened Ash's control. "Fuck... fuck, Eli... gonna come." He eased his grip on Eli's hair so the man could pull off of him if he wanted.

Eli moaned, his tongue lashing the head, his hand working the lower half of Ash's cock in silent encouragement. Just a little bit longer. Ash chanted curses under his breath, interspersed with Eli's name. Then the tension exploded as fingertips rubbed his spot just right.

Ash groaned low in his throat, lifting his hips in tight, hard rocks into Eli's wicked mouth. "Oh fuck... oh fuck, Eli." His heart pounded fast enough to make him dizzy as he came. He lifted his head, groaning at the sight of Eli's lips wrapped around him as he continued to suck and stroke with his tongue until Ash was spent.

Ash released his grip on Eli's hair, and Eli lifted his mouth slowly, his eyes gleaming in the faint light. He crawled up Ash's body, pressing kisses to his stomach and chest until he reached Ash's mouth. "Feeling warmer?" he asked with a husky laugh.

Ash drew him down for a deep kiss, tasting himself on Eli's tongue. "You've definitely made me forget that New England hell is about to descend with a vengeance."

Eli curled up against him, head on Ash's shoulder, his thigh over Ash's and his arm around his waist. Ash could feel the throb of Eli's hard cock against his side. "I can keep you warm all winter."

"I have no doubt about that." Ash captured his mouth, sinking into the kiss as Eli moaned. "You don't have to run downstairs to make sure nothing burns, do you?"

"I set it to warm earlier. Stay. I'm not ready to move just yet."

Ash wrapped his arms around Eli and held him close. This was what drew him to Eli again and again—the warmth of his smile, the closeness he allowed with a select few, the way that he seemed to look out for everyone but himself. When Eli had used his prickly temper and that cool reserve to hold Ash off, it had driven him nuts because he knew what Eli was really like underneath.

"No more pushing me away, okay, Eli?" Ash ran kisses over Eli's jaw, lips nibbling as Eli tensed. "Let me stay in. I don't know why you do that."

"Because...." Eli's arm tightened around Ash's waist as he lifted his lips for Ash's kiss. "You're leaving, and I just don't want to think about that."

"Then don't." Ash kissed him until the underlying tension left Eli's body and his cock throbbed rhythmically against Ash's thigh. He wished he could meet the guy who had hurt Eli enough to make him afraid. He'd punch him in the face. "We never know what tomorrow is going to bring. I learned that the hard way. We make each other happy now, let's enjoy that."

Ash slid his hand over the curve of Eli's ass and then between his thighs to cup his hard cock through his underwear. "After all this time of thinking of touching you, now that I'm here with you, I don't think I'm ever going to get you out of my blood." And he couldn't find a damn thing wrong with that.

"I know what you mean." Eli's lips moved on Ash's skin, teeth lightly scraping as he rocked his hips into Ash's touch. "Don't stop, please don't stop."

Desire surged again at the plea in Eli's voice. Satiation never seemed to last long before Ash was eager to have him again and again, until they couldn't move. He rolled Eli under him and knelt up just long enough to pull the underwear down Eli's long legs. "I'm not going to stop. Not unless you tell me no."

"You said no more games, no more bets. We're together now, Ash. I'm sure as hell not going to say no to you right now." Eli wrapped his arms around Ash, tugging him down. They both groaned as their bodies came together, fevered skin against fevered skin. Ash's cock hardened a little more as it rubbed against Eli's rampant shaft, slick with precome.

Ash kissed him, his tongue delving into Eli's mouth. The man made him so hungry with his hot mouth and eager hands, those wicked sounds that lodged in his throat. Eli's hands gripped his ass, rocking Ash against him as Eli ground his own hips. "Ash," Eli gasped as he tore his mouth away. "Reminds me of that encounter behind your apartment."

"A memory that has kept me company more than one night lately." Ash shuddered as Eli's mouth found his ear, and he nipped hard enough to make it sting. Eli pressed the lube into his hand and curled his fingers around it.

"I've been dreaming of you fucking me for the last two weeks. And I've been about to come out of my skin since you cornered me in my office."

Ash smiled on a rush of satisfaction. Eli played it so damn cool sometimes that it was hard to tell how much he was getting to him. "Really, do tell," he whispered as he popped the cap on the lube. "How close was I to being able to indulge in my fantasy of having you bent over your desk?"

"Too close. Britton would've heard me screaming your name."

Ash groaned at the thought of Eli screaming his name, period. "Well, I'm glad you didn't give in because I would've hated for us to get caught. Even if I still want to get you into a compromising position in that office."

"I still want to pull you down on one of those overstuffed chairs in the special collections library and let you have your way with me," Eli said, sliding one leg up to hook over Ash's hip. "I guess some things are going to have to remain fantasies."

Ash snickered and slicked his fingers. "Saying something like that is waving a red flag in front of a bull. Damned if I'm not going to find a way." Both his fantasy and Eli's. Anything could be done with the proper amount of planning.

Eli moaned as Ash stretched him, nipping at his ear again. "Hurry up, I'm impatient for you."

It was hard to concentrate on getting Eli ready when he kept whispering wicked encouragements in Ash's ear. How the hell was a man supposed to concentrate? "Behave yourself."

"That entirely defeats the purpose. And you're not one to talk after I've been trying to get you to behave for how long now?" Ash heard the fumble of fingers on a box, the tear of foil, and then a few moments later Eli rolled a condom over Ash's cock and gave it a squeeze. Ash groaned as Eli wiggled out from under him and pushed up onto his hands and knees. He tossed Ash a smile of pure deviltry over his shoulder. "Be bad with me, Georgia."

Ash rose up behind him, his heart pounding as he stroked his hand over Eli's back, following the flow of muscles from shoulder to hip. His cock nudged against Eli's cleft, and he moaned, arching his back and rocking toward Ash. "I'd be a fool to ignore an invitation like that."

He guided his cock, groaning as it found Eli's entrance. They began to push together, Eli pressing back as Ash thrust forward. They both moaned as his cock sank deep inside Eli. "Fuck, yeah, just like that," Eli breathed.

Ash wanted to hear the sound of Eli's voice just like that for a very long time. Ash's hands clutched Eli's hips as Eli clenched around him. Ash leaned over him, hands braced on the mattress, teeth grazing Eli's shoulder as he thrust. The man got under his skin and made him crave more. He couldn't remember another lover getting to him like this.

"Harder," Eli groaned, grinding back against him. "Been too long."

Ash pressed his forehead against Eli's shoulder, panting as he snapped his hips harder. Eli continued to encourage him between moans and soft gasps. *Harder. Faster. Rougher.* Until Ash's head swam. He straightened again, his hands braced on Eli's shoulder and hip as they ground against each other.

Damn, Ash loved the long line of Eli's back, broad at the shoulders and lean at the waist. He wrapped an arm around Eli's stomach and hauled him up against him so that Eli was straddling Ash's thighs. Eli groaned and slipped an arm around Ash's neck, twisting around to kiss him as Ash drove into him.

"Feels so good," Eli groaned against his lips. "More."

Ash smiled and cupped Eli's balls in his hand, gently rolling them, fingers playing with the silky, fragile skin. "How's that? You like me touching you there too, don't ya?"

Eli shuddered and clenched around him. "Damn right I do."

"How about this?" Ash teased, wrapping his hand around Eli's cock and starting to stroke him in rhythm to his thrusts. "You like that, my sexy professor?"

"Oh fuck." Eli's head fell back on Ash's shoulder and his Adam's apple bobbed as he swallowed. "You're a dirty fuck, Ash. What do you want me to say? 'Please pound your teacher's ass and I'll give you a B'?"

"B? I'm insulted. I guess I'll have to try harder." Ash ran his thumb over the head of Eli's cock, savoring the slick wetness. He circled his thumb around the stiff peak of Eli's nipple and gave it a pinch.

Eli jerked in his arms with a rough groan. He curled his fingers over Ash's hand on his cock, urging him to stroke faster. "I revise... my opinion. You're the teacher's... pet. Just keep doing that."

Despite the cool air in the bedroom, Ash felt overheated. Eli's throat was damp and tasted of salt, his hair clinging to his sweat-slicked skin. Ash groaned, pressing his face against the curve of Eli's neck as the tension rose. His balls tightened, aching, as Eli cursed between panted breaths. Then Eli clenched around him and the tension shattered.

Ash groaned and thrust hard up into him, coming, and just seconds into his orgasm Eli came, too, clenching around his cock in rhythmic bursts that only extended the intensity of his climax. They both trembled and panted, and Ash couldn't remember the last time he'd felt so shaky inside after sex.

Eli slid, boneless, back onto the bed with a groan, and then reached back to tug Ash down beside him. Ash stared up at the dark ceiling, listening to Eli breathing next to him. It took several long minutes for Ash's heart to stop beating so wildly and his breathing to even out. He rolled onto his side, slinging his arm over Eli's waist and brushing a kiss to the top of his head. "Dinner is really going to burn now. I don't feel like moving for a couple of days."

Eli's shoulders shook with silent laughter. "What, you expect to be served in bed now?"

"Mmm, I like the sound of that. No getting up and getting dressed," Ash said as he nuzzled Eli's cheek. "I could get used to that."

"I refuse to have crumbs in my bed or Jabbers clambering all over us so he can steal what we have." Eli sat up and leaned over the side of the bed to grope for his clothes.

"He wouldn't do that to me." Ash ran his hand over Eli's hip. He couldn't stop himself from touching him if he tried; trying to play it cool in class was going to be impossible by the end of the semester. He wanted everybody to know that Eli was his for now.

"He's got you fooled, my friend. He will take shameless advantage of your lapse in judgment." Eli smiled over his shoulder and then leaned back for a quick kiss. "Hot stew on naked parts is no fun."

"You sound like you're speaking from experience."

"A long story for another day." Eli rose and shrugged into his shirt. "I do have some other news for you. I meant to tell you when you arrived, but you distracted me."

"Good news?" Ash asked, only half paying attention as he ogled Eli's ass while he searched for his jeans.

"Very. I found the baseball card."

It took a moment for that to sink in as Eli looked at him with an air of expectation. "Whoa, wait a minute. *The* baseball card?" Ash asked as he sat up. "The one that dipshit has been scouring your house for?"

"That would be the very same one."

"You'd better not have given it to Wayne." Ash snagged his clothes off the floor, and at Eli's silence, he looked over to find him studying Ash with his arms crossed over his chest. That card was the ace up their sleeve, and frankly, Wayne hadn't done a damned thing to earn it. "Jesus, please tell me you didn't give it to him. Eli, I'm going to strangle you."

"Is that any way to speak to your lover?" Eli pressed his lips together in a way that made Ash think he was trying not to laugh.

"Strangling me would be a bad mark on your record. You'd never be able to keep it out of the headlines."

"Eli," Ash growled.

"I didn't give it to him, so you can calm down." Eli gave him an exasperated look and brushed a kiss over Ash's knuckles. "Wayne's dad has the card, and no, I didn't give it to him, either. Even though if I could've, he'd have been the only one who I'd give it to. It does belong to him."

"How did Mr. Grayson get it?"

"I guess after hearing about Mr. Grayson's stroke, Dad felt bad. He sent me to see him in the hospital this summer with an envelope. Ironically enough, Mr. Grayson has had the card this entire time and Wayne doesn't know it."

"What are you going to do?" Ash asked as he began to get dressed.

"I'm not sure. I figured we could sit on it for now. Mr. Grayson doesn't want Wayne to know because Wayne will sell it. I've talked with his nurse and butted my nose into their business. Money is tight, but maybe not as tight as Wayne seems to fear. I don't want Mr. Grayson to be forced to sell it if he doesn't have to. That card made him smile every time he looked at it. It seems cruel to take it away now."

Ash frowned, but there really wasn't any point in pushing the issue. He'd decided when he came here that he wasn't going to strong-arm Eli into going to Cooper. Not since Wayne had decided to behave, at least for the moment. Maybe the threat of proof had only been a bluff or maybe the confrontation had scared Wayne enough that common sense had returned.

"Okay, we'll sit on it for now. To be honest, I don't want to waste my time giving that man a single thought for the rest of the weekend. If he wants to stay silent and off my radar, that's fine by me."

"I was hoping you'd say something like that." Eli ran his hand over the short fuzz of Ash's hair, and his gaze turned vulnerable. "Can I talk you into staying tonight?"

"I think I can be persuaded," Ash teased and was rewarded by a smile that brightened Eli's eyes as they headed back down the stairs. He had a ridiculous pile of homework to do this weekend and he liked the idea of doing it in this cozy house instead of his drafty apartment.

Knowing Eli, he'd probably work on his research or read a book with those sexy glasses and distract him often. At least at the house he could act out several of those fantasies he had about his professor.

"You've got a wicked gleam in your eyes all of a sudden," Eli said, his lips quirking as he headed toward the stove. The rolls were definitely on the dry side when Eli pulled them out with a groan. "Damn. Oh well, she left me a bunch, I can heat up more." He cast Ash a quick, wicked glance of his own. "They were sacrificed for a very good reason."

Damned if the man didn't have him tied up in knots.

CHAPTER 17

ELI rubbed his brow as he made his final notations on the student composition in front of him. He had a good group of freshmen, for the most part, but the way some of them strung an argument together made his eyes cross. At least this lot was almost done. Only one more paper to go for that class and his suffering would be over. He was pretty sure his students would say the same, now that one of their English requirements was coming to an end. And they would probably all pass his class, which should please Britton.

He shouldn't have thought the devil's name because his door opened and Britton entered yet again without knocking. Eli bit back a sigh of exasperation. The man wasn't going to change any more than Eli was going to change for Britton. They were just going to have to get used to each others' quirks, even if Britton's made Eli grind his teeth.

"May I help you?" Eli asked, stacking the papers together and sticking them inside his portfolio. At least he was looking forward to reading the papers from his Historic Letters class. He had faith in Ash and the rest of the students.

Britton's brows drew together as he looked at Eli in suspicion, and Eli gave him a sunny smile in return. "Please, have a seat." Wasn't that what Lu always told him? Kill them with kindness and if that didn't work, use a shotgun.

"I looked at that student's papers and I have to agree that his claims are spurious."

Eli fought to keep from smiling at the disgruntled note in Britton's voice and he certainly shouldn't give him the sarcastic reply he deserved. "Do you want to give him the bad news?"

"I already did." Britton ignored the seat as he continued to stare at Eli as if he could see right through him and ferret out every secret he had. Eli gazed right back at him evenly. "I know you're hiding something, Hollister. You're a terrible liar, and I'm going to find out what it is."

There were times when Eli was just sick of the high school bullshit. This was borderline harassment. Britton wasn't going to stop breathing down his neck until he either got rid of him or Eli made tenure. Or maybe Britton would give it a rest if he did discover a so-called secret of his. He could tell him that he was gay. Eli's stomach lurched with a sickening twist.

His personal life was not something he wanted to discuss with someone whose mind was so narrow he could stab out both his eyes with a needle. Britton gave him enough scorn without Eli fueling it. To face it over his work ethic was one thing. The thought of dealing with it on an even more intimate level made him feel like a terrified teenager again, facing the sick look on his dad's face.

No. He wouldn't tell Britton he was gay. He did not make a big deal of his sexuality at work. If someone asked he wouldn't deny it, but there were only a few people with whom he had shared that personal detail of his life. Britton would respond in one of two ways: either he would stomp out in utter disgust and leave him be because he wouldn't want to be contaminated by him, or he'd think it was some kind of joke and accuse Eli of lying.

Eli didn't feel like putting up with or responding to either of those scenarios. His patience for diplomacy was rapidly coming to an end. "Can't we just call a truce? Because I have to tell you, this constant war is getting old. We should be concentrating on our jobs and not trying to one up each other all the time. When are you going to realize that I'm not thinking up ways to break rules or spite you? I like to teach and I'm a good teacher. I like to hole up with my books and write papers the same as you do."

Britton's eyes lit up with obsession as he sat down in the chair opposite Eli. "I knew it. You're plagiarizing your papers, aren't you?"

Eli's mouth dropped open in surprise. Where the hell did the man come up with these ridiculous ideas? "No, for good or bad, all the papers I've published are my own. Sorry."

"Then what is it?"

"It's nothing! Christ, Britton, what the hell is wrong with you?" Eli snapped, ready to haul the old bastard out of there by his bushy eyebrows. "You know what, never mind. There's nothing I can say that's going to convince you that I don't have a damn thing to hide."

As soon as the words left his lips, he thought of Ash. Maybe he should tell the dean about the relationship now, just in case. He wasn't going to be able to stay away from Ash, and while there wasn't a steadfast rule against seeing a student, it was frowned upon. He wanted steady ground to stand on if their relationship did ever come out.

Eli glanced at the clock, already cursing himself for losing his temper. "If you don't mind, I have class in thirty minutes and I need to prepare. And don't bother threatening me again before you go. It makes you sound like some clichéd villain."

Britton's face turned a furious red, but Eli's last words worked as he'd intended, and the old man kept his mouth shut as he stalked out. Eli dropped his head in his hands with a low groan. One of these days he wasn't going to let the man get under his skin, but until then Britton won, whether the other man considered it a victory or not. Maybe he should talk to Dean Newton. Britton's behavior was becoming more and more erratic with every passing week.

WAYNE stood outside of Eli's office, stunned by the angry words being spoken inside. He'd heard Eli complain about Britton, but he'd never realized that the man rode Eli so hard. Flushing with shame, he shoved the envelope deeper into his coat pocket. He couldn't, in good conscience, slip that note under Britton's door.

As angry as Eli had made him when he confronted him at Dingers, it was time to make a full confession and hope that Eli was more forgiving than Wayne had been. He stepped to the side as Britton came charging out. The man didn't even see him. Wayne took off his hat and crushed it in his hand as he peeked inside.

Eli sat at his desk, his profile to Wayne as he stared out the window. He seemed so defeated that once again Wayne was ashamed of his recent actions. He knocked on the door, and Eli's head whipped around. At first his eyes widened and then a wary expression settled on his face. He'd never looked at Wayne like that before. There wasn't even a hint of a smile.

Eli sighed and lifted his hand. "Come on in, Wayne."

Wayne took a step closer and twisted his hat between his hands. He hovered for a minute just inside the door before coming all the way in and shutting it. "I have a couple things I need to get off my chest."

"I'm listening." Eli sat back in his chair and gave Wayne his undivided attention.

Wayne's stomach churned and he took a deep breath. He just had to get it all out. "I didn't mean for Jabbers to get hurt. That was an accident. I swear I didn't put that fisher cat in the shed."

"I didn't think for one minute you had." Eli's expression softened. "You've never been deliberately cruel."

Wayne let out a sigh of relief and sat down in the chair. His knees were knocking so bad he thought he might fall on his face. "So you're not going to go to Cooper? I swear, I've been jumping at the sound of a siren for weeks now. My nerves just can't take it anymore."

"No, I'm not, despite advice to the contrary. I don't want you to lose everything or have your dad end up in a home. That's what could happen if you went to jail. And I have a friend who keeps reminding me that attempted blackmail is a felony, not to mention his outrage over you sneaking into my house."

Wayne flinched and felt all the color drain from his face. A felony? He'd never thought of that. His dad would've gone to a home for sure if Wayne had gone to jail. Thank goodness Eli was a decent man. There were so many other ways this could've gone, all of them very bad.

Eli's gaze became stern. "But I'm not going to put up with having my privacy violated, my belongings being vandalized, or having the threat of my dog getting hurt hanging over my head. You keep pushing me and I will talk to Cooper."

Wayne looked down at his hat, unable to meet Eli's eyes any more. "You and me go back a ways. I shouldn't have treated you like that. Wasn't like you were some outsider."

"You shouldn't have done it, period, outsider or not. There are better ways to make money." Damned if Eli didn't know how to make a man squirm inside. Wayne wanted to disappear, until Eli's next words hit him. "I know you felt betrayed by my family, so I talked with my dad."

His head jerked up as hope came alive once again. "What did he say? Did he admit to having the card?"

"My dad is not one to talk much about anything he deems personal business. Especially with me. But he doesn't have the card anymore and it's definitely not in my house."

Wayne slumped in the chair as that last flicker of hope died. "I thought he might've sold it. I found some appraisals in a box in your home office. I got so mad, thinking that you were saying one thing to my face and doing something else behind my back. I'd hoped that the card was still there, since the appraisal wasn't for that one, but that's pretty much dead now."

"I'm sorry, Wayne. Why don't you talk with your dad? I saw him the other day, and he seems as sharp as ever. Ms. Parisot thinks he's recovering better than you think he is. I bet between the three of you, you'll be able to come up with a solution for your bills that doesn't involve crime or selling off cherished possessions."

"I think he wants to sell the business," Wayne said, miserable over that thought. "It was supposed to be mine. All my life, I understood that he wanted me to take it over one day, and when that day came I couldn't hack it."

ELI sympathized, he really did, and not just for Wayne, but for Tilly and the others who worked there, and Jonas, who liked the convenience of the hardware store when something unexpected came up at a job. But the truth was, Wayne was not a businessman like his dad. He did not have the patience or acumen to run the store, and it had been going downhill steadily the past six months.

"The store needs a manager, and you're not right for the job, Wayne. You like to be out tinkering and working with your hands, not dealing with invoices and employees. And Tilly hates the paperwork even more than you do. Have you given any thought to hiring a manager? I bet Jonas might know someone who'd do a good job. You should ask around, delegate."

"Maybe," Wayne said in a dubious voice, and Eli decided not to push it further. He'd planted the seed, whether or not the other man did anything with it was up to him.

"I'm glad you came by, Wayne, but I have a class starting soon. I really should get going." Eli thought longingly of his next class, where he'd get to see Ash for seventy-five minutes and have the promise of a weekend hidden away at home with his lover.

"How'd you know?" Wayne frowned at him as he rose, his gaze puzzled. "How'd you know it was me? I mean, you never treated me like you suspected. How'd you figure it out?"

"I didn't. I trusted you even when others said I shouldn't. A friend of mine figured it out after you broke into my office, and I didn't believe him for a while." Eli shook his head. Ash had better instincts than he did. He'd thought that Wayne was more honest than that. He could've been straight with Eli from the beginning and saved them both the angst.

"Well, I guess I should thank you for not going to Cooper." Wayne stood up, once again twisting his hat in his hands and not quite meeting Eli's eyes. "Your friend isn't going to, is he?"

"He promised me he wouldn't as long as you leave me alone." Eli stood up to get his coat for the walk to class. "And you have no damned idea how much it took for me to get him to agree to back off. He's a little twitchy about it. He even thinks you were following me about campus, and it really bothered him. So consider yourself warned."

"Heard loud and clear. I don't understand, though, why would he think I was following you? I swear I wasn't."

Eli frowned. There was genuine puzzlement on Wayne's face. "Well, I thought that theory was going a little far myself. You have better things to do than skulk after me. Hanging around on campus and watching me teach isn't going to bring you any money."

"You can tell your friend that I wasn't following you, and I don't have any proof or any pictures of...." Wayne's face turned a dull red. "Of anything that I really have no interest in seeing. I never took it that far."

Eli shot him an amused glance, even as another knot of tension inside him eased. Pictures could do Ash far more damage than himself. There were still arguments over DADT, and it seemed like the repeal was stuck in a holding pattern. He didn't want it to bite Ash in the ass when he was so close to finishing. "I'm glad to hear that. I'd be really pissed off if my friend got hurt because of it."

"Yeah, well." Wayne stuffed his hat on his head and then dug an envelope out of his pocket and threw it in Eli's trash can. "I'm ashamed to say that I was thinking of forcing the issue. It's over with, and I'll not be bothering you again. I swear it."

"Is that what I think it is?" Wayne nodded and Eli eyed the envelope with a groan. "I wish you'd just burned it and not told me." Ash would flip his shit if he found out and Eli hated keeping things from him. At least he could point out that Wayne's confession and his tossing of another note was a step in the right direction. He just hoped that Ash concentrated more on the tossing than on the existence of a second note.

"Well, I really needed to come clean. It's been bugging me for months." Wayne shrugged. "I guess I'm not cut out to be a criminal. My conscience kept eating away at me, and then when you told me that Jabbers got hurt that bugged me even more. He's a good dog, always friendly."

"Why did you? I know you were pissed about what my dad did to yours, but damn, Wayne, I thought we were friends."

If anything, the other man looked even more shamefaced. "We are, or were, I guess. I wouldn't blame you if you wanted to have nothing to do with me. After you offered to help last summer, my dad told me what had happened way back, and I got pissed. It felt like you were deliberately mocking me. I guess I went off a little bit, and Dad clammed up and refused to talk about it. So I just got it into my head that if I could find the card I'd just be recovering what was ours."

Eli did not want to give Wayne his easy out and crush his dad at the same time by telling him about the card. Dammit, how the hell did he get into the middle of these things? He just wanted a nice, quiet life and a hot man beside him. That wasn't too much to ask for.

"I can understand that reasoning, but I really wish you'd told me everything instead of searching my home and trashing my office." The damage to his book still rankled.

"I was getting desperate. The medical bills were piling up, and I'd come to the conclusion that there wasn't a box of cards buried in that junky attic of yours. You might want to clean that out. It's a fire hazard."

Eli's lips twitched. "I'll keep that in mind."

"Then Dad told me he was thinking of selling the store. I figured if I just put a little pressure on you, you'd hand the card right over. After I left the note, I realized I'd fucked up. So I went to get it back and accidentally let Jabbers loose. I didn't mean to, I swear. You never come home early from camp."

Eli dug the envelope out of the trash and waved it before slapping it down on his desk, thoroughly exasperated. "Then for God's sake, Wayne, if you felt so bad what made you write another note?"

"I was pissed about the way you confronted me, even more pissed because I can't go into Dingers now without Neil eyeballing me or Lu saying something snippy. I was going to demand you give me the card or I'd slip that note under Britton's office door. Then I heard the way that old bastard rode you and it didn't seem right. And since I came clean about everything else, I had to tell you about the note too."

"See, I told my friend that you weren't a hardened criminal. It's nice to know that my instincts aren't completely off base." Eli ripped the envelope into many pieces and tossed it in the trash.

"Thanks Eli, for the advice, and giving me another chance."

Eli smiled at him and clapped him on the shoulder. "You'll figure out a way, and if not we'll find that damned baseball card together."

They walked out together, and Eli locked the door behind him. He wanted to get out of there before another one of his nemeses showed up. It was like convergence of the bad guys. All he needed to make it complete was to have Whitney show up with a ball gag and restraints.

At least that was one worry he could check off his list. His confrontation with Britton continued to grate on him, but at least his meeting with Wayne had gone far better than he could've hoped. It was over with, and he couldn't wait to tell Ash.

Only Ash didn't show up for class.

JABBERS scrambled up the stairs to Ash's apartment, his tail wagging in anticipation of seeing his favorite friend. Ash hadn't shown up for class today and he hadn't answered any of Eli's calls or text messages. Perhaps Ash had a good reason for missing it and not calling, and here Eli was, rushing over, worrying over nothing. But it wasn't like him to skip class, period. He took his classes far more seriously than Eli had when he was in college. He had to trust his intuition. And his intuition screamed that something was wrong.

Eli knocked on the door, then again, harder, when there was no response. Ash's truck was parked around back. With the cutting wind, Eli couldn't picture him walking anywhere, so he had to be home.

"Go the fuck away," Ash snarled from within.

Eli's brows shot up. A prudent man would take Ash's words and belligerent tone of voice to heart and leave. He wasn't a prudent man. He banged on the door again, louder this time. "I'm not going anywhere until we talk."

There was more cursing, followed by the sound of breaking glass. Jabbers sat back on his haunches and scratched the door with a little whine. His concern growing, Eli tried the door and found it unlocked. The scent of bourbon hit him first as he stepped inside.

Ash looked over from the couch, his eyes bleary and bloodshot, his face florid. "Dammit, ya made me break the glass." He scrubbed a hand over his face, the anger in his voice fading to misery. "Go away, Eli, Ah don' wanna see anyone right now."

Eli shut the door behind him, shocked to his core. Of all the scenarios he'd imagined, finding Ash dead drunk in the late afternoon didn't even make his list. "For Christ's sake, Ash, what happened?" His heart twisted as he came closer and saw the shimmer of unshed tears in Ash's green eyes.

"What the fuck do you care? Jus' leave me alone." Ash groped for the bottle on the table, with maybe an inch of bourbon left inside, and Eli swooped down and took it right out of his hand. "Jabbers, you stay over there!" Eli snapped as the beagle tried to come toward the broken glass littering the floor to one side of the coffee table. Jabbers sat down and let out a mournful howl. "And quit that."

"Fuck," Ash muttered, trying to grab for the bottle and missing. "That sound goes right through my skull. Fuckin' give it back and go 'way."

"I care more than you think, and you're not touching the rest of this." Ignoring Ash's protests, Eli went into the kitchen and dumped the bourbon down the drain. What the hell had gotten into him? Had Ash's superiors found out about their relationship and he was being dishonorably discharged? The thought made him fucking furious.

The sound of retching broke through his thoughts, and Jabbers started howling again. Eli cursed and ran back to the living room. Ash had managed to stumble his way to the bathroom, the beagle pawing at him with little yelps between his howls. A headache started to throb at Eli's temples as the reek of vomit clung to the sickly sweet odor of bourbon. Eli had never been so grateful for having a strong stomach.

"Get out, Jabbers, now," Eli said firmly, wishing that he'd left the beagle behind. The dog slunk away, head down, tail dragging, his entire body slumped in dejection. He was the worst for getting his feelings hurt at the most inopportune times. Eli grabbed a washcloth and dampened it, laying it on the back of Ash's neck as he heaved his guts out.

Eli pressed his lips together and started the shower. By the time he had found some towels for them both, Ash had stopped and knelt up to bury his head in his arms on the sink. "Come on, Georgia," Eli murmured, helping the trembling man to his feet. He didn't look good, his freckles stood out stark against skin drained of color. "Let's get you cleaned up."

He forced Ash to drink a glass of water, undressed them both, and pulled him into the shower, letting the hot water rush over them. On a normal day he never would've been able to manhandle Ash into doing a damn thing he didn't want, but clearly this was far from a normal day.

"Ah don't need yer help," Ash growled, pulling away and bracing his arms against the tiles.

Eli refused to let that rejection sting. Not now, when Ash needed him. "Too bad, I'm not going anywhere."

A low animal-like moan came from Ash's lips, and Eli thought his heart would break. He rubbed a hand over the short fuzz of Ash's hair. He wanted to ask what had happened, but Ash was such a private man, rarely speaking about himself. Eli didn't want him spilling his guts and then regretting it in the morning. If Ash wanted him to know what had caused this meltdown, he'd tell him when he was sober.

Ash shook his head hard, which turned out to be a mistake when he dry heaved again. Gently, Eli wiped a washcloth over Ash's face and held him as his shoulders shook. He'd never seen Ash with his guard down, fuck down, it was completely shattered to pieces. "Come on, Ash, let's get some more water in you, some boxers on, and into bed you go. You need to sleep this off."

Ash clutched his arm with surprising strength and looked at him with bloodshot eyes. The vulnerability in them made Eli's throat close up. "Don't leave me alone here, Eli. Ah'm sorry Ah yelled at ya. Don't leave."

"Don't worry about it." Eli ushered him out of the shower and wrapped a towel around him, leading Ash to his bedroom. "I'll be here in the morning when you wake up cursing a blue streak over the throbbing in your head and the fire in your guts."

He wasn't going anywhere. God help him, he was in love with the man.

"Yer too nice. Anyone ever tell ya that?" Ash slurred as Jabbers crawled out from under the bed to watch them.

"I have a temper that's too short and I've let it loose more times than I care to remember," Eli replied and gave Ash a slight push. He stumbled and sprawled out across the mattress with a soft groan, immediately wrapping his arms around the pillow.

"But not a mean temper," Ash mumbled. "Ya keep givin' people chances long after they've stopped deserving them. Wow. Ah think the bed's spinning. Make it stop."

Eli tugged the damp towel from Ash's hips and pulled a blanket over him. It would be too much effort to wrestle him into a pair of boxers. "I think you're gonna have to suffer for a little bit, love. You're completely sloshed with bourbon." He patted Jabbers's head as the beagle jumped up on the bed and laid his head across Ash's ankles.

"Ooooohhh, that's better."

Eli's mouth twitched as toes wiggled out from under the blanket. What was he going to do with Ash? There was no denying how he felt any longer, and the thought of Ash leaving in the spring would give him a fit if he wasn't determined to take this whole relationship one day at a time. Just as Ash had said, they didn't know what each day would bring. Eli wasn't going to worry about tomorrow anymore. He was going to enjoy every moment he did have.

He closed the blinds, dimming the room. Night was falling and soon there wouldn't be anything to disturb Ash sleeping off his drunken fit.

"Ya gonna give me another chance?"

"I wasn't aware that you needed another chance." Eli walked back to him and sat on the edge of the bed. Ash's eyes were half-closed and focused on him. "But if it would make you feel better, you can have as many chances as you want."

Ash tensed as grief crumpled his face again. "Ah left 'em behind. All of 'em, Mike an' Kurtis an'…."

Eli frowned and touched his finger to Ash's lips as his heart sank. "Everybody has to decide for themselves when to stay and when to get out. Isn't that what you said to me?" Something must've happened to one of them. Weren't they due to come back home any day now? He hated seeing Ash like this and being helpless to soothe his pain. "You can't start blaming yourself for knowing when it was your time to find something else to do with your life."

"Can't go ta sleep. Ah need another drink." Ash tried to push himself back up, and Eli pushed him back down again.

"Ash, if you try to get up again, I'll tie you to the bed."

Ash snorted, getting tangled up in the sheet. "Like ta see ya try."

"I'm closer to the kink drawer than you, and your coordination is shot." Eli wrestled Ash back down as Jabbers got into the mix, licking both of them impartially. Ash cursed and threw his arms over his face, groaning.

"Why'd ya bring that demon mutt?" Ash muttered, grabbing the blanket and tugging it up again.

"Because he loves you too and was just as worried as me." Eli tensed but Ash didn't seem to notice his slip of the tongue. Now was not the time to confess his feelings or wonder whether or not they were returned.

At least the man was distracted from his grief. Kurtis and Mike.... Eli recognized their names. Ash had served with them and considered the men to be like family. There were two others that Ash sent care packages to, but Eli couldn't recall their names at the moment. Something had to have happened to one of them. At least he hoped it was only one of them and not all of them. That would be the only reason why Ash would've gotten so lit up. "Now close your eyes. We can talk about it when you wake up."

"Ah need the phone. Case Jamie calls." Eli worried that Ash would try to get back up, but whatever reserves he'd had left seemed to have deserted him. His eyes were closed now, his words coming out slower and softer as Eli gently rubbed his back. "Don't leave."

"Georgia, you're going to have a tough time getting rid of me. I'll wake you up if Jamie or one of your sisters call." He didn't think Ash even heard the last part, the sound of his even breathing telling Eli he'd passed out. "You staying for me?" he asked Jabbers, who'd entrenched himself by Ash's feet, and the beagle thumped his tail. He never left Eli when he was sick, so he trusted the dog to stay by Ash and raise a fuss if he got sick again.

Eli began picking up the broken glass in the living room and then mopped up the spilled bourbon. Ash would not appreciate smelling that when he woke up. A black box had fallen on the floor and been half-kicked under the couch. Curious, Eli scooped it up. Nestled inside was a Purple Heart, the medal bordered with gold.

He sighed and set it on the coffee table where Ash would be able to find it in the morning. The cleaning done, Eli settled down on the couch with the laptop he'd retrieved from the Jeep and prayed that the phone wouldn't ring and bring more bad news.

CHAPTER 18

ASH groaned as he awoke to a pounding head and a churning stomach. He pulled a pillow over his head with a curse as he tasted the stale bourbon in his mouth. What the fuck had he been thinking? He never got drunk, and for the life of him he could not remember partying the night before. He hadn't partied in years.

Then the frantic phone call from Melanie came back to him. Ash's stomach lurched, and he almost hurled right there in his bed before he managed to clamp down the reaction. Gritting his teeth, Ash turned his face into the pillow.

Mike was dead and Kurtis injured. She didn't know how bad, only that he was coming home to go to Walter Reed Hospital. That had to be a good sign, that he was stable enough to travel. *Please, God, let it be a good sign.*

Ash rolled onto his back and threw an arm over his eyes to block out the trickle of light coming through the blinds. Mike. Ash's hand flexed, and he touched the scars on his side as memories ripped through him. The stunned pain, the absolute panic as he realized he was pinned and the fires were creeping closer. Couldn't move, couldn't barely breathe past the smoke and fumes.

He'd known he hadn't had a chance in hell in making it out, and then Mike appeared. He was the most beautiful damn sight that Ash had ever seen, with sweat tracking through the soot and grime on his face. The memory of that moment, the realization that he had a chance because Mike had risked his own ass to pull him free, clenched his chest in a viselike grip.

Now Mike was dead. The tightness in his chest moved up to his throat as he allowed himself to indulge in a few more memories. How much Mike had loved video games and tinkering with anything electronic, swearing he could make it better. Most of the time, he did. How he never talked about his parents, but idolized his older brother. The way he'd push his glasses up with his middle finger when the others would rag him too much.

Goddamn, Ash would miss him.

Mike had saved his life, and Kurtis had saved his damned sanity when Ash had been ready to wallow in the guilt and remembered terror after he'd been injured because he'd screwed up. Fuck. He had to be there for him when Kurtis returned to the US. He had to call Jamie and check on her and the twins.

What the hell had gotten into him yesterday? His memories were vague and hazy after the phone call. He'd only been looking to have one drink to ease the shock. That one must've turned into several, based on how he felt today. What a fucking asshole moron he'd been.

As Ash sat up and swung his legs over the side of the bed, he heard an odd skittering noise outside his bedroom door. Before he could make sense of what it was, the door banged open and a white, black, and brown blur leapt at him with a happy bark that made his head ring. "Jabbers, what are you doing here?"

Ash jerked on a pair of sweat pants and rubbed the beagle's ears as Jabbers tried to lick him to pieces. Despite his hangover, heartache, and worry, he found himself smiling at his enthusiasm. "So you were the one licking my toes last night. I thought that was just a dream," he mock growled. "Does this mean your daddy is here too?"

Through the bourbon haze, he thought he remembered Eli pounding on the door and him yelling at Eli to go away. He frowned, struggling to bring back more details, and all he got were fragmented memories of Eli standing by him as he hurled and then tossing him into a shower. "Not my finest moment, huh?" he asked Jabbers as the beagle settled down for a good tummy rub.

"I wouldn't worry about it too much. How are you feeling today?"

Ash looked up at Eli in the doorway, and damned if the sight didn't ease his heart even more than slobbery beagle kisses. Eli wore only his faded jeans, his hair unbound and hanging in a tumbled mess around his shoulders. Ash followed his long, lean chest and tight stomach with his eyes down to the two steaming mugs in his hand.

"Dear God, is that coffee?" Ash held out his hand for the mug and nudged Jabbers over so Eli could sit next to him on the bed. "I think you're my guardian angel."

"If you think I'm an angel you must still be drunk." Eli handed the mug over, his blue-gray eyes shadowed with worry. He didn't ask what had to be on his mind, just sat down and quietly sipped from his own mug. It was one of the many reasons why Ash had come to the realization that he didn't want this relationship of theirs to be just a fling before moving on. "I can make you a light breakfast if you want me to."

Ash grimaced at the thought of any food, light or not. "No thanks, at least not right now. My stomach just might rebel, and you've already tended to me enough." He leaned over and laid a light kiss on Eli's lips. "Thank you, you didn't have to do that, or stay."

"I promised you I would."

And Eli kept his word; at least Ash had yet to see him break it even if it cost him in the process. He took a sip of coffee, feeling both awkward and the need to bare his soul. "Do you have to get to your office anytime soon?"

"I can stay as long as you need me to," Eli replied softly. "Do you want me to stay?"

Ash nodded, his throat tightening. "If ya don't mind. Ah need someone to talk to. Melanie didn't call, did she? Or Jamie?"

"No, but it's still pretty early, not quite seven. You passed out before dark and only got up once in the middle of the night."

Ash didn't remember that at all, though he had dreamt of Eli pressed up against him with an arm around his waist. Perhaps it hadn't been a dream. "I'm going to take a quick shower so I'll feel marginally human, and then I'll tell you everything."

"I'll fix you my hangover cure. I get the impression you're going to need all the energy you can get." Eli rose and then paused by the door. "Do you remember anything we said last night?"

Ash frowned as he scrubbed a hand over his head. Oh damn, what had he said? He'd been pretty pissed when Eli had come in and taken away the rest of the alcohol. He was sure there had been a broken glass in there somewhere. He just hoped he hadn't thrown it at him.

"Whatever I said, ignore it. In fact, I probably said a lot of things that I didn't mean so I'll apologize now." Ash searched Eli's face for any sign that he'd hurt his feelings, but he couldn't tell.

"You just cursed quite a bit and told me to go away several times," Eli said with a chuckle. "And when you realized I wasn't going anywhere, you calmed down. Nothing to worry about."

Ash scratched his head as Eli disappeared; maybe he was missing something. His brain had not yet caught up to his body. It still wanted to crawl back into the bed, pull a pillow over his head, and forget that the world existed for another couple of hours. He downed the rest of his coffee and went to go drown himself in the shower instead. He'd chosen to drink yesterday and now he was just going to have to man up and deal with the consequences.

By the time he emerged, he felt at least up to tackling whatever Eli decided to make for breakfast. Eli pointed to a glass of orange juice and a banana, then took Ash's coffee mug to refill it. "Start with that, the peanut butter and toast is coming."

"Thank God for simple. I was afraid you'd go overboard in your zeal to pamper me."

"Another day." Eli slid two pieces of toast onto a plate and handed it to Ash. "Besides, you know I try not to cook if I can help it. My problem is, I like to eat, so sometimes I get stuck with the chore."

Ash listened to Eli's small talk, just enjoying the sound of his smooth voice as his gut churned while he ate. It probably had as much to do with the hangover as it did with the news of his friends. Finally, he set down the rest of the breakfast, unable to take another bite.

"I appreciate you staying with me and checking in on me. I know it must've worried you when I missed class and didn't respond to any of your texts."

Eli sat back with his mug. "What happened?" he asked softly, his expression compassionate, not pitying. Ash couldn't take pitying right now.

Ash's poked at the toast on his plate. "I've told you about Kurtis and Mike, right?"

Eli nodded and reached over the table to lay his hand on Ash's. "And the rest of the men you talk with on your webcam."

Ash finished the rest of his juice, though it did nothing to dissipate the lump in his throat. "There was an ambush on the convoy. Kurtis was hurt, Melanie didn't know how bad. He might lose his leg," Ash said in a hoarse whisper. "And Mike was killed, by friendly fire, they say. God, Eli, he took a gut shot and there was nothing they could do where they were. He was in pain for hours."

The lump grew larger, threatening to strangle him as he thought of Mike's last hours. The only consolation he had was knowing that Kurtis and Mike hadn't been alone. Lewis and Jamison would have kept vigil with them until help arrived.

Eli squeezed Ash's hand, empathy in his gray eyes. "I'm so sorry, Ash."

"Mike saved my life." Ash felt the sting return to his eyes, the same stinging that he'd tried to drown in bourbon yesterday. He blinked against it and focused on his coffee. He couldn't believe that he would never see him again. It was like he'd woken up to find a piece of himself neatly excised away. "If it wasn't for him risking his ass and pulling me out of that wreckage…. I just can't wrap my mind around it; they were going to be coming home next week."

"Are they bringing Mike home?"

"Yeah, and Kurtis is going to Walter Reed in DC. Melanie's supposed to call me when she has all the details." He should've called Jamie already. Dammit, he should've left yesterday and been down there with her. That was his duty as Kurtis's best friend.

Guilt weighed down on him. Guilt that he'd been safe in New Hampshire while his brothers had been stuck over in that hell. Guilt that for one brief, horrible second he'd been relieved that it wasn't Kurtis who had died. How could he ever think anything like that?

He could never admit that to anyone, much less his best friend or the man currently sitting across from him, fingers twined with his with that steady, calm expression on his face that made it so tempting to lean on him more.

"Let me know what you want to do, and I'll make arrangements with your professors. We can head down to Georgia tonight, or to DC, depending on what your sister says."

It took a moment for Eli's words to sink in, and then amazed gratitude filled him as he stared at Eli, unable to quite believe what he heard, what Eli was offering. It touched him deep inside, a place where Ash hadn't let anyone in before. "You'd go with me?"

"If you'd let me. I don't like the thought of being away from you when you're hurting, whether you'd admit it or not."

Ash shouldn't take him up on his offer. It was selfish with everything Eli had riding on him at work, but he couldn't bring himself to refuse. He felt like he was coming apart on the inside and he couldn't. He had to be strong for Kurtis and Jamie and their twins, just like Kurtis had been there for him.

"Thanks, Eli, I appreciate it." He tugged on Eli's hand and the other man rose, coming around the table toward him. The light in Eli's eyes, the expression that he reserved just for Ash, made his chest tighten and ache. Ash stood up and sank his hand into Eli's tumbled hair. There was so much he wanted to say to him, but the words tangled up nonsensically in his brain and wouldn't translate to his tongue.

So Ash kissed him instead and hoped that maybe what he meant would somehow magically transfer to Eli. Eli slipped his arms around Ash, pulling him close. As bad as he still felt, he sure as hell didn't want to drink it away today. He'd rather drown himself in Eli.

The sound of the phone ringing broke them apart. Eli smiled and nuzzled Ash's mouth before letting him go. "You should go get that."

Ash took a deep breath and nodded, feeling much steadier he picked up the phone to console Jamie. "Hey, darling, how are you holding up? How's Kurtis?"

"Ash, what am I going to do? He's going to take it so hard." She sounded so distraught that it tore at him. He should've already been on a plane south. Eli squeezed his shoulder before moving on to clean the kitchen.

"Talk to me, Jamie. It's going to be okay. Kurtis is the toughest guy I know," Ash said in a soothing voice, anxiety for his friend tearing at him. "Did they have to take his leg?"

She broke down crying, and Ash stared up at the ceiling, his own eyes burning. That was an answer in itself. He'd never heard Jamie cry before, not even when Kurtis had been shipped out again. "Not yet, but it's still a possibility. I-I'm sorry. I didn't call you to wail in your ear."

Ash closed his eyes as relief swept through him. There was still hope. "It's okay. Are you still at home? I can catch a flight out of Manchester and be there tonight."

"I can't ask you to do that." Jamie cut off his protest before it started, her voice firming. "Melanie's here and your mama's driving up. You have school, and I really want you to be there for him when he gets to Walter Reed. Take some time off then. Kurtis is going to need you."

"Do you know when they're bringing him home? Is he stabilized?" And what about Mike? He had parents that he was estranged from and an older brother he looked up to that he hadn't seen in years. He was some kind of doctor. Ash wasn't sure how far the estrangement went with his parents; Mike had never wanted to talk much about it. Ash had to make sure the brother knew so he could go to Mike's funeral. He should have one blood relative there at least, if his parents continued to act as if they didn't have a Marine for a son.

"I'll call you as soon as I know. I promise, Ash."

Ash talked with her a few more minutes, and she sounded calmer by the time they hung up. Kurtis was lucky to have her. There weren't many women who could handle being a Marine's wife. He turned to see Eli watching him as he cradled a cup of coffee in his hand. Damned if he wasn't lucky to have Eli too. He wanted those blue-gray eyes on him all the time, sometimes calm, sometimes stormy, sometimes laughing. He'd take him in any mood.

Ash tossed his phone down and absently patted Jabbers. "I need to talk to Sheriff Cooper."

Eli blinked, and then his brows came together in a frown. "What for? Wayne came to the office to apologize to me."

"He did? When?" Ash stuffed his feet into his sneakers. "Wait, tell me on the way."

"Okay." Eli disappeared into the bedroom and came back out shrugging into his shirt. "I'd still like to know why we're going."

"I need his help tracking down a person the fast way. I'm not sure if Mike had his brother listed as his next of kin or not, but I'm not going to take any chances by assuming that he is. Mike would want him to know what happened to him."

Ash tossed Eli his coat and held the door open for him. "Now tell me all about your meeting with Wayne."

ELI studied Ash as the cab crawled through the DC traffic toward Walter Reed Hospital. Ash was a doer, and the inactivity these past several hours was beginning to wear down his patience. Ash glared, tight-lipped, at the cars packed around them, and drummed his fingers on his knee.

"It's always a disaster when it rains," the cabbie said with a grimace as he laid on the horn and cut off another driver.

"And I'm reminded, yet again, why I'll never move to a city," Eli murmured under his breath.

The drumming ceased as Ash turned his face toward him. "Not even your beloved Boston?"

"If you think this is bad, try dealing with that commute every day." Eli briefly touched the back of Ash's hand. "We're almost there."

"Am I that bad?"

"I'm half-expecting you to get out and start directing traffic," Eli teased, though deep down he was worried. Ash hadn't shown one more crack in his demeanor since that morning. He'd buried himself into self-appointed tasks, finding Mike's brother, getting ahead on his schoolwork, and coordinating with Jamie. Now he was here in DC, to bury one friend and console another, and Eli wasn't sure how he was handling the pressure because Ash wouldn't talk about it at all.

"Don't tempt me. I just might." Ash leaned forward with an explosive breath as the hospital came into view. "About damned time," he growled. "Good thing we didn't stop by the hotel first."

Eli stifled a flutter of nerves as they got out of the cab and retrieved their bags. He would be meeting some of Ash's family, and others he considered family. At least Ash had shown no indication that he remembered Eli tossing around the L word the night he was drunk. And it wasn't that he didn't want to tell him, but Ash was under enough stress right now. If he didn't return the feeling, it would be just another pressure point on Ash. More guilt when he was already wrestling with an armful.

"Are you ready?" Eli asked as they stood outside, cold drizzle coming down from leaden skies.

"As ready as I can be," Ash said with a sigh as he shouldered his duffel bag. "Come on, they're waiting for us."

Eli had the nagging suspicion that something was eating at Ash. Something more than the circumstances, something that had made him get out that bottle of bourbon and drink himself into a stupor. It bugged Eli because he wanted to get it out of him before it began to fester. He just hoped that Ash wasn't blaming himself for not still being with his brothers in arms when the convoy had been attacked.

They walked down the hushed corridors, Ash's expression set in stone until they reached Kurtis's room. Green eyes flicked toward him, and Eli smiled, touching his shoulder. "Right behind you, Georgia."

Chaos erupted as soon as Ash opened the door. Eli held back as Ash was swarmed under women and toddlers. A petite dark-haired woman with short hair got to him first and hugged Ash fiercely as a taller, slightly plump redhead waited behind her, shifting in impatience. Two equally dark-haired children attached themselves to Ash's leg, babbling for attention.

"Out of the way, Jamie," the other woman said with a good-natured smile. "It's my turn to maul my brother."

The bed in the room stood empty, and there were signs that it had been occupied. One of the toddlers peered around Ash's leg and gave Eli a wave. He crouched down and waved back. "You must be Brandon."

He nodded and stopped trying to climb up Ash's leg in favor of attaching himself to Eli instead. "Unca?"

"Oh, no, buddy, I'm afraid not," Eli said with a spurt of panic. He'd never handled a kid this small before; what if he accidentally hurt him? "I'm a friend of Ash's."

"I'm so sorry about that," Jamie said, coming forward to scoop Brandon up in her arms. "He isn't stranger wary at all. I'm Jamie."

"Eli, I've heard so much about you." To Eli's surprise he found himself engulfed in a hug from Ash's sister. "I'm Melanie, Ash's older sister." The babble of greetings continued for a few more minutes, and it reminded Eli a bit of what it was like at his cousins' homes in Tennessee, family everywhere and all talking at once.

"Where is he?" Ash asked, glancing toward the bed. "Is he okay?"

"They're running some more tests on him. He should be back soon." Jamie worried her lip. "Physically, I think he'll recover and adapt. I don't know, he just seems so worn down right now."

"He just needs some time," Ash murmured to her, rubbing her back. "I think he was a little worn down before he was hurt. The best thing for him now would be to get him okay enough to be able to leave the hospital so he can go home. Brandon and Danielle are going to be the best medicine he's ever had. He can do all the rehab he needs in Atlanta."

"I hope you're right."

There it was again, Ash's tendency to take charge. He couldn't not do it when there was a situation to be dealt with. Eli watched Ash console Jamie, holding Danielle in his arms, as he wished Ash would let Eli console him in return. He longed to take Ash into his arms and hold him until his barriers broke down and he let a little more of his heartache pour out. It made Eli ache to see him so strong and know that Ash was hurting so bad inside.

"So you're the one who's finally run off with my brother's heart," Melanie said in an undertone as she plopped into a chair next to him.

"Oh, I don't know if it's gone that far yet," Eli replied in a voice just as soft. "I'm working on it."

Melanie's hair was a more brilliant copper than Ash's, and her eyes were a merry blue, but she had the same smattering of freckles on her face and her smile was as warm. "He brought you with him, didn't he?" She cocked her head, giving him an appraising look. "Aren't you his professor too?"

Eli could feel his cheeks warm under the scrutiny as he resisted the urge to shift in his seat like an abashed teenager. "I do have that distinction, but the, uh, the relationship started before we realized he was going to be in my class."

"He seduced you, didn't he?" Melanie shook her head as Eli coughed in surprise at her directness. "Dirty dog."

"Actually, it was mutual, or you could argue that I started by making eyes at him when I first saw him, but yeah, the actual seduction, very mutual." Now Eli did shift and cast a pleading glance toward Ash.

"Melanie, stop trying to dig smut details out of him," Ash said, giving her a narrow-eyed glare. "At least give him a chance to get used to you before you embarrass him to death."

Melanie snickered and patted Eli's hand. "It's so refreshing to see you protective over a boyfriend." She glanced at her watch and rose to take Brandon. "They should be back any minute, and the doctor's not going to want a ton of people around while they get Kurtis back into bed. I'll take the twins and Eli down to the cafeteria and you can text me when it's safe to come up again."

Eli stood up as well, seeing the sense in that, even if he hated leaving Ash. He cast his lover a questioning glance, and Ash nodded as he handed Danielle over. "I'm fine, Doc. I promise."

"You'd better be." Eli gingerly shifted Danielle in his arms, and she looked at him with a little frown at being disturbed. He hoped that he hadn't upset her; he knew nothing of toddlers. "I promise not to drop you if you promise not to start screeching on me, okay, sweetie?"

Melanie laughed as she led the way out of the room. "I wouldn't show any weakness to these two if you can help it, Eli. They are expert manipulators."

"I'll try to keep that in mind." Eli waited until they'd gone down the hallway a bit. "How is Kurtis, really? Ash is awfully worried."

"As good as he can be under the circumstances. He needs time. Time and care." Her eyes were serious as they entered the elevator. "How's my brother holding up? He sounded like ass when I first talked with him."

Eli choked out a laugh as Melanie shot him a quizzical look. "Sorry, Ash told me who your mom named you after, and the thought of Melanie Wilkes saying ass or asking about her brother's sex life...."

"Well, Mom got us all dead wrong. Our personalities couldn't be further from those characters if we tried."

The cafeteria was fairly quiet at this time of day, and they found a table in the corner. Melanie held onto Brandon when he tried to wiggle and get down. "Oh, no, boyo, it's time for you to nap. Look at your sister, she's already half gone."

Eli glanced down at Danielle, and sure enough her eyes were half-closed, her cheek pressed against his chest. "Poor girl, they must be exhausted with all of this uproar around them."

"Everyone is." Melanie studied him as she rocked back and forth with Brandon in her arms. "So you never answered my question. How's Ash?"

Eli hesitated, weighing Ash's tendency to be private against the obvious close relationship he had with his family. "He took it hard at first, but I think being down here and being able to do something, no matter how small, is good for him. He's not one to wait by the sidelines for news."

"No, not when he can throw himself into the thick of things," Melanie said as she patted Brandon on the back. "So you're the reason why my brother is hedging on taking that job offer in Atlanta."

Eli's heart lurched, and he glanced down at Danielle to mask his dismay. Ash had a job offer in Atlanta? That was news to him. "I don't think Ash has made any decisions about his career after college."

"I don't think he has either. But I do know that he's fallen in love with that town he moved to. He won't stop talking about it. He seems to have made a lot of friends there. I thought most small towns were supposed to treat newcomers like they didn't belong there."

"Amwich is a college town, so they're used to new faces coming and going." Ash had made himself at home there and he'd gotten close with Jonas and Cooper and several others. "I don't think it's me so much as he's comfortable there." He didn't dare believe that Ash might stay for him.

"That's what you think." Melanie shot him an amused smile. "Eli, my brother never would've brought you along if he wasn't a goner for you. And I just want to make sure that Ash isn't going to suffer an epic disappointment if he decides to stay."

"You know, you and my cousin Lu would get along very well." Eli hated the poking and prodding, but now that he thought about it, he was sure Ash had suffered the same at his cousin's hands. "I'll say this and no more: Ash means more to me than anyone in a long time, both as a friend and, well, you know."

Eli refused to tell Ash's sister that he was in love with him until he'd told Ash himself.

Melanie laughed and shifted the now-sleeping child in her arms. "Okay, I'll leave you be. I've got what I wanted."

Eli's lips twitched into a smile, despite his discomfort with the grilling. "Remind me to stay on your good side."

"Good idea."

CHAPTER 19

ASH'S stomach churned as he heard Kurtis's voice coming down the hall, and he steeled himself for his first glimpse of his best friend. It lurched again when the door opened and he came into view. Ash's gaze flicked down to the leg swathed in bandages. All of his half hopes that it was just a nightmare died and it was a struggle to remember the blessings. Then Kurtis saw him and his eyes lit up.

"Who the hell let you in here? Fuck, Ash, it's good to see your ugly face."

Ash grinned back at him, and some of the tightness in his throat eased. "Confused again, buddy, you're the one with a face like a horse's ass."

He resisted the urge to help Kurtis lever himself onto the bed by jamming his hands in his pockets. Kurtis wouldn't appreciate being treated as an invalid no matter the circumstances, and Ash put his hand on Jamie's arm as she started forward. Kurtis heaved himself over and pulled the sheet up to his waist, grimacing in pain until he got himself settled.

"Good thing I have such a big dick. It keeps me centered."

Ash burst out laughing and bumped fists with Kurtis, who winked at him. "You are a big dick, donkey."

Jamie made an exasperated sound and punched Ash on the arm before dropping a kiss on Kurtis's lips. "On that note, I'm leaving. I'm going to lay the twins down at the hotel before they start terrorizing people. You going to be okay?"

"No need to hover with Ash around, he'll do it enough for you both."

"Bullshit, I am not hovering."

"You're dying to. You're practically twitching where you're standing." Kurtis made a shooing motion at his wife, but tempered it with a smile. "Go, but don't be gone too long." He didn't come out and say the words. He didn't need to. His eyes said how much he'd missed her.

"And get some sleep yourself while you're at it," Ash added in as Jamie headed toward the door. Kurtis leaned his head back against the pillow, the pleasant mask fading as the lines on his face deepened. Ash had thought Kurtis had lost weight before all this happened, but it was hard to tell on the screen sometimes. Judging from his appearance, he'd lost even more since they'd last talked.

"Damn, Kurtis." He hooked a chair and sat down, struggling for a joke that would ease the knot in his chest and lighten the sudden serious mood. "I know MREs taste like shit, but you could've packed a few more of them on you. You look like Skeletor."

"You, sir, are no He-Man." Kurtis touched his thigh and grimaced. "And I'm lighter because of this. There is a good chunk of muscle missing from my calf."

An awkward silence fell between them, and Kurtis closed his eyes. "The worst part is, there's a tiny part of me that's relieved," he whispered.

Ash shifted uncomfortably, reminded of his own feelings when he first heard the news. "How so?"

"Not that I'm hurt and have to bust my ass before I walk again, but because now I can't re-enlist when my time's up. I've been struggling with the decision for months, to stay or to go. It was killing me. I wanted to be home with Jamie and the kids, not worrying when I was going to be shipped out again. But I also couldn't bring myself to say I was quitting because I knew what I was signing up for and I believe in it."

Ash stared down at his hands, remembering another hospital room that time he'd been the one in the bed and it had been Kurtis sitting beside him. "You can't let the guilt eat at you, man. It'll tear you apart if you let it."

"It has been." Kurtis plucked at the blanket covering his battered limb. "And I keep telling myself that this doesn't make me any less of a man, but it just seems so fucking hollow when Jamie looks at me. It's going to be a long time before I can stand on my feet again."

Ash didn't know whether to let go of some of his tension because Kurtis wasn't questioning *if* he'd walk again, just *when*, or worry more because the doctors were still considering amputation because of blood flow problems to the surrounding tissues. That would be another blow. "She's damn happy to have you home alive. We all are."

"I know that. Fuck, it's just knowing and believing are two different things. What if I lose it? How can she not look at me and not think she's tied to a—"

"Don't say it; you demean both you and her. I'm not going to pretend like she's not going to notice that your leg's messed up when she looks at you, and that for a while it might be the first thing she does see. It's going to be a reminder that she almost lost you. But she isn't going to stop loving you because of it. She's not like that. Come on, you know that."

"What about Brandon and Danielle?" Kurtis looked so damned troubled that Ash wished Eli were with him. He'd know what to say. Ash wasn't as good with expressing himself, the words seemed to get all tangled up inside him at the worst times.

"You've never not been able to do something that you set out to do. You've got to fix in your mind what kind of an attitude you want toward this. If you let it bitter you, then they'll grow up knowing you to be that kind of a man." Which Kurtis wasn't. He wasn't a fucking quitter, but Ash wasn't sure how to remind him of that. "Or they can see you as a man who overcame a pretty harsh setback, but still remained the guy that Jamie fell in love with."

Once again, silence fell between them as Ash struggled to think of something to say. Had it been like this for Kurtis when Ash had been injured? All he could recall was pain and being muddled with drugs and knowing Kurtis was there. "You've got to find a way to keep going on, even if you're angry right now, or scared, or whatever, you know? And you've got to give yourself time. This isn't something that's going to get straightened out in your head overnight."

Kurtis cast him a sideways glance, as if he was unsure whether or not he should say something. "I knew how freaked out you were when your Reserve unit got activated and you had to miss your spring classes for training. I never said anything, but I knew. And you still went back to Iraq without one word of complaint to anyone for the whole seven months you were there."

That had been one hell of a rough time. He'd known it was a possibility, but he hadn't been as prepared as he'd thought he was when it had happened. For a while there, he'd thought he'd never get a full night's sleep without reliving getting hurt in his dreams. Eventually that had faded. "I swore an oath."

"Yeah." Kurtis rubbed his thigh with a grimace. "What was going through your head when you decided to opt out?"

Ash remembered the same stay-or-go argument keenly, but it hadn't been as much of a struggle for him as it seemed to be with Kurtis. "I was disillusioned," he said, staring down at the scars on his arm. "With the military as a whole, not with the individual men I served with. It made the decision easier."

"But it still bugged you. I remember." Kurtis laid back and looked up at the ceiling. "I never thought less of you for getting out when you did. I don't know if I ever told you that."

Ash glanced down at his hands and nodded. "Thanks, that matters. I don't think any less of you, either, you know that, right? I can understand being torn between two different duties, both of which you take seriously."

Kurtis nodded, but didn't say anything as he continued to stare up at the ceiling.

"You're going to be okay."

"Yeah."

The room grew quiet as they both got lost in their own thoughts. Ash was still worried about Kurtis. His recovery was going to be long and challenging, but at least he didn't seem to be withdrawing in on himself as he'd seen other men do, as he'd almost done himself. Even if

Kurtis was quieter than normal, there were still those moments, the jokes and teasing, that gave Ash hope.

"You up to a little bit of company?" Ash asked, breaking the quiet. "I have someone I want you to meet."

Surprise flickered across Kurtis's face. "You brought someone with you?"

"I did. I hope you don't mind." Ash pulled out his cell phone to send Eli a text. "I can send him on to the hotel if you do."

"Wait a minute. You brought that professor you've been chasing after? Hot damn, Ash, I knew you were a goner."

Ash shifted in his chair as animation lit Kurtis's face. "I wouldn't go so far as to say that. We're taking it slow."

The energy faded and Kurtis sighed. "I would like to meet him, but not today. I have therapy in an hour, and that always gets me shagged. After that I have to meet with the fucking shrink. Right now I just want faces around me that I recognize. He'll understand, right?"

Ash quickly sent Eli a message and nodded his head. "He will. You'll see when you do get to meet him. He's pretty damn... I don't know... special."

"Oh God, you've got it bad, man. Sap is oozing from your pores."

"Shut the fuck up. I'm not that bad," Ash replied, shifting in his chair once again. Kurtis started chuckling, and Ash told himself that his friend's teasing had to be a good sign.

"Yes, you are. You should see your face right now." It was hard to come up with any defense to that when Ash really wanted to have Eli here with him.

"Don't think I won't kick your ass just because you're in the hospital."

Kurtis snorted, his eyes brightening in challenge. "Don't think I still can't take you because I've got a fucked-up leg."

ASH came through the hotel room door and slumped against it, weariness etched across his face. It made Eli ache to see that stoic mask drop. The last couple days had been rough on Ash, and he hoped that Mike's funeral this morning had brought his lover some closure.

"What time are you going to go visit Kurtis?" Eli asked as he shrugged out of his coat and tossed it over the back of a chair.

"Not for several hours. He's got physical therapy and he usually needs some time to himself afterward."

Eli brushed his fingers over the medals on Ash's chest. The midnight-blue coat stretched across his broad shoulders and was cut to fit his chest. The belt emphasized his trim waist. As good as the man looked in his dress uniform, he'd be more comfortable with it off. "Come on, Georgia, I think you need a little R & R."

A tired smile flickered over Ash's lips. "You know, ever since I've met you, you've been tending to me."

"I think you're imagining things." Eli took Ash's hand and drew him through their suite.

"So you're not the one who gave me a massage that first night? Or threw me into the shower when you found me dead drunk and poured me into bed afterward?"

"Maybe you have a point," Eli said as Ash began to get undressed, hanging up his uniform as he went. "I think a repeat of both is in order." He slipped his arm around Ash's waist and kissed his shoulder as Ash leaned back against him. "A hot shower followed by a massage."

And a long nap. Ash hadn't been sleeping very well, and they both had to be back home and at school before they knew it. He did not want Ash going back exhausted and stressed, not with finals coming up.

"That does sound good." Ash turned his head and kissed Eli lingeringly. "But only if I get to tend to you right back."

Eli smiled, stroking his fingers along the tense muscles of Ash's stomach. As hard as these last few days had been, he loved going to sleep next to Ash and waking up beside him. When the semester was over, if Ash felt the same way he did, Eli wanted to talk Ash into moving in with him.

And if Ash wanted to leave for Atlanta come spring, Eli would deal with that then. He'd asked Melanie some more questions about that job offer, and it sounded like everything that Ash could want. He'd be near family and his best friend, who'd be able to use his support. He'd be working toward national defense security and protecting US soldiers.

Thinking about inviting Ash to live with him had to be the biggest step he'd ever made. His grandparents' house had always been a haven to him, and the idea of opening it up to someone else shouldn't be so easy, but with Ash, it was. That in itself was scary. In the back of his mind he kept telling himself that Ash would leave, just like everyone else. And his damned foolish heart kept replying that Ash was different, and even if he did leave, this time with him was worth it.

"I like the sound of that." Eli's heart skipped a beat as he undressed and followed Ash into the shower. There wasn't much room, not that Eli needed an excuse to mold himself to Ash. Hot water poured down their bodies and steam filled the air as Ash turned around in his arms to face him.

"I'm sorry you've been stuck in the hotel while I visit Kurtis," Ash murmured, pressing his forehead against Eli's.

"I didn't come for him," Eli replied, cupping the nape of Ash's neck. "I came for you."

Ash's eyes warmed as he pressed Eli back against the tiles. "And it's what kept me together, so let me thank you."

Eli's heart flipped again as Ash kissed him slow and deep. Damn, he loved Ash. It was on his lips to say it when the kiss broke, but he stopped himself. No, now wasn't the time. Later, when Kurtis was steadier and Ash wasn't so vulnerable.

Then Ash knelt, and Eli groaned as he took Eli's cock into his mouth, sinking all the way down. Eli couldn't get enough of Ash's mouth, and the expression in his eyes tore down all of Eli's defenses. He sighed, leaning his head back on the tiles. "Fuck... I do love you."

His heart lurched. Oh God, he couldn't believe he'd just blurted it out loud like that. He was such a fucking idiot. Already flushed from the shower, his cheeks heated even more. His heart pounded and his stomach clenched as he waited for Ash to push away. Eli glanced down at him, and his embarrassment faded at the sparkle in Ash's eyes and at how goddamned sexy he looked with his mouth stretched around Eli's cock.

"I'm that good, huh?" Ash teased, after slipping his mouth off and flicking the head with his tongue.

"Something like that," Eli replied, both relieved and disappointed that Ash seemed to think he was joking. Then Ash took him into his mouth again and it was hard to feel disappointed about anything. Not when Ash was going down on him like he was worshiping Eli's cock. "Oh dear God."

Eli slid his hands over Ash's short hair. The combination of the hot suction of Ash's mouth, the steamy air, and the light in Ash's eyes as he looked at Eli as if he were the only person that mattered in the world made it hard for Eli to catch his breath. Ash's hands slid up Eli's thighs, cupped his hips and pinned him to the tiles as his mouth worked him. "Fuck, Ash."

Ash bobbed his head faster, his tongue alternating between lashing and stroking as Eli panted curses and pleas. He had Eli caught good. A blunt finger sank into him, and Eli's thighs trembled. "Dammit, keep doing that and I'm yours for life."

Ash answered that with a harder suck and a swirl of his tongue that left Eli gasping. His balls tightened as he groaned, and Eli vowed that in just a few minutes he'd give Ash a taste of the same pure torment.

"You have the sexiest expression on your face," Ash said, pausing in his sucking to nuzzle at Eli's balls. Another finger sank inside of him, twisting, teasing as Ash mouthed his sac.

"My turn," Eli panted, and Ash shook his head, thrusting hard with his fingers.

"Not until I'm done with you." Ash continued to thrust as he sank his mouth down again. Fuck, the man could deepthroat. Ash quickly found a rhythm between his fingers and mouth that had Eli on the edge and begging. But it was that happy sparkle in Ash's eyes that sent him roaring over. He was so in love with Ash it wasn't even funny.

Eli's orgasm left him gasping, leaning against the tiles for support as Ash grinned up at him, the tension and exhaustion gone from his face. "You get the hottest expression on your face when you come."

"And you say the damndest things." Eli held out his hand to help him up, but Ash shook his head and grabbed the soap.

"I'm not done yet," Ash said as he lathered up a washcloth. "We're tending to each other remember? I'm going first." The cloth slid up Eli's legs, soaping him from his toes to the tops of his thighs. "You know, I really love your legs."

Ash made a sexy sight himself on his knees, his skin flushed from the heat, his body cut from working it hard. And as much as Eli wanted to get his hands on him, Ash wouldn't let him budge until he'd washed every inch of him. "My turn," Eli breathed, snatching the washcloth away.

Eli turned Ash toward the wall and started with his back, watching the way the water ran the soap off of him almost as soon as it touched his skin. The burn mark on his side extended an inch or two onto his back, and there were other smaller scars, white with age, but they didn't take anything away from how beautiful Eli found him. It made him ache instead, with love and desire, and the persistent nagging wish that Ash would remain his for the rest of their lives.

He knelt behind Ash and was faced with the tightest ass he'd ever had the pleasure to lay his eyes on. Small and perfect, just the right size for Eli to lay his hands on. He tossed aside the washcloth and soaped his hands instead, running them over the taut skin, teasing his fingers along the cleft as Ash caught his breath.

Eli grinned and pushed his cheeks apart, watching the water run down to his puckered hole. "Don't want to miss this spot," he murmured and leaned in, rubbing his tongue over Ash's entrance.

Ash groaned, laying his cheek against the tiles. "Aw, damn, Eli."

Eli smiled at the sound of that husky voice and pressed a kiss against Ash's contracting hole. He flicked his tongue again, teasing, probing as Ash shuddered, making the sexiest pleading sound in the back of his throat. It wasn't something Eli had heard from him before and he wanted more. "Spread your legs wider, Georgia."

He had Ash shift until he was leaning against the tiles, arms braced and legs spread. There wasn't any room in the shower, but Eli didn't care as he went right back to tormenting Ash. He slid his hand between Ash's thighs and cupped his balls. Then he returned right back to Ash, spread out before him, and pushed his tongue inside him.

Ash groaned, his body jerking, and Eli would've smiled again if his mouth wasn't so busy. He worked his tongue, alternating between circling it and pushing it inside. "I never would've taken you for a squirmer," he teased, nipping one smooth cheek.

"You never seen me with the devil kneeling behind me," Ash said, looking over his shoulder at him. "You're enough to make any man crazy."

"I'm just getting started." Eli pushed his hair out of his face and ran his hands over Ash's legs. He wasn't going to stop until Ash was as crazy about him as Eli was for his lover. There was no getting Ash out of his system. And one way or another, he'd get Ash to realize just how good they were together.

ASH stared up at the ceiling, fingers playing with the ends of Eli's hair as his thoughts whirled in endless circles. Eli didn't stir when he slept, and his head was heavy on Ash's shoulder. He was enjoying that weight right now and the feel of Eli's breath on his bare skin. It kept him grounded.

His thoughts returned to Kurtis, struggling to cope with the sudden changes in his life. Guilt. His friend felt guilty for surviving. Guilty for that brief moment of relief that it hadn't been him who was being buried in Arlington. It made Ash writhe inside for the same reasons it no doubt made Kurtis writhe.

What the hell was wrong with him? That moment of relief ate at him like acid in his veins.

Beating himself up wouldn't make Mike come back, but telling himself that didn't help much. Seeing Mike's brother at the funeral had helped some, because sure enough, the man's parents hadn't come to bury their son.

Still, that hadn't been as much comfort as Eli's quiet, solid presence next to him as they lowered Mike into the ground. Ash wouldn't have ever met Eli if it wasn't for Mike. He wouldn't have had a chance to hold Kurtis's kids or help his friend come to terms with his injuries. Fuck that moment of relief. Ash squeezed his eyes shut as they burned. If only he could take that thought back. Just remembering it made Ash want another drink.

He wasn't going to go down that path.

Ash turned his head and brushed his lips over Eli's forehead, breathing in the scent of his hair. His thoughts skittered back to Mike with a brief surge of remembered fear as he recalled the day he almost died. He could still remember that woman's eyes, large and dark, fringed with long, black lashes. They'd been beautiful eyes that didn't belong to a killer. He'd never forgotten those eyes.

Every time Ash thought he'd left the past behind him, something would remind him vividly of that day. Like when his reserve unit had been activated, or getting that phone call about Kurtis and Mike. And he'd be right back there, remembering those eyes and the stony expression in them that he'd so stupidly missed at first. He'd seen what she'd wanted him to see until it was too late.

Caught between being asleep and wakefulness, the memories overwhelmed him until Ash jerked himself out of them. He froze, his breath unsteady as Eli stirred next to him. He slid his hand soothingly along Ash's side and tipped his head back to look at him with a sleepy gaze.

"Your heart's pounding."

"It's nothing," Ash replied, laying a kiss on those upturned lips. "Go back to sleep."

Concern darkened Eli's blue-gray eyes, and he hesitated before speaking. "You know, you can talk to me. I'm not going to suddenly think you're hateful just because you tell me what's been bugging you. It goes deeper than Kurtis and Mike, doesn't it?"

Ash's hand stilled on Eli's back, the other man's hair still tangled around his fingers. "Isn't that enough? Anything more would be selfish of me, wouldn't it?" he said lightly, looking back up the ceiling as his heart started to race again.

"You're not selfish."

"Known me only a couple months and already you can say what manner of a man I am?" Ash replied, his insides roiling into a tumbled mess. "You're not the best judge of character."

Eli spoke of love during the heat of sex, but he never said anything like that any other time. What did he really feel for Ash? And how would that change when Ash told him about all the ugly things from his past? When he told him his initial reaction when he heard about Kurtis and Mike. Eli was fiercely independent, and Ash couldn't see him sticking with one man for very long. Best not to let himself get too caught up in how good Eli made him feel.

Eli stiffened next to him and then propped himself up to give Ash an intent look. "Don't try to pick a fight with me. Wayne's a good man who made stupid decisions. I think we've all been there at some time."

"Didn't stop you from misjudging him when his intentions were staring you right in the face."

Eli's gaze narrowed and his jaw squared. "Who's this really about, Ash? Me or you?" Ash closed his eyes, hiding from blue-gray eyes only to be confronted with darker ones. Eyes he'd misjudged. Fingers brushed his side, and Eli's hand splayed on Ash's stomach. "What is it?" Eli asked quietly.

Ash loved the sound of Eli's voice, warm and compelling, just like the man. He loved him. Ash's eyes popped open as he took in Eli's face, hovering close to his own, and all those feelings that he hadn't realized he'd been holding at bay flooded through him.

He was in love with Eli.

"It's an ugly story."

"Maybe it's time you told it to me. Maybe I'm not the best judge of character, but I am a good listener."

Eli wouldn't press him if Ash told him he wasn't ready or didn't feel like talking, and that was what decided him. Eli would give him all the time he needed. Just knowing that was enough.

"We were in Iraq, and damn, it was such a hot mess that year, suicide bombings, car bombings, people getting kidnapped everywhere. The tension was so fucking brutal."

All the chaos was enough to make a man crazy. There were days when it seemed like the entire world had gone insane or the real world had ceased to exist and all that was left was this hot hell that he couldn't escape. Talking about it put him right back in his memories, smelling the stink of his own sweat and the fear that permeated everything, until Eli started rubbing a thumb over his skin.

"We were trying to help the police force get a handle on things, and it was so damned difficult when you couldn't trust anyone. It was so fucked up, Eli, you just don't know. They were using kids to trigger some of those bombs. Who the fuck does something like that?"

That still fucked him up inside, all those little bodies and haunted eyes.

"I can't begin to imagine what it was like for you." Eli's fingers continued to soothe, stroking Ash's stomach. "Or how close you must be with Kurtis. He was there with you, right?"

"Yeah." There was no jealousy in Eli's expression. Some guys might not understand, might resent that closeness, but not him. It filled Ash with a profound sense of relief. He'd had one too many lovers who'd been threatened by that and had given him hell. If there was no trust, then what was the point? "He kept me from going nuts in the burn unit after I got hurt."

"And you're keeping him from going crazy now. And from what you've told me of him, he doesn't seem like the kind to turn his back on the world and his family."

"He's not." Ash had to remember that, had to believe in it so Kurtis saw it when they talked.

He tightened his arm around Eli, determined to get the rest of the story out. "We were on patrol, trying to make it so people could come out of their damn houses without wondering if they were gonna get their guts blown out when they did. This woman ran toward me, staggering as if she were in shock, her belly big. And I didn't see what I should've seen. I saw what she wanted me to see."

A pregnant woman mourning.

"It all happened so damn fast. I've got her eyes seared into my damn brain. I don't think I'll forget them as long as I live. She began shouting, hell, everyone did. I should've shot her, but I froze. Dammit, Eli, I hesitated. My instincts screamed that she was a suicide bomber, and I still couldn't pull the trigger. It's what I was trained to do and I didn't."

"They didn't train you to kill mothers and kids, Ash. Despite what you know now, when you looked at her at that moment, that's what you saw. Hindsight gives too many opportunities to say, I should've done this or that without really taking into account what was going on at the time."

"Yeah, well, that hesitation cost too damn much. Domingo shoved me, and the next thing I knew I was waking up in the middle of a firestorm. Rubble had me pinned down. A truck was on fire and when the tank blew, it was going to take me with it. Domingo was dead, staring at me no more than a foot away. And that fucking fire kept snaking closer, moving so damned fast. There was nothing I could do to stop it, not even when it reached me." He ground his teeth together. "I couldn't move."

Eli's eyes darkened as his fingers traced the scar on Ash's side. "Jesus, Ash."

"I think the anticipation was almost worse. As soon as it reached me, Mike was there, yanking me out from under the rubble, carrying me free. He wound up in the hospital with me, both of us with shrapnel and burns. Mike saved my ass."

Ash's throat closed up. "Damn, Eli, you're going to think I'm the biggest jerk-off fucker in the world, but when I heard about Mike and Kurtis...." He stopped, unable to say more.

Eli cocked his head, his brow furrowing, his fingers stilling. "What, Ash? You had a thank God moment or something? That Kurtis hadn't died instead?"

"How'd you know?"

"You're human, Ash. Just because you had that momentary thought doesn't mean that you wanted Mike dead or that you weren't grateful for what he did for you. It doesn't make you any of those things you've been calling yourself. Is that why you got drunk?" Ash nodded, and Eli slid his hand around the nape of Ash's neck and pressed their foreheads together. "You were a man who was hit with the terrible truth of one friend dead and another hurt. Ripping yourself to shreds isn't going to bring Mike back."

"Not agonizing over it is easier said than done," Ash whispered, blinking away the stinging in his eyes. "He deserved more."

"That could be said for a lot of people." Eli relaxed against him, curling his arm around Ash's waist. It absolutely amazed him that there was no condemnation in Eli's eyes, no disgust. It made Ash wonder if there had been more behind those words that Eli spoke in the heat of passion. Maybe Eli did love him back, Ash just wasn't sure. "But you brought his brother when he never would've known that Mike had died. Maybe that will balance out your sense of karma."

"Maybe." Ash trailed his fingers through Eli's hair then turned, bearing him back to the bed and pinning Eli under him. "I think you balance me more."

"You're pretty balanced all on your own, Ash. You don't need me."

"Bullshit. I need you plenty." Ash glanced at the clock and decided they still had a little time before he had to go to the hospital. "Let me show you."

CHAPTER 20

ONLY two more weeks and the semester would be over. Eli stole a glance at Ash, who had his head together with Nori as they went over the final points for their joint presentation. Ash would keep her from holding back out of shyness. Anybody else in the class would've overwhelmed her with the force of their own personality, whether they meant to or not.

Ash glanced up and gave Eli a quick wink and a grin, filling him with a rush of warmth. Two more weeks, and he could be with that man openly. He couldn't wait. Well, maybe he should wait until grades were posted, but that was only another week. Three weeks seemed like forever.

It didn't help that Eli was still trying to work out how Ash felt about him. The man had opened up quite a bit since they'd been in DC. He wasn't the kind of man to usually talk about himself, and Eli hadn't realized how much Ash had held back until he started sharing. It wasn't much, little tidbits about himself that he hadn't offered before. More talk about his admiration for Sheriff Cooper. Nothing about his future plans, though.

Now that Kurtis was responding to therapy and he'd been able to keep his leg, Eli didn't have the same reservations over talking about their future. He'd have to ask Ash about that job offer over dinner tonight. That wasn't the only good news. There had been no more break-ins or blackmail notes; Britton had even stayed away. This was almost the life he'd dreamed of for himself. His gaze drifted to Ash once again. He was worse than a teenager pining over a crush in class. At least no one was paying attention to him.

"Daydreaming, Doc?"

Eli fiddled with the ring on his cuff as he met Ash's eyes. "Just making notes for later."

Ash turned his attention back to Nori after one more secret smile for him. Eli stared back down at the papers on his lap, suppressing a sigh. Once the semester was over, he could feel out where Ash stood. And he hoped Ash was right where Eli was and wanted to take that next step forward. He wanted Ash in his home permanently, not just for weekends here and there.

Eli forced his thoughts back to the task at hand and scribbled a few more notes. The sudden quiet amongst his students had him raising his head again, and he blinked at the sight of Britton standing not two feet away from him with a pleased look in his eyes.

"Dean Newton wants to speak with you right now."

Eli's heart sank into his stomach. What was it this time? "Can it wait until class is over? It's only another ten minutes."

"No, he insisted that it be now," Britton replied, an aggravated, petulant note creeping into his voice. Eli wasn't sure what was going on with the other man, but there were times when he seemed to be losing his grip on things. Petulant did not suit him at all.

"Of course." Eli rose and turned to face eight pairs of curious eyes and one pair of angry, worried green ones. "I trust you will carry on without me? We'll start the final presentations on Wednesday."

"Sure, Doc," Ash said, cutting a hard glance at Britton. "We'll be ready."

As Eli followed him out, he heard whispers springing up behind him. As always, Britton's timing sucked. He could've waited another ten minutes. But why do that when he could make a situation as uncomfortable as possible for Eli?

He didn't bother with making small talk or trying to figure out what was going on as they walked to the dean's office. There was little point, and he was too busy trying to keep his stomach from churning. Eli could only think of one reason for an interruption of his class and that was a family emergency. A lump rose in his throat. *Please let Lu be okay.* Eli wouldn't ask Britton. If it was bad news, he'd rather hear it from a friend.

Dean Newton's secretary showed them in, and one look at the grave expression on the man's dark face had Eli's hands turning icy with fear. It was bad. The dean always had a genuine smile on his face. "It must be huge for you to pull me out of class," Eli said as soon as the door shut behind them. "May I ask what's going on?"

The dean's expression became even more serious as he looked at Britton. "You interrupted a class?"

"It was almost over." Britton waved dismissively.

Eli gritted his teeth. He could almost hear the man's thoughts: *it was a Cultural Studies class so what did it matter?* It certainly didn't bear the same prestige as Britton's own focus with Eighteenth Century Literature. "Final presentations are due to start on Wednesday. I should've been there in case any of them had any questions or concerns. But since we're already here and it's too late to go back, we might as well get on with it."

"Please, sit, both of you. Eli, I'm sorry that your class was interrupted. That shouldn't have happened." Dean Newton gestured toward the chairs. Eli quelled his unease and sat down, acute distaste going through him as Britton elected to remain standing, no doubt so he could loom over Eli. Asshole.

The dean kept giving him glances that told Eli whatever bullshit Britton had stirred up this time was something that the dean was taking seriously. So Eli needed to as well. "A very serious accusation has been brought against you, Eli, one that I have to look into. Especially since Britton claims to have some proof."

The lead ball dropped in Eli's stomach. He knew he should've come forward to the dean about Ash; he'd meant to and then he'd promptly forgotten his vow in all the chaos surrounding Ash's friends. Fuck, what kind of proof could Britton have? Ash wasn't over every night, and his house was very isolated. Eli couldn't picture anyone in town talking to Britton, not when he treated most of the people in Amwich as being beneath his notice.

"What's the accusation, sir?"

"That you're having a long-term affair with a student and skewing grades in their favor." The guilt that had assailed Eli as the dean started talking was immediately swallowed by hot anger as he continued.

"Britton has already looked into a complaint over unfair grading." Eli glanced at Britton who looked too entirely self-satisfied for Eli's comfort. "And he deemed that those charges were unfounded."

"I do recall that concern. But this matter of an affair changes things." Dean Newton turned his attention toward Britton. "Randall, you said you have proof? I would like to see it and I'm sure Eli would as well."

"Is this enough to hold a hearing?" Britton dug into his breast pocket, pulled out an envelope and handed it to the dean. It didn't look as if it contained any pictures, and Eli breathed an inward sigh of relief. He didn't want Ash's name dragged into this mess if he could help it. "I found it in Eli's office."

Eli could not figure out what that envelope might hold, but whatever was inside it made the dean's brows leap up into his hairline. He passed the note to Eli without a word and Eli stifled a groan as he recognized Wayne's untidy scrawl on the taped-together page. There were pieces missing, but enough remained to damn him.

Last chance, Eli. You have my card. Give it over or I'm going to the head of college about your affair with your student.

Fucking son of a bitch. Britton had gone through his trash. What kind of low life, dipshit asshole went through someone's trash searching for dirt? The violation from Wayne was bad enough, but at least he'd been looking out for his dad. From Britton it made him ill because there was just no sane reason for it.

The recognition must've shown on his face, because when he looked at the dean next, there was a profound disappointment in his eyes. How could he explain the note while keeping Ash's name away from Britton? He trusted Dean Newton, but he didn't trust Britton not to bring Ash up on a hearing as well. Fuck, and how could he explain it without sounding like a certified lunatic or getting Wayne tossed in jail for breaking into his office? Britton and the dean were both still hot about that.

"I can explain that note," Eli said with a calm in his voice that he sure as hell didn't feel.

"I think it speaks for itself," Britton began, but Dean Newton waved him to silence.

"I would like to hear what Eli has to say."

Eli's mind raced as he handed the note back to the dean. "I was having a personal problem over some heirlooms that belonged to the man who wrote this note. He believed that I had them. He let his emotions get the best of him and tried underhanded tactics, but we worked things out."

"Eli, that is not enough," the dean said with a hint of exasperation. He frowned as he read the note again. "How could he blackmail you if he didn't at least believe it to be true?"

"There was no blackmail. I never paid him a dime, and he admitted to me that he had nothing to back the accusation on. He's just been in a rough spot and not thinking clearly lately, and we had worked it all out."

"Would you be willing to tell us who wrote the note?" Dean Newton leaned forward in his chair, fixing Eli with an intent look. "Would he corroborate your story?"

Eli frowned, worrying one of the cuff rings. He didn't want to lie. Lying now would make it even harder for Dean Newton to trust him when he spoke to him in private. And he sure as hell didn't want to tell Britton who wrote the note. What a fucking messed-up tangle. When had everything gotten to be so confusing?

"If he's telling the truth, then we can figure it all out during a hearing," Britton said smoothly. "I know who Hollister was speaking to, and I'm sure I can get him to testify before the panel. I'll also get the student in question. I've seen them together on more than one occasion. A student, might I add, who has a history of trouble with the university."

Eli tugged harder on his cuffs at the thought of Britton spying on them. He would bet that it had been Britton hiding in the woods that day. And the idea of Ash having a bad rep at Amwich was ludicrous.

"In the meantime, I'd like to suggest that Eli be suspended from classes until the hearing is over."

"The hell you will," Eli snapped, jumping to his feet. "I have presentations this week, and final exams to prep for. I think you've disturbed my students enough this semester with your hysterical, paranoid rantings."

Britton's face flushed a bright red and his jowls quivered. "You are done here, Hollister. You might as well pack it up now before you bring this institution any further disgrace."

"Bullshit!" Eli opened his mouth to say everything he'd been dying to say to Britton for a long time and then forced himself to get a grip. It would solve nothing, it wouldn't change Britton's opinion of him one bit, and he was already picking his way through a minefield. He didn't want to alienate Dean Newton even more by sinking down to Britton's level.

He unclenched his hands, turned to the dean and blocked out Britton. "With respect, sir. Either have my hearing tomorrow so I can be back in class on Wednesday, or have someone nondisruptive observe me for the rest of the semester, if that would ease your mind. But please don't let my classes be disturbed any more than they already have been."

"Don't—"

Once again the dean cut Britton off with a quick gesture. "I think it'll be difficult for Randall to get everyone he'll need together by tomorrow. We'll schedule the hearing for Friday. I'd like to get the matter resolved quickly and quietly as well. And I won't suspend you, not yet, however, I will agree to having someone observe your classes."

Eli nodded, unhappy with the idea of having someone breathing down the back of his neck, but that alternative was better than being banished completely. If it wasn't for the fact that turning in his resignation would be letting Britton win, he would do it right this damn second. He was sick and tired of the constant suspicion hanging over him, even if, in this case, some of the allegations were true. "Yes, sir."

"In that case, I'll observe his classes."

Eli stopped himself from blistering the air with curses and turned on Britton. "I said nondisruptive. You would be the worst of distractions. Besides, shouldn't you be busy gathering your so-called evidence and witnesses against me?"

"You also have your own classes to attend to, and to be honest, Randall, you're not objective when it comes to Eli. I'd hoped you two could work out your differences on your own, but it's clear that I'm going to have to step in, and I'm not at all pleased at having to do so."

Dean Newton paused and stared them both down, his dark eyes fierce. "You're both dismissed. Randall, I'll see you on Friday. Eli, when is your next class?"

Eli grabbed a pen and pad of paper so he could write out his schedule for the dean, and the snick of the door closing told him that they were now alone. He could feel the other man's eyes on him, and the sick feeling returned to his stomach, worse this time. He might not care for Britton's good opinion, but he respected Dean Newton.

"Sir, I meant to bring this to you before, and I didn't. I thought I could ride out the rest of Britton's year as head and maybe my own pride got in the way." Eli set the pad down and met the dean's eyes. "But there are some things you should be aware of."

Dean Newton sat back in his chair and folded his hands against his stomach as he studied Eli. "I'm listening."

"Britton's behavior has deteriorated rapidly over this semester. Barging into my office is one thing, but bringing up student complaints in front of other students, which he has done, is an ethical violation, so is breaking into my office to get that note. I don't care how friendly he is with the departmental secretary. I ripped the note up without reading it and threw it away in front of the man who gave it to me. Not to mention interrupting my class today. There have been times when he's forgotten things I've said from one minute to the next, and his temper has been out of control."

Dean Newton sighed and leaned forward. "Those are very serious accusations as well. This witness that Randall plans on getting, would he corroborate that you tossed the note?"

Eli hoped that Wayne would, but he'd rather not bring him into it. What if Britton was able to offer Wayne money or something? Wayne would jump all over that and not care if he screwed Eli in the process. He hated to think like that, especially since Wayne had apologized, but he didn't trust Wayne like he used to. "I don't know, to be honest. I'd like to think he'd tell the truth, but I just don't know anymore."

He closed his eyes. Fuck, he felt so damn worn down. He didn't even know right now if he cared anymore. Then, one more thought struck him and brought back all of his anger. "Another thing, sir. How would Britton know if I've changed any grade, for any student? He doesn't have access to my grade book. He wouldn't know who's getting what unless he broke into my office."

"A good question, and one I'll look into." Dean Newton held out his hand for the schedule and looked it over with pursed lips. "I'm sure others in the department will have noticed his behavior if it's as erratic as you say. If he's harassing you as much as you claim he is, and if he's breaking into offices and disclosing student information, I'll remove him as head. If he's got proof that you're sleeping with one of your undergraduate students, you'll be gone too. Understood?"

"Understood." Eli pressed his lips together and tried to console himself that it was only his head on the line, not Ash's. He supposed he could send out some more feelers over the semester break and use the rest of the year to hopefully land another job. "Who will be overseeing my classes?"

"I'll observe, and it'll be just your Historic Letters class since Britton alleges the student is in there. I'm not concerned about the others. You can go now."

The tone of dismissal was absolute, and Eli realized it was pointless to try to argue his case further. He gathered his things, and as soon as he was back out in the hallway he sent a quick text to Ash to make sure he was not waiting for him in his office. No need to make things easier for Britton than they already were. It was going to be hard enough to mitigate the damage as it was.

AT THE last minute Ash remembered that Wayne's dad was living with him, and that he still hadn't fully recovered from the stroke, so he just knocked on the door when he really wanted to beat it down with his fist. A tight, fearful expression crossed Wayne's face as he opened it and saw Ash on the porch.

"I don't have anything to say to you, so you can just turn around and go back to town."

Ash stuck his foot in the door before Wayne could shut it again, his temper simmering even hotter. "Trust me, Wayne, you do *not* want me heading back into town." He'd thought of landing a good, hard punch on Wayne's jaw a couple of times for good measure. Only the thought of having to tell Eli that he'd done it was enough to keep his fury under check. He also had to remember that was assault and that it would look very bad on his record.

"Britton already called and asked me to testify. I suppose I should've known you'd be on by. Come on in." Wayne stepped back and held the door open for Ash. "You going to have me arrested now, like Eli said you would? I swear I didn't give that note to Britton. I don't know how he got it."

"Believe me, it did cross my mind. Eli has managed to convince me that this didn't happen on purpose. He seems to think that Britton was listening at his door. I guess I shouldn't be surprised you already know what happened. It's not going about town, is it?" Ash nodded toward his truck. "We need to talk, but not here. I don't want to get your dad worked up. So let's go for a little ride."

Wayne's face became pasty, and his eyes widened. "It was an accident. Don't turn me in to Cooper."

Ash grabbed Wayne by the front of his overalls and dragged him out onto the porch. "You know, I really don't give a shit how you feel about this, Wayne. Everything you did, you brought on yourself. The only one I'm concerned about it is Eli, who's in a lot of fucking trouble between your bullshit and Britton's vendetta. Get in the damn truck."

From what Eli had told him, it seemed that Wayne was Britton's ace in the hole. The whole hearing had to be based on what Wayne could tell them. Ash had received a demand from the man to show up at the hearing as well, and a few quick phone calls had let him know that everyone else in their class had received the same e-mail. Ash was pretty certain Britton didn't actually know which student it was, or else Britton would've tried to pin him down personally to come. He was looking for Wayne to out Eli and him publicly.

Ash had hated seeing that look of stunned helplessness on Eli's face and having him try to hide his expression out of some mistaken belief that Ash would think Eli had regrets about them. He didn't like hearing Eli talk about other possible colleges when Ash knew that he'd be miserable moving away. Ash wouldn't accept that, which meant Britton needed to be discredited beyond any hope of recovering his reputation.

"I can't leave my dad behind." Wayne glanced back at the house, and Ash knew that if he gave the man an opportunity to scurry back in he'd never have another chance at him. Wayne was too afraid of the consequences of his actions to speak out in Eli's defense. There was no way they'd be able to keep what he did silent, and when the rest of the town found out, his reputation would be ruined, possibly what was left of his business too.

An older woman with graying hair came out onto the porch, drying her hands on a paper towel. "Is everything okay?"

"Everything is fine, ma'am. I just need to talk to Wayne about a situation." This had to be Mr. Grayson's nurse. The way Wayne wouldn't meet his eyes told him that his excuses about his father had been just that, fucking excuses to get out of this confrontation. "Wayne and I were just leaving. He'll be back soon." Ash shot the man a hard look, daring Wayne to contradict him.

Wayne mumbled something under his breath that Ash couldn't make out and then stomped over toward Ash's truck. Ash nodded at the nurse. "Ma'am." Then he turned to follow. Okay, now to convince Wayne that testifying for Britton would be a very bad idea. He sure as hell wasn't going to let that bastard boot Eli out of a place that he loved.

CHAPTER 21

ELI tried to quell his nerves, with little success. It didn't help that he was pretty sure Ash was up to something, though it was hard to be certain because after he'd told Ash everything, he hadn't seen him once outside of class. And during that class, the dean sat in his own armchair and thankfully made himself a part of the discussion instead of sitting back, staying silent, and just taking notes.

His students had gone from being sullen and withdrawn to opening up before the class had ended. The only one who hadn't seemed affected at all was Ash, which only deepened Eli's suspicions. How the kids had found out about the whole mess was still a mystery to him. If Ash had told them… Eli couldn't think of anything dire enough, but he'd figure something out.

Eli laced his fingers together as the committee took their seats with Dean Newton and Britton. Today, it didn't matter how long he'd known them or how good his track record was as a professor. It all depended on how Britton was going to twist things to suit his own worldview, and Eli still didn't know how the hell he was going to defend himself.

His mood darkened even more as the door opened again and his students filed in one by one. Nori and Whitney looked as sick as he felt. Ash's expression was impossible to read, and Kerry, bless her, looked downright militant. He was grateful that Elsa and Hannah sat on each side of her; maybe they would keep her from starting a ruckus. Eli ground his teeth together and glared at Britton.

"Don't you think involving them is taking this a little too far? Wouldn't this be a violation of student privacy?"

"It already involves all of them. The rest have a right to know that they're not getting the same perks as your lover," Britton snapped right back, with a glance in Ash's direction.

"We want to be here, Dr. Hollister," Bron said, giving him a tight smile before turning to the dean. "Please, Dean Newton, we already know that what's said here stays here. We'll take an oath if you want."

All the students nodded, determination on their faces. The dean studied them all in turn. "I'll allow it."

Britton shuffled his papers and checked his watch again. "My witness should be here any minute."

"He'd better be. I don't care to have my time wasted," one of the other committee members said as he leaned back in his chair. "This whole thing's a joke."

Britton looked as if he was about to take umbrage when the door opened a final time. Eli's heart sank as Wayne came in, worrying his cap in his hand. His eyes darted to Eli and then darted away again. Fuck. He really was done for, and Ash might get caught up in the backlash with him. That's what really ate at him.

Another glance at his lover showed Ash sitting back, legs stretched out before him, with the rest of the students strung out on either side of him. He looked as comfortable as if he were sitting at home. Damn the man.

"Good, you're here, Mr. Grayson. We can get started now." Britton couldn't look any more self-satisfied if he tried. Eli ground his teeth. "I don't see any reason to drag this out. It's fairly simple. Dr. Hollister not only had an affair with a student, but he also used his position to waive his own rules when it came to attendance and grades. Here is a copy of his syllabus, clearly outlining his policy."

Eli pressed his lips together, the urge to speak almost choking him. There were allowances for letting a student off for funerals and emergencies, dammit. Ash had missed no other days. Britton should not be allowed to twist that around. The only thing that kept him from shoving Britton's words down his throat was the promise Ash had extracted from him that morning when he'd called.

Ash didn't want him to speak or interrupt until it was his turn to plead his case. He'd be going last, and God help him, he might just swallow his tongue in the meantime. Several members of the committee, those that knew him best, looked at him curiously, as if wondering why he hadn't reacted. Eli's foot started tapping.

"What's your proof?" John Sanmarina asked. "Eli's been here for years, and I've never ever heard any rumors like that before. And we all know which colleagues have had affairs with students. Eli's name has never come up once."

Eli's nostrils flared as Britton pulled out that damn note. If anybody should get in trouble, it should be Britton for going through a man's trash. Weren't there laws against that?

Britton passed the note around to the committee members, giving everyone a chance to read it. One by one, they all looked toward him with expressions of speculation on their faces. "Mr. Grayson sent that note to Eli. Isn't that correct?" Britton asked as he turned toward Wayne.

"I didn't send it." Eli blinked in surprise as Wayne flushed. "I mean, I wrote it, but I handed it right to Eli to show him I wasn't going to try to play any more games." Wayne twisted his cap between his work worn hands. "I'm not explaining this well. It's kinda complicated."

"No, it's fairly simple," Britton said. "Were you blackmailing Dr. Hollister?"

"No. I was trying to, but it's kinda hard to blackmail a man when he won't cooperate with you."

Irritation flashed across Britton's face as someone snickered. It sounded like Isaac, but when Eli glanced over at his students, he couldn't tell who the culprit was. "I tried to scare Eli into paying because I knew he was on shaky ground with you, so I thought maybe he'd give me some money if I threatened him with you."

Some of Eli's anxiety for himself eased, only to be replaced with worry for Wayne. "You don't have to say anything else, Wayne," he spoke up quietly. No need to get Wayne in trouble over something that had been resolved. Ash glared so fiercely at him that Eli clamped his lips shut again and began drumming his fingers on his thigh.

"I can see why you wouldn't want him to implicate you any further," Britton said with a smirk. "But I'm not done with my questions. Mr. Grayson, is it true that you were blackmailing Hollister because of his relationship with a student?"

Wayne expression became even more miserable as he looked down at his hands. "No, sir, that's not why. I was blackmailing him over a baseball card that I thought his family had stolen from mine ages ago. When Dad got sick, I needed the extra money and I took my anger and frustration out on Eli. Figured I'd just get what was owed to me from him by threatening to make his life hell with you. Everybody knows you ride his ass. I figured he'd give me anything I wanted so as not to get you harassing him more."

Britton snatched up the note and waved it in the air. "What about the proof? Where are the pictures of Hollister with a student? Stop playing games, Mr. Grayson. This is serious business."

"There weren't ever any pictures. I lied. Dammit, it was a stupid thing to do but haven't you ever been desperate?"

Britton shot him a withering glance. "No."

Wayne's eyes narrowed as he glared right back at him. "Seems to me you must've been to go through someone's trash." Britton bristled, but Wayne was already turning his attention to the committee. "I threw that note away in front of Eli to show him that I really wasn't going to harass him anymore. He could've told Sheriff Cooper about what I tried to pull and he didn't. He gave me another chance. He even gave me ideas for helping to get my store running more smoothly. Does that sound like someone who'd cheat on a student's grades for his own gain?"

"I think you've said more than enough," Dean Newton said. "Thank you for clarifying the matter for us."

"Then I'm done?" Wayne's face lit up as the tension disappeared when the dean nodded. "Hot damn. Then you'll keep it just between yourselves? So nobody else has to know what an asshole I've been?"

The committee assured him, and Eli gave Wayne a smile as he stuffed his cap on his head. It was over. Damn, Eli was surprised he hadn't sweated through his clothes on that one. He touched Wayne's arm as he hurried past him toward the exit. "Thanks for coming. You didn't have to."

"Yeah, I think I did. Maybe this makes up for the book I damaged at least?"

"It makes up for everything," Eli assured him with a smile. Wayne had probably been terrified he'd be hauled off to jail after admitting to blackmail and he'd still come to clear Eli's name. Even if it didn't work out in his favor today, that cleared all debts, in his opinion.

"If I'd known Dr. Hollister was going to tamper with my witness then I wouldn't have asked him to be here," Britton said, biting off each word.

"Give it up." John glanced at his watch again. "A man's not going to admit to a criminal offense unless it's true. I can't see why he'd have any reason to lie for Eli, especially if your allegations had any merit. Wayne would have the upper hand."

"I didn't want to have to do this," Britton started to say, and Eli bit his tongue to keep himself from calling the man a bald-faced liar. The only thing that would make Britton happier would be if he won. He seemed to thrive off of making people uncomfortable and unhappy. "But his students will testify to his favoritism to the student he's been sleeping with."

"Keep dreaming, Britton," Kerry called out. "We haven't seen anything like that. You're a dirty old man for thinking up such things."

"Enough, Dr. Britton, either tell us who Eli's supposed to be shacking up with and get them to corroborate or end this ridiculous farce. I have another meeting this afternoon and would like to have time for lunch in between," John said.

"Fine. As I've said, this student has a history of inappropriate relationships with her professors. As you can see by this record, she's missed more days than she's allotted for that class without automatic failure and her grade has improved significantly in the last several weeks."

Eli's heart sank as he remembered turning around to find Whitney in nothing but a scrap of lingerie. No, there was no way Britton could've known about that incident, or else he wouldn't have waited this long. He should've gone to the dean immediately after that incident to protect the both of them instead of hightailing it out of town. He had only himself to blame for this part of the fiasco.

His eyes flew to Whitney, whose face had turned scarlet as she tried to sink down into her chair and hide. That stupid, blind son of a bitch. Fury reared as Eli straightened in his chair. He knew Ash was probably glaring at him so he didn't look at him sitting next to Whitney and opened his mouth to speak.

"She?" Dean Newton asked in a neutral voice.

"Yes, Whitney Grenier, come forward, please. The committee has a few questions they'd like to ask you."

Whitney's hair whipped her face as she shook her head violently. "I-I want to be excused," she said in a bare whisper. "Please."

"You're in enough trouble as it is, young lady, and—"

"Stop it," Eli snapped, standing up. God, Ash was going to kill him, but he couldn't let Britton continue to degrade Whitney in public. It was his turn to say his piece, dammit.

"I'm not going to have you humiliate or harass my students anymore. There is no relationship between Ms. Grenier and me. Yes, she missed quite a few classes at the beginning, enough to technically flunk her. But we sat down and worked out a plan for her to turn it around. Since then she has not missed or been late one day. She has completed all of her papers and presentations. And if she does well on her final exam, she'll probably end up with a low C. Maybe it's bending the rules a bit, but I'm not in the habit of drumming students out of my classes if I can help it. She had one more chance and she took full advantage of it instead of continuing to slack off."

"You would try to foist it off with an excuse like that," Britton sneered. "But I don't think the other students in your class would like that you're making special arrangements for one student when they've done all the work and attended the classes as they were supposed to."

"And their higher grades reflect that," Eli bit off. "Let me tell you this in simple terms that even you cannot possibly misunderstand: I am gay. I assure you that I've never had an affair with any woman, ever."

Britton's face went blank, and he looked between Eli and the students and the panel, his mouth working like a landed fish. "What?"

"Dude. He's, like, totally gay," Isaac said. "It came up in class once when we were talking about Oscar Wilde and Kerry grilled him on it."

Britton closed his mouth with a snap, and his back went stiff. "You're lying."

"Randall, I can attest to Eli's truthfulness. I've known for years," the dean said. "It's time to drop this. Students, you may be excused, you too, Eli, though I'd like to speak with you later. Randall, please meet me in my office."

"Wait," Britton said with a note of desperation. For a moment, Eli almost felt sorry for Britton. The expression on the man's face was that of someone watching all their dreams slip through their fingers. But the look of lingering, acute embarrassment on Whitney's face as she slipped away was enough to harden Eli's heart. "There must be some mistake."

Ash stood up to follow the rest out, and Britton's eyes widened as he stabbed a finger in Ash's direction. "That's who Eli's been sleeping with. I caught them together several times in his office."

"Oh, for the love of—" John threw up his hands and then rose. "If you caught them together, then why did you think he was with Whitney? Clearly, you don't know what's going on in your own department."

"But I saw—"

"Dean Newton," Eli said, cutting Britton off. The man sickened him. "There is one more thing that I would like resolved before the committee breaks up. I'll make it quick."

"Go ahead."

"Please let my decision regarding Ms. Grenier stand regardless of the missed days." He gave Britton a hard look. "I know what was in my syllabus regarding absences, but I think the humiliation she suffered needlessly today should account for something, not to mention the hard work she's shown since I made it plain that she would fail if she continued on as she had been."

The committee members glanced at each other, and then John shrugged. "If she's done all of her work and hasn't missed any classes after your agreement, I don't see why not. I trust your judgment."

"I concur." The dean rose and glanced at Britton. "Randall, I would like a word with you."

Eli turned away, his stomach doing crazy flips. He couldn't believe it really was over. No more Britton hanging over his head, scrutinizing everything he did. The relief was palpable. He hadn't realized how much it had weighed him down until it was gone.

He glanced up to catch Ash's eye, only to see that he had disappeared along with the rest of the class. That was who he wanted to celebrate with, but it would have to wait for tonight. Maybe they could head up to the camp for the weekend... no wait, dammit, Ash had drill this weekend, which meant Eli probably wouldn't get to see him before he left.

Well, that was just depressing. Eli's heart sank all over again, and his victory turned hollow. To be honest, staying in Amwich if Ash wasn't going to be there would be misery. Eli was a military brat. He was used to bouncing around from coast to coast. Ash might end up moving around often in whatever job he took, and Eli thought he just might be able to handle that, if he was with Ash.

At least next week was the final week of classes. As soon as the last grade was posted, he was telling Ash how he felt about him and asking him to move in. They could figure out their future together after that. His phone buzzed as he said the last of his goodbyes to his colleagues, and the text there had him grinning like a loon.

Congrats, Doc. Up for a new bet? Winner gets kink drawer rights. Think of that over the weekend.

ASH thought class would never end, not that they'd gotten too much accomplished. The rest of the kids were too keyed up over the hearing on Friday and over finally getting the chance to say their piece to Eli, not to mention celebrating the fact that Britton was stepping down as head of the department. There were even rumors that he wouldn't be back at all in the spring.

What kept Ash's blood going was all those little glances Eli kept giving him. Heated and loving looks, no matter how much Eli tried to keep himself focused on the class as a whole. After a long week of zero satisfaction, those glances were playing havoc with Ash's control.

And when Eli headed toward his office after class, Ash was two steps behind him until Kerry's giggle stopped him. "Good thing the dean wasn't here today taking notes. You two would've been so busted."

"You're just seeing it because you'd already figured it out before today." They probably could've been more circumspect. There was only one more class to suffer through. "Besides, you're hard-wired to see romance and forbidden affairs in everything. You who named your cat Lancelot and did your project on Abelard and Heloise."

Kerry's cheeks turned pink. "Maybe. Still, you should've done something to help Dr. Hollister on Friday instead of staying quiet."

"You think me declaring my undying love in front of the whole committee would've helped him? More like gotten us both into trouble, and then Doc would be pissed at me as well. Romantic it might've been, my starry-eyed girl, but not a good idea."

"Maybe," Kerry said in a doubtful voice. "I still think you ought to make some kind of gesture. Something big."

"You'd like that more than he would, I think," Ash said with a laugh. "And I'm ending this conversation before you try to talk me into opening the final class with a serenade or something equally overdramatic. I'm not catering to whatever fairytale love story you have going on in your head about us."

"Ha, make fun of me all you want, Mr. Southern Gentleman Ashley!" Kerry called after him as he made a strategic retreat. "I know a happily ever after when I see one."

Ash couldn't stop thinking about Kerry's parting shot as he walked toward Eli's office. Happily ever after. He liked the sound of that. The Hermitage might not be a castle, and Amwich was more of a village than a bustling capital, but those two places were what Ash thought of when he heard the word "home." That and Eli himself. And he'd been looking for a place to call home for a long damn time.

His lover had his feet propped up on his desk and his eyes closed when Ash slipped into his office and locked the door behind him. A smile tugged at Eli's lips, though he didn't open his eyes. "I have no office hours today. You'll have to wait until tomorrow."

"What if I have a problem that just can't wait?"

Eli's eyes opened, and Ash was struck by the heat and love in them. "I suppose I can make an exception for you. Come here, Georgia. I missed you like crazy this weekend."

Ash walked over to him, his heart thumping harder. It jumped with a hard, lurching throb as Eli grabbed the front of his shirt and pulled him down for a kiss that left his senses reeling and his thoughts scattered. "I missed you too," he said when Eli finally let go of him.

"So the dragon is gone, I hear," Ash murmured as Eli released him. "The meeting with the dean must've gone well."

"Britton's stepped down as head of the department and he'll be retiring at the end of the year. The rumor is that he's been diagnosed with dementia, even if it's probably too early to tell for sure. I'm pretty much guaranteed my tenure, now that he's not around to jeopardize it." A faint line appeared between Eli's brows and then disappeared just as quickly.

"That's good news. That's what you've always wanted, isn't it?"

"Plans have a way of changing sometimes. This has been the craziest fucking semester ever. I think I'm going to go to Tibet and become a monk."

"Liar. You love it here too much to leave." Ash laughed and stole another kiss. "Kerry just yelled at me, she seems to think that a white knight should've swooped in and rescued you on Friday."

"I think one did. I wasn't expecting Wayne to be there. He'd told me that he'd turned Britton down. I suspect you might have had a hand in changing his mind."

"I might've said a few words." A smile curved Ash's lips as he lifted his head. All those lines of tension that had always been around Eli's mouth and eyes when he was in this room were gone. "I have to say my opinion of Wayne went up a notch or two. He'd originally told Britton he wasn't interested in talking to him. I convinced him that testifying for you would be a much better idea. I even promised to put in a good word to Cooper for him."

"You could've told me your plan." Eli tapped his finger against Ash's chest. "It would've kept me from going crazy beforehand."

"Couldn't do that, Doc, sorry. You have the worst poker face of any man I've ever seen. You're too expressive, and Dean Newton was going to be watching you. The more genuine your emotions were during Wayne's testimony, the more credible you were going to look. Your worry over seeing Wayne there was taken as worry for a friend by the time you were done having your say, not worry over what Wayne might have told the committee."

"You have a streak of deviousness in you that I never imagined." Eli drew Ash down for another lingering kiss. "Thank you."

Ash grinned at him, too buoyed up to be subtle. "So how long have you been in love with me?"

ELI blinked, his mouth falling open as his heart skipped a long beat. "What?"

Ash plucked the rubber band off the end of Eli's braid and threaded his fingers through his hair, unwinding it. Anticipation rose, and Eli found it hard to catch his breath. "It's a simple question, and I'm dying to know the answer. But if it'll make you feel better, I'll go first."

Ash wrapped Eli's hair around his fist. Eli's heart sped up until it was slamming rapid fire in his chest. "I want to stay in Amwich and be with you," Ash said in a husky voice.

It took a moment for that to sink in and then warm pleasure lit up inside Eli. "You do, hmmm? So is this your way of saying you feel the same way about me?"

"It is. I've never told a lover this before." Everything went still inside as Eli looked at Ash, waiting for those words. He'd never seen Ash look so damn nervous when he finally spoke. "I love you."

A grin split Eli's face as everything in his world seemed to right itself and settle into place. He tugged Ash down onto the chair with him, needing him close. The chair squeaked and Eli chuckled. "I don't think this chair was made for two. I'm going to need to get a couch in here for you."

"So you've given up on the idea of going to Tibet?" Ash asked as he nuzzled Eli's smiling lips.

"Screw Tibet, I've got everything I need right here." Eli wrapped his hand around Ash's nape and tugged him down for another breathless kiss. "I was going to wait until the end of the semester to ask you, but I can't wait any longer."

"You're only giving in by a few days. I won't tell if you won't." Ash's green eyes gleamed with silent laughter.

"Move into the Hermitage with me."

Ash pretended to consider it, his face drawn in thought, as nerves jumped in Eli's stomach. "I don't know, are you still going to insist that the American League is better than the National League? And what the hell kind of a position is designated hitter? I mean, really."

"Just wait. I'll convert you yet."

"The hell you will. You're a bit of a fanatic. I don't know if I can handle all of that Red Sox talk every day, and Jabbers has a cold nose in the morning."

"I prefer to think of myself as a true believer," Eli huffed.

"That's what all fanatics say." Ash's hand tightened in Eli's hair as he lowered his mouth for a kiss. "I would like nothing more than to move in with you. Being with you only part-time has been driving me crazy."

"I've changed my mind. You're definitely a grand slam." Eli sighed against his lips. "I love you."

"I know." Ash stole another lingering kiss. "Now, about that bet...."

MARGUERITE LABBE has been accused of being eccentric and a shade neurotic, both of which she freely admits to, but her muse has OCD tendencies, so who can blame her? Her husband and son do an excellent job keeping her toeing the line, though. Together with her co-author Fae Sutherland, Marguerite has found a shared passion for beautiful men with smart mouths.

When she's not working hard on writing new material and editing completed work, she spends her time reading novels of all genres, enjoying role-playing games with her equally nutty friends, and trying to plot practical jokes against her son and husband. Her son is learning the tricks too quickly and likes to retaliate. You'd think she'd learn.

Visit Marguerite's website at http://chasethedream.net/.

Also from MARGUERITE LABBE

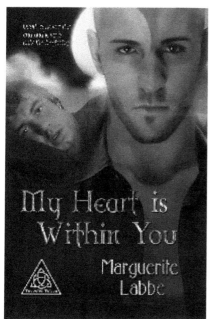

http://www.dreamspinnerpress.com

For more of the
best M/M romance,
visit

Dreamspinner Press

www.dreamspinnerpress.com